T0146493

Eternal Reign

Also by Melody Johnson

Sweet Last Drop

The City Beneath

Coming soon

Day Reaper

Eternal Reign

A Night Blood Novel

Melody Johnson

LYRICAL PRESS
Kensington Publishing Corp.
www.kensingtonbooks.com

LYRICAL PRESS BOOKS are published by

Kensington Publishing Corp.
119 West 40th Street
New York, NY 10018

All Kensington titles, imprints, and distributed lines are available at special quantity discounts for bulk purchases for sales promotion, premiums, fundraising, educational, or institutional use.

Special book excerpts or customized printings can also be created to fit specific needs. For details, write or phone the office of the Kensington Sales Manager: Kensington Publishing Corp., 119 West 40th Street, New York, NY 10018. Attn. Sales Department. Phone: 1-800-221-2647.

Lyrical Press and Lyrical Press logo Reg. U.S. Pat. & TM Off.

First Electronic Edition: April 2017
eISBN-13: 978-1-60183-425-6
eISBN-10: 1-60183-425-X

First Print Edition: April 2017
ISBN-13: 978-1-60183-426-3
ISBN-10: 1-60183-426-8

Printed in the United States of America

ACKNOWLEDGMENTS

This installment in the Night Blood series is especially dear to my heart because I wrote it during a uniquely stressful and blissful time in my life—my engagement—and released it the same month as my wedding. In acknowledgment of the many people who made my engagement special and memorable, and who traveled across the country to celebrate our big day, this book is dedicated to . . .

My mother, Nancy Johnson, who listened to me alternately lament and rejoice in wedding planning for hours every week throughout my one year and four month engagement, and who helped me find the absolutely perfect wedding dress.

My father, Leonard Johnson, who has always supported my dreams, even when doing so meant me being far from family—from going away to college to the big move to Georgia. My dreams for a fairytale wedding were no exception.

My parents-in-law, Theresa and Dick Bradley, for welcoming me into their family and making me feel like I was a Bradley long before I ever took their name.

My best friends—Stacy Flick, Meredith Bause, Caroline Dempsey, Erin Jones, Carli Feldman, and Chrissy VanScoten—who stood by my side. We live states away from one another, but no matter how far away we are physically, your love and memories of our crazy antics remain close to my heart.

My family and friends, who didn't let the distance stop them from joining me in celebration of my big day. Having you here to witness our vows and join together as one family meant more to me than you'll ever know.

My husband, Derek Bradley, who carried my engagement ring for six months and across five states to plan the perfect proposal. Like any romance novel, our adventure has had its ups and downs, but as much as we've already experienced on this journey together, our story is really just beginning.

And I can't wait to experience what happens next.

Vampires Bite in the Big Apple—deleted, restored & rewritten notes from draft 3
Cassidy DiRocco, Reporter, *Sun Accord*

A reliable witness is as valuable and elusive as the pot of gold at the end of a rainbow. Without anyone to quote what "really happened," I may as well be writing fiction—what sane person would believe that vampires exist on my word alone?—but multiple people often tell various and conflicting versions of the same event even without vampire intervention, and not intentionally. Memory is subjective, and perception can be biased. Even the most reliable witness needs corroboration.

Advances in forensic science, unlike eyewitness testimony, are dead-on accurate. DNA evidence isn't subjective. Trace evidence can't be prejudiced. Ballistic evidence isn't biased. Forensics separate reality from memory, so despite what witnesses think they saw—or what they want others to believe they saw—science uncovers the truth.

For the first time in my life, I was the main witness. I was writing *my* story—possibly the most important, life-altering, jaw-dropping story of my entire career—and all I needed was corroboration. Without proof, without undeniable, scientific evidence to validate everything I'd seen and experienced, no one would ever believe me, so I waited, forcing myself to practice patience over the instinct to snatch up the proverbial bullhorn and shout my discovery to the world. I thought I had time to gather my evidence, build my corroboration, and protect my loved ones while I carefully crafted the article that would not only change my life but the lives of everyone in New York City—hell, the lives of everyone on earth.

I was so worried about the people I'd put at risk by exposing the truth that I never considered the weight of their deaths from my unwritten words . . .

Three Days before the Leveling

Night bloods cannot prepare for or against the transformation. Once we are transformed, life as we know it is altered in every way imaginable. On one hand, we can no longer tolerate sunlight, food, and silver, but on the other hand, we receive heightened speed, senses, cognitive functions, and strength. Unimaginable strength and perfect health. I don't know why we fight the transformation—no matter how devastating the changes to our former way of life and thinking, the pros far outweigh the cons—except for the simple, unforgivable, unacceptable notion that we must change.

—Dominic Lysander, on becoming a vampire

Chapter 1

Dominic looked pretentious and posh, as usual, leaning against the wall in the hallway outside my apartment. Even gazing at him through the fish-eye lens of my door's peephole—from the top of his immaculately cut and styled black hair to the bottom of his shiny Cole Haan wing-tipped dress shoes—he was a hopeful-mother's dream, a shrewd-woman's nightmare, and the reason I no longer bothered trying to sleep at night. Knowing the truth beneath the pretty wrapping—that he was the Master vampire of New York City—didn't stop my heart from jumping and dropping in confused anticipation and adrenaline. After I'd nearly lost him last week, I'd come to the implausible, unwelcome conclusion that I actually preferred my life with him in it, but since I'd completely lost the protection and mental strength of my night blood, his unexpected presence also twisted my gut with pure, unadulterated fear.

I hadn't seen Dominic in five nights, not since he'd entranced his name from my mind and confirmed our worst suspicion: I no longer had night blood.

Without night blood, I didn't have the potential to transform into a vampire, I couldn't reflect Dominic's commands if he attempted to entrance me, and I no longer had any of the qualities that Dominic held in such high esteem, that he'd planned to leverage during the Leveling; the one night every seven years that he lost his strength and abilities as Master to his potential successor, allowing a new Master to rise in his stead. Without those qualities, I couldn't help him survive the coming battle to keep control of his coven. I was nothing but another human.

I was nothing but food.

Dominic knocked a second time, this series of staccato raps on the door more insistent than the first.

"Who's at the door?" Meredith asked. Her eyebrows rose and disappeared behind her bangs.

Of course, on the one night Dominic finally decided to confront me, I had company. I should be grateful; he was knocking on the door rather than inviting himself in through one of the third-story, living room windows. That would have been difficult to explain to Meredith. Longtime best friend and wing woman at the *Sun Accord* she was, but night blood she wasn't.

"I'm hoping if I wait long enough, he'll give up and go away."

"*He?*" Meredith asked. A mischievous smile curved her lips.

"It's probably best to answer the door of your own will," Nathan murmured.

I stared at my brother, surprised that he'd uttered a full, intelligible sentence beyond "We're out of milk" or something equally inane. Inane seemed all he was capable of lately.

"He'll make it worse for you otherwise," he added.

I ignored Meredith and narrowed my eyes on Nathan. "How do you know who's at the door?"

Nathan dropped his gaze to the cereal bowl in front of him and continued spooning scraps of shredded wheat and milk into his mouth without further comment.

Maybe he'd actually keep the food down this time. Then we could work on gradually introducing warm meals and protein back into his diet.

I worried the doorknob with my thumb. Nathan might have been monosyllabic and near bulimic since returning to the city, but he was right. If I didn't open the door of my own will, Dominic would probably force me to grant him entrance into my new apartment. A tenuous spring of hope coiled in my gut. Maybe, just maybe, my efforts to create a fallout shelter here in the city had been a success; maybe I didn't need to worry about entry, forced or otherwise.

I might have put my newly fortified apartment to the test, but with Meredith sitting at my kitchen table, a slice of sushi roll halfway to her mouth, the risk of exposing her to the danger standing on my doorstep wasn't worth the pleasure of denying Dominic entrance.

I opened the door.

Dominic smiled, deliberately flashing his sharp, elongated fangs. "Good evening, Cassidy."

His voice purred in a deep timbre that plucked at the taut cords in my stomach. I squelched the feelings, but after weeks of denial, I could finally admit that they existed.

"What are you doing here?" I whispered.

He raised a perfectly arched eyebrow. "No 'Hello?' No 'What a pleasant surprise?'" Dominic tsked his tongue against the back of his teeth. "Where are your manners?"

"What a surprise," I muttered, deliberately omitting "pleasant." "You should have called before coming, Dominic."

He inhaled sharply. The fragile hope that softened his expression shamed me.

"Don't," I warned, keeping my voice low in an effort to prevent Meredith from overhearing. "I didn't remember your name on my own. Nathan reminded me. It still feels like a void, like Nathan telling me your name four days ago was the first I'd learned it."

His face fell. "That's unfortunate."

I sighed. "Are you only here to antagonize me, or was there an actual purpose to this visit?"

"Antagonizing you would be purpose enough, but yes, I have a greater purpose than even that," Dominic said, magnanimously. "Must we converse in the hallway? I don't believe I've had the pleasure of seeing your new apartment. Won't you invite me in?"

I shook my head. "Now's not a good time. I'm busy tonight."

"You haven't seen me in five nights. What could you possibly be doing at this late hour?" His expression hardened with a sudden realization. "Or is the proper question, *who* could you possibly be doing?"

I blinked. "What?"

"After everything that he's done, how could you allow Ian Walker to—"

"Cass, who's at the door?" Meredith poked her head between us, widening the cracked door. She panned over Dominic, from the perfection of his hair to the shine of his shoes, and turned a lascivious smile on me. "Won't you introduce us?"

"Yes, Cassidy, won't you introduce us?" Dominic mocked, his expression losing its edge. He looked amused.

"No," I said to Meredith. I turned to Dominic and cocked my head. "What were you saying about Walker?"

"Never mind about him. I'm much more interested in her," Dominic said, inclining his head toward Meredith.

I narrowed my gaze on him. "Unfortunately for Meredith, she's already made your acquaintance."

Meredith shook her head. "I don't remember making his acquaintance."

"He has that effect on people," I said smartly. "Even me."

A growl rattled from his chest.

I rolled my eyes. "You know my sarcasm better than that. Knock it off."

"It's not your sarcasm that angers me. It's the reminder that you were taken away from me."

I was never yours to begin with, I thought, but I knew better than to further antagonize him. I bit my tongue and said instead, "I'm right here."

"You know what I'm referring to," he said.

I sighed. I did, but I'd been dreading this conversation all week. "You should consider yourself lucky that I even—" I sneezed.

"Gesundheit."

"Thank you," I managed before sneezing three more times in rapid succession. "I—"

Dominic raised an eyebrow. "Are you ill?"

"I'm fine." I dismissed his concern with a wave of my hand. "If you want to come back tomorrow, we—"

"A sneeze often indicates that one is ill or is about to become ill," he interrupted.

I rolled my eyes. "Once upon a time, yes, that was the case. People sneezed one day, and the next, they were on their deathbed. But with the advance of modern medicine and vaccinations, a sneeze is oftentimes just a sneeze."

Even as I finished my sentence, I sneezed again. Somehow, sneezing made my point less credible.

Dominic shook his head. "There are people—for many years now we've referred to them as physicians—who study your symptoms, diagnose your illnesses, and treat them with medication. I believe modern medicine refers to these medications as antibiotics, and the sooner you receive them, the better."

Meredith laughed. "I like him." She offered Dominic a California roll from the plastic container. "Sushi?"

Dominic patted his stomach. "Unfortunately, I've just eaten. Otherwise, I'd surely be ravenous for anything you offered me."

"Just meet me upstairs on the rooftop in two minutes," I snapped, flabbergasted, and shut the door in his face.

No sooner had I shut the door than I sneezed again. And again and again in rapid succession.

I could hear Dominic's fading laughter even through the closed door.

"Bless you," Meredith mumbled around a mouthful of sushi. She swallowed before saying, "I don't suppose you might be developing allergies." Her eyes glinted with amusement when she glanced away from the door to grin at me.

"No," I sighed, "but we may want to eat out of separate containers from now on. I think I'm coming down with something."

"I don't mind coming down with whatever you're catching," she said. Her tone sounded innocent, but her grin was absolutely wicked.

Nathan, upending the final drops from his cereal bowl, choked on his milk.

Her gaze suddenly turned thoughtful. "But seriously, of all the men in this city, you could do worse. He seems like an old soul."

I locked the front door. "You have no idea."

"Then why give him the cold shoulder?" Meredith asked. "The least you could do is invite him in and give me a proper introduction to the man who drops in unexpectedly on your doorstep at nine o'clock at night."

And therein lay the very problem with being best friends with a non–night blood: all the damn unanswerable questions.

Meredith's eyes widened, her expression salacious, and I knew without having to hear the words about to come out of her mouth that she'd jumped to the wrong conclusion. "Or is he just a booty call?" she asked, wagging her eyebrows hopefully.

"You know me better than that." I laughed.

She sighed dramatically. "Unfortunately, but one day you will officially get over your rat-bastard ex, and when that day comes, I want to hear every detail."

A door slammed shut, and I realized Nathan had escaped to the bathroom. Maybe he wasn't in the mood for Meredith's teasing—

and honestly, neither was I if it involved dredging up conversation about Adam—but then I heard the gagging and retching noises coming from behind the closed door. Five days, and he hadn't been able to keep down anything but water. I couldn't think of anything more bland and stomach-settling than chicken broth and cereal, but if I didn't think of something soon, I'd have saved my brother from being Damned only to lose him to starvation.

Maybe I could borrow Dominic's IV.

"Is he okay?" Meredith whispered.

I leveled a look on her. "It's your fault. Talking dirty in front of my little brother, shame on you."

Meredith made a rude noise in the back of her throat. "He's your brother, but he's not little anymore. He should move out."

I frowned. "He just moved in."

"He's cramping your personal life."

"I don't have a personal life."

"You would if you didn't live with your little brother," Meredith argued. She had a valid point if we'd been normal siblings, but Nathan and I were anything but normal.

Night blood ran in our family genes, and Nathan was no exception. Unfortunately for our sanity and safety, we'd discovered our heritage separately and attempted to stop the rebel vampires terrorizing New York City without telling each other: I'd ended up playing bait for Dominic to smoke out their leader, and Nathan had sought out their leader to stop her on his own. If we'd had the courage to tell each other the truth and fight our enemies together, maybe Jillian Allister, Dominic's former second, potential successor, and leader of the rebel vampires, wouldn't have so easily attacked and transformed Nathan into the Damned—a ravenous creature whose insatiable thirst for aortic blood consumed its every thought and action.

I'd thought moving in together and being close to family would bring a sense of normalcy back into our lives after everything had been knocked so off-axis, but besides not being able to stomach solid food, one little detail of Nathan's time being Damned had escaped my consideration and prevented us from feeling at home, even here in the city: Jillian had wiped Nathan's existence from everyone's memory after transforming him and their memory hadn't been restored when he had.

Every friend forgot they'd known him. Every touch he'd ever shared was suddenly someone else's touch. Every relationship he'd ever formed and every gift he'd ever given or received was suddenly nothing but a reminder of everything he'd lost. I'd even had to reintroduce him to Meredith, which was especially strange considering she was practically family. She was like his sister, too, but after thirty years of friendship, she smiled and held out her hand like a lovely, polite stranger.

"Your life's a clean slate." I'd tried to bolster his spirits, but we both knew that was bullshit. Nathan was stranded, and I didn't know the first direction in helping to guide him home.

Meredith pointed her thumb at the door. As she sensed my somber mood, her expression suddenly turned serious. "Should I leave?"

I pulled down the drop staircase to the roof. "This won't take long."

"Quick and dirty. I'm liking him more and more." Meredith winked.

"Shut up," I said, smirking in spite of myself.

"Slow and thorough is good, too, I suppose. But if that's what you prefer, then I should definitely leave."

I shook my head and laughed at Meredith's teasing. It would be funnier if she wasn't partly right.

"If you're not back by the time I finish this California roll, I'm gone," Meredith warned.

I pointed my finger at her. "Don't you dare finish our food." And then, deliberately, I added, "Dominic is not worth missing out on sushi."

Meredith shrugged. "Better make it quick and dirty then. I've only got three more rolls to go."

Chapter 2

My new place was smaller than my last apartment, especially with Nathan skulking in the shadows, but more important than size, I'd needed an apartment that could easily transform into a fully functioning fallout shelter. Keagan McDunnell, one of the many fellow night bloods lost during my disastrous visit to upstate New York last week, had shared his wealth of knowledge with me about vampire fallout shelters before going missing, and according to his expertise, my new apartment needed three essential anti-vampire ingredients: large, open windows and a southeast-facing apartment to let in sunlight; original metal locks and hinges and silver stuffed in every nook and cranny; and human blood.

With the exception of dried, stale human blood lining the apartment's perimeter to mask the appealing scent of my fresh, circulating blood, I had the other ingredients to my fallout shelter covered. The large, bay windows in my living room and bedroom allowed the sun to flood my apartment with natural light, and I'd draped gauzy fabric over the curtain rods instead of hanging drapes to let the apartment soak in all that natural protection. The apartment had its original, rusted hinges, skeleton key locks, and chain on the door, and I'd added a few additional metals of my own. I'd splurged, drawing on my savings for real silverware, silver curtain rods, metal wall decorations, and vintage silver floor lamps. And in addition to purchasing all that hardware, I'd used my remaining silver nitrate spray on every doorframe.

Everything I'd purchased for the apartment was to fortify it against Dominic and his vampires. The rooftop access, however, was just for me.

Everything seemed bigger on the rooftop—the city, the sky, my dreams, and perspective—while my problems and I seemed inconsequential in the giant, cosmic scheme of things. They weren't inconsequential, and neither was I—the very weight of my problems and their consequences were oftentimes crushing to contemplate—but when I lay on my hammock and watched the sun rise from the rooftop with just my thoughts and a glass of cabernet, I was lifted from beneath the weight of my problems. On the rooftop, with the warmth and protection of the sun on my skin, I could breathe.

When I emerged from the rooftop access staircase of my newly vampire-proofed apartment, Dominic was lounging in my hammock.

"That was longer than two minutes," he chided.

I glared down at his reclined form and crossed my arms. "Don't get comfortable. This is one of the few nights I have with Meredith, and I don't want to waste it."

He lifted an eyebrow. "You see Meredith every day. Sometimes you see her every night. And she's obviously not good for your health."

"I *work* with Meredith every day and sometimes every night. We're having girl time tonight. There's a difference." I narrowed my eyes on his last comment. "How does she affect my health?"

"She's human; with your weakened immune system and night blood, your body is obviously having some kind of allergic reaction to her."

I stared at him blankly.

"The sneezing. You—"

I rolled my eyes. "That's the most ridiculous thing I've ever heard come out of your mouth, and that's a lot, considering we're talking about you. I don't care how weakened my blood is, I am not allergic to my best friend."

Dominic patted the minuscule space in the hammock next to him. "Come here, and I'll explain it to you."

I shook my head. "I believe that would constitute 'getting comfortable'."

Dominic leveled his eyes on me, those otherworldly, icy-blue eyes. They often looked through me—seeing my innermost fears and desires—more than they looked at me, but they looked at me now. He knew how I felt about him. He didn't need proof of it by reading my mind when he could taste it on my skin, feel it like the heat from a wood-burning stove wafting from my thoughts, hear it in the cadence of my breath. He knew, but I'm sure the confirmation of it on Technicolor display was gratifying too.

He grinned, confirming my suspicions. "Would getting comfortable really be so bad?"

I nodded. Dominic was my ally, but that didn't change who and what he was. "Getting comfortable could be deadly," I said.

"Being comfortable and becoming complacent are two very different things, and I would never accuse you of complacency." He tilted his head, smiling. "Is this a hard-and-fast rule of yours, remaining uncomfortable?"

I sighed, knowing from experience what was coming next. "No, it's not a hard-and-fast rule. It's more of a personal preference."

He lifted an eyebrow. "You prefer to remain uncomfortable?"

I rolled my eyes. "Fine. A cautionary measure."

He growled, deep and predatory, but it didn't have anything to do with anger.

Involuntarily, I took a step back.

"Cassidy DiRocco," Dominic rumbled through the growl. I could feel my mind perk at the call of my name, like the way a dog cocks its ears forward to receive its next command. I envisioned a silver-framed mirror protecting my mind, like he'd taught me, but I knew that it wouldn't work against him. Not anymore.

"Come and lie next to me in this hammock," he commanded.

Instantly and uncontrollably, I stepped forward. I went to him as he commanded, my actions not my own, and lay next to him in the hammock. To my credit, I lay opposite him—my head at his feet—but that was only because he hadn't specified the exact position I should take.

Dominic shook his head at me from across the hammock, his lips tugging into a reluctant smirk. "Even now, you're impossibly obstinate."

I smiled. "Thank you."

"Did you try to deflect my command?"

"Of course. I'm obstinate, remember?" I scoffed.

His lips twitched. "Well, besides your stubbornness in refusing to lie 'next to me' properly, I didn't sense any resistance from you. Not like I used to," he added softly.

I sighed. "You didn't see my mirror?"

He shook his head.

"When I spoke to Dr. Chunn, she mentioned that the female body typically takes sixteen weeks to replenish blood cells after donation. It's possible that—"

"We don't have sixteen weeks," Dominic interrupted. "It's been five days since your blood transfusion. The Leveling is in three days, and if you haven't regained the advantages of your night blood by now, it won't matter if you regain them sixteen weeks or sixteen years from now. We need them for the Leveling."

"I'm sorry my recovery isn't on your schedule," I said dryly.

"Me too," Dominic said gravely. "If you don't have them for the Leveling, I need to consider an alternate plan to protect my position as Master."

I crossed my arms. "It's not my fault that this happened. I didn't ask for a blood transfusion. I didn't want to lose what little protection I had against you and the other vampires. I was dying, and the doctors were just trying to save my life. They succeeded, if you haven't noticed, but you've been less than grateful."

"You're damn right I'm less than grateful. If I was there, I could have—"

"But you weren't," I interrupted. "You weren't there, and the doctors did the best *they* could."

Dominic looked away. "I'm just telling you what must be done."

"And what exactly must be done?" I demanded. "What are you trying to tell me?"

He stared off into the distance, across the expanse of city lights. We couldn't see the stars here, not like I could upstate when I visited Walker last week. Some people might miss details like that—the natural serenity of country living—but despite the promises that Ian Walker had made me—and he'd made and broken many, as had I— the country had not been the reprieve from the doom and gloom of my life that I'd needed and anticipated. Worse, Walker hadn't been the man I'd needed or anticipated.

Under the pretense of writing an article about country versus city crime rates for Carter, my cranky boss and editor in chief of the *Sun Accord,* I'd visited Walker at his hometown of Erin, New York, for three reasons: to learn more about vampires from a man who'd known about his night blood his entire life, to uphold my end of a deal I'd struck with Dominic to find Nathan, and to explore my developing and deepening feelings for Walker. I'd thought that, of those three reasons, the third was the most likely to blossom. He'd thought I'd only had one reason to visit him. We'd both been disappointed. In that brief, disastrous excuse for a vacation, I'd missed the city. I'd missed the bustle and life and conveniences I'd taken for granted, like streetlights and taxis and the absence of wild animals. I'd especially taken for granted the protection of Dominic's presence.

Before my visit upstate, I'd felt constricted by his visits and considered his limitless reach an unwanted invasion of my personal, physical, and mental boundaries.

Until he'd been out of reach.

I would have died last week without Dominic, killed by my own brother when he didn't know anything but how to kill. When I'd needed Dominic most, despite the risk and distance and my own reluctance, he'd been there. He'd protected me against Walker when everything had turned south, and he'd more than upheld his end of our bargain concerning Nathan. He'd nearly died saving him, and undoubtedly would have if not for the metaphysical bonds he'd forged between us, linking our life forces. Granted, he'd forged those bonds without my prior knowledge or consent, which I found unforgivable, except for the pesky fact that I'd been grateful for their presence when we'd needed them most.

On a day-to-day basis, those bonds were easily forgotten, or in Dominic's case, easily hidden until I'd discovered them. It wasn't until he'd been shot through the heart with Walker's wooden stake and I'd coughed up physical blood from the metaphysical injury that I'd realized how our lives were linked and the repercussions of those bonds. Now that I knew, if I concentrated hard enough, I could feel the sting if Dominic had a hangnail, but unless one of us was egregiously injured, Dominic held the bonds in check, keeping my pain and ailments and injuries within my body and his within his body.

I stared at the scarred side of Dominic's face as he continued studying the expanse of city below us, and I had the sudden, insane impulse to kiss those luscious, imperfect lips. In this form, his lips were the only feature that was imperfect, and I cherished that reminder of his former life, a life that despite our age, gender, and moral differences, was very similar to my own: we were both at one time night bloods, and we bore physical reminders of our mistakes.

He met my gaze, and I looked away, embarrassed by my thoughts and urges. We wanted two very different futures for ourselves and this city, but the one want we agreed upon—very recently and only sometimes, although with increasing and alarming regularity—was his lips against mine. He hadn't kissed me since that crazy moment upstate in Erin, New York, when he'd healed me and I'd been drained enough to become high on his blood, but I'd thought about that moment every day since. I'd relived the smell of his longing and the heat of his breath and the demand of his lips in the quiet solitude of my hammock on this very roof every night.

But I wasn't alone tonight.

I forced myself to meet his gaze. Judging by the intensity in his eyes, he thought about that moment as often and with as much longing as I did.

"I've never faced a situation quite like this before," he said. When he finally spoke, his voice was hoarse, as though he needed to clear his throat. "A human knows of our existence, knows about me and the inner workings and location of my coven intimately, and I have allowed her memory to remain intact. If my coven knew, it would ruin both of us."

I frowned. "Who are you talking about?"

Dominic blinked at me. "My dear Cassidy DiRocco, I'm talking about you."

"Oh," I said. I remained quiet, waiting for his next words. My gut churned; I didn't like the direction this conversation was headed.

"What would you have me do?" he asked. "Would you prefer to keep your memory of the existence of me and my coven, putting us both at risk, or become blissfully unaware?"

He knew my preference, and if he didn't, he didn't know me as well as I thought he did. "I'd prefer to keep my memory." I gave him a look. "Obviously."

"Think on it, Cassidy. Without your night blood, you have no protection against other vampires, and if I don't survive the Leveling, Jillian will come for you. She knows where your loyalties lie. She will not tolerate you or any of my supporters, but if you no longer remember me or her or any of us, if you don't know that vampires even exist, she may allow you to live. You might be able to carry on with your life as you did before we met. Isn't that what you truly want, anyway, to live your life as it was before you met me?"

I shook my head. "What I truly want is for vampires to not exist at all, but they do. To pretend anything else would be a lie, and didn't you once say that I'm in the business of exposing the truth?"

Dominic nodded. "I have no interest in living a lie, no matter how pretty that lie is. You know me better than that, or at least I thought you did."

"I suspected you would say as much, but knowing what may become of me and also knowing what Jillian may do to you, I couldn't live with myself if I didn't at least offer that option."

"Wiping my memory doesn't ensure my safety anyway," I argued. "If Jillian comes for me, I want to know exactly why she's here and why I'm being killed. I wouldn't change anything I've done for you or Nathan, so if Jillian wants to kill me for it, that's her prerogative. I don't want to forget it happened."

Dominic reached across his body and touched my ankle. "You say that now, but you may feel differently when she breaks you. I couldn't bear to witness your suffering."

"You won't be witness to anything. If Jillian comes for me, you'll already be dead," I reminded him.

He leveled a look on me. "I couldn't bear the thought—"

I pulled my foot from his hand. "Save it. You watched Kaden break every bone in my body, literally, limb by limb, as he tortured me to get to you."

"I intervened before he went too far," Dominic growled.

I laughed. "Your threshold for 'too far' is much higher than mine."

"We did what was necessary for the bigger picture."

"That's exactly what I'm asking you to do now. If you fail, Jillian won't come after just me. New York City as we know it will be devastated. Vampires will be exposed. People will need someone who knows what the hell's going on and who can anchor them in the truth. I can be that person."

Dominic was quiet for a long moment.

I bit my lip.

"Allowing you to keep your memory puts you at risk, but it also puts me and my coven at risk," Dominic finally said.

"That's typical!" I snapped, exasperated. "As usual, your coven comes first, even before common sense. This was never my choice at all, was it?"

"Cassidy, please—"

"No! If you think I'm going to agree to let you wipe my memory for the benefit of the coven, you've lost *your* mind. I'm not letting you off the hook so you can feel better about mind-raping me. I'm not agreeing to this. I'm not your martyr!"

Dominic's face tightened. "If you would shut up and listen—"

"Screw you," I snapped.

Dominic was suddenly on top of me, his hands gripping my shoulders, his body pressing across my body, his face in my face. "I'm not going to wipe your memory!"

I blinked up at him. Squished into the hammock from the crushing weight of his body, I could barely breathe, let alone think. "Oh," I murmured. "But you said—"

"I said for you to shut up and listen." His voice was a growl, and I could feel the hard proof of his anger and excitement against my hip. He was a vampire, and he was dangerous—there was no denying the facts of his existence—but in many ways he was still very much a man. Lately, he seemed determined to remind me of that fact, too.

I shut my mouth.

"Are you listening now?"

I nodded.

"Allowing you to *keep* your memory compromises the security of me and my coven, so I need you to promise me that you will keep our secret. Promise me that you will not expose our existence before Jillian does, that you will only acknowledge our existence after I'm gone, after she makes vampires a known threat to humanity."

I glared at him. It was impossible to press an advantage from my prone position beneath him, but I glared anyway. "I don't want to expose your existence," I said, "but if your existence is going to be exposed anyway, why can't I—"

He put up a hand. "You don't want to be out-scooped. I understand, but this isn't your career on the line. It's your life."

"My career is my life," I grumbled.

"Not anymore. To survive, you need Jillian to take the fall for exposing us."

"Why? What's the harm in writing my article if she's going to expose you anyway?"

"It matters; when the Day Reapers come, and believe me they will come, they will come for her and not you."

I closed my mouth. I hadn't considered the Day Reapers. Dominic spoke of them like boogeymen in the shadows, wielding justice and order like swords, but I'd never experienced their wrath. Based on what I'd heard about the horror of Dominic's personal experiences with them, I wanted to keep it that way. The Day Reapers were members of the Council, the governing body who ruled the Masters ruling their covens. Their law was final and breaking that law a death sentence. According to my conversations with Walker when he was still willing to share the vast depths of his vampire knowledge and experience, a night blood transforms into a vampire in three days, but on rare occasions when the transformation takes longer, a Day Reaper is born. They are more powerful, more adept at mind control, and have heightened senses and more abilities than other vampires—including the ability to tolerate sunlight—making them the perfect judges, juries and executioners of vampire-kind.

"Promise me," he insisted.

I sighed. "I promise."

He opened his mouth.

"I promise by the certainty of time that I will not expose the existence of vampires before Jillian," I clarified. "I promise to keep your secret unless it's already exposed."

Dominic smiled.

"What's another bond here and there when we're already linked for life, right?"

"Right." He eased his grip on my shoulders and lay next to me the way he'd intended from the start. "Kiss me before I leave."

I raised my eyebrows. "Is that a request or a command?"

"If I'd commanded you, your lips would already be pressed against mine instead of arguing with me, would they not?"

I pursed my lips.

"Almost, but not quite. You need more of a pucker."

I smacked his shoulder. "And why in the world would I do that?"

"I want to say good-bye. I need to make other arrangements to secure my standing in the coven since my original plan has failed me, and I need a token of courage to give me strength."

"That's a reason why you should kiss me, not why I should kiss you."

Dominic raised an eyebrow. "I should kiss you because I ache for you." He pressed against me again, as if I wasn't already perfectly clear on the part of his anatomy that was aching.

I nudged him away with my shoulder. "If it's just physical satisfaction you're looking for, I'll pass."

Dominic groaned and flopped back on the hammock to gaze at the sky. "You're insufferable. What about allowing you to keep your memory is just physical satisfaction?"

I rolled my eyes. "If you're looking for a thank-you for allowing me to keep something I already have the right to keep, then fine. *Thank you*," I said snottily.

"Wiping your memory was never truly an option. I just needed to ensure that you'd considered all possibilities. That we were, as you say, on the same damn page."

I couldn't help but smile. He really did listen to me when I spoke. "And why is wiping my memory not an option? Not that I want to encourage you, but it's the option I'd thought *you'd* prefer."

"If I wiped your memory of vampires, I'd be wiping your memory of my existence. Of everything I can and can't bear, everything I'd do for the bigger picture and for my coven, I could never do that."

I stared at him, trying to determine the truth in his words.

He gave me a long look. "I can't bear that you forget my name on command. I can't imagine you forgetting me entirely." He made a strange noise in the back of his throat that clogged my own. "It's unthinkable."

I touched the scar on his chin and urged his face toward mine. He looked at me, wary now that I'd pissed him off, but still willing.

"I'm sorry that I can't help you on the Leveling. I really am. And I'm grateful that you're allowing me to keep my memory, that you're choosing me over your coven. I understand how big that is."

He nodded.

"But you and I, whatever this is between us, is wrong. I'm human, and you're—"

"And I'm a monster," he interrupted bitterly.

"And you're a vampire," I said firmly.

"It's just a kiss."

I laughed. "With you, it's never just anything."

His focus honed on my lips, and my laugh died at the seriousness of his expression. I wanted him. God help me—vampire or not, monster or not—I wanted to kiss him.

"Tell me you don't want to kiss me," he demanded.

"Stop reading my thoughts," I snapped.

"I'm not. I'm reading your expression. Say it," he urged.

I shook my head. "I want to kiss you, damn it. But that's not the point—"

"That's exactly the point," he growled. Taking my acknowledgment as permission, he kissed me.

And damn me, I kissed him back.

His lips pressed hard against mine—longing, searching, needing—and I moved my lips over his, matching his need and passion with my own. I licked a smooth line over his bottom lip, over the jagged pull of his scar. Like a shark drawn to the source of a blood trail, he growled at that sensitive lick and feasted on my mouth. He stroked my tongue with his tongue, sucked my bottom lip into his mouth, and bit it between his flat front teeth.

I could tell he was being careful. His fangs were lethal, and if he wasn't careful, he could tear my mouth apart as easily as kiss it. But I didn't want careful. I wanted him as lost and drowning as I felt.

I bit him back.

I slanted my mouth over his, scraped his lip between my teeth, and pulled him closer. Without his heightened vampire senses clouding my perception, I could feel Dominic's kiss for exactly what it was, not the snapping warmth of a hearth or the bursting orange glow of our colliding auras or the millions of other indescribable sights, scents, tastes, textures, and sounds of a kiss while on his blood. That kiss had been like a dream: I remembered it happening, but even in the moment while it happened, nothing about it seemed real. Nothing about kissing Dominic or the feelings he made me feel had made tangible, lucid sense.

Without the heightened senses, as his hand cupped the back of my neck, as he tilted my head to gain better access, and as he growled into my mouth, I knew the truth: the reality of his kiss was better than the dream. I wanted more.

I wanted him.

He moved away from my lips to nip a line down the side of my neck. I tried to breathe, to think, to speak, but the chill of his breath against the hollow of my shoulder shot goose bumps down my side, and all I could do was feel. I scraped my nails down his back.

He growled again, like the revving purr of a '69 Cobra Jet. He was the perfect combination of power and muscle and badass design that even someone like me, who knew next to nothing about cars beyond their look and feel, knew on sight that I wanted to drive. This close, with nothing, not even air, between us, I felt the vibration of his growl from my neck to jawline to the roots of my teeth.

His hand still cupped the back of my neck, controlling and dominant as always, but his other hand shifted gears, stealing slowly under my shirt. I felt his long fingers and the calluses on his palm scrape a long, hot line along my side and over my stomach. I knew where that hand was navigating as it drove fractionally higher. I tried to ignore the rush of my heart as it pounded panic in a cold wash over Dominic's heat, but the panic was undeniable.

Dominic was not Adam, I reminded myself. In every way possible for two men to be dissimilar, Dominic and my ex-boyfriend were two completely different people. Dominic was more animal than man. Where he was wild and dangerous, Adam had been sensitive, sweet, caring, and harmless, yet Adam had hurt me in ways I'd never thought possible. The deepest wounds never heal—you just learn to live with them—but this one wound, the hole Adam had left in my heart with his absence, was the one I still hadn't learned to live with.

Dominic's hand cupped my breast.

I tore my lips from his mouth, panting.

"Never just a kiss," I murmured lightly.

Dominic wasn't fooled. I could see by the disappointment and concern battling in his eyes that he knew my stopping him again was more pain than modesty, but unlike Adam, he didn't pin me down with accusations like knives.

"Did I hurt you?" he asked.

I shook my head.

"Do you want to talk about it?"

I opened my mouth to automatically deny there was anything to talk about, but the penetrating steadiness in his stare stopped me. He wasn't turning away from me. When I was ready, we could face the pain together.

I shook my head again. "Not yet."

"All right," he said. He touched a lock of hair that had sprung wildly out of place in our frenzy and smoothed it down behind my ear. His thumb grazed the side of my cheek, and the Adam-shaped hole in my heart, the promises and hopes and future I'd let die along with my parents, ached.

"Then before I bid you good night, *Cassidy DiRocco...*" he murmured, but the soft comfort of his tone couldn't mask the command in his words. My mind sang like a tuning fork in response to his voice, and I groaned.

"No, just this once, just for tonight, let it go. Please," I pleaded. "We were having a moment. Why ruin a perfectly good moment?"

"You will forget my name," he commanded.

And just like that, immediately and unforgivably, his name disappeared from my mind.

I turned away from him, feeling useless and weak and angry—wildly, burningly angry—and, if I was honest, disappointed in myself.

He let me roll out of the hammock. I was under no illusion that I'd escaped him. He let me leave.

"Well?" he asked.

I shook my head. "Nothing. Once again, it's like empty space in my mind where your name used to be."

He sighed. The pain he exuded from that expulsion of breath was almost enough to let me forgive him. Almost.

"I'm sorry," he said, and in one graceful move, he stood from the hammock to face me.

I crossed my arms. "Me too."

"Good night, Cassidy."

"Good night," I said shortly, my voice pinched. My mind struggled and failed to find his name in the gray matter of my brain.

And as part of the smoke-and-mirror games he could play on my mind, I blinked, and Dominic vanished into the night. The only proof of his presence from one moment to the next was the slight swing of the hammock and the tingling formation of a hickey on the side of my neck.

Chapter 3

Apparently, my conversation hadn't classified as a "quickie." Meredith was gone when I returned to the kitchen, the only proof of *her* presence the empty sushi container on the counter.

I picked up my phone to check the time—our conversation had only been twenty minutes, thirty tops considering the kissing—and stared at the six missed calls and four voice mails from Carter.

"Crap, crap, crap," I said in a panicked litany. "What the hell's going on?"

I pounded the voice mail icon and listened to Carter's impatient voice blast me from the office. "You'd better not be picking up your phone, DiRocco, because you are already at this crime scene. Meredith assures me, as she always does, that you are with her, but I know from her previous assurances that isn't always the case. I need you at the corner of East 56th Street and Avenue D in Brooklyn at Harry Maze Playground, and I need you there yesterday. The police are being tight-lipped on this scene, but you and I both know who can squeeze out a sentence or two even if they aren't releasing an official statement. Get it done, DiRocco. I fell back in love with you after that piece on crime fluctuation, but ignoring my calls on the first major murder we've had this week is not going to keep you in my good graces. Not at all!"

I rolled my eyes at Carter's melodramatic tone and swiped my leather satchel off the counter on my way out.

Why hadn't Meredith interrupted my conversation with the Master vampire? I thought, angry with Meredith for ditching me on a case and with myself for having to refer to him as "Master vampire" even in my own thoughts.

I could still feel the churning ache and fireworks of kissing him, but I couldn't for the life of me find the consonants and vowels to form his name. I ground my teeth in frustration.

"I'm going out to a crime scene. Duty calls," I shouted through the closed bathroom door in Nathan's direction.

He didn't respond, but I hadn't expected him to.

If a certain Master vampire could find the patience to wait out my wounds, I could find the patience to wait out Nathan's. Although, to be fair, patience had never been my strong suit.

Just as I reached the front door, someone knocked.

Relief washed over me, and I grinned as I turned the knob. "I knew you wouldn't leave without me, Meredith. If you're trying to teach me a lesson on quickies, it worked."

I swung the door open, but the skeletal, fanged, twitchy woman standing outside the threshold of my apartment was decidedly not Meredith.

"Ronnie?" I asked, carefully. Hopefully, I didn't look as horrified as I felt.

The first time I'd made Ronnie Carmichael's acquaintance, I'd felt a twinge of jealousy. She'd welcomed Walker home after he'd picked me up from the bus terminal, and the gesture had been mostly platonic—she'd waited for us on the porch in an oversized, green sweatshirt, boot-cut jeans, and fuzzy green socks—but it wasn't the casual clothes, warm hazel eyes, or wide, bright smile that had made my heart hurt. It was the warmth in Walker's responding smile that had churned my stomach.

Despite the smile, Walker had never noticed how much Ronnie cared for him; he'd missed a lot of things. In the fifteen years they'd lived together, she hadn't left the house for fear of vampires. She was pale from hiding in the house, and thin, either naturally or from depression—too thin considering the amount of banana nut pancakes she'd made every day for everyone else. She'd been scared of her own shadow, even tucked safe and sound inside Walker's house, and, just looking at her, I'd been torn between smacking her and feeding her. I remember thinking that evening on Walker's porch, when she'd been healthy and human, that her pale skin and sharp features reminded me of fine china, something of high value but easily broken.

Now she was in pieces.

Her auburn hair, which once fell thick and shiny in soft waves,

was thin and hung from her scalp like tinsel. I'd thought her thin before, but now she was skeletal. Her features were no longer sharp;
they were gaunt. Her protruding bones formed hollows beneath her
cheeks, and her thin, purple lips pulled tight against teeth that looked
too big for her mouth. Her eyeteeth were pointed into delicate fangs,
but they couldn't with any true comparison compete with Dominic's
fangs. They were pointed and sharp enough to break skin, but I didn't
tremble at the sight of her. She was the one trembling. Even as a
predator, Ronnie was still a victim, and God help me, I still wanted to
feed her.

Unfortunately, I'd learned my lesson the hard way when it came
to letting Ronnie drink from me. I wouldn't be making that mistake
again anytime soon.

Ronnie Carmichael was a vampire.

That sentence still didn't make sense to me. Even staring at her
physically in front of me, emaciated and fanged and trembling, it
didn't make sense. She'd lived with Walker, a vampire hunter, and
somehow, even hiding inside Walker's anti-vampire fortress, she'd
been attacked and transformed into the very creature she feared most.

I had my suspicions about that day and who had transformed her;
those suspicions pointed to the same vampire who had inexplicably
been capable of saving me the day I'd bled myself dry attempting to
transform Nathan back from being Damned. Bex, Master vampire of
Erin, New York—and thanks to me, Master vampire of New York
City's new ally—had carried both my brother and me, half-dead and
mostly unconscious, out of the woods and to the hospital, and she'd
done so in broad daylight. The one person I'd told, whose name still
eluded me, had said I was mistaken, and if I wasn't, I should keep my
mouth shut about it. Because if Bex had saved me and transformed
Ronnie in broad daylight without bursting into flames, then that only
meant one thing: Bex was a Day Reaper.

"May I come in?" Ronnie asked. She twitched her head up and to
the side, looking down the hall. Then she twitched her attention back
to me.

I opened my mouth, automatically about to invite her inside, and
then I snapped my mouth shut. This was Ronnie, sure, but she was
also a vampire.

I peeked down the hall where she'd been looking, but the hallway
was empty. "Are you running from something?"

She rubbed her hands together methodically, worrying the scabbed skin at her knuckles. The movement reminded me of a fly.

This is Ronnie, I reminded myself, and although I couldn't let her in, I couldn't be rude either. I patted the silver knife in my leather satchel, assuring myself of its presence. I'd always preferred silver nitrate spray over weapons that could be turned against me, but I didn't have Walker in my corner anymore. Without Walker, I didn't have a ready supply of silver nitrate. I still wore a vial of Dominic's blood on a necklace around my neck, but that was useful only if my other weapons failed. If I was injured, assuming I survived an attack, I could heal myself with his blood, but I had to be very careful. If I lost too much of my own blood, using his blood to heal myself would transform me into a vampire. Although, considering that the blood pumping through my veins was no longer night blood, Dominic's blood might actually kill me now before it saved me.

Against my better judgment—with only my knife, silver jewelry, and crossed fingers to keep Ronnie at bay—I stepped across the threshold and joined her in the hallway.

"What's wrong, Ronnie? What are you doing here?" I frowned at the fear and gaunt lines etching her face. "Does the Master of New York City know you're here?"

Ronnie shook her head frantically. "No, Lysander doesn't know I'm here. No one knows."

Lysander! His last name filled half the gap in my mind. It wasn't great, but anything was better than nothing. I'd take what I could get. "Then what's going on?" I asked, focusing on Ronnie.

She tried to swallow. I could see her throat struggling to move before she succumbed to a bout of racking coughs. When the coughing subsided, she rasped, "I need help."

"I know." I reached out a hand to pat her back and froze. Her eyes caught my movement. Her head twitched, and her gaze focused with unwavering intensity on my wrist. I let my hand drop back down to my side. She looked at me again, pathetic and still trembling, and I sighed. "You haven't visited Walker, have you?"

Ronnie shook her head.

"I know it's hard. Walker, the house, the night bloods: they were your family. And now," I stared at Ronnie and swallowed, "now, everything's changed. It's a huge adjustment, an unthinkable adjustment, but it happened. You have to move on from Walker, move on from that life, and make a new life for yourself with other vampires. Have you talked to anyone about it?"

She shook her head again.

"They were night bloods once too, you know. That's something you have in common," I said, trying and failing miserably to be positive. She'd been attacked and transformed against her will, not spending time in day care. She shouldn't have to find something in common with her attackers. She shouldn't have to try to make friends.

"It's not just me," Ronnie said. She looked over her shoulder and down the hallway again.

I followed her gaze, but the hallway was still empty. I glanced at my watch and suppressed a sigh. I was already late to the crime scene. I didn't have time to play therapist, not even for Ronnie.

"You really need to eat something. You don't look well," I said, unthinkingly, and then I held up a hand. "But not here. Eat something on your way home, after you've left the city. I have enough crime here without you feeding, too." I narrowed my eyes on her, remembering how she had struggled with the powers that came so naturally to other vampires. "Can you entrance a human?"

Ronnie growled. I didn't recognize it at first because it was higher and threadier than the deep, clicking rumble I was accustomed to hearing from other vampires, but even higher pitched and softer around the edges, it still spiked the hairs at the back of my neck to attention.

I rummaged in my leather satchel for the hilt of my silver knife, wishing it were silver nitrate spray. I could stab Ronnie if I needed to. If it came down to her or me, I'd choose me, no question, but I didn't want to. I couldn't imagine the frail, kind woman I'd known, now a vampire, reduced to nothing but ash.

My breath caught as my thoughts drifted to Rene, Bex's Second and the only vampire I'd ever witnessed crumble to ash from a silver broadhead to the heart. I swallowed down the pressure in my throat, compacted the ache deep in my chest, and slammed the lid shut on the burning behind my eyelids until my feelings were once again locked into a very tiny box. I couldn't deal with the nightmares of my past now when Ronnie was standing before me here in the present, a living nightmare right in front of me.

"Ronnie," I said, the warning in my tone sharp, "don't do this."

"You're not listening," she said, clearly distraught, but still growling and still inching closer.

"Calm down, and I'll listen."

"You don't understand. We're all like this." She raised her hand, and her fingernails had pointed to claws. They didn't lengthen to talons, like *Lysander's*—the frustration of not knowing his full name still stung—but they could still do some serious damage against my easily wounded, human skin.

"I'm your friend, but I will hurt you before I let you hurt me. Do *you* understand?"

Ronnie stopped inching closer. "Hurt you? Why would I . . ." she began, and then she saw her own hand, raised and clawed, and dawning horror broke over her expression. "I won't hurt you. This is just how my hand is. This is how I look now."

"It doesn't have to look that way, not if you would eat properly. But like I said, not here." I relaxed my grip on the knife now that she'd stopped advancing.

"That's what I'm trying to tell you," she snapped, and then she closed her eyes, took a long, deep breath, and retreated a step. Her claws rounded to nails again, and when she opened her eyes, her expression, although still haunting, was less frantic. "We're all weak. We don't know how to use our vampire senses to our benefit. I heard a bird squawking while I was deep underground, within my room in Bex's coven."

"Well, you have exceptional hearing now," I said.

Ronnie shook her head. "It was the sound of Keagan's annoyance at the grate of my voice. I never even knew he thought of my voice as grating. I never knew someone's annoyance had a sound, let alone that it sounded like a squawking bird."

I nodded knowingly. "I'm sure it's confusing, but you'll get the hang of it. You have lifetimes to get used to it," I said half-jokingly, trying to make light of her situation.

She stared at me with her crazy, otherworldly eyes, and I swallowed my jokes.

"I won't have another week, let alone lifetimes, if I can't eat," she said. "None of us will. I don't want to hurt anyone. You remember what happened to your wrist when I drank from you?"

"Well, yes, but—"

"I can't heal a wound, so if I bite someone's neck, they'll die. Even if I managed not to kill them, I can't use mind control to make them forget the attack." She touched my arm. I flinched, but she didn't hurt me. She was reaching out. She was trembling. "We need help. None of us can do this except you."

"Me? How can I help? I'm not a vampire." *I'm not even a night blood anymore*, I thought, but *Lysander* and I had both agreed it was best to keep that knowledge between the two of us.

"We're vampires, and we can't use mind control," Ronnie whispered, her voice soft and sincere and so damn hopeful it gave me goose bumps. "But you're only a night blood, and you can entrance vampires. Please, Cassidy, you have to help us."

I narrowed my eyes and focused on the one word in her argument that I could legitimately argue back. "'Us'? Who are you referring to besides yourself?"

"Keagan, Jeremy, Theresa, and Logan. We were all in the house the day Bex attacked and transformed us."

I breathed in sharply. Although that was exactly what I'd suspected had happened the night I'd returned from Bex's coven to Walker's empty house, having my suspicions confirmed was like a stake through the heart. I'd saved my brother during that fateful visit to Walker's hometown, but the events that had unfolded because of my visit had irrevocably destroyed two families and the home that Walker had built literally with his own hands. I wouldn't undo saving my brother even if I had the power to turn back time, but looking at Ronnie, at the sorrow in her eyes in her corpsey face, I could regret everything that happened to Ronnie and Keagan and all the other night bloods. I wouldn't take it back, but I regretted it.

I reached out—wanting to help, needing to comfort—but before I could touch Ronnie's shoulder or squeeze her hand in support, she twitched her head sideways, eyeing my arm like a bird will its prey.

I let my hand drop. The Ronnie I might comfort and support was dead and in her place was a creature that fed from my blood, and I couldn't forget that. "Are you certain Bex was the vampire who attacked you?"

"Of course I'm certain," Ronnie said, her voice rising in exasperation. "I saw her face, plain as day."

"Keep your voice down," I hushed. "The night has hundreds of ears, and that is not something we want everyone to overhear."

"She might be your ally through your precious *Dominic*, but I don't owe her a goddamn thing," Ronnie snapped. "She attacked us, transformed us, and left us to die in her coven. I'm by far the weakest of the five of us, but we all need help harnessing our new abilities. We won't survive much longer without your help, Cassidy, *please*. I'm begging you."

Dominic! My mind soaked the name deep into my memory, fully refilling the gap from his command. I remembered his name again. *Dominic Lysander*, I thought to myself and smiled in relief. I finally felt whole again.

"This isn't funny," Ronnie said, and her voice cracked. She was near tears.

"No, it's not." I wiped the smile from my face. "Have you talked to Bex about any of this?" I asked, and Ronnie's expression hardened. I held up a hand. "Not about you coming here. About harnessing your senses and mind control."

"How can I talk to her when she's not there?" Ronnie said slowly and loudly, like one might speak to the elderly.

I blinked. "What do you mean, she's not there? You haven't seen her lately?"

"I haven't seen her at all. No one has since the day you transformed Nathan back from the Damned. She's gone."

I raised my eyebrows. "No one knows where she is? Not anyone?"

"I can think of only two people who might know where she's hiding: Rene and Ian."

My heart ached at the mention of Rene, but I ignored it. "Walker and I aren't speaking."

"Well, Ian and I certainly aren't on speaking terms either," Ronnie said, exasperated.

"I doubt she'd leave her coven unprotected," I said skeptically.

Ronnie shook her head. "We're not unprotected. In fact, it's just the opposite. There are several aged, very powerful vampires keeping order in her absence. No one knows where she's gone, but everyone was prepared."

"That's good. Maybe one of those vampires could—"

"They're busy being Master by proxy, and I don't know them, Cassidy. They're vicious and evil and horrible and—" Ronnie's voice broke. She took several deep breaths before she was able to compose herself again. "They're vampires."

"Well," I said softly, very softly, "so are you."

"They're not my friends. I don't know them. The only thing I *do* know about them is that they've attacked and killed people. They're animals. *You're* my friend, Cassidy, and I need *your* help. Please, teach me to harness my vampire abilities."

I rubbed my forehead, an expanding headache throbbing between my eyebrows. "I'll do what I can, but to be honest, I don't know if mind control is the same for vampires as it is for me. I barely know how I do it myself."

"Anything you can teach me is more than I know now," she said, the hope in her expression overflowing.

"I can think of another person who might know where Bex would hide," I said thoughtfully. "And he might be able to help you harness your abilities better than me."

Ronnie's expression fell flat. "No."

"Formally introducing you to Dominic is a good thing. You'll have a resource if something ever happens to Bex."

"Something *has* happened to Bex!"

"Don't jump to conclusions, but that's exactly why you should meet Dominic. He's your ally. He can help, and if there's one thing I've learned over the past month, it's that you need to gather as many allies as possible and surround yourself with them like Kevlar."

"I don't want more vampires involved. No one knows I'm here. I just need *your* help, no one else's, and especially not Lysander's."

I dropped my arms to my side and shrugged. "I'll do what I can," I muttered, feeling defeated. How could I teach anyone mind control when I'd lost the ability to do it myself?

"Thank you, thank you, thank you!" Ronnie shouted in a litany. She launched herself at me and wrapped her arms around my neck.

I patted her back carefully, wincing at the feel of her bony ribs through her tissue-paper skin. "You're welcome. I'll see you back here tomorrow night. Meet me on the rooftop."

She pulled back. "Tomorrow? But I thought—"

"I was just on my way out. I have business tonight, but I'll see you tomorrow." I stared into her eyes, trying to decipher what else was wrong, what else I was missing, but I couldn't see anything in those otherworldly, swirling orbs except my own reflection. "Okay?"

Ronnie was struggling with something. She bit her lip, and since she was still unaccustomed to having fangs, one punctured her skin.

I watched it embed in her lip and winced for her, but she didn't even blink. She just licked at the wound and stared at me, trying to find the words.

"Okay?" I pushed, feeling bad that I was pushing at all, but if I didn't show my face at Harry Maze Playground tonight, Carter would have my ass on a platter.

She nodded. "All right. I'll see you here tomorrow night."

"On the rooftop," I reminded her.

"On the rooftop," she murmured back, and I wondered if maybe I hadn't lost my mind-control abilities. Ronnie had always been meek and compliant, even as a night blood, but I was missing something. Judging by the lost, frantic expression on Ronnie's face as I walked away, that something was big. For the life of me, though, as I rounded the corner of the hall, the same corner that Ronnie had kept in her peripheral vision, I couldn't see any holes I'd missed.

Nothing sprang out from around the corner as I turned toward the elevator. Nothing attacked me as the elevator doors opened, and Ronnie didn't stop the elevator doors from closing as I left, but it didn't matter if I couldn't see the hole. Unseen, it would still leak until I was drowning. By then, even if I found the leak, it'd be too late. After over five years of investigative journalism, I knew that no matter how big or small, a missing piece to the puzzle was the piece that inevitably got people killed.

Chapter 4

Harry Maze Playground was still in massive chaos when I turned the corner onto East 56th Street. Detective Greta Wahl and her team were efficient and diligent and damn good at their jobs, but assessing them on this scene alone, I would have thought rookies were running the show. Barriers hadn't been properly established, and members of the media were going wild, snapping close-ups of victims, trampling across the playground to snag statements, and wrestling one another to interview witnesses.

Five years ago, I might have joined the mob. I might have elbowed my way into the thick of it, shouting questions at sobbing victims and scrapping for quotes, but my hip couldn't tolerate that kind of pressure. If someone threw an elbow my way—based on the groans and grunts and sway of the mob, I'd say more than a few elbows were landing on target—I didn't have the strength to elbow back. I'd easily become one of the victims being trampled. Since I couldn't join the big boys in the trenches anymore, I had to snake along the sidelines and fight my battle more strategically.

Even without a busted hip, evidently Meredith felt the same way. I caught her speaking to two women sitting on the curb next to an ambulance. Judging from the yellow tags around their wrists and the fact that they hadn't been loaded into the ambulance for immediate transport to the hospital, there must be other, more critical victims on scene for the medics to triage.

I stepped forward to join Meredith at the ambulance when someone caught my arm. I turned to set straight whoever was manhandling me, but the hand belonged to Officer Harroway. His grin, as usual, was part genuine and part mischief. If the gleam in his baby blue eyes was any indication, I'd say mischief won the majority.

Officer Harroway was a handsome, block-jawed, stubborn man. He never knew when to stop teasing or when a joke was more inappropriate than funny, and our shared history only made his inability to resist a joke at my expense that much more frustrating.

My limp, my reputation at the precinct—hell, my very presence—were all reminders of that fateful Mars Killington stakeout five years ago. It should have been the breakout of all our careers, Greta's and Harroway's as well as my own, but my source had set us up. When we'd been caught in the cross fire, I'd covered his back with mine and took the bullet meant for him. The precinct would never forget my heroism for saving one of their own, but Harroway, the bastard, had never forgiven me for it.

Despite his bruised ego and survivor's guilt, or maybe because of it, Harroway gave me the inside scoop on cases when the rest of the police in his department were being tight-lipped. His way of saying thank you, since he suffered from the inability to express his gratitude directly, but given the choice between the two, I'd take the scoop.

His sappy baby blues stared down at me now, sparking with delight, and I waited for whatever ridiculous statement was about to crawl out of his mouth. I wasn't a patient person, but when it came to Harroway, I preferred not to encourage his antics.

"Will you come with me? Detective Wahl needs to speak with you," Harroway said, his voice the epitome of professionalism.

I frowned. The teasing gleam in his eyes was unmistakable, but for the first time in the five years I'd known and loved-hated him, Harroway refrained from stabbing me between the ribs with his wit.

"Greta needs to speak with me?" I said, trying to act like he hadn't thrown me a curve ball. "Now?"

"That's what I just said," Harroway replied. He stepped toward the scene, assuming I'd follow. "Hard of hearing tonight, DiRocco?"

Of course, he'd assumed right. I followed fast on his heels, or at least as fast as my grinding hip allowed. "Why does Greta want me on her crime scene? Shouldn't she be processing the evidence, interviewing witnesses, and chasing down suspects?"

Harroway shrugged. "She sent me here to chase you down this time."

"I'm not a witness or a suspect, am I?" I asked.

"No, you're a pain in my ass," Harroway said, but his grin took the sting from his words. "What's gotten into you? If Detective Wahl wants to talk to you, that means you get to talk to her. You can shake her or squeeze her or whatever it is you reporters do to get information. It's a win-win."

I raised my eyebrows. "It doesn't look like the other reporters are getting one-on-one time."

"Nope, but the other reporters aren't you." He held up the yellow police tape for me to duck under. "Ladies first."

The other reporters glared at me as he escorted me on scene, the combination of jealousy and respect coloring their expressions. Some of them were more jealous than others. A few looked downright pissed, but the attention, no matter how unwanted or unwarranted, wasn't anything I wasn't used to.

"…environmental science expert."

I'd only caught the tail end of his sentence, distracted by the crowd and chaos. "What did you say?" I asked.

"You really might want to have your hearing checked, DiRocco." Harroway snapped his fingers next to my ear.

I backslapped his hand away. "Hands off, Harroway."

"The environmental science expert Greta called to consult on this case is here," he said, chuckling. "This scene is messier than any case we've seen in a while, and, as unlikely as it seems, we might be looking at an animal attack."

I raised my eyebrows. "Animal attack?"

Harroway held up a hand. "I know it seems impossible here in the middle of Brooklyn, but animal bites don't lie. Whatever killed these people certainly isn't human. Unless humans are evolving claws and very sharp canines," he said, shaking his head.

Vampires, I thought, but Dominic usually altered the evidence before the police arrived to ensure the safety of his coven and the continued secrecy of their existence. The last time he'd allowed a scene to remain unaltered and everyone had suspected an animal attack—everyone, that is, until Dominic had entranced them all the next day—he'd been betrayed by Jillian and her rebels, attacked, and left exposed to sunlight, incapacitated and unable to alter the evidence.

I just saw Dominic tonight, I reminded myself. *He's fine.* But that didn't stop a knot from tightening in the pit of my gut.

Then the other ball dropped as I realized the full extent of what Harroway had just said. Greta had called in the advice of an environmental science expert for animal-bite victims. Regret and anxiety doused my worry for Dominic.

Walker was here.

Forcing one foot in front of the other was always physically painful, but continuing to follow Harroway to the crime scene, knowing he was also leading me to Walker, was excruciating. The thought of facing Walker after everything we'd said to each other—and left unsaid—was unthinkable. He didn't even know about Ronnie.

Harroway turned at the fence corner to enter the playground, and I gaped at the scene in front of us. I should have prepared myself. He'd warned me that the scene was gruesome, but actually seeing the mess of bloody victims scattered over the wood chips with my own eyes was something else entirely.

Some of the victims were still moaning and trembling in pain, waiting for medical treatment. Most were splayed across the ground, their wounds embedded with dirt and wood chips, but a few were bent back over teeter-totters and lying at odd angles across slides. One man was hanging halfway from the bottom monkey bar, his upper back on the ground, his lower body raised upside down, and his broken leg jammed between two of the bars.

Other victims were already bandaged and wore yellow tags around their wrists, waiting for transport to the hospital. A medic wrapped a red tag around the wrist of a young woman whose stomach had been impaled on a metal fence post. Miraculously, she was still conscious and responding to the medic's questions. Several other medics joined them, one with a power saw, and they prepared to cut the post from its cement casing.

As many victims as there were waiting on medical treatment, the majority of the bodies were still and silent, many with missing arms and legs, some with missing heads, and those detached appendages were also scattered across the wood chips among the dead and still-suffering victims.

I took a deep breath, glad we were outside—the air was crisp and clean despite the carnage—and tried to collect myself.

"How many?" I asked, gazing over the scene as a whole and trying to not focus too closely on any one person or injury.

"At our most recent count, forty-two people were injured. More people were here than usual at this time of night because of a Night Owl fund-raising event, something about raising money for kids and literacy. A few survived with only minor lacerations, but the majority of the victims were mauled. Some were obviously dismembered." Harroway wiped his hand down his face. "It's grisly here, DiRocco. Old hamburger meat."

I winced at his description. "You had to go there," I muttered.

"Squeamish, DiRocco?"

I shook my head. "Tired. Just so damn tired of covering the same scenes over and over again."

Harroway raised his eyebrows. "You've covered an animal attack in Brooklyn before?"

I can't get away from them, I thought.

The last "animal attack" in Brooklyn had been attributed to gang violence, and the "animal attack" I'd covered while visiting Walker upstate had been officially deemed a rabid-bear attack, but I was one of the few people who knew the unofficial truth about both cases.

And thanks to my recent promise to Dominic to keep the existence of vampires a secret, I thought bitterly, *the truth would remain unofficial.*

"If you can't handle this, DiRocco, maybe you shouldn't be on scene."

I met his eyes. "Can't get rid of me that easily, Harroway."

"Glad to hear it," he said and turned to forge a path through the mess of pain, blood, and death to find Detective Greta Wahl.

She was speaking to a tall, dark-haired man when we approached. Greta was average height, but the man next to her made her look petite in comparison. Her curves were hidden beneath a bulky, second-hand blazer, and she'd slicked back her thick, curly hair into her usual tight, no-nonsense bun. Greta exercised that no-nonsense attitude with more than just her hairstyle; her pragmatic, direct approach to life had been a catapult to her career and our friendship. The jut of her chin and her wide stance telegraphed that she wasn't letting anyone, no matter their height, gender, or position, stand in the way of solving this case. If he wasn't helping, he was hurting, but luckily for this man, he was nodding his agreement to whatever Greta was saying, the epitome of team work.

The dark-haired giant looked familiar, but I'd worked my fair share of crime scenes in Brooklyn; I knew almost every detective, officer, and forensic scientist by face if not by name. I dismissed the man and kept a wary eye out for golden-blond, curly hair and a pair of velvet brown eyes. If Harroway was right about Greta calling in an environmental science expert, Walker was working this crime scene somewhere, measuring bite radii, snapping pictures, and pretending to be just as dumbfounded by an animal attack in the middle of Brooklyn as everyone else.

The shared secret of being night bloods and knowing that vampires existed had bonded us more quickly and tightly than I'd ever experienced with another person, but the last time we'd seen each other, Walker had killed Rene, turned his back on me, and left me to die, effectively severing that bond.

I wasn't in any rush for a reunion.

"I found DiRocco wandering the perimeter," Harroway said, gaining Greta's attention. "She was last on scene, as usual."

I glared at him. "It doesn't matter when I start the race as long as I finish first."

Harroway snorted. "With that bum hip, I'd say you need the furthest head start you can get."

And there was the Harroway I knew and couldn't stand to be around, slipping the knife quick and dirty between the ribs.

"Thank you for finding DiRocco. I can take it from here," Greta said, turning to face me and effectively dismissing him. "I need you back on blood spatter. Janson needs help transporting samples."

Harroway's face reddened slightly, but if he disagreed with her assignment, he wouldn't disrespect Greta, not directly and not in public. Without another word, he nodded and walked away.

I turned to Greta, shaking my head. "I'll take a dose of whatever mind-control powers you have over Harroway, please."

Greta laughed. "It's called pulling rank. But I'm not fooled, DiRocco. You might not enjoy Harroway's sense of humor, but you do like biting him back with it."

"Well, yes, there is that," I admitted. I held out my hand. "Always a pleasure, G, despite the circumstances."

She took my hand and pumped it once. "I thought you'd take a special interest in this case, considering the evidence."

I cocked my head. "What evidence is that?"

Greta held up her hand. "We'll get there. I was just explaining the history and sensitivity of this case to our environmental science expert. Nicholas Leander, meet Cassidy DiRocco. She's the investigative journalist I've been bragging about, and my personal friend. DiRocco, this is our expert witness, Dr. Leander."

Dominic gazed down at me, his scarred lips quirking into a smile as I stared, dumbfounded. He was the tall, dark-haired man who had been conversing with Greta when I'd approached. The implications were slow to seep into my shocked brain, but when they did, they fired like a rocket launcher.

I wouldn't be working with Walker on this case, but God help me, the only thing worse than working with Walker was working with the devil grinning down at me.

Chapter 5

"Dr. Leander," I said numbly. He'd had the nerve not only to forge a degree, but a doctorate.

"Nicholas is just fine," Dominic said, holding out his hand. I resisted the urge to smack the smirk from his face.

I'd never imagined Dominic having a career, let alone posing as having one. I'd envisioned his nights being spent as a creature of darkness—whatever that entailed—but never in my wildest dreams did I ever expect to have to interact with him in a professional setting. I'd never interacted with Dominic in front of anyone besides other vampires. Our brief conversation tonight with Meredith had been the first time that I'd witnessed him speak with a human and not mind-wipe the conversation from her memory.

Every time I thought I'd come to grips with reality, some new discovery reared its ugly head and tore the life I'd come to accept from my numb grasp. I'd accepted the improbable existence of vampires only to discover my night blood. I'd embraced my night blood only to discover the existence of Damned vampires and my brother as one. I'd transformed Nathan back from being Damned only to lose the protection of my night blood.

And now, Dominic had allowed me to keep my memory of the existence of vampires despite my lack of night blood only for him to pose as a human, and not just any human but an environmental science expert investigating vampire attacks, of all things.

He'd gone too far. As usual, he expected much more from me than I was ever willing to give.

"You've got to be kidding me!" I burst out.

Dominic's grin widened, but I noticed that he didn't allow himself to part his lips entirely. No flashing fangs in front of Greta. I glared at him.

Greta looked back and forth between us. "Are you two already acquainted?"

I sighed in defeat. As much as I abhorred lying to Greta, telling her the truth was out of the question. If I told her that a coven of vampires was living beneath the city and was responsible for several of the murder cases she'd already closed, that said vampires were likely responsible for tonight's murders, that Dominic was not only one of them but was their leader, she would think I'd lost my mind. Dominic knew I was bound to silence by the risk of tarnishing my reputation as well as by my promise to him, and he was using that knowledge to his advantage.

I crossed my arms and settled on what might be the next best thing to exposing the truth: taking advantage of *his* secret. This investigation was my playing field. For once, we weren't in his coven or deep within a coal-mining shaft or in the middle of an upstate New York wilderness. We were in the city, surrounded by humans—and not just any humans, but my close, personal friends—and at a crime scene. This was my turf, and he'd be playing my game for once.

I smiled coyly and took Dominic's proffered hand. "No previous acquaintance, and I'm sorry for the outburst. To be honest, I was expecting someone else."

"That makes two of us," he said.

Dominic pumped firmly and released my hand, but I could feel the tingling of his skin against mine even after he let go. Working together was going to be torture.

I raised my eyebrows. "Who were *you* expecting?"

"Certainly not this," Dominic said, waffling his hand between Greta and me. "According to Detective Wahl, you are quite extraordinary. I'm looking forward to witnessing the magic of your investigative skills for myself."

I narrowed my eyes. "Are you mocking me?"

"Not in the least. If anything, I'm mocking Detective Wahl." He nodded at Greta, and she grinned back, obviously on good terms with a fraud, a fraud I'd brought into our lives. I could spit. "I was just telling her how rare it is for a detective to admire and trust a reporter as highly as she regards you," he finished.

"I assure you, the feeling is mutual," I said, turning to Greta. "It's never a good sign when we need an environmental science expert on the case. What are we dealing with this time?"

"That's what I'm hoping you can tell me," Greta said. She jerked her head toward the opposite end of the playground. "Come on, let me show you. Both of you."

Greta stepped forward to lead the way. With her back turned, I glared at Dominic, trying to express the depth of my annoyance in a glance. He grinned at me, open-lipped and flashing those long, sharp, pearly fangs at me in amusement. I wasn't amused. I didn't know if he or his vampires were responsible for this scene or how he'd obtained the credentials to pose as an expert witness, but no matter how he'd done it, he was here. I'd have to deal with it.

But that didn't mean I had to like it.

"This isn't funny," I said, indicating the carnage and suffering around us.

"No, it's not," Dominic said, "but the look on your face when you saw me certainly was."

"This investigation is important to me—you know how important my work is to me—and I don't appreciate you being here. These people are suffering; they deserve a team of people dedicated to finding the monster responsible for their suffering and bringing that person to justice."

"That's precisely why I'm here. If you find that vampires are responsible, you can't bring them to justice." His smile widened. "But I can."

"And you usually do so without interjecting yourself into the investigation." I narrowed my eyes on him. "Why introduce yourself to Greta and pose as an environmental science expert?"

"Is it wrong for me to better acquaint myself with the facts of this case? My insight and perception might be helpful, considering the evidence. We both know an animal isn't loose in the middle of Brooklyn."

I crossed my arms, not budging. "You can acquaint yourself with the facts of this case without lying to Greta, and without forcing *me* to lie to Greta."

Dominic sighed, the world's troubles, evils, and uncertainties apparent in the weight of his gaze. "You're not a night blood anymore, and without those few abilities you once had, you're more vulnerable than most humans. You have a reputation among the vampires now, but you no longer have the muscle to back it up. I'll be your muscle."

I shook my head, still unconvinced. "Nope, that's not it either."

Dominic blinked. "Excuse me?"

"You're here for something specific, but protecting me isn't the reason. You could protect me without directly interjecting yourself into the investigation." I pinched my lower lip between my fingers. "It must have something to do with the role of being an environmental science expert."

Dominic's expression turned to stone, and I knew by his lack of reaction that I'd struck a nerve.

"Walker would freak if he knew you'd scooped his case," I muttered to myself, and like a spiritual revelation, the truth slammed home. "You're here because you don't want Walker here."

Dominic didn't say anything for a long moment. When he finally spoke, his voice was terse. "You're certainly competent at uncovering the truth."

I snorted. "You don't think Walker is going to catch wind of this investigation and wonder why he wasn't invited to consult?"

"I don't care what he wonders. Detective Wahl did not invite him here, so if he comes, it won't be with any legal authority."

"Since when do you care about legal authority?"

Dominic's jaw tightened. The muscles in his cheek flexed and twitched, and I knew I'd hit another nerve.

"Detective Wahl didn't invite him, so if Walker comes, she'll kick him off the case without you needing to intervene," I said, working through the logic aloud. "Why does that matter? You could just entrance everyone to forget he was here and kick him off the case yourself—" I sucked in a sharp breath and met his gaze. "Except Greta is too stubborn and strong-willed to completely forget."

"Ian Walker can't be trusted, not near my coven and especially not near you," Dominic snapped. "I don't want him here, so either I pose as an environmental science expert in his place, or I kill him. Which do you prefer?"

I opened my mouth and closed it, shocked by his outburst. Even after everything Walker had done, I didn't want him dead. Granted, I didn't want him here investigating this case, but I certainly didn't want to work with Dominic either.

Dominic's expression softened as he gazed into my eyes, and I hated that my anger softened along with it. "I know my presence here chafes you on many levels. You resent that you must keep my secrets from people you deeply respect, but I assure you that I'm not posing in a capacity in which I can't be of service. I want to find the monsters responsible for this atrocity, and if these crimes are vampire-caused, you can be sure I'll bring those responsible to justice."

I frowned, annoyed that his logic made a strange sort of sense. "If you hinder this investigation in any way—"

"I'll be helping you, not hindering you," Dominic interrupted.

"—whatever *this* is," I said, pointing between the two of us, "is over before it ever really began."

He nodded, his expression grave. "I agree to those terms."

Whether he agreed or not wasn't the point. He was bound to hinder this investigation—I could feel the inevitability of his hindrance like the ache in my hip before a storm—and when he did, I'd have a legitimate concrete wall to erect between us.

I turned my back on Dominic and quickened my pace to catch up with Greta. She stopped at the far side of the playground, away from the chaos and the media, and I realized that this section of the crime scene had been secluded with properly established barriers. The stretch of playground adjacent to Avenue D was basically a decoy to keep the sharks busy on the blood Greta wanted them to see, so she could keep them off the scent of this.

The victims here on the far side of the playground were just as mangled and dismembered as the victims scattered across the wood chips, slides, and teeter-totters, but what made my skin crawl in horrible, vivid remembrance was the fact that each victim had a gaping, hole beneath the sternum.

Each of these victims was missing their heart, the same telltale wound that Nathan had left on his victims when he was Damned.

A Damned vampire was here in New York City, and only one non-Master vampire was powerful enough to transform a night blood into the Damned.

Jillian.

I swallowed my nerves and glanced at Dominic. The look in his eyes when he met my gaze made the skin on the back of my neck prickle. Jillian was here in New York City during the week of his Leveling, and she wasn't here alone.

I turned from Dominic to face Greta. "Your team certainly did a better job cordoning off this section of the crime scene," I commented. "Not a camera in sight."

Greta nodded. "And why would I do that?"

I looked out over the victims and their missing hearts and played dumb. "You need to spell it out for me, G. This just looks like more of the same carnage to me."

Greta eyed Dominic and me with her cutting gaze, the way Dominic sometimes looked into me rather than at me, and I felt as if she could peel apart the layers of my mind, too, in search of the truth. Bex had fixed the reports from our case upstate to support a rabid-bear attack and hide the involvement of vampires, including the evidence of missing hearts. No one except Agent Harold Rowens remembered the truth, but as usual, Greta always seemed to know more than she should. She wasn't a night blood, but she was too strong-minded, clever, and stubborn to blindly accept the lies that everyone else so easily believed.

"I'm going to tell you something about these victims that we aren't releasing to the public," Greta said. "You need to sit on this until I give you the go-ahead, got it?"

I nodded. "You know I'm a steel trap."

"The majority of these victims, almost all the victims who died on scene, are missing their hearts."

I frowned, trying—and by the skepticism on Greta's face, probably failing—to fake disbelief. "Missing their hearts?" I asked. "That's not something easily misplaced."

Greta shook her head. "Nope. We'll know more when we get the bodies back to the lab, but preliminary findings suggest that something sharp punctured beneath the sternum and ripped the hearts from their chests whole. Granted, there are a lot of blood and body parts to sift through, but from what we've gathered so far, not one shred of cardiac muscle has been found on scene."

"I don't know much about wild animals, but I can't think of one that specifically hunts humans for their hearts. Maybe we should ask the expert," I said pointedly, raising my eyebrows at Dominic.

He nodded, looking very sage. It made me want to smack him, again. "You're right, Ms. DiRocco," he said, and I felt appeased slightly by the affirmation, which was probably why he'd said it. "There are no wild animals that I know of that deliberately hunt humans for their hearts."

"The evidence we have here suggests otherwise," Greta said grimly.

"Are other organs missing?" Dominic asked.

I felt a pang of guilt. Dominic knew that a Damned vampire was responsible for this massacre. He knew that Jillian was back with one look at those bloody, punctured chests, but despite the anger and fear and festering betrayal that realization probably wrought, he would still play the role of an inquisitive expert witness.

Maybe he wouldn't hinder this investigation as much as I feared after all.

Greta shook her head at Dominic, but when she answered, she was looking pointedly at me. "No, just the hearts are missing. Everything else, although shredded and dismembered, is accounted for."

"My God," I said. I remembered saying that last time. I remembered thinking it over and over again like a mantra, and despite the fact that this scene was nothing but a bad rerun, I was thinking it again.

"The scene's been processed, so do what you need to do, Dr. Leander, before we bring it all back to the lab. We'll have a report from the medical examiner tomorrow, but the faster we close this case, the better."

"I'm assuming photography and measurements are allowed?" Dominic asked. He pulled out a DSLR digital camera from a side satchel I hadn't noticed hanging at his hip. He whipped out a ruler and notepad as well.

As much as I tried to hold in my reaction, I gaped. The Dominic I knew had fangs and pointed ears and transformed into a gargoyle when he got angry. He'd needed directions to operate a cell phone and could barely text. He certainly didn't know how to work a digital camera. He normally didn't wear a side satchel.

I narrowed my eyes, wondering what else he was hiding in his bag of tricks.

Greta extended her hand. "Please. Whatever you need to do. The scene is yours."

Dominic nodded graciously and approached the nearest victim.

I shook my head, not knowing which disaster I was more disgusted with: the crime scene or Dominic's charade.

"DiRocco," Greta said sharply. "A moment?"

I nodded. "Sure, G."

Greta led me away from the carnage. She turned to me, and her voice was low when she said, "Tell me this scene doesn't look familiar to you."

I sighed and looked away, unable to meet her eyes. What the hell could I say?

"This scene is identical to the scenes we had two weeks ago, but back then, we had one victim, not eleven. These were the murders that followed you upstate when you visited Walker. These were the cases that were attributed to a rabid-bear attack, but I'll be damned if a rabid bear was here two weeks ago and double damned if there's a rabid bear here now," Greta pushed, and when Greta pushed, she pushed hard.

I crossed my arms. "What are you getting at, G?"

"You were there in the thick of it. You helped solve that case. Whatever it was, bear or not, you faced it," Greta insisted. "What the hell is going on, DiRocco?"

"You read the report. You know what it says," I said. "Who am I to say differently?"

"Yeah, I read the report," Greta scoffed. "I read your face too, when you saw the victims. You recognized those wounds. Why were the missing hearts omitted from the final police reports?"

I shrugged. "You'd have to ask the officer who wrote the report."

"I'm asking you."

"I didn't write the report, so how should I know what facts, if any, were omitted and why? You never mentioned anything about missing hearts to me before. Why should I know why they're pertinent now?"

"You knew a lot more about that case than was written in that report, and you know more about this case now."

I crossed my arms. "What are you accusing me of? Am *I* under investigation?"

"Do you honestly think that I'd invite you into this investigation, introduce you to my expert witness, and have you very publicly escorted on scene if I thought you were a suspect?"

I narrowed my eyes. "You had Harroway find me and escort me on scene in front of every city reporter on purpose?"

"You've been in the hot seat before, and I don't want to put you there again. What I want is your help. You have inside information on this case, DiRocco, and it's time that you shared it. I'm not accusing you. I'm encouraging you."

I shook my head, not knowing how to respond. This might be my chance. Greta was obviously prepped and ready for the facts, but could any amount of readiness really prepare someone to accept the existence of vampires?

Dominic had made his way across the scene—I could see the flash of his camera from a distance—but whether he was two inches away or two miles, he'd still hear our conversation.

"I just need a direction, DiRocco. I had squat two weeks ago; now we've got five times the victims, and I've still got squat. If you need immunity, you've got it. If you want witness protection, it's yours. However you're tied to this case, however you know what you know, it doesn't matter. No one has to know, not even me, but you've got to throw me a bone. Work with me, DiRocco."

"I don't need your protection." I laughed humorlessly, as if Greta or the police department or anyone could protect me against Dominic's wrath and the subsequent wrath of the Day Reapers. "We all need protection," I muttered.

"DiRocco, please. Give me something. I'm asking you, as your friend, off the record, off my investigation, what the hell is happening?" She leaned in close, and I could see the desperate uncertainty in her eyes. She was scared, and I didn't blame her. I was petrified. "What eats human hearts, and who has the power and resources to cover it up?"

She wanted the truth, and I could tell by her tone and that look in her eyes that she wouldn't give up until she found it—if not from me, from someone else. She might be desperate enough to believe almost anything, but I couldn't expect her to believe something as impossible as the existence of vampires on my word alone. I needed what I always needed when I covered a case. I needed hard evidence to prove my point.

And I needed to prove it without breaking my promise to Dominic.

You're right. I have a lead, I mouthed to her. I couldn't whisper because Dominic would hear. Hell, he could probably hear the movement of my lips. "I'm sorry, Greta," I said aloud. "But you're wrong. I don't know anything about this case. It's as new to me as it is to you."

Greta hesitated. She didn't move a muscle, but her eyes were everywhere, searching the scene, scanning her officers, glaring at someone over my shoulder.

When she met my eyes again, I mouthed to her again. *We need privacy.*

Greta nodded. "I understand. Thank you for being honest." *Tomorrow morning at the morgue. I'm meeting with Dr. Chunn.*

"Anytime."

Greta reached out and squeezed my shoulder. *8:00 a.m.*

I nodded.

Greta returned to the scene—toward blood, guts, carnage, and Dominic—and I felt sick with dread. This was my moment: I was going to prove the existence of vampires, and I felt like vomiting.

Harroway was walking toward the forensics van, carrying a long rectangular box, but when he passed Greta and noticed that our conversation was finished, he changed course and walked toward me instead.

I rolled my eyes. I did not need his crap right now. Before he even opened his mouth, I held my hand up. "I don't want to hear it."

Harroway raised his eyebrows innocently. "Hear what?"

"Whatever you're about to say. Just swallow it."

"I really hit a nerve with that bum hip joke, didn't I?" Harroway said, looking less than repentant. If anything, he sounded proud of himself.

"That's your problem: you think you're joking, but no one's laughing." I leaned in and whispered, "You're not funny."

"Not possible," he said, but then something miraculous occurred. Harroway's face sobered. He jerked his head back toward Greta. "Is everything all right?"

I smiled. "You worried about little ol' me, Harroway?"

"When Detective Wahl told me to bring you on scene, she had a tone, that same tone she saves for interrogation rooms."

"Is there a question buried somewhere in that statement?" I lost the smile and crossed my arms.

Harroway shifted his weight from one foot to the other, looking more uncomfortable than I'd ever seen him look in my life. "If there's something going on that you can't tell Detective Wahl, you know you can tell me, right?"

I raised my eyebrows. "That's flattering, really, but there's nothing to tell."

"You don't understand. What I'm trying to say is—"

"Don't." I cut him off with a slice of my hand. "I know exactly what you're saying, and I don't appreciate it, Harroway."

He frowned. "I'm saying that I have your back."

"Greta's your superior and the lead detective on this case. You should have *her* back. You should be protecting her and the integrity of this case, not me," I said, angry knowing that the integrity of this case was already compromised, and it had nothing to do with Harroway. We'd wake up tomorrow, and the evidence would no longer support an animal attack. The animal bites would be smooth and clean from knives, and after Dominic finished entrancing our witnesses, no one would remember this scene in its entirety, not even Harroway.

But that wasn't Harroway's fault, and I'd just bitten his head off. I sighed. "I'm sorry. You didn't deserve that. I—"

"You're right," Harroway said, but his voice was clipped and cold. "I should get my priorities straight."

"That's not what I—" I began, but Harroway was already continuing on his way toward the forensics van. "Shit," I muttered under my breath. I had enough real enemies. I didn't need to make more, especially not out of former friends and definitely not out of officers on this case.

As I watched Harroway hand the box of evidence to the attendant in the forensics van, something clicked. This case would likely never go to trial—hell, after Dominic was finished entrancing everyone, I would be lucky if anyone remembered a crime had even been committed—but if they'd collected blood samples, Dr. Chunn might test those samples in time for her meeting with Greta tomorrow morning. And if no one tampered with the evidence, Dr. Chunn might discover something unexplainable in those blood samples.

I rubbed the little pendant of Dominic's blood between my fingers, my brain working in overdrive.

Chapter 6

Meredith finished shooting the scene shortly following my confrontation with Harroway, and we shared a cab back to our office at the *Sun Accord*. Even after being back in the city nearly a week, I still settled into the cab with a feeling of overwhelming gratitude. Walker's hometown of Erin, New York, was quaint and secluded, but I'd grown up in a city of lights, bustle, and conveniences that I wouldn't trade for all the best scoops in the world. People feel a sense of security in their houses, with their furniture, pictures, and the familiarity of their belongings surrounding them, but houses can burn to the ground, reducing life's treasures and memories, and the people I loved most, to ash. I hadn't felt a sense of home since my parents died, but having returned from Erin, New York, with a new-found appreciation for public transportation, city lights, and crowded streets, I realized that home wasn't necessarily four walls to fill with your belongings as much as a feeling of belonging, and I belonged here in New York City.

My parents died in a home fire five years ago, nearly six now, but the pain of their loss still burned my heart as if they'd died five days ago. I'd learned how to contain the pain in a little box hidden deep in the darkness inside me—the same box where I'd hidden my fear for Nathan when he was Damned, my anxiety concerning relationships after my experience with Adam, and my conflicting feelings for Dominic. Since Dominic had helped me save Nathan, I'd been forced to examine those feelings, but I couldn't just pluck him from the box without disturbing the rest of my unresolved nightmares. Everything I'd forcefully and successfully repressed for years was suddenly coming back to light.

The cab dropped us off at the office. Meredith dove into her work, editing and sorting pictures as if we were on a tight deadline, but the paper was already put to bed. Carter would want an insert printed, but we could submit that in the morning. Without the urgency of a pressing deadline, I couldn't muster Meredith's level of enthusiasm for my work. Never mind the fact that by keeping Dominic's secret, my article would once again be a lie, a con to the public instead of a beacon of light exposing the truth, and I felt tainted by my contribution to keeping everyone in the dark.

An hour later, Meredith plopped herself in front of my desk, having completed her work while I was still staring at a blank page and a blinking cursor. My stomach growled.

"Can't write on an empty stomach," she said. "Sorry for eating all the sushi."

I smirked and shut off my computer. "No, you're not."

"You calling it quits?" she asked, obviously surprised.

"For now. I need fresh air and food and—" I looked around at our drab cubes, scratched doors, and flattened carpet, searching for the words. "—something, but whatever it is, it's not here."

Meredith raised an eyebrow. "This office has certainly seen better days, but it's never cramped your style before."

That was before Dominic pinned me to this seat and ravished my lips, I thought wistfully. *And long before Walker lifted me onto this desk and kissed me senseless.* I'd discovered my ability to entrance vampires at that door and wrote my first retracted article on this computer.

Reminders of the loop-de-loop of my life were everywhere.

I shook my head, feeling flushed. "You up for sushi?"

Meredith laughed. "We just had sushi four hours ago."

"Correction: *you* had sushi four hours ago. How about—" I sneezed. "Sorry, what if we—" I sneezed three more times in rapid succession and gave up on talking.

"Bless you!" Meredith plucked two tissues from the adjacent desk and handed them to me. "You weren't this sneezy at the crime scene."

"It's obviously you," I quipped, hating that Dominic was right, once again, about the most ridiculous things.

"I recommend soup and sleep," she said. "Sushi sounds lovely, but it's been a long night. I'm heading home."

I looped my leather satchel over my shoulder. "I'll join you. If

I'm going to stare at my computer screen and bang my forehead against the keys, I may as well do it from home."

We locked the office doors behind us and took the elevator to the lobby. Meredith was hailing a cab when I noticed a pair of green-tinted, reflective eyes staring at me from across the street. My eyes couldn't penetrate the darkness of the alley, so I didn't know who was staring and whether it was deliberately lying in wait for me or just looking for a meal. Either way, it didn't matter. I wouldn't drag Meredith into the darkness with me, not when she didn't have any means or knowledge to protect herself.

A taxi pulled to the curb in front of us.

Meredith opened the back door and ducked inside. I rummaged in my leather satchel, stalling.

"What is it?" she asked.

"You go ahead. I forgot my article notes on my desk," I lied, shutting the door.

She leaned out the window. "Just run inside. I'll wait."

"Me, run?" I said, forcing a laugh.

She stared at me, deadpan. "You've been mugged after late shifts at work before. Don't be stupid. Going home by yourself is just asking for trouble."

"I'll be fine." I glanced over the taxi to the vampire waiting across the street. Since it hadn't attacked yet, it was probably waiting specifically for me. Whether I asked for it or not, trouble always seemed to find me.

"I was mugged too, you know. Maybe I'm the one who doesn't want to ride home alone. Did you think of that?" she asked pointedly.

Meredith thought we'd both been mugged that fateful night five weeks ago because that's what Dominic wanted her to believe, but in reality, he had attacked her, entranced her, and coerced her into writing a retraction of my article on an animal attack in Brooklyn. At the time, I couldn't believe she would betray me like that—writing a retraction of my article, especially when the article didn't need one—but as I came to understand Dominic's powers of influence, I realized that Meredith couldn't help but believe his lies. No one could, except for me.

Now, even I couldn't.

If I couldn't protect myself, I couldn't hope to protect her.

I tapped the hood of the taxi. "You're not walking home, so unless your mugger is lying in wait for you outside your apartment, you'll be fine, too."

She sat back in the seat and crossed her arms, looking petulant. "Don't jinx me."

"I'll see you tomorrow," I said firmly.

"Bright and early," she said, interjecting false cheer into her voice.

"Just how we like it," I quipped back.

She winked, her smile swift and bright, and then the taxi took her away, far away from me and the vampire who was stalking me in the night.

Chapter 7

Two weeks ago, I might have run from the vampire across the street. Hell, three weeks ago, I would have sprinted, and two weeks ago I might have hidden inside the taxi with Meredith, but no matter how fast I ran or where I hid, I wouldn't be safe until sunrise. Then again, as Ronnie knew all too well, sometimes even the sun can't save you. Hiding only delays the inevitable, and after everything I'd experienced, I wasn't waiting for the inevitable to find me.

I gripped the silver knife in my leather satchel and crossed the street to face the inevitable waiting for me in the shadows.

"It's not nice to stare," I said.

My voice sounded smooth and sure, not at all betraying the quaking inside my chest. I still couldn't see the creature inside the alley except for the doubled glow of its eerily reflective eyes, but I didn't need to see it to know its unimaginable strength and otherworldly capabilities. The same capabilities Dominic used to save me could easily be used by any other vampire to kill me.

"Following me?" I asked.

"Yes," the vampire said. He hissed the *s* at the end of "yes," so his voice reverberated from the alley, creepily snake-like.

I swallowed. "What do you want?"

"To talk privately."

"So talk," I said, shortly.

"'Privately' being the operative word," the vampire insisted.

"No one's paying us any mind at the moment."

"Come into the alley, and I'll talk," he said.

"I believe 'at the moment' is the operative word. No one's paying us any mind *at the moment*, so talk, and I'll keep it that way," I countered.

"'At the moment' isn't a word; it's a phrase," he said haughtily.

I waited him out in silence, knowing from experience with interviewing witnesses that an extended silence can be telling. In most cases, it makes a person hesitate and rethink their next move. If I was lucky, he'd let loose the very thing he wanted to keep secret.

"Well?" someone else whispered. There was another vampire in the alley.

"Shut up," someone else hissed. Three vampires.

"We don't have all night, and Lysander didn't want—"

"Are you in or are you out?" the vampire who'd originally been talking to me threatened.

"I'm in, but—"

"Then shut up," the other vampire hissed again. "If she's as powerful as they say she is, she can hear us."

They went silent again.

I rolled my eyes. *They* were afraid of *me*. Rumors of my power had spread, but I hadn't imagined they had multiplied to such an extreme that vampires would be as cautious of me as I was of them. Their fear was unfounded now that I didn't even have night blood— hell, their fear was unfounded even when I'd *had* night blood—but it was their inability to whisper silently, not exceptional powers, that allowed me to hear them.

Impatient, I spoke, breaking my own rule and the silence. "If you don't have anything to say to me, you're wasting my time."

I stepped away from the alley, just one step, and in the next instant, I was surrounded by vampires.

My heart throbbed painfully in my chest, and in a burst of blind adrenaline, I lunged sideways into the street to dodge away from them.

A taxi honked. Headlights flashed, and the shriek and stink of brakes lit the air. One of the vampires caught me around the waist and dragged me back to my feet on the sidewalk. The taxi missed my body by inches.

I lifted my arms to struggle, but the vampire had already let me go. He didn't step back, and his friends were still surrounding me, but he'd let go.

I froze, taking stock of what had just happened.

I'd nearly been killed by a car to escape a vampire, and the vampire had saved me.

There were three vampires total, and although they hadn't attacked me yet, they surrounded me, two from behind and one in front. The vampire standing directly in front had a classic widow's peak, but his hair was dirty-blonde and long, nearly shoulder length. One of the vampires behind me was incredibly tall and made only more gigantic-looking in proximity to my shortness. He had a scar along the line between his nose and upper lip from a cleft-lip repair during his human life.

I'd always been snappy placing names to faces, a trait necessary in my profession, and I knew with one glance that Sevris was the vampire in front of me and Rafe was the uncommonly tall vampire at my back. Even if I wasn't good with names, I'd have recognized Neil, the third vampire. He had unmistakable, plum-colored eyes, but it wasn't his eyes that had made an indelible impression on my memory.

Neil had tried to kill me. Twice.

Rafe had goaded him the first time, and because of Rafe's teasing and the tempting smell of my blood, Neil had burned himself on a silver cage in a failed attempt to drink from me. The cage had held, and as much as Dominic had kept me caged to keep me in, the silver had kept hungry members of his coven out.

The second time, I'd been dying and vulnerable without the protection of a silver cage surrounding me, but I'd had Dominic's protection. In punishment for trying to drink from me again, Dominic had severed Neil's heart from his aorta and ripped the still-beating organ from his chest.

Despite his past injuries, Neil looked hale and healthy now. His plum-eyed stare was unnerving. I swallowed to make sure my voice was solid and unwavering when I finally gathered the nerve to speak.

"Thank you, Sevris, for pulling me from the street. That taxi was obviously not going to stop, not even for me."

Rafe snickered, sharing my sense of sarcasm, but Sevris didn't so much as flinch. I'd deliberately said his name, and he'd recognized the gesture. He knew I remembered him—although not one of the active rebels, he'd never been Dominic's biggest supporter—and he knew I knew his name. Knowing a vampire's name was power; if I'd still had night blood, all I'd need to control his mind would be for him to drink a drop of my blood.

Hopefully that knowledge was enough to keep him from drinking.

"You seemed more worried about us than about that taxi," Rafe commented.

"Your speed still takes me by surprise. You startled me."

"Your instinct was to run," Rafe said, and his smile was all teeth. I recognized that smile on another face, and it took me aback. He reminded me of Rene, whose sharp teasing was often accompanied by that relish-filled, toothy grin.

I glared at him, turning my grief into something just as familiar but much more comforting: anger. "I'll know better next time, Rafe."

Rafe lost the smile at the mention of his name, and Neil's eyes flitted frantically between Sevris and me.

The look Sevris shot over my head at Neil was cutting. Neil took a step back and physically took a breath. He didn't need to breathe to live, and he didn't have a heartbeat to slow with a deep breath.

I shook my head at myself, always trying to make sense of creatures that shouldn't even exist.

"It's lovely running into you, even Neil, but it's been a long night. I'd prefer not to make it much longer," I said slowly and calmly. Despite the space he'd given me, I could feel Neil's presence behind me like an exposed wire about to spark. "How can I help you, gentlemen?"

"Actually, we're here to help you," Sevris said.

"You're here to help me," I repeated, not sure I'd heard him correctly.

He nodded, deadly serious.

I laughed.

Sevris continued to stare at me with his flat-eyed glare, not amused by my amusement.

I cleared my throat. "Sorry, but the last time we spoke, none of you were interested in helping me. In fact, you encouraged Nervous Neil over there to eat me," I said, pointing my thumb behind me at Neil.

"I'm sorry," Neil stammered. "You smelled delicious, and I couldn't help myself. I couldn't—"

Sevris cut him another look.

"Sorry," Neil finished lamely, and I wasn't sure if he was still apologizing to me or to Sevris for speaking out of turn.

"Apology accepted," I said magnanimously, "but apology or not, your attacks," I met Sevris' gaze, "and your teetering loyalty isn't something I'd easily forget."

"We aren't strong enough to rebel against Lysander and survive, but neither are we strong enough to stand by his side if the rebels rise again," Sevris said. "If Lysander is challenged, make no mistake, we will take shelter and follow whoever is left standing. We don't want to make waves. We just want to survive the storm."

"How pragmatic of you." I crossed my arms. "What does that have to do with me?"

"We'd prefer if Lysander was the vampire left standing."

"Right," I said noncommittally, still trying to piece together how I fit into their puzzle.

"We can get you human blood," Rafe said, his smile widening.

I opened my mouth and closed it. That statement was the furthest thing I'd expected from him. "I don't understand what—"

"Don't play coy," Sevris said, that cutting glare now aimed at me. "It's a waste of our time. You are Lysander's night blood, his right hand in sunlight, and you are an unforeseen factor in his arsenal for the Leveling. We need to ensure your safety and, if possible, enhance your power to enhance his. We heard that you crave human blood," Sevris said, the barest hint of a grin tugging at his lips. "Being vampires, we can help with that."

I blinked, playing the longest game of catch-up in my life. "How did you hear that I crave human blood?" I stalled.

"The same way we heard that you had the power to entrance Jillian and strengthen Dominic's alliance with Bex. The same way we know you transformed a Damned vampire back into a night blood." Sevris sighed deeply. "If Lysander is to have a chance of surviving the Leveling, he needs you."

I nodded grudgingly, pretending he was right. I didn't actually crave human blood, but for a time, I'd felt Jillian's cravings. At first, I'd mistaken them for my own. I knew better now, but apparently, they didn't. If it meant they weren't going to attack me, I'd let them believe whatever they wanted to believe.

"And you can get me human blood? Discreetly?" I added. I did not want to be responsible for another crime scene.

Sevris nodded. "It's already done."

Neil moved behind me, and I turned, deliberately and slowly, even though my instincts told me to bolt. When I faced Neil, however, his hand was extended, offering me four vials of blood.

I took them, at a total loss.

"Gratitude often has no words," Rafe said, his voice shaking with laughter.

"Er, of course. Thank you. I just—" I shook my head at the vials of blood and then at each of them. As strange and unnecessary as the vials were, Sevris, Neil, and Rafe were trying to help me. "This gesture, although unexpected, is very much appreciated," I said honestly. "I won't forget this."

"You're very welcome," Sevris said. "If you need anything— more blood, protection, anything—you call for me."

I blinked. "I don't have your number."

I didn't think it was possible, but Sevris' face actually broke into a brief, but genuine smile. "Just call my name. Wherever I am, I'll hear you and come."

"Right. Thanks," I said, feeling a little unnerved. Dominic wasn't the only vampire whose reach was unfathomable, and now, apparently, he wasn't the only vampire who had my back.

Sevris nodded. With a flick of his eyes and an undetectable signal between them, Sevris, Rafe, and Neil disappeared in a whirl of wind and cloaking darkness as spontaneously as they'd appeared.

I turned, trying not to look conspicuous, but we were on the sidewalk, under the glow of streetlights, and they'd just taken flight in plain sight. Someone must have noticed. Maybe after all this time, I'd finally find a witness who remembered what they saw.

Everyone walking past or standing nearby continued about their business as though nothing extraordinary had just occurred, as if three dangerous-looking men, one of which stood over seven feet tall, hadn't just bled into the shadows, into thin air, before their very eyes. I glared at them, all of them.

I shouldn't be disappointed. How many times had I dismissed a movement in the night as a trick of the darkness and my own paranoia? Now that I knew vampires existed, however, such willful blindness was maddening.

I tucked the vials of blood into my leather satchel and walked toward the intersection to hail a cab. The alley Sevris and the others had hidden within was the same alley I'd crawled through to escape from Kaden several weeks ago. God, had it only been weeks? It seemed like just yesterday, yet somehow, I felt years older.

I peeked inside the alley as I passed, and a pair of glowing blue eyes stared back at me.

I jerked back instinctively, tripping on the edge of the sidewalk and back onto the street.

A taxi honked. Its headlight blinded me, and I screwed my eyes shut, braced for the impact twice in one night.

Dominic's arms wrapped around my waist, and before I bit asphalt, the ground fell away from my feet. We launched high across the cold night sky, leaving the danger of speeding taxis and their headlights miles behind us.

Chapter 8

We landed on a rooftop. As soon as my feet were firmly beneath me, I pushed away from Dominic, and just like Sevris, he let me.

"What the hell? Are you trying to kill me?" I snapped, clutching my heart.

He raised an eyebrow. "I saved you from the taxi, did I not?"

"Saving me from the taxi doesn't do much good if I die from heart failure. What were you doing in that alley? Were you following me, too?"

Dominic raised an eyebrow. "Is hiding in the alley to hear your conversation with my vampires without interrupting considered 'following'?"

I blinked at him. "Actually, yes, that's the exact definition of following. That actually crosses the line into 'eavesdropping' and 'stalking.'"

"If Neil had attacked you again, as he is prone to do, or if Sevris had smelled the absence of your night blood, I would have intervened on your behalf to prevent them from harming you. In that scenario, how would my actions be defined?" Dominic asked, cocking his head to the side.

I blew wild strands of hair out of my face and regarded him non-committally. His question was serious, but I could tell by the glint in his eyes and the smirk pulling at the corner of his lips that he was enjoying himself.

I crossed my arms. "You're arguing semantics."

Dominic shook his head. "I'm arguing intent. I was protecting you, not stalking you."

"Except that you didn't make your presence known when Neil, Sevris, and Rafe left. You just stared at me from inside the alley with your creepy, glowy eyes." I glared at him, making my point. "Like a stalker."

Dominic's expression broke into a full smile, the scarred half of his lip and chin remaining stiff in a downward pull, so his smile was lopsided and charming, nearly endearing, if one could see past his fangs. Which lately and unfortunately, I could.

"I didn't expect you to look in the alley. Most people would have simply walked past, and I would have gone unnoticed," he said, still smiling and shaking his head at me. "My mistake for expecting you to act like most people."

"Right," I muttered, trying to hold onto my indignation, but his smile, which was so rare and fleeting, was like a blanket over flames, suffocating the source of my anger. I lifted my arms and waffled my hands at our surroundings. "What are we doing here? This isn't my roof."

"No, it's *our* roof."

I raised my eyebrows. "We have a roof?"

He nodded, and the anticipation in his expression was unmistakable.

I studied it, but besides the view, the roof itself was unremarkable. I shrugged. "I don't remember."

"I suppose you were distracted at the time."

"What was distracting me?"

Dominic's smile widened. "Me."

He grabbed my waist and dipped me back in one swift motion, so I was lying prone in his embrace. A squeak escaped me—a high, girly, scared little squeak that made me hate myself—and then Dominic's face was buried in the hollow of my neck, tipping my face to the side to gain better access.

I struggled because I'd hate myself even more if I didn't, but even as his growl hummed low and steady, like the constant undertone of a well-oiled motor, goose bumps puckered over my neck and down my side. The cool softness of his lips against my skin sparked a deep, burning heat that scorched me from cheeks to toes. My eyes rolled back from the sensations he forced me to feel, and I wanted more.

I could deny my feelings and pretend that I wasn't attracted to a monster, but the monster I'd labeled him as at first sight wasn't the monster he'd proven himself to be. He was still dangerous and devious and oftentimes more instinctual than intellectual. He was probably manhandling me for personal gain, but God help me, I wanted his hands handling me.

His tongue flicked against my throat, and I felt the thrill of his touch shoot down my spine.

I gasped.

"Do you notice anything familiar?"

He breathed on my neck, and my wet skin, slick from his tongue, sizzled.

I moaned in response.

"What do you see?"

Considering that my eyes were closed, I was seeing the back of my eyelids, but he was trying to prove a point. I should oblige before I melted into a mindless puddle. Pulling my concentration away from his lips and tongue, away from the delicious pressure and movement of his hands, I opened my eyes. Strangely enough, the view *was* familiar. Granted, I saw the cityscape from my rooftop every day, but something about this particular view—the position of the buildings, the lights, the angle of my prone position beneath him—tickled a faint memory.

"Have we been on this particular roof before?" I asked, doubtfully.

Dominic nodded, and I tried and failed to repress the shiver that engulfed me from the movement of his stubble scratching against my neck.

I frowned, questions cutting through my desire. "Do you shave?"

Dominic paused mid-nuzzle. "Excuse me?"

"I don't think I've ever felt your five o'clock shadow. Your cheeks are usually smooth, and I guess I assumed—" I swallowed, hesitant to voice my question.

"Please, don't censor yourself now." Dominic lifted me upright, setting me back on my feet. When he stepped back, the space between us left me feeling oddly bereft. "Finish your question."

He was annoyed, but he was also right. I started my question. I should see it through. "Does your hair grow?"

He stared at me.

"It's just a question. You know I need to ask questions. I think of them, and they nag me until—"

"Does *your* hair grow?"

I blinked at him, thrown off by the question. "Well, yes, but—"
But I'm alive, I thought. I shut my mouth.

We'd had this conversation before, and I'd debated the nature of
Dominic's existence in my mind since meeting him. By human stan-
dards, he was dead—he didn't breathe and he didn't have a pulse. By
every other standard—walking, talking, bleeding—he was alive and
well. Better than well; Dominic was Master of his species, and if his
species happened to have hearts that didn't beat and lungs that didn't
breathe, I suppose a different measure of differentiating life from
death was necessary.

Or at least, that's what Dominic would say.

The man in question raised his eyebrows. "But what?" he asked,
waiting to hear how I'd finish that sentence before reacting. He was
keeping his expression deliberately blank, so I couldn't tell if he was
amused or angry.

I sighed. "*But* I also don't burn in sunlight or drink human blood to
survive. We are fundamentally different creatures. I'm just curious."

He shook his head, some of the tension seeping from his stance.
"Your never-ending curiosity," he murmured.

"Is trying your never-ending patience?" I finished for him.

He smiled, reluctantly. "We've come a long way, Cassidy, you
and I," he said.

I smiled back. "Really? How so?"

His smile widened, flashing fangs, and we both burst out laughing.

"Considering everything you've been through, at both my hands
and the hands of others, I'm shocked by how far we've come," Dominic admitted, the residual hiccups of laughter still lingering.

I nodded my agreement. "And by how far I still want to go."

The words slipped out of my mouth so fast, I hadn't realized I'd
uttered them aloud until they lingered like a blade between us. Part of
me wanted to snatch them back from the air and hide them in the
dark, unfathomable depths of the box where I locked all my secrets.

The other part of me—the ridiculous, asinine, foolhardy part that
loved risk far more than its reward—saw the muscles shift in his expression, how he lost the last of his laughter and stared at me like I
was more than a woman or a meal. He stared at me like he was consumed by me. To want him back with such force would be more than
asinine and foolhardy—it was deadly—but I couldn't help how I felt,
and God help us both, he could sense it.

I opened my mouth to try to take it back, but Dominic wouldn't have any of that. He took advantage of my open mouth, and his tongue locked with mine before I'd uttered one syllable.

Whatever I'd been about to say was scorched from my mind. His lips rocked against mine. His hands wrapped around my back so every inch of me, from thigh to chest, was pressed against him. I bit him, needing to fight, to feel like there was still a woman inside of me that I recognized and respected, but he bit me back. I gasped from wanting more—more tongue, more lips, more teeth, more hands—more than I'd ever imagined wanting. Most especially, more than I'd ever imagined wanting from him.

My leather satchel hit the concrete roof. I clutched the front of his button-down in my fists, wrinkling and ruining another one of his immaculate shirts, trying to anchor myself in the moment. He'd taught me to focus on the pressure and warmth of his hand in mine when I was overwhelmed—to anchor my mind with skin-to-skin contact while enduring extreme physical or mental pain—and I needed that mooring now. The walls he'd broken through to touch my heart had been cemented in a foundation of betrayal, abandonment, rage, and grief so deep and solid that they were long overdue for breaking. I felt as if the surrounding pieces of myself that had anchored them in place for half a decade—pieces that I'd never intended to lose—were becoming uprooted with them.

I was losing them now, whether I'd intended to or not; I could either pull away, like I probably should, and attempt to make an excuse for leading him on despite my feelings, or rip down the remaining ruins of those walls myself before he caused more damage. Since I'd always prided myself on asking the hard questions—and Dominic was undoubtedly the hardest question of my entire life—I gave him the only answer I could possibly give.

I released his shirt, curled my hands around his neck, and angled my head to kiss him more deeply.

He groaned, and the rumble of his growl wasn't dangerous this time. I recognized it as more male than vampire, and it sparked an answering weakness in me. My knees were unaccountably shaking. My body felt unnaturally hot and aching and reliant on his strength. I didn't recognize myself; the feeling should have been terrifying. I'd never been one to embrace change, but the change in this moment was so delicious and I was so hungry for more, hungry for him, that I didn't care. His hands tightened around my back, pulling me closer and deeper into him. I didn't think I could feel so surrounded by another person, nearly invaded by his touch and strength and the fresh pine scent of his skin embracing me, but Dominic was everywhere—in my mouth, around my body, flooding my nose and ears and shivering down my spine—so every nerve sparked like the brilliance and danger of an exposed, live wire. And I reveled in it.

I swiped my tongue over his, deep and soft and trembling, acting on the unexplainable urge to somehow meld myself inside him, desperate to feel the heat and texture and exposure of skin on skin, when something sliced the side of my tongue.

Blood instantly filled my mouth. I jerked back, touching my hand to my mouth. I'd cut myself on his fang. I'd lost myself and forgotten I was tonguing a vampire, and I'd *cut myself on his fang.*

I not only lost myself, I thought, *I lost my freaking mind.*

My blood smeared the seam of his lips. His tongue darted out to lick it clean.

"Sorry," he murmured, but he tightened his grip and leaned down for more.

I turned my head and forced myself to step back from his embrace. I'd been through many difficult and heart-wrenching milestones in my life—the breakup with Adam, the death of my parents, fighting Percocet addiction, and recently, surviving the near loss of my brother—so I couldn't honestly say that pulling away from Dominic Lysander was the hardest thing I'd ever had to do, but I'd be lying to myself if I didn't say it came close. The monstrous form he wore during the day and the danger he posed to humans at night was a danger that recently, and likely mistakenly, didn't seem to apply to me. The strength and increasing depth of my feelings for him was more terrifying than Dominic himself.

I may have torn my lips from his, but his lips didn't stop their torment. He trailed a blazing path of kisses and careful nips down the side of my neck to the sweet spot in the curve of my shoulder. I gasped.

"I didn't mean—"

"Yes, you did," Dominic murmured between kisses.

"Well, yes, I meant what I said, but I didn't mean more than this. We can't continue—"

"The hell we can't."

He moved up to nibble on my ear, and I shivered. If he continued, I might not be able to form coherent sentences much longer, let alone argue, but my tongue was throbbing in a bone-deep ache. Blood swelled inside my mouth, and in another moment, I'd need to spit.

"Stop. I can't," I said, my words garbled from trying to keep the blood from welling over and running down my chin.

"You can't or you won't?" Dominic asked, his voice rough and short, but he did as I asked. He stopped. His lips stopped their sharp, nibbling kisses, and his hands loosened around my waist.

I turned my head, unable to hold in the blood any longer, and spat.

Saliva, thickened and darkened by my blood, dripped in a long rope from my mouth and hit the cement rooftop. I cringed and wiped the back of my hand over my chin.

"I can't," I said, honestly.

Dominic's face lost its edge as he searched my face. I don't know what he saw in my expression, but his own softened. He leaned in for another kiss.

I shook my head. "I said no."

"Just one last kiss for tonight. Don't let it end on blood and pain. We are beyond that now."

His eyes were so blue, nearly white toward the pupil, and so otherworldly and fascinating that seeing such raw emotion in his gaze was spellbinding.

We shouldn't, last kiss or not, but hell, when did I ever do anything that I should?

When he ducked his head down, I didn't pull away this time. I was wary and uncertain, and if I was truthful with myself, still hungry for him—which only made me more wary and uncertain—but he was careful this time. We both were. He pressed his lips gently to mine, coaxing and softly asking permission. I opened my mouth slightly, and his tongue darted inside, smooth and sure, to swipe along the side of my tongue. I held still, afraid to participate, knowing that if I lost myself in the whirlwind and raging fire of our heat I'd hurt myself again.

The sizzling burn of his healing saliva enflamed my mouth. He kissed me again, just the soft press of lips and lingering heat, before pulling away.

The silence was suddenly awkward between us. Our eyes met, and for the first time, we both let our eyes slide away.

"Good evening, Cassidy DiRocco," he murmured.

I felt the burn of tears sear the back of my eyes. I was an idiot. He was only saying good-bye for tonight—I knew better than to think he would bid me a permanent farewell—and yet that's how this felt, like we were on the edge of something gaping and if neither of us bridged that distance, we never would. In coming physically closer, we'd somehow pulled further apart. And why did the thought of his permanent good-bye make me feel the keening regret of grief?

"Enjoy your article," he added. "I know it's long in coming, and I dare say, you deserve this one."

I snorted. "Right. Will you be using the wolf pendant again to fool everyone into thinking this was a gang hit, or should I prepare a different lie for the public this time?"

Dominic shook his head. "Meredith took pictures of the animal-like bites and dismembered bodies, did she not?"

I blinked at him. "Of course she did. She's under the misguided impression that she'll get to print the truth, since she doesn't remember otherwise from our last animal-attack article."

"Write the animal-attack article."

I blinked at him, sure I'd misheard him. "You want me to write the truth? I thought you didn't want me to expose Jillian. I thought you didn't want me to encourage the Day Reapers to come for us."

"No, I don't, but with my waning strength, it might be helpful to have the Day Reapers come for her."

"That's your plan B now that I'm out of the game?" I asked, shocked. "The Day Reapers?"

"Do you want to write your article or not?"

"Well, yes, but—"

"Only write the evidence you have based on the scene, not on what you know based on your experience with Jillian and the Damned. Write your original animal-attack story, and I'll let it be printed unredacted this time."

"I can't write about the missing hearts anyway," I admitted. "Greta wants to keep that information out of the press again. The story *is* the animal attack." I met his gaze, feeling the wonder of receiving presents from Santa on Christmas, a joy that I hadn't experienced since childhood. "I can write my article, and you won't alter the evidence?"

"Write your article without revealing Jillian, the Damned, vampires, or the missing hearts," Dominic nodded, "and I won't alter even a fingerprint."

I breathed in sharply. Hope was a powerful thing. It could save a person from the edge of despair as easily as it could prevent that same person from facing the hard truth of reality. I gazed into Dominic's eerie, otherworldly eyes, the hardest truth I'd ever had to accept, and felt hope. He was encouraging me to write this article, maybe not the exact article I wanted to write—I still couldn't reveal the existence of vampires—but this article would warn the public against a very real danger in the night. Did leaving that danger unnamed make it any less real?

"The bites are more ragged this time. There's more dismemberment and a higher body count," I thought aloud, my heart racing. "Meredith needs a photo that captures that without revealing the missing hearts. I need to comb through the evidence."

Now that I was actually writing an article worthy of being written, I had a million things to accomplish tonight and only a few hours to get it done. Adrenaline, not unlike the side effects of drinking Dominic's blood, honed my thoughts, focus, and senses. I met his gaze, and he had a strange expression on his face. I ignored it.

"I need your statement," I said.

He cleared his throat. "My what?"

"You're the expert witness covering this case, are you not, *Dr.* Nicholas Leander?"

"Yes, I am," he said tightly, but he didn't seem angry. His expression was still strangely unreadable. After a moment, I could see his chest shaking, and I realized he was struggling not to laugh.

I glared at him. "This is serious! You may have bumped Walker from the case for your own purposes, but his position has many responsibilities, one of which is relaying the facts of this case to the public."

"I could plead the fifth. The evidence is, after all, self-incriminating," Dominic teased.

"I have made grown men cry during interrogation without even trying," I warned. "Don't make me try."

Dominic threw his head back and laughed, letting loose the bellows he'd been so valiantly containing. He held up a hand before I lost my mind completely and hit him. "I don't intend to be coopera-tive with the media, but for you, I'll make an exception."

"Wonderful. Then, in your expert opinion, did the attack involve multiple animals or one?"

"Multiple."

I raised my eyebrows. "You have evidence to support that claim?"

He nodded. "Of course."

"What have you determined about the animals based on evidence at the scene?"

"They're the same species. Massive strength and size. They don't need finesse or grace to complete their kill. They likely don't even need each other."

I cocked my head. "Expand on that. How don't they need each other?"

"Other animals—like chimpanzees, for example—hunt in packs. Each chimp has a role—to distract, give chase, lead astray, or kill. Our creatures didn't do that. They chose individual targets, hunted them, and killed them without a strategic plan or cooperative effort. We are looking for multiple creatures who hunt, but they don't hunt with a pack mentality."

"In your *expert opinion*," I continued, "how should people pre-pare against such an attack?"

"The kill occurred at night, so the creatures may be nocturnal. Stay indoors after dark. Travel in groups even during the day, and don't travel at all if you already have an open wound."

"Nathan didn't seem too picky about his prey when he was Damned. Whether we were in groups or alone didn't matter. If he was hungry, he attacked," I said skeptically.

Dominic shot me a level look. "As if you're going to tell people not to wander after dark with an open wound."

"If I do, I won't word it like that," I muttered, "but I have to try."

Dominic touched my cheek with his thumb. He smoothed it along the line of my cheekbone, but I could feel his touch heat parts of my body that had never seen sunlight. I held my breath.

"Why is this so important to you?" Dominic asked.

I blinked at him, surprised by his genuine interest. "I've built my entire career on exposing the truth. If people are aware of the world around them, if they're informed, then maybe they have a chance to protect themselves and their families. Maybe they can learn from other people's mistakes and live better lives."

"You want to inspire people to live better lives by reading your article on an animal attack," Dominic said, and I got the distinct impression he was being deliberately obtuse.

"I want to inform people about the world around them."

Dominic shrugged. "They're strangers."

"They're New Yorkers." I sighed, trying to think on his terms to better explain myself. "Just like you protect your coven, I need to protect the people in my city. I can't transform into a gargoyle-like beast to physically protect them, but I can keep them informed, so they have a chance to protect themselves."

"Gargoyle-like beast?"

I froze, wondering how he'd take that, and more pointedly, wondering how I'd let myself become so glib in his presence. Not too long ago, I would have checked my every word, but astonishingly, despite my glibness, Dominic's lips quirked. Maybe we'd come even further than I'd imagined.

I shrugged. "I'm just calling it—"

"Calling it as you see it. Everyone knows you're a straight shooter. Your temperament wouldn't have it any other way." Dominic shook his head, but he didn't lose the smile. "Other reporters write about ribbon cuttings, check donations, and bakery openings. Someone reading your article would think this city is nothing but doom and gloom."

"Now you sound like Carter." I repressed the stab of grief and regret following his comment about bakery openings and shook my head. "Sure, this city is more than murders and rapes and animal attacks. The good things that occur in the city deserve coverage, too, but if people don't know about the doom and gloom, they can't guard against it. And if they can't guard against it, they're at risk of losing the little good that's left, or even worse, they're at risk of losing their lives. People deserve to know how to protect themselves, and if that means telling them to stay indoors after dark, especially if they have an open wound, it's my job to figure out how to deliver that news so that they'll not only bite, they'll swallow it whole."

Dominic's smile widened. "You love a challenge."

"Things certainly seem more valuable when you must fight to attain them."

Dominic snorted. "Now you sound like me."

I nodded. "We've been hanging out too much. It's a problem."

"On that note, I bid you farewell, but only for tonight," Dominic said softly. He cupped my face in both of his hands, and I realized that sometime between my cutting my tongue on his fang and now, we'd bridged the seemingly insurmountable distance between us.

His lips brushed against mine, gentle, sure, lingering, and all too brief. I instinctively leaned closer as he pulled away and had to check myself. He was Dominic Lysander, the Master vampire of New York City, and I was Cassidy DiRocco, the unwilling night blood he'd coerced, using her missing brother as leverage, to play the part of his loyal day servant.

Except lately, I wasn't quite unwilling.

Dominic looked deep into my eyes, and I braced myself for what I knew was coming.

"Cassidy DiRocco," he commanded, invoking the power of my full name to wrap my mind and will around his little finger, but this time, I didn't feel the pull of his mind on mine. "You will forget my name."

I frowned, thinking *Dominic, Dominic, Dominic, Dominic.*

He turned away, believing his name was entranced from my mind. I gaped. His powers had failed him. Even when I'd had the full power of my night blood running through my veins, I'd felt his power. My mind had always remained my own, but I'd been physically helpless against the force of his commands. Now, I didn't even feel his presence invading the space in my mind.

"Dominic, wait."

He halted in mid-motion, and the expression on his face made my throat clamp in a dry squeeze.

"What did you just say?" His voice was nothing but a growl.

I swallowed. "It didn't work. I still remember your name."

His body was suddenly, unaccountably flush against mine. He trapped me in his embrace, buried his face in my neck, and inhaled deeply.

"You still don't smell like you," he said, sounding resigned. "Did you feel the compulsion? Were you able to resist my command?"

"No," I admitted. "Your command was just words without any power behind them."

"Two nights to go, and it's already begun," he growled softly.

I shook my head. "What does that mean? Is my night blood returning?" I asked doubtfully.

"I am still hopeful that your night blood will eventually return, given enough time for your blood to fully regenerate, but that's not why you remembered my name. It doesn't have anything to do with you."

"'It's not you, it's me?'" I asked, jokingly.

Dominic didn't laugh this time. He didn't even crack a grin. "Precisely."

I shook my head. "I don't understand."

"I'll slowly lose my strength and abilities until I am completely powerless on the night of the Leveling. The first of many powers that I'll lose this time, it seems, is the ability to entrance minds and alter memory."

I blinked, thinking of Ronnie and her subsequent feeding problems from that particular inability. "How will you eat if you can't entrance a human to forget the attack?" I asked, but I already knew the answer before his eyes deadened. He would never risk exposing his coven by allowing someone to know about his existence. If he exposed himself by feeding and couldn't alter the person's memory, he would kill them to ensure their silence.

Walker was radical in his efforts to kill vampires, willing to risk his life and the lives of his loved ones, willing to kill a human, in the name of killing a vampire. In his mind, nothing was beyond sacrifice if it meant furthering his cause. Gazing into Dominic's eyes, I knew he would be just as radical in his efforts to protect his coven.

I pulled away from his embrace.

Dominic sighed. "I don't have much of a choice. Would you rather I starve?"

"You have loyal vampires in the coven who are willing to help you, willing to die for you, to keep you as their Master, or so you've said."

"Yes, the majority of my coven supports me in my position," he said.

"In all that majority of vampires, surely there's one who can entrance your victims for you, so you don't have to kill them."

"I no longer have a second in command. Jillian was my most trusted vampire, my right hand, and she betrayed me. She was the vampire I'd have trusted to admit my weakness to and ask for aid." He snorted. "Obviously, that's out of the question now."

I lifted my hands, exasperated. "There's no one else?"

"Yes, there's someone else." He swiped his thumb over my cheek. "But until you regain your night blood, I fear you're not much help either."

I opened my mouth and closed it, at a loss.

"I bid you good night, Cassidy."

Before I could recover, he launched from the rooftop and disappeared into the shadows of the night sky.

Two Days before the Leveling

You think it's an acquired taste, like beer or coffee, that will become more palatable as your tongue adjusts to the nuances of its flavor and texture, but you're wrong. Blood is universally delicious, like water, without adjustment needed. You simply need to be a vampire.

—DOMINIC LYSANDER, on drinking blood

Past experiences and future ambitions are only excuses to justify your present actions, but present actions define you for a lifetime. When your lifetime is as long as mine, you either learn great patience while deliberating your choice of action or you act by instinct and damn the consequences.

—DOMINIC LYSANDER, on surviving an extended existence

Chapter 9

"You're fired!"

Only by the herculean strength of my will did I stop myself from rolling my eyes in the face of Carter's outrage. He'd punctuated his outburst by slapping that morning's newspaper on my desk and jabbing his forefinger at the headline, but I didn't need to look at the front page to know what was plastered across it. I'd pulled an all-nighter to complete that very article and pulled every string I had at the printer to make sure it ran front page despite the late submission. Meredith's photo was by far more graphic than the bite mark we'd attempted to print last time, but not the most graphic we could have chosen from last night. Through the blood and gore, you could clearly discern some body parts, which was more than could be said of her other photos. The shot should have made me cringe nonetheless, but I was so excited to finally print a kernel of truth about the danger overtaking this city, I couldn't help but smile.

"You're punishing me," Carter accused. "One retraction, DiRocco, I make you write one retraction, and this is how you thank me? Both you *and Meredith* are fired."

Smiling might have been worse than rolling my eyes. I sighed. "You didn't ask me to write a retraction. You made Meredith write one behind my back."

"I knew it." Carter narrowed his eyes. "You're punishing me."

I shook my head. "You should be thanking me."

"In all the years you've worked for me, there's only one topic I forbade you to write about, and that was another animal-attack story. We took a huge hit because of that article, and if anyone else had written it, they would have been fired on the spot. You put our credibility with the public and the NYPD on the line."

"That article strengthened our connections with the police. Greta credits me for helping her solve that case," I said, more angry now than exasperated.

"I'll admit that you strengthened our connections, but it wasn't because of that article. You risked everything on that story, and I'm not letting you get away with that unpunished again."

"I'd hardly say I got away unpunished. I got caught in the crossfire of a gang war and ended up in the hospital," I snapped. "And I'm not getting away with anything *again*. This," I said, pointing at today's headline, "is a completely different article."

He picked up the paper and shook it at me. "I said it before, and I'll say it again: no more animal attacks! No more bite marks! There are no animals on the streets of New York City!"

"That's debatable," I muttered.

"DiRocco—"

"I didn't write about an animal attack," I interrupted.

"No? Then what's this?" he asked, pointing an accusing finger at the gore splattered across the front page.

"Did I write 'animal' somewhere in the article?"

Carter narrowed his eyes as he looked at me, his bushy eyebrows frowning so low over his eyes that they must have obstructed his vision.

"Has Greta called to demand a retraction?"

"You're splitting hairs," Carter said, warning plain in his voice.

"I'd say there's a big difference between having and not having Greta's support," I said calmly. "In fact, I'm meeting her at the ME's office in half an hour. She invited me on the case. I'm getting inside scoop." I popped the "p" at the end of "scoop," and Carter's eyes bugged from his skull. "You're welcome."

"If I get one complaint from her department, just one, you're finished here," he warned, shaking his forefinger at me to punctuate "one."

I smiled. "Fine with me."

He stared at me hard, harder even than my stare from more years of practice, but what he saw in my expression must have convinced him of something my words hadn't. He sat down across from me, letting the paper rest on my desk without poking or shaking it in my face. "You believe in this story."

I nodded. "Like nothing else I've ever believed in."

"So this wasn't an animal attack?" he asked.

"Greta doesn't know what it is," I evaded.

"What or who?"

I met his gaze, just as hard.

"This story sounds a little too similar to that first one for my liking, whether you included the word 'animal' or not."

"It's not—"

Carter held up a hand, and I closed my mouth. I'd pushed his buttons for enough years to know when to keep pushing and when to just shut up and listen. I shut up.

"Last time, you kept me out of the loop. Don't make that same mistake. If you're in over your head, let me know. I'll help you in any way I can. Got it?"

I blinked, surprised and uncommonly touched by Carter's sincerity. "Got it."

He pointed his finger at me. "But don't push me, DiRocco. No animal bites."

"Yes, sir," I said, looking at the paper between us. "I'll stick to dismemberment."

He snorted.

"Greta called in an environmental expert on this one," I hedged.

"So I read," he said, raising an eyebrow. "Just like last time."

I pursed my lips. "There's bound to be more victims before this is all said and done."

"Good, then you'll have more to write about." He stood. "Do me a solid, DiRocco, and don't be one of them this time."

"Careful, Carter, people might think you actually give a damn." I grinned.

"You've got my support, not my love, DiRocco, and that's assuming no one calls," he said, holding up a finger as he walked away. One finger. One call.

I clutched my hand to my heart. "Break it to a girl gently next time," I called after him.

Carter raised his hand in acknowledgment, but he didn't turn around.

Meredith waited until his office door shut behind him before jumping from her desk and taking a seat in front of mine.

She let loose a long whistle as she took in the headline. "Should I get a box for my office supplies?" Meredith asked. She didn't seem particularly concerned at the prospect of being canned.

I shook my head. "By the end of our conversation, he was excited about our next scoop."

"Only you could flip Carter on a dime," Meredith said, shaking her head at my antics.

"On many dimes." I pointed my finger at the paper, and then, realizing I looked like Carter, I curled my finger back in. "People are going to eat this up, and Carter knows it. As long as there's no backlash from the bureau, he wants all he can get."

"Well, no one demanded a retraction this time," Meredith said, her voice neutral. Her eyes were on the article, but I knew better than to believe she wasn't waiting for my reaction.

"Nope, no retraction."

"No one really bought the whole rabid-bear-attack explanation for that last bout of serial killings, and now, whoever this creep is, he's escalated."

"I didn't mention the bear-attack case," I hedged, hoping people would make the connection anyway.

"You didn't have to. A picture is worth a thousand words." She tapped her cover photo. "Where there was one, now there's a dozen. People are going to piece it together."

I tried to suppress my smile, I really did, but heaven help me, I couldn't contain myself. "Good," I said.

She shook her head and met my gaze squarely. "What the hell is going on? God knows I should know—we work together on every case and I join you at every crime scene—but somehow, you still manage to cut me out."

I'd debated the risks of breaking my word to Dominic for Meredith. She was my best friend, the sister of my heart, and the only person besides Nathan whose mouth was more padlocked than mine. Keeping such an integral part of my life from her was killing me as surely as it would eventually kill our friendship, but I couldn't risk her life in the hopes of preserving our friendship. I hated that she was on Dominic's radar; I wouldn't bring further attention to her by giving her more information for Dominic to entrance from her mind.

Now that Dominic couldn't wipe her memory, I couldn't bear to think how he'd ensure her silence.

I shook my head. When in doubt, deny. "I don't know what you're talking about. You know everything I know, which isn't much."

"That's bullshit. Last time, you knew there were bite marks on the victims. You convinced Greta to order a second autopsy to prove your point, and you didn't take me with you."

I laughed bitterly. "Do you remember the bite marks?"

Meredith crossed her arms, her green eyes piercing me like a bug on corkboard. "You know I don't. I don't even remember shooting the front-page picture, even though it's on my memory card and saved in my file; I obviously took it." She leaned on the edge of her chair. "It's been weeks, and my memory of being mugged is still nothing but fog and shadows. You were attacked that same night, by the same man, but you remembered every detail."

I glanced around at the other writers, reporters, and photographers milling in the bullpen, but everyone was putting out their own fires and running to chase their own leads. No one cared about our conversation.

"After all these weeks, why are you bringing this up now?" I whispered.

"I tried to ignore the facts and move on. I was ashamed and humiliated and wracked with guilt that I wrote your retraction, that I couldn't remember my mugging, that I couldn't be a stronger person and stand shoulder to shoulder with you against whatever you were fighting. I wanted to forget all of it had ever happened, but now it's happening all over again. The attacks, the bite marks, the secrets—but it's so much worse." Meredith held up the paper, and this time, I did cringe. "The body count and viciousness of the attacks are escalating, and I've got a bad feeling it's only just begun. Don't leave me behind, Cass, not this time."

I stared at her, feeling wrung. Even if I didn't lie, even if I put her at risk and told her the truth—the whole truth about Dominic and Walker, about vampires, night bloods, the Damned and the Day Reapers, about everything—would she even believe me? After hiding behind so many lies for so long, where did I even start?

My cell phone vibrated next to the keyboard on my desk, and a rare snapshot of Greta smiling flashed at me in time to the rhythmic buzzing.

I unlocked the screen with a swipe—grateful for the interruption—and turned to give myself a false modicum of privacy. Meredith strained forward in her seat.

"DiRocco here."

"I'm on my way to meet with Dr. Chunn. She doesn't have much more to show us that we didn't see on scene last night, so we're meeting in her office," Greta said without preamble. "You still want in on her report?"

"Always," I said. Meredith was just shy of climbing over my desk to hear Greta's side of the conversation. I dug my phone more forcefully into my ear, as if that would keep the sound waves from reaching her.

The secrets were tearing me apart. How could she accept the truth when I'd only recently accepted it myself? My life wasn't just about uncovering the next scoop anymore. My life was dangerous and insane. I carried knives now instead of pepper spray, and not just any knives—I carried silver-plated knives express-shipped from a paranormal antiquities shop in California. Four vials of human blood were still in my satchel—amid my notepad, pens, and lipstick—and my intention to smear their contents around the perimeter of my apartment was probably more strange than carrying them in my purse. Who could understand that?

I fingered the vial of Dominic's blood hanging around my neck, tucked out of sight beneath my shirt, and inspiration struck me. "Meredith's coming too," I told Greta.

Meredith's smile was brilliant. She mouthed, *thank you thank you thank you* as she did a little butt-dance on her seat. I remembered the first time Greta had invited me for an exclusive on one of her cases. I'd been just as excited—hell, the thrill of getting the scoop still made my heart race—but in this particular case, anticipation of revealing my secrets, even only a fraction of a secret, was terrifying. No one would believe me if I told them point-blank that vampires existed. Like I told Dominic, I needed to make the news palatable enough for people to swallow. I needed corroboration.

I waved away Meredith's thanks and focused on Greta.

"Dr. Chunn doesn't like a crowd in her morgue, but since we're meeting in her office, that should be fine."

"Who says three's a crowd?"

"They'll be four with Dr. Leander."

I glanced out the window. The brilliant beams of morning sun bathed the bullpen in light. "Dr. Leander is joining us for the meeting? Dr. Nicholas Leander?"

"That's what I just said," Greta said, her voice measured. "Is that a problem?"

"Not at all," I said. "Did he agree to the meeting?"

"I left a voice mail," Greta answered. "Why do you ask?"

"No reason. Just curious."

"You always have a reason. What do you know?"

"I got the impression that he's a night owl," I said, choosing my words carefully. "The crack of dawn seems a bit early for him."

"The sun's been up for an hour, no crack about it. I'll see all of you in fifteen," Greta said, her tone final. She added, "No cameras."

Meredith opened her mouth, about to argue. I waved her away, already on it.

"Aw, G, cut a girl off at the knees, why don't you?"

"You already got her in, DiRocco. Don't push your luck."

"Her camera's her lifeline, like my recorder. When have you ever demanded I not bring my recorder?"

"You might bring a recorder, but you don't use it."

"Not without permission, and neither would Meredith. Cameras allowed, but no photos without permission."

I could hear the exasperation in her sigh even over the phone. "You never know when to quit. You're lucky Dr. Chunn even permits *your* involvement."

"And I'm grateful for the opportunity. If she ever needs anything from my end, it's hers for the asking."

"I vouched for you, DiRocco. Don't make me regret it."

"And I vouch for Meredith. Did you like this morning's article?" I asked, switching gears.

Greta grunted. "It was one of your better works," she admitted.

Damn right it was, I thought proudly, but that wasn't quite the point. "Did you notice everything I didn't say? Did you notice how Meredith cropped the photo and—"

"I know you can keep a secret, DiRocco. That's no surprise. You wouldn't be where you are if you couldn't," Greta interrupted.

"Meredith can keep a secret, too. I wouldn't bring her along if she couldn't."

Greta let loose a strangled noise. After a strained silence, she finally said, "Bring Meredith and her damn camera, but if she takes so much as one photo without permission, just one—"

I met Meredith's eyes, and she shook her head vehemently in agreement.

"She won't."

"—we're done."

I was getting a lot of "just one" conditions on my deals lately, first with Carter and now with Greta. I must be getting on everyone's last nerve. "I understand."

"Good. See you there," Greta said, and without another word from her, the line went dead.

I met Meredith's gaze. "Happy?" I asked.

"Ecstatic," she said, but her smile tipped into a serious expression despite her excitement. "Wouldn't just telling me the truth be easier than dragging me into the investigation?"

I raised my eyebrows. "Are you in or not?"

Meredith lifted her hands. "I'm totally in, but Greta obviously wasn't. Why push it? What's your angle?"

"You'd never believe me if I told you what's going on," I admitted. I tipped my voice low, and Meredith leaned closer to hear me over the background noise of the bullpen behind her. "The truth is so incredible that no one will believe me unless I can prove it."

Meredith blinked. "Greta doesn't even know, does she?"

I shook my head. "I'm not even sure I can prove it, but if I can, and you finally know the truth and actually believe me, there's no going back." *Unless Dominic wipes your memory*, I thought and then winced at the alternative. "Knowing the truth puts you at risk. People have killed to keep this secret."

"I figured as much," Meredith said. She lowered her voice and whispered, "Will this secret explain why I can't remember who mugged me and why I was compelled to write that retraction?"

Jesus, first Greta and now Meredith. Everyone was so ripe to know the truth, they might actually believe me. Hope spread through me, like a spiderweb crack through ice.

I nodded. "Yes."

"I didn't want to know the truth when this all started," Meredith admitted. "I was scared."

"I know," I whispered. "So was I."

"But you plunged headfirst into that investigation, like you do every investigation. Like you're doing again now."

"That's how I do everything. All in or get out. But you don't have to do this, Mere. My life isn't any better for knowing this city's deep, dark secret."

She met my eyes squarely. "If you could take it back, would you unknow it?"

I breathed in sharply, reminded of my conversation with Dominic last night. "Never. But I don't think you understand the risk. Knowing could kill you."

"Not knowing is killing me, too. It's just a different kind of death."

I shook my head—a person could endure a variety of different kinds of deaths, but only one would actually kill her—but I'd already made my decision. I wouldn't back out now. "Then we'd better get going. Greta and the lovely Dr. Chunn are waiting for us."

Meredith stood. I looped my leather satchel over my shoulder and followed her to the elevator. She waited until we were inside before speaking again. "I overheard Detective Wahl mention a Dr. Nicholas Leander."

"Yep. What about him?" I asked, trying to breathe. If I proved the existence of vampires, I'd face a lot more questions than this and from worse people than Meredith.

"Just getting a handle on who will be at this meeting."

I shook my head. "It'll be just the four of us, no Dr. Nicholas Leander."

Meredith raised her eyebrows. "Wahl seemed pretty sure that he'd be there."

I shrugged. "I'm pretty sure he won't be."

An image of the gargoyle-like creature Dominic transformed into during the day rose in my mind's eye. His strong, muscled legs bent back at the knee joint, his nails transformed into talons, his nose—normally straight and regal in his stubbornness—flattened at the front and raised to points at the corners, and his ears elongated to long points on either side of his head. I'd classified him as a vampire because he drank blood and burst into flames in sunlight, but in all my research for my article—in both historical retellings and popular fiction—nothing had prepared me for the creature he became when the sun crested the horizon.

And yet, even after transforming into that creature, he'd protected me, shielding my body with his and preserving my humanity when he could have stolen exactly what he wanted.

The man I was slowly coming to know and understand and grudgingly respect was still the same man, even as a monster.

I shook away the thought. "At least, I certainly hope not."

Chapter 10

Dr. Susanna Chunn's office in Kings County Hospital Center was remarkably warmer than our last meeting location inside the morgue, and I wasn't referring to the temperature. Instead of the sleek, polished gleam of chrome, her office was cozy and dimly lit. The smell of antiseptic was replaced by the smell of a floral diffuser, and instead of congregating around gurneys and buckets of severed body parts, we could sit. A dark brown leather couch spanned one wall, bracketed on either side by shelves stuffed to overflowing with binders, books, and framed photos. A light cream area rug spanned the floor, and canvases of waterfalls, sailboats, and ocean sunsets decorated the walls. Opposite the couch was a window with a view of the peak-roofed townhomes on Winthrop Street; the office was just a few hallways short of having a real view of Wingate Park.

The room was more crowded than I'd expected, but not because Dominic had arrived for the meeting. He hadn't, but Harroway had. Greta and Harroway sat in the chairs facing Dr. Chunn's desk while Meredith and I sat on the couch. The tension between Harroway and me was palpable; neither of us acknowledged the other beyond a polite head nod. No razzing from Harroway, and no heckling from me. Anyone who knew us well would know something was wrong based on our good behavior.

Dr. Chunn was a petite woman, slender and middle-aged, but her subtle style lent her a youthful presence despite the frown lines between her eyes. Her hair was cut pixie short in the same punk hairstyle that reminded me of my brother—short at the sides and long at the top. The style was as faux hawk as she could get and still work in a professional setting. She wore glasses that were new since the last time we had met. They still featured thick, hipster frames, but while the old pair had been black, these were gray on the outside and yellow on the inside. Besides the edge to her hair and beautifully impractical glasses, Dr. Chunn was a consummate professional, from her clothes to her expression. She took her job and this case, like all her cases, extremely seriously.

Her evidence, however, was everything we already knew and nothing that could help further this investigation.

Greta sighed with frustration. "You've got to give me something to go on, Dr. Chunn. We already know that most of the bodies are missing their hearts. The mutilation and body count have escalated since the last spree of attacks, so please, tell me that we have more leads than we did four weeks ago when this all started."

Meredith stiffened beside me, and I remembered that she didn't know about the hearts.

"Considering the increased mutilation, there's actually less physical evidence," Dr. Chunn said morosely. "Matching the severed body parts and organs to complete a whole body for each victim will take time. Once we do, I may have more evidence for you, but until then," Dr. Chunn shook her head sadly, "there's unfortunately not much more to go on than we had last time."

"What do we know about this guy?" Harroway asked. "Maybe we can start there instead and work from his profile."

"Guys," Dr. Chunn corrected. "Or women, although the brutality of these kills does suggest a size and strength that would rule out female perpetrators. Whoever they are, men or women, they're not acting alone."

"You're sure?"

"Unequivocally. Dr. Leander left me his findings along with his regrets that he couldn't be here in person—"

Greta huffed, and that harsh exhalation expressed exactly what she thought of Dominic's regrets. I bit my lip to keep from smiling. Someone was getting fired, but it wouldn't be me this time.

"—and his notes indicate, in congruence with the evidence I've found, that more than one perp caused this kind of damage," Dr. Chunn finished.

Dr. Chunn spread a series of photos and ledgers with measurements on the desk between us, and I winced. Photos were less gruesome than being there in person, but not much better. Meredith squirmed in her seat.

Dr. Chunn pointed to one of the photos and its corresponding measurements. "This victim alone has wounds from mouths with three different bite radii."

"Just this victim?" Meredith asked.

"Many of the bodies have been completely dismembered. Bites from teeth as well as bruises from blunt force trauma and slashes from claws are evident on each victim, and in some cases, like this one, from multiple perps. Analyzing and cataloging each injury on each victim will be a time-consuming process."

"Got it," Meredith said, pursing her lips as if she regretted her question. Her face paled, and I knew why; even after everything I'd seen and experienced at the hands of both humans and vampires in this city, I felt queasy myself.

"Fine, we're looking at multiple perps," Harroway amended. "What do we know about them?"

"They're brutal and indiscriminate in their brutality," Greta said. "Men and women of all different ages and ethnicities have been targeted."

"They attack primarily at night. Their victims who survive always suffer amnesia, and they're confident and skilled enough to attack in populated areas, causing mass casualties, without leaving witnesses," I added.

"How do you know their victims suffer amnesia?" Harroway asked.

"I haven't found a single witness who could give me a credible lead," I said. "Have you?"

Meredith slumped minutely, no doubt thinking of her own memory loss.

"And there must have been a recent trigger for our perps to progress from one kill a night to this massacre," she said, gesturing to the photos spread across Dr. Chunn's desk.

"Or, where there was one perp killing one victim a night, there are now multiple perps killing multiple victims per night," I said.

Jillian's escape was the recent trigger. It had to be. And she'd obviously transformed multiple night bloods into Damned vampires since losing Nathan. My heart ached at the thought. Nathan and I hadn't been the only night bloods in the city after all, but we might be now.

"None of that explains the problem we have with the footprints," Harroway grumbled.

"We have a footprint problem?" I asked.

Greta nodded. "We have several molds from animal tracks in the park," she said, "but they don't lead anywhere. It's as if the animals leaving those tracks just vanished into thin air."

I bit my lip. Telling them that the perps could fly—or at least jump so far and high that the difference between jumping and flying seemed inconsequential—without any corroboration probably wasn't wise. Besides, the real question wasn't how they left the scene but rather where they went once they left. Where did a group of massive, heart-eating monsters hide during the day in a city as densely populated as New York City?

Dominic had built an entire city of vampires beneath New York City where hundreds of his kind could live in secret from the human population, but he would know if the Damned were hiding in his own coven, wouldn't he?

Dr. Chunn nodded, and it took me a moment to come back to the conversation. She wasn't answering my unspoken question. She was agreeing with Greta. "Dr. Leander's notes indicate that the tracks seem to disappear as well. He notes that the perps may have jumped or climbed into a nearby tree and suggests we revisit the tree trunks to study any trace evidence that may have transferred on their bark."

Harroway nodded. "Will do."

Greta frowned, not as convinced. "The lowest branches on those trees are well over twenty feet high. Jumping that height on a whim would be impossible. If they fled through the trees, they must have had a premeditated exit plan, but the random brutality and rage of these murders indicate a disorganized mind who kills on opportunity, not planning. It doesn't make sense."

"No, it doesn't, not for a person," Harroway said. He clenched his hands into fists and pounded the arms of his chair absently. "Working from the perp's profile won't work if it's an animal. We can't predict its behavior if it doesn't have a motive to kill beyond pure instinct or survival."

"They're bites, for sure, but not necessarily animal bites," Greta said. Her eyes flicked to mine, and I stifled a smile. She'd caught the subtext in my article. "Which is why I needed Dr. Leander here today."

I lifted my hands in mock surrender. "I'm not the one who brought him in on the case."

"Not that I know Dr. Leander or have any previous experience with his work, but from the level of detail and insight of his notes, personally, I'm impressed with his skills and perception," Dr. Chunn stated. "One of the details I found interesting was his note here." She pointed to another photo and set of margin notes. "He noticed something sprinkled over the asphalt, something metallic that wasn't organic to the area."

Greta leaned closer to the photo and frowned. "Are those fish scales?"

I clenched my hands into fists, remembering the impenetrable hardness of Nathan's skin when he'd been Damned; reptilian-like scales had covered his entire body.

"I don't know about fish, but they certainly appear to be some sort of scales," Dr. Chunn confirmed. "They're burnt, some of them completely charred, so it's difficult to determine. I've sent samples to a wildlife forensic DNA lab for testing. By tomorrow, we might have a better understanding of the creature we're dealing with."

Harroway raised his eyebrows. "We didn't find fish scales at any of the other scenes. Maybe the cases aren't related after all."

"Look at the size of this sample," Greta said, jabbing the photo with her finger. A penny was in the photo for perspective, and the little fleck of the fish scale was smaller than Lincoln's eye. "We never would have found something like that in the rubble."

"Dr. Leander did," Harroway pointed out.

"Now that you know what to look for, can you search for remnants of scales at previous scenes for comparison? If you find anything, we could potentially link the cases with hard evidence," I suggested.

Harroway snorted. "It's been weeks. If scales were at those scenes before, they've been contaminated to hell and back by now."

"Do you still have photos of the scenes from those previous cases?" Meredith asked.

Greta nodded. "Of course."

"Well, the sites might be contaminated, but the photos haven't changed. I have software that can blow up photos and heighten their resolution," Meredith said. "If the scales are there, I might be able to find them in the crime-scene photography."

Greta glanced at me as if for confirmation.

I nodded. "Meredith's my go-to tech girl, always has been. If you're willing to share the evidence, she can do whatever you need her to do with it."

"If you're worried about the originals, you can keep them. I just need copies on a USB," she said.

"Have you ever worked with the department before in this capacity?" Harroway asked, his expression pinched.

She shook her head. "No, never."

"You'll have to sign a confidentiality agreement," Greta said. "Anything we give you to use for the investigation is for investigative purposes only."

"I have my own camera to use for the newspaper, and I pride myself on my own photography. I wouldn't use yours—I wouldn't *want* to use yours—if that's what you're implying."

"I'm not implying a damn thing," Greta said, smiling, "Just informing you of the process."

Meredith nodded. "Understood. And I'm glad to help. These psychos need to be stopped."

Harroway nodded. "Amen to that."

"Doc, did you find anything else on the victims, any residue that might indicate a location other than the park?" I asked, contemplating the possibility of the Damned hiding within Dominic's coven in the sewers.

Dr. Chunn cocked her head. "Not that I saw from a visual examination, but I'm waiting on test results from swabs of the victims' skin, wounds, and fingernails. I should have those results tomorrow as well."

I nodded. "Great. Thank you."

Greta raised her eyebrows. "Is there a residue in particular that you're expecting to find on the victims?"

I shrugged. If I mentioned my suspicion, Greta and her team would investigate the sewer systems. They'd risk their lives facing Dominic's coven, and the Damned might not even be there.

Greta pinned me with a look. "If these attacks are anything like last time, these bastards will attack again tonight and every night until we stop them, and we don't have any leads. If you've got something, anything, let's hear it."

I met her hardened gaze with one of my own. What she didn't realize, what no one realized, was that even with all the evidence laid out in front of them, even with the proof of their existence before their very eyes, they still might not comprehend the reality that vampires existed. And not only did they exist, they weren't even the most dangerous creature in the night.

My breath caught as I realized something I'd never considered before now. When Dr. Chunn's scale samples returned, she would discover an unexplainable truth about the creatures we were hunting, but if she didn't know that there were two unexplainable creatures roaming the shadows of this city, Dominic's vampires might take the fall for Jillian's Damned and their slaughter.

"Well?" Harroway prodded.

Greta glared at him. She'd been trying to smoke me out with silence.

"There is one thing." I reached into my leather satchel and pulled out the little vial of Dominic's blood that I usually wore as a charm around my neck.

Dominic's blood was a deep crimson, nearly black, and shimmered inside the engraved glass charm. I handed the vial to Dr. Chunn, and the moment the charm left my fingers, I felt trapped in a snare of my own design.

Technically, I wasn't exposing his existence to the public with one of my articles, so I wasn't breaking my promise. But I knew Dominic wouldn't see the technicalities of my actions. He wouldn't see that I was actually protecting him, distancing him and his coven from the real monsters destroying this city. No matter my intentions, Dominic would surely see my actions as a betrayal. I knew that, and I was giving her his blood anyway.

Dr. Chunn took the charm from my hand and studied it. "What is this?"

I swallowed my fear. "Blood. I need you to run a DNA test and compare it to the scales found at the scene."

"Whose blood is it?" Dr. Chunn asked.

"We're about to find out."

Harroway met my eyes for the first time that morning and pinned me with his frustration. "That's a bullshit answer, DiRocco, and you know it."

"To prove the truth to you, we need this DNA test." I turned to Greta. "You won't believe me otherwise."

"More bullshit," Harroway spat. He turned to Greta, too. "I say we take her downtown till she squeals. I say—"

"Let it go, Harroway," Greta interrupted. She eyed the two of us. "Whatever you two are arguing about, I don't want to know. I just want it fixed."

"There's nothing that needs fixing. Harroway and I said some things we didn't mean at yesterday's crime scene, but we're good now."

Harroway snorted. "Speak for yourself."

"I am."

He glared at me, cutting me more with his silence than he ever had with words.

"I said that I don't want to know," Greta insisted. "Just fix it. Am I clear?"

"Crystal," I said.

Harroway nodded curtly, but he broke eye contact, keeping his gaze locked on the wall behind Greta to avoid both of us.

Greta shook her head and focused on the reliable, emotionally mature Dr. Chunn. "Run the tests, please, Susanna."

"You got it," Dr. Chunn said. "I'll try to turn it around in time for tomorrow, but with such late notice, I can't make any promises."

Greta pointed her finger at me. "If this doesn't shed a scrap of light on this case, I'm listening to Harroway's advice, got it?"

"Dear God, anything but that," I said snarkily, but she didn't understand that even when she had all the facts, nothing would shed light on this case. If anything, the truth would just lead us all deeper into the darkness.

Chapter 11

Nathan watched as I smeared human blood in the crevice where the wall met the floor, across the doorframe, and under every window ledge. The three vials Sevris had given me didn't contain much in terms of volume. Although I hit the main entry points—front door and bedroom windows—I needed more for the living room bay window, the bathroom skylight, and the rooftop access. I'd deliberately chosen this apartment for its windows and daily sun-baths, as per Keagan's advice, but all those windows were potential thresholds for a vampire to cross. Keagan had assured me that more windows and access to sunlight were better than physical barriers. Walls were a false sense of security; although I couldn't see a vampire through them, vampires could certainly still sense me, and walls, unlike sunlight, wouldn't stop them.

"Whose blood is that?"

I jerked mid-smear, surprised by Nathan's voice. He'd spoken so seldom over the past week that I was growing accustomed to the yawning silence. I glanced over my shoulder. He was picking at his cuticles, which were chapped and scabbed from habitual worrying, but he wasn't looking at me. He was staring fixedly at the crevice between the wall and the floor beneath the doorframe.

He was staring at the smeared blood.

"I don't know," I said cautiously.

I emptied the last of my fourth vial and stood. I knew Nathan was in pain. I knew he was tormented by everything he'd experienced. But I'd thought that everything he was tormented by was in the past. Judging by his tightly corded forearms as he flexed his fists and the set of his clenched jaw, he was tormented by the present, by something here and now in this room.

His eyes were still fixated on the blood.

"I know how you feel," I whispered.

Nathan's eyes jerked up and met mine.

I swallowed, remembering the driving, relentless thirst that had been Jillian's bloodlust, the thirst I'd mistaken for my own. "It's consuming and confusing and disgusting, and it's the dual emotions—the craving and self-disgust—that drives you insane."

Nathan frowned. "Are you talking about being addicted to Percocet?"

I frowned back at him. "No, I was referring to the blood." I held up the empty vial in my hand.

Nathan's expression hardened. His eyes narrowed on the vial and then at me, and my breath caught at the pain in his gaze. "You don't know shit."

I crossed my arms. "I know more than you think I know. I'm right here. Whenever you're ready to share, I'm here to listen. After everything I've seen and been through, I can—"

"Everything you've seen and been through," Nathan scoffed. "What about everything I've *done*?"

"You weren't yourself," I whispered, taken aback by the heat of his rage. "No one blames you."

He laughed, and the sound was bitter and grating and awful. "Of course, no one blames me. No one remembers me."

"I remember you, and I don't blame you."

"I blame me! You want to tell Lydia Bowser's parents, Alba Dunbar, Logan McDunnell, and Riley Montgomery's family that I wasn't myself when I clawed their loved ones to pieces and ate their hearts? You think that makes what I've done okay?" Nathan stepped forward, his fists clenching and unclenching at his sides.

My brother would never hurt me—not as himself, anyway—but in that moment, I had to physically stop myself from stepping back.

He didn't wait for my reply.

"I'm a murderer, Cassidy," he growled.

"Don't do this to yourself. You're not—"

"I *murdered* Lydia, John and Priscilla Dunbar, the McDunnell brothers, and Riley Montgomery. I tried to murder Rowens, Bex, Walker, and Rene. Jesus, I tried to murder you! You can spin the facts however you want, but the truth is that I would have torn you to shreds, eaten your heart, and relished the taste of your blood. I'm a murderer."

I slammed my fist on the kitchen countertop. "That's enough. I won't stand here and listen to you whine over something you couldn't control. You are not a murderer. The monster that Jillian made was a murderer, but that monster wasn't you!"

"I sought out Jillian to stop the monsters, but I became one instead. That was my choice. I have to live with that and atone for the wrongs that choice wrought."

"You never could have known what would happen, the creature you would become, when you made that choice."

"We never do," Nathan said. "If we knew the consequences of our actions in advance, how many choices would we make differently?"

"Every choice." I held up the empty glass vials in my hands and shook them at him. "You think I *want* to smear human blood around the perimeter of my apartment? It's unsanitary and disgusting and inhuman, but it's a countermeasure to protect us from the vampires."

He crossed his arms. "Whose blood is it?"

I blinked. "Does that matter?"

Nathan stared at me, waiting.

"I don't know whose blood it is," I admitted.

"Where did you get it?"

"I won't apologize for doing what's necessary to keep us safe," I hissed.

"If you got that blood where I think you got it, someone was attacked to keep us safe. I'd rather stay in danger, and the sister I knew and respected would agree with me." Nathan turned away before I could respond and slammed his bedroom door behind him.

He was right; the sister he knew four weeks ago, before his disappearance, might have scorned a gift from the vampires. Now, questioning whose blood I was holding hadn't even crossed my mind. I wasn't the same person I'd been before his disappearance. The grief of losing him, the nightmare of finding him, and the struggle to bring him back had forged the person I'd become, a person who knew that, to survive the coming storm, we'd have to do a lot worse than smear a few vials of blood around the perimeter of the apartment.

I blew out my breath and decided that the moral battle with my brother could be waged another day, a day when I'd had more than three hours of sleep in twenty-nine hours. I glanced at the clock and groaned. Make that thirty-one hours.

I washed and disposed of the empty vials, scrubbed my hands clean, and was just about to finally seek the comfort and oblivion of my bed when my phone buzzed.

No! I thought, but against every instinct I had shouting at me to ignore my phone in favor of my pillow, I answered the call. The moment I glanced at the screen and saw "Supervisory Special Agent Harold Rowens" in block letters blinking at me, I knew going to bed was a lost dream.

I swiped my thumb across the screen. "My story ran this morning. What took you so long?" I teased.

Rowens didn't say anything. He could rival Dominic with the discomfort caused by his silence.

"Hello?"

"I thought you turned him back. The last I saw, your brother was a man again."

I shut the door to my bedroom and hoped that Nathan wouldn't hear our conversation through the wall. Supervisory Special Agent Harold Rowens had been the lead FBI agent investigating the serial murders in Erin, New York, while I was visiting Walker last week. After I'd transformed Nathan back from being Damned, Bex had wiped the witnesses' memories, replaced them with memories of a rabid-bear attack, and the investigation had concluded, but Rowens was the only person who, despite Bex's influence, had remembered the truth: my brother had been a twelve-foot-tall, indestructible, gargoyle-like monster who feasted on human hearts.

Considering Rowens' resistance to mind control, I had the sneaking suspicion that Nathan, Walker, and I weren't the only night bloods in town.

"Nathan is still himself." *Kind of*, I thought with a wince.

"Were the hearts missing?" Rowens asked.

"You do realize that a leave of absence means actually being absent, right? How's physical therapy coming along?"

Silence.

I sighed. "You know I can't—"

"Where's your brother?" he asked, his voice hard and unwavering.

"In his bedroom. The creatures are somewhere in the city, but this time, they're not my brother."

"Creatures," he said. "As in more than one?"

"We believe so, yes."

He was quiet for a long moment, but I could hear him breathing, processing the fact that we were royally screwed. "We barely survived against just your brother," he said.

"I know."

"Can you transform the creatures back into humans like you did Nathan?" he asked.

I rubbed my forehead. "It's more complicated than it sounds."

"It gets more complicated than creatures that eat your beating heart?"

I smiled. "Was that humor I just heard from your mouth, Rowens?"

"No, it was sarcasm. There's a difference."

"Can't be, because then no one would think me funny."

"No one does," he said, but I could hear the smile behind his words.

I took a deep breath. Maybe he was ready. "What do you think about visiting a friendly face? I have answers to your questions, and you just need to brave a city full of heart-eating monsters to get them."

"I'm already on my way. I just need your new address."

"As in here, to my apartment?" I blinked, taken aback. "I take it back. You didn't waste any time after reading my article, did you?"

"Nope, not a second," he said. "I want to know why no one remembers the facts from last week's investigation. I want to know why people are turning into these creatures and how we prevent more from turning. I want to know what the hell is going on, DiRocco."

"Once you know, you can't unknow," I warned him. "Life as you know it will never be the same, and your worst nightmares will be a reality."

"My nightmares are already a reality since the night your brother tore my arm off," he said succinctly.

"Nathan lives with me now," I reminded him. "Can I trust you to play nice?"

"Me playing nice with your brother is the least of your worries," he said, his voice taking on a dangerous edge. "I wasn't Nathan's only victim, and so far, I haven't said a word. Yet."

"Are you threatening me?" I asked, shocked.

"I want answers, DiRocco, and, like you, I'll do what needs to be done to get them."

"No one would believe you," I said. "Those deaths were ruled a rabid bear attack."

"No one would believe me? Not even enough to make someone doubt you? Not even Greta?"

I gave him my address.

"See you soon," he said and ended the call.

I stared at my phone and thought of all the ways that having an FBI agent and newbie night blood here in the city—hell, here in my and Nathan's apartment—would royally screw me. Then I looked at my pillow. *Nope, not going there*, I thought, and snuggled under the comforter to sleep the day away. Night would bring about an entire world of problems, but at the moment the sun was still shining. Sleeping in sunlight meant sleeping in safety, so I closed my eyes and let myself escape from reality, if only for a few hours.

Chapter 12

I opened my eyes, and a man was standing next to my bed in the pitch dark, watching me sleep.

I screamed.

A hand clamped over my mouth. "Chill out. It's me," he said.

Panic flushed from my body at the sound of my brother's voice. I expelled a heavy sigh, but that didn't stop my heart from trying to beat out of my chest. Nathan removed his hand.

"What the hell?" I hissed. "Why are you creeping in my room?"

He snorted. "I've been trying to wake you for a full minute. We've got company."

"Wonderful," I said, recalling my conversation with Rowens.

"Who are you meeting with first?"

I froze in the middle of smoothing crazy bed hair out of my face. "What do you mean?" I asked.

"Meredith and Agent Rowens are in the living room, and Ronnie's waiting on the roof."

"Ugh," I groaned. "Fucking Ronnie. I can't babysit her right now. Why is Mere here?"

"Carter called. According to Meredith, you're both already on scene."

I stilled. "Another animal attack?"

He nodded.

"Where?"

"Wingate Park."

Nearly adjacent to the medical examiner's office, I thought. I covered my face with my hands, trying with every fiber of my being not to scream in frustration.

Nathan nudged my shoulder.

I glanced between my fingers, and he offered me a mug of steaming fresh coffee.

I cupped the mug between my hands, stunned. "What's this?"

"You drink it, and it makes the day more doable," he said with a grin. "I'll keep Rowens and Meredith busy while you deal with Ronnie. Meredith will run ahead to the scene like she always does, and Rowens will understand that the investigation comes first. Your conversation with him can wait until morning. After hours on the road, he looks beat anyway."

I sipped a slug of coffee and sighed. "Best brother ever," I murmured.

"You're welcome. Now hurry up to the roof before Ronnie eats someone. I'll tell the gang in the living room that you're getting dressed."

Nathan slipped out of my room, shutting the door softly behind him as I held my coffee and stared, incredulous. Nathan had my back. He had brought me coffee, was distracting the mob, and was organizing my crazy. I chugged down all eight ounces, grateful for the caffeine, but the coffee wasn't the only reason my stomach spread with warmth.

I wasn't in this alone anymore.

As promised, when I had finally dressed, armed myself, and climbed the rooftop access, Ronnie was waiting for me, but she wasn't the only vampire on my roof.

Keagan, Jeremy, Theresa, and Logan were there too, looking just as skeletal and twitchy as Ronnie. A rattling growl swelled in the air as I climbed the final step onto the roof. They shifted closer.

"Ronnie, you brought friends," I said, trying to keep my voice as neutral as possible while five pairs of glowing, otherworldly eyes trained on me.

"I'm not a baby who needs a sitter," Ronnie said, but her voice was rough and guttural.

I frowned. "Excuse me?"

"Isn't that what you said? 'Fucking Ronnie. I can't babysit her right now.' Your annoyance tasted like grape cough syrup," she said.

Shit, I thought. *Fucking Ronnie and her vampiric hearing.* "Yes, that's what I said, but that was before I had my coffee. I'm more optimistic now."

Keagan snorted.

"Well, as optimistic as I ever get," I amended. "I'm here, aren't I?"

All five vampires just stared at me, watching me squirm, listening to my heart beating, probably fantasizing about ripping me apart. Despite their inhuman stillness, or maybe because of it, they seemed to draw closer.

"I'm sorry you heard me say that," I said. "It wasn't kind of me."

"But you're not sorry for saying it," Jeremy pointed out.

Keagan rolled his eyes. "She calls it how she sees it. That's why we're here."

"She's sorry because we heard her," Logan said. "And now she's frightened." His growl grew louder.

I crossed my arms. "Did you come here to frighten me?"

Ronnie pouted. "You know why we came."

"No, I know why *you* came," I said, pointing at Ronnie. "I have no idea why everyone else is here. You never said anything about a night blood reunion."

Logan, Theresa, Jeremy, and Keagan swiveled their heads to stare at Ronnie. Their movements were jerky and unnatural, and I felt the relief of having their targeting gazes on someone else, anything else, besides me.

"She didn't know we were coming?" Keagan asked.

Ronnie looked sheepish. "She agreed to help," she said weakly.

"Fucking figures," Jeremy spat.

Theresa looked near tears. "We'll die if we don't learn to control our powers enough to feed."

"No, we won't," Logan said grimly. "We'll live in hunger until instinct wins and we murder someone."

"It won't come to that, because Cassidy's going to help," Ronnie said, looking at me. "Right?"

All five pairs of glowing vampire eyes turned to stare at me again.

I raised my eyebrows. "You *all* want my help?"

Ronnie looked down at the roof's cement top for a moment, and when she finally met my eyes again, the pain in her expression made me ache for her. "We're helpless and starving, and we need guidance. Without help, we're not going to survive."

I groaned. Even if I didn't have a heart, I couldn't refuse her with all five vampires surrounding me and only a single silver knife in my pocket. But my heart was pounding a hard rap against my chest cavity, exactly where I wanted it to remain, and bleeding for the desperation in Ronnie's eyes.

"We need some ground rules," I said.

"Thank you, thank you, thank you," Ronnie gushed.

I held up a finger. "One, I'm sarcastic and ornery on a regular basis. You know that, and you came here for my help anyway. If I say something that rubs you the wrong way—like that you need a babysitter, for example—you need to deal with it nonviolently. No bites and no threats."

"Of course, no biting," Ronnie agreed too quickly.

I met their eyes individually, and everyone nodded in agreement, even Jeremy who typically made it a point to unconditionally disagree with everything.

I sighed. "Two, we may need to entrance each other to practice, so this rule goes for everyone's protection. While we are entrancing, we must respect the person being entranced. No commands that are dangerous or damaging, nothing that we wouldn't be willing to do to ourselves. Okay?"

Everyone nodded in agreement.

"Lastly, we're allies. Our Masters have a tenuous truce, one that is in all our best interests not to break. Hurting one another, being disloyal to each other, or in any way risking the anonymity of your existence will sever that truce. We need to make sure these meetings to hone your powers—as I'm sure we'll need several—are not only to strengthen yourselves, but to strengthen our bond as allies."

Jeremy crossed his arms. "I couldn't care less about my coven. I just need to eat. Who gives a shit if we break the truce?"

"Masters give a shit," I said. "You're not a night blood anymore—you're a vampire—and your survival is dependent upon your Master. You care about surviving, don't you?"

Jeremy narrowed his eyes on me, obviously annoyed, but he nodded.

I met each of their eyes again, their reflective, nocturnal gaze so different than the eyes I'd come to know last week. I knew them little better than acquaintances as night bloods, but looking into their eyes now, I didn't know them at all. "And that's the ultimate goal, isn't it? Ensuring everyone's safety and ultimate survival?"

Jeremy still looked unconvinced, but once again, everyone nodded.

Keagan raised a hand.

I tamped down a groan, truly feeling like a babysitter. "Something to say?" I asked.

"I just wanted to thank you. Had our positions been reversed, I don't know how many of us would have the open-mindedness and courage to help like you're helping us, and I appreciate the effort."

I nodded in silence, waiting for the next shoe to drop. Coming from Keagan, it was sure to be a doozy.

"Suck-up," Jeremy muttered.

Keagan must have physically retaliated; although I didn't actually see him move, Jeremy flinched and stepped away from him.

Keagan didn't bat a lash. "I have something for you to show *our* appreciation," he said, glancing at Jeremy when he emphasized "our." He swung a backpack off his shoulder onto the rooftop and unzipped the top. "These are for you."

I leaned infinitesimally closer to peer inside and narrowed my eyes at the contents of his bag. A few wristwatches, a handful of pens, stacks of tuna cans, pepper spray, and a pair of gloves were piled amid a few other random, innocuous-looking items that I didn't recognize as weapons. But I knew better than to believe something wasn't a weapon from looks alone.

"What is all this?" I asked, although I had a sneaking suspicion I knew exactly what it was, and I struggled not to smile in glee.

Keagan didn't struggle against his smile. He shared a grin that, without the fangs and creepy, reflective eyes, could melt a girl's heart. As it was, he melted mine. "It felt wrong to barge in on you empty-handed."

I stared at the weapons before me and gave into glee. "You are so clutch."

"I know." His grin widened. "You've got a compartment here with some blood bags, so you can line the rest of your apartment and rooftop. I can feel some gaps in your fallout shelter at the bathroom window and dining room."

I nodded. "I didn't have enough for the entire perimeter."

"Now you do. Also, we have the oldies here—pressurized silver spear, clicky wooden stake, silver nitrate spray," he said, holding up a watch, pen, and pepper spray, "and some newbies. In particular, a few prototypes for the Damned and tracking devices Walker has been experimenting with."

I shook my head in wonder at his loot. "How did you get all this? I doubt Walker is giving away anything for free."

Keagan lost a little of his grin. "He's not giving it away at all. Colin was worried that one of Walker's new weapons would catch Dad and me off guard. We know what to expect from the watches and pens and such, but something like this," he said, hefting what looked like a small bazooka out of his bag, "could be our undoing. It looks like a really big gun and fires like a really big gun, and the bullets that hit their target feel like bullets from a really big gun, but they're actually silver-lined tracking devices. If he shot us with one of these, and we thought they were just silver bullets, we'd hide, wrongfully thinking we were safe inside the shadows or the coven. But wherever we hid, Walker would find us."

Logan didn't say anything. He simply reached out and squeezed his son's shoulder before letting his arm drop back down to his side. The grief and pride etched into the weathered planes of his face said it all.

"Handy for Walker. Not so much for you," I noted.

Keagan nodded. "Exactly. So Colin sneaks me the weapons that Walker gives to him, so we can be as prepared as possible when Walker hunts us. And now," he said, tossing me the bag, "they're handy for you."

"Thank you," I said, feeling an elation and excitement I could only compare to a child's on Christmas morning.

"I can give you a lesson on those bad boys after you teach me how to entrance, so I don't starve and kill someone," he said, not-so-subtly reminding me of the purpose of our rooftop meeting.

I laughed. "Now that is a deal worth taking." I looked at each of my former night blood companions and then at the bag of toys Keagan had given me, feeling more optimistic than I could have imagined at the prospect of giving vampires entrancing lessons. "Let's begin."

Chapter 13

An hour later, every drop of hard-won optimism I'd had was sucked dry. Ronnie, Logan, Keagan, Theresa, and Jeremy weren't any closer to mastering mind control, and I was very late to join Meredith at the crime scene after taking the time to fully line my apartment in human blood. Granted, I was now sporting a shiny, new Invicta skeleton watch, and my pockets were filled with goodies that could make even the most stalwart vampire drop to his knees. Overall, the night had started off on a promising note, but a mass murder scene could darken even the lightest of moods.

Live victims were already en route to the hospital, and the mob of reporters and cameras was in full force, straining the perimeter. Roadblocks and yellow tape lined Winthrop Street, keeping civilians and media so far back from Wingate Park, I couldn't see anything beyond the chain-link fence.

Members of the media were becoming obviously impatient. Considering the article I'd written and the exclusives I'd managed to scoop, I would've been impatient, too, in their shoes. These murders were swiftly becoming national and international news; I could only imagine the fire their editors had lit under their desks. As it was, I just felt on edge. Meredith wasn't throwing elbows in the mob, and I couldn't find her scouting the perimeter; Greta must have pulled her on scene. Tardiness was a relatively new habit of mine, thanks to unwanted and unexpected midnight visitors, and a niggling unease turned my stomach.

"Nice of you to join us," Dominic purred from behind me.

I suppressed an audible gasp and turned around. Posh and polished, Dominic gazed at me with that lopsided grin from behind the police barricade, decked out in full environmental-science-expert garb. A black duffle was slung over his shoulder, and a DLSR camera hung from his neck. Notepads and charts were shoved in the side pocket of the duffle, along with tape measures and rods. He was dressed a little more casually than I was accustomed to—a purple, striped, button-down shirt tucked into charcoal pants, no jacket—and I wondered if that was deliberate. He was working the investigation now, like Walker, and Walker was more casual. Although, to be fair, Dominic's casual didn't quite match the jeans and cowboy boots of Walker's casual.

"Meredith said you were getting dressed and would join us momentarily," Dominic said. He glanced at his watch—his brown, leather Fossil watch, I noted, not a Rolex—and then met my gaze, one eyebrow raised. "If I'd thought getting dressed would take you over an hour, I'd have gladly assisted."

I narrowed my eyes, not liking the double entendre of admonishment and invitation. "I'm sure you would have, but I made it here all on my own."

"Too bad," he murmured. "Maybe if I'd helped, Greta wouldn't want your head on a pike."

"If you hadn't ditched our meeting with the medical examiner, maybe she would be in a more forgiving mood," I snapped back. "Will you get Greta or Harroway here?" I glanced over my shoulder at the mob of media. A few heads were already turning our way.

"To what purpose?"

I blinked, surprised it wasn't obvious. "To invite me on scene."

His smile couldn't have possibly been more radiant. "You need an invitation from me to cross a threshold?"

The irony wasn't beyond me; I just didn't find it nearly as amusing. "Dominic, we don't have time to—"

"It's Nicholas," he interrupted. "'Dr. Leander' is acceptable as well."

I rolled my eyes. "I don't—"

"And you're very right. We have very little time to solve these murders and gain control of the city before the Leveling, before we lose control entirely," he interrupted, his voice measured. "What could have possibly kept you?"

I stilled. Coming from Greta or Harroway, the question was hard enough to shake, but coming from Dominic, with his otherworldly eyes staring into mine and his unimaginably heightened sensory receptors feeding him information, it was an entirely different game. I schooled my face to show my annoyance and hoped he couldn't smell or taste my anxiety. "I'm sure Greta will slap me with the same reprimand once I get on scene, so save it. Everyone can crucify me all at once."

Dominic snorted. "I hardly think my question warrants comparison to crucifixion."

"And yet, here I am on the other side of the police barrier, still uninvited. Will you tell Harroway or Greta I'm here? Has a sign-in been established?"

"You're an hour late; everything has been established." He lifted the yellow police tape and gestured me forward. "I give you permission to enter."

I rolled my eyes. "As much as giving me permission to enter must tickle you, I need someone running this investigation, like Greta or Harroway, to invite me on scene."

"I am helping to run this investigation."

"Could you just—"

Dominic held up a hand. "Calm yourself. Greta told me to invite you on scene should I see you."

"Wonderful," I grumbled, knocking the tape and Dominic's hand aside as I ducked under the barrier. "You could have led with that when you found me."

"Not much in this life still 'tickles me,'" Dominic said, following hot on my heels as I walked on scene. I swear I could feel the wind of his breath chill the back of my neck as he whispered, "But the fire in your eyes warms me in places I'd never thought to feel heat again."

I ignored him and walked faster.

Wingate Park spanned the entire block between Winthrop Street and Rutland Road, and just like the previous crime scene at Harry Maze Playground, it offered several recreational attractions, including a playground, a football field, handball and basketball courts, and a running track with stadium seating. Situated as it was next to the hospital in a decent neighborhood, people often brought their children here to play. Concerts were held here. People trained on the track and used the field for intermural sports. For the Damned, Wingate Park must have been a damn smorgasbord.

As I stepped on scene from Winthrop Street, my first view was of the track, the football field directly in front of me, and the stadium to my left.

My second view was of a torn, dismembered left foot a few yards shy of the goalpost.

I closed my eyes for a moment to anchor myself, and when I opened them, I deliberately kept my eyes on the field in front of me and not on the limb on the ground next to me. Police were clustered in four groups: two on the far side of the track, one on the field not far from the first two, and the last on the opposite end of the field.

I frowned. "How many victims were there tonight?"

"Four."

I raised my eyebrows. "Only four?"

Dominic nodded. "We have at least twenty injured witnesses who claim to have been attacked 'by a freakin' minotaur.'"

I stared at him.

"That was a direct quote."

I shook my head. "The Damned don't have horns."

Dominic shrugged. "Their rows of pointed fangs and their disjointed hind legs obviously made an impression, despite the lack of horns."

Gazing out over the scene at the four groups of police officers and medical personnel, I shook my head. "The Damned have never shown restraint before. If there were two dozen people here, why only kill four?"

"And that, DiRocco, is the question of the hour," Harroway boomed from behind me.

I flinched, wondering how much of our conversation Harroway had overheard, but I managed to school my expression before facing him.

"Harroway," I acknowledged.

"Jumpy tonight, DiRocco?" He grinned.

"Only when people sneak up behind me and say, 'boo,'" I said, sourly.

Harroway offered his hand to Dominic. "We missed you this morning at the medical examiner's office."

Dominic shook his hand and nodded. "I trust my notes as well as my findings were helpful to the investigation."

"Dr. Chunn assured us on your behalf that they were, since you couldn't bother to assure us yourself," he shot back.

Dominic's eyes darkened, and I resisted the urge to step between the two men. Harroway didn't know or understand the creature he was prodding. Normally, Dominic might entrance Harroway and send him on his way, but since he had lost that ability, I couldn't guess at Dominic's reaction.

Luckily, Greta and Meredith stepped out from the nearest group of officers and chose that moment to approach, interrupting Dominic's reply. Greta's face was an unreadable mask, crafted over years of hard police work and training, but Meredith's expression spoke for both of them. Her naturally pale complexion had soured to a sickly paste, and the pinched line of her lips was probably the only barrier keeping down her breakfast.

I knew the feeling well. Having seen the Damned's damage in person multiple times, I knew that each time was just as sick as the first. I don't know if anyone really gets over the shock and horror of seeing a human heart being ripped from a person's chest and eaten raw.

"Your thoughts?" Greta asked.

I raised my eyebrows, waiting for the crucifixion I'd anticipated, but Greta was nothing but business. "Four deaths instead of dozens? I don't like it."

"What's not to like?" Meredith asked. "The fewer victims the better."

"They changed their MO," I answered. "Why?"

Greta shook her head. "Nothing else was different. The victims are missing their hearts and were torn limb from limb, just like last time. We found scales and some dead-end exit tracks—again, like last time. The only difference is the number of victims and that they allowed live witnesses."

"They're getting sloppy, leaving witnesses," Harroway said, thoughtfully. "Maybe they were interrupted? If they felt rushed, that would explain the limited victims and the witnesses they left behind."

"Interruptions never interfered with their slaughter before," I pointed out.

Greta nodded. "Something changed, something big enough for them to limit their kill count." She met my eyes, and her gaze was hard and penetrating. "Have you seen the bodies yet?"

I shook my head.

"You don't want to," Meredith murmured. She was wearing a beautiful silk scarf that matched her belt and shoes and camera strap—more color, coordination, and fashion in one accessory than I'd ever managed with my entire wardrobe—and she'd double-wrapped said scarf around her nose and mouth. Considering the balmy, seventy-degree air, I doubted the extra wrapping had anything to do with the weather. Whether she was trying to keep her breakfast in or the smell of putrefaction out—likely a combination of both—I knew she was unequivocally right. I didn't want to see the bodies. I'd seen enough blood and guts and death to last me multiple lifetimes, but it didn't matter what I wanted. There might be evidence at this scene that wasn't present at the last, evidence that others might miss and that could be the big break this case needed.

"You coming?" Greta asked, and without waiting for my answer, she turned on her heel and walked back to the scene.

She knew me too well. I'd follow her just about anywhere, for anywhere she led, a scoop would inevitably follow.

I squeezed Meredith's hand to give her strength for another round and stepped forward to follow Greta.

I'd taken only three steps onto the sidewalk when something slammed into my back. The impact didn't necessarily hurt—except for the jarring tweak to my hip and the ache of air being knocked from my chest—but the landing pounded my face and body hard into the ground.

I struggled onto my side against the weight of whatever was grinding me into the asphalt. "What the—"

Dominic was on top of me, shielding my body against the creature on top of him. Rows of razor fangs snapped in a snarling frenzy. Its flat, black shark eyes honed in unsettling focus on Dominic's chest. It drew back its massive hand, each nail a thick, pointed talon, and I screamed.

The creature's arm was a blur as it struck, but Dominic was faster. He wrapped an arm around my waist, and with my body pressed flush against his, he launched into the air. We soared a few feet and then landed back on the grass, out of arm's reach but not out of danger. I gazed out over the field, over what mere seconds ago had been an organized, neatly labeled crime scene, to what was now the bloodbath I had expected upon arriving. Dozens of Damned vampires had descended on the officers, reporters, medical personnel, and bystanders. Where there had once been a dozen victims to slaughter, there were now several dozen, and the Damned weren't showing any restraint this time.

"Dear God," I murmured, horrified. People were being torn apart like rag dolls, their innards exposed, their blood fountaining over the field, their empty chest cavities gleaming in the moonlight.

"I assure you, God has nothing to do with this," Dominic said, his voice as sharp and clear and cold as glass.

"Meredith!" I shouted. I scanned the crowd, but all my mind could register were creatures and blood. "Greta!"

"Quiet," Dominic hissed, pulling me tight against him before the mob drove us apart. "You'll make us a target."

I shook my head. "They already fed tonight. Why attack again? Why here, of all places?"

"The first attack wasn't to feed. It was just to create the scene, to draw more people in for the real attack," Dominic said, his luminescent eyes raking over the bloodbath. "For this attack."

"The Damned aren't cognizant enough to plan something like that. They act on pure instinct and hunt as individuals. They don't organize a planned, collaborative attack."

The lines around Dominic's mouth deepened. "The Damned can't, but I know a very cognizant, very organized, manipulative vampire creating Damned vampires who would do exactly that."

A creature lunged forward, swiping at me with its talons. Dominic slammed into me again, knocking me to the ground and scraping my cheek on grass and gravel, before launching us another few yards back, once again out of arm's reach.

I touched my cheek gingerly, my hand shaking as I watched the creature blink at the spot we'd just occupied. It looked up, searching for us, but between people running and creatures chasing, through the chaos of screaming and blood and death, it couldn't find us in the crowd. Taking advantage of its confusion, I dug the silver nitrate spray out of my pocket and gripped it tightly in my palm. I was prepared with weapons, Dominic was at my side—on my side—and these were creatures we'd battled and won against before. Granted, where there had been one there were now dozens, but despite our dismal odds, I also held tight to the one thing that had saved Nathan, Dominic, and me the last time we'd faced the insurmountable: hope and the unrelenting drive to survive.

Chapter 14

When we'd faced Nathan as a Damned vampire, we'd formulated a plan and executed it. The plan hadn't gone particularly well—it certainly hadn't gone according to plan—but we'd been successful as far as Nathan was concerned. We'd transformed him from the Damned back into a night blood. In the process, however, Jillian had escaped. I surveyed the carnage in Wingate Park—the people fighting and running, the pitch of their screams as the creatures tore them apart, and the swift cut of their silence as they died, dozens upon dozens of people who would have lived had Jillian never escaped—and I felt sick.

A high screech pierced the air, cutting through the chaos and my heart.

Meredith.

I searched the crowd, but like the creature who'd lost sight of us, I couldn't pinpoint any one person in the chaos. Dominic and I were the only people not moving in a sea of panic and death, but I'd unmistakably heard her, and if I could hear her, Dominic had undoubtedly heard her, too.

I touched his arm, still straining fruitlessly to find her in the mob. "Did you hear that? It's Meredith."

"I heard," Dominic said grimly. "But I can't—"

Another creature crashed through the crowd toward us. Dominic wrapped an arm around my waist, and I lost my bearings in the whirling twists and jumps as Dominic dodged the creature and cut through the crowd with me in his arms.

"We need to find her," I said, but Dominic didn't respond. The creature was still hot behind us, tearing through the crowd as Dominic spun and somersaulted in nauseating acrobatics.

I swallowed bile. "She doesn't have someone like you to protect her. She doesn't even know what's really happening. We need to—"

"We will," Dominic growled.

The creature jumped overhead and swung its talons in a desperate lunge, raking the earth behind us. Dominic wrapped his body around me, shielding my back from its razor-edged claws with his, but the creature was faster than even Dominic. One of its talons caught my shoulder and split my skin to the bone. Blood poured down my arm.

Dominic growled. Even though I knew his growl wasn't aimed at me—was, in fact, in defense of me—it still chilled the skin on the back of my neck. Dominic was suddenly half-transformed—his nails lengthened to claws, his mouth elongated into a razor-toothed muzzle, his knees snapped back into hind legs—and he stabbed the creature's arm with his own talons.

The creature's scales were indestructible; Dominic's claws didn't so much as leave a scratch. Dominic's skin wasn't nearly as impenetrable. The creature's claws swiped over his back, and I felt Dominic stiffen behind me before blood drenched both of us.

He'll heal, I reminded myself. *He's healed from worse injuries.* But with the coming Leveling, he didn't have all the strength and abilities he used to.

The creature lunged forward, swiping at us a second time. I lifted my arm, aimed the silver nitrate spray at the creature's face, and pulled the trigger. The creature reared back, clutching its eyes and letting loose a demonic howl. Dominic took advantage of its distraction and put yards of grassy park, screaming bystanders, feasting creatures, and dismembered bodies between us and our creature, letting ourselves once again become lost in the chaos.

Dominic turned suddenly, tucking me behind him as he scanned the crowd and giving me a view of his back. His shirt was sliced from the small of his back to the top of his shoulder blades, and through its tatters, I could see that his back was flayed, his skin flapping and bleeding, and as I'd suspected, not healing in the least.

I reached for the vial of his blood around my neck and was startled when my hand touched only the silver chain. I mentally smacked my forehead; I'd given the vial of Dominic's blood to Dr. Chunn for DNA testing.

I leaned forward, careful not to brush my front against Dominic's raw back. "We can't keep this up much longer. You're not healing."

"I know," Dominic wheezed. He didn't need to breathe to live, yet he was gasping. "I thought you'd run out of Walker's silver nitrate spray."

"I came across some more," I said. "Get us out of here. Now."

Dominic raised an eyebrow. "What about Greta, Harroway, and Meredith? Are you abandoning them to this?" he asked, waving a hand at the field of blood and suffering.

"You have supporters within the coven. Call on them to help us fight until you regain your full powers."

"And reveal how quickly and thoroughly I've weakened?" Dominic shook his head. "I'd lose what little support I still have."

"We don't have many options. It's either that or—" I lost my train of thought as a flutter of yellow silk caught my eye in the crowd. Meredith's scarf.

My eyes honed in on the scarf, hoping against everything sane and plausible that she was still wearing it, but when my brain processed what my eyes were seeing, my heart dropped. I wanted to stuff my hopes in a glass jar and smash everything—the jar, my heart, and my stupid hopes—into a million pieces. Meredith was certainly still wearing her yellow silk scarf; a creature was holding her off the ground and choking her with it.

Her legs kicked and swung as she struggled a good three feet from the ground. The creature was snarling and slavering, literally drooling over her, and in the face of such ravenousness, she did the only thing she could; she tried to alleviate the pressure from her neck by pulling herself up on the very scarf choking her. She was obviously trying, but just as obviously failing.

As she dangled in midair from her own scarf, the creature drew back its massive claw in preparation for ripping out her heart.

"Dominic!" I shrieked, pointing at Meredith.

Dominic's head whipped up to where I pointed, and then he was gone. I gasped, too afraid to hope anymore, too afraid to breathe. More afraid than I'd ever been for myself. The creature's claws came down in a swift strike, and I screamed.

A black and blue blur of movement slashed Meredith's scarf in half, and she dropped to the ground in a boneless heap. The creature's claws missed Meredith by inches but caught Dominic instead. He materialized midair, no longer a blur of movement but a bleeding, very visible man being impaled in the ribs by one of the creature's talons.

The creature slammed Dominic onto the ground, pinning him in place with an impaled claw. He raised his other claw high overhead.

My gut clenched. *No. Please God, no,* I thought.

Bex had nearly died from having her heart ripped from her chest. She'd only survived because I'd doused both the gaping wound of her chest cavity and her heart in Dominic's healing blood and stuffed her heart back into place. I lifted my hand to my throat, fingering the chain around my neck. If Dominic couldn't even heal the claw rakes on his back, he might not survive losing his heart, even after I returned it to his chest, and especially not without his healing blood.

The creature's claw swiped through the air, aimed at Dominic's chest.

I lifted my arm and aimed, hoping the silver nitrate spray would span the distance between us.

A burst of light flashed next to Dominic, dousing the field in garish, gory, Technicolor detail and just as quickly blinding me. I blinked, trying to see past the light spots dotting my vision, but just as my sight was clearing, another rapid burst of flashes blinded me again. The creature let loose a rumbling howl, and the flashes became more regular, almost a strobe, so in jerky, halting movements between flashes, I could see the creature, its head thrown back as it howled in rage and pain. The claws intended for Dominic's chest were raised over its eyes, trying to block the light. Dominic was bleeding and prone on the ground, but no longer pinned by the creature's claws, his heart still whole and unharmed inside his chest, where it belonged.

But no matter how I squinted through the darkness or scanned the scene between flashes, I couldn't find Meredith.

With one arm covering its eyes, the creature reached out with its massive claws and batted the air blindly. Dominic crawled, hand over hand, beneath the whipping slashes. The creature lashed out desperately, blindly. Dominic must be crawling blind, too. That would be the only explanation for why he wasn't crawling away from the creature. If anything, he was crawling closer, toward the source of the flashing.

Get out of range, you idiot, I thought, resisting the urge to shout. The creature swatted low and to the left, missing Dominic's head by hairs. I covered my face with my hands, staring through my spread fingers. I couldn't help. I couldn't bear to watch, and I couldn't for the life of me look away even though my own helplessness was killing me.

Dominic disappeared behind the flash. In the next instant, the flashes stopped, plunging the field back into impenetrable darkness.

Meredith screamed. I strained through my light-blinded eyes to find her, but her scream was fading, like she was inside a speeding car, being driven far away.

Eventually, my spotted vision began to clear, and in the semi-darkness of glowing street lamps and what was left of our crime scene spotlights, I stared in gaping shock at the scene before me. Dominic was across the field, halfway between me and the ambulance at the edge of the park. Medical personnel were ducking out of the ambulance with a stretcher and army-crawling unobtrusively toward Meredith, who lay scarily still but otherwise not visibly injured on the sidewalk next to the ambulance. She clutched her camera to her chest, protecting her scoop even in unconsciousness, and I realized belatedly with the impact of a bulldozer that the flashing had been Meredith snapping photos with her camera.

With Meredith across the field and out of harm's way for the moment, I took in the scene around me. The creature was closer than I'd imagined in the strobe of Meredith's flash, closer than I preferred—but then, considering its single-minded consumption of human hearts, across the field would have been too close. And not only was the creature directly in front of me, it was enraged.

Its nocturnal eyes were still recovering from the camera flashes as it swung its massive head around, slashing its claws right and left, up and down and sideways, searching for its prey. It growled in snarling, unforgiving fury, realizing Dominic and Meredith were gone. And there I was, standing with my hands over my eyes and staring through my fingers—as if that would make *me* less visible—the perfect target for its anger and blame.

I took a small, careful step back.

The creature snapped its head forward and locked its eyes on me.

I froze, rooted by fear and horror. I tightened my grip on the silver nitrate spray, feeling woefully under-armed even with my new arsenal.

The creature charged for me.

I didn't have time to move. I didn't even have time to scream. One moment the creature was staring at me, slavering with accusation and rage, and the next moment, Dominic wrapped me in his arms, and we were airborne. The creature attacked the spot I'd stood the moment before, shredding the earth with its lethal talons, and I shuddered at the thought of how those talons would have shredded me.

It stared at the earth, suddenly stock-still, as if just realizing it had slashed dirt and grass to ribbons instead of flesh and bone, and looked up. Its eyes were luminous and haunting; I could choke on the hate suffocating that gaze. It locked its eyes with mine and let loose a gut-churning, hair-raising howl from the depths of its soul.

I reminded myself that two weeks ago, this creature was a night blood, just like Nathan, who'd known nothing of the nocturnal, blood-thirsty creatures that lived beneath our city and certainly nothing of the war that waged between them. I hated thinking that the only way to stop this madness was to kill them, but when the key to saving Nathan when he'd been Damned was love, how could I save dozens of people I didn't even know?

We'd flown only a few yards when Dominic landed. We were still on the baseball field; no sooner had we landed than he did a backflip to avoid another charging creature.

"Thank you," I gasped, once I'd found my breath. "For saving Meredith."

"You're welcome."

"We need to find Greta and Harroway, too."

Dominic dodged another attack, whipping me around in graceful arcs and inhuman somersaults. "We need to get *us* out of here," he growled.

"What are you waiting for?" I asked. My split shoulder was still gushing blood and ached as he moved, avoiding the claws and teeth closing in around us. "Why did you land back in the field? I thought you were flying us the hell out of here."

"I'm trying," Dominic snapped. "What about Greta and Harroway?" he asked, but his tone was more sarcasm than question.

"You're injured, and we're outmanned. We need to heal, get help, gather reinforcements, and regroup. We need—"

Dominic lunged forward to avoid one creature's snapping jaws from behind as another creature swiped at us from the front. He spun out of reach, dodging both creatures, but he was a millisecond too late. A claw sliced across my forearm, knocking the silver nitrate spray from my hand.

I cursed and clutched the wound as it gushed, joining the waterfall of blood from my shoulder.

The rattling hiss of Dominic's growl vibrated against the back of my neck. "How bad is it?"

"Just get us out of here."

Dominic's arms tightened around me, and we launched into the air, for real this time, above the bloodbath beneath us, over the field and surrounding chain-link fence, past the screaming and crying of hundreds of people dying.

And then we were falling.

We crash-landed a few blocks from Wingate Park onto the concrete sidewalk. Dominic turned onto his back, his body cradled around mine to take the brunt of our fall. Even with his body as a makeshift toboggan, my head snapped back into his jaw, my hip gave out with a sickening crack, and my left leg scraped at fifty miles an hour into concrete as we slid across the sidewalk.

We lay still for several seconds after coming to a stop. The shouts and crunch of carnage were loud around us, but like a bug twitching and half dead on a windshield, I couldn't move, no matter the surrounding danger. I tried to turn my head to brace against whoever had knocked us from flight, but the creature, wherever he was, wasn't here now.

Dominic shifted beneath me, and something sharp stabbed through my leg.

I groaned.

"My apologies. Are you all right?" He sat up with me draped over him. The movement was dizzying and painful.

I held in a gasp. "No," I gritted out between my teeth. "Where did it go?"

Dominic made a choked sound. I snapped my gaze up, searching for the creature he'd seen, but nothing dangerous was near at the moment. Or rather, nothing dangerous was near that *I* could see.

"Where is it?" I whispered.

"Keep still until I heal your leg," Dominic replied. He was suddenly gone from beneath me, and my butt bit into the sidewalk.

"My leg?" I regrouped and looked down at my leg. And then I gagged. The skin had been completely de-gloved from the muscle, and blood was pouring onto the pavement. The white bone of my shin gleamed under the streetlights, and I could see it was broken. I could literally *see* the break. The world spun, and I had to look away before I passed out.

Dominic appeared in front of me, reaching for the flap of skin dangling by gravel-shredded strands.

I flinched back from his outstretched hand. "Don't," I gasped.

"I'll work quickly," he said grimly, and before I could protest a second time, he pressed the dangling skin against the wound and licked.

I could feel the quick swipes of his tongue's intrusion beneath my skin, in and out and side to side, as he coated my wound in his saliva. I pressed my hand more firmly against my mouth to hold back both my screams and the contents of my stomach.

Any second now, my leg would start to burn from his healing, from blood vessels, muscle, bone, and skin fusing back into place. Being injured always hurt, but whether I healed human slow or vampire fast, recovering from injury always seemed to hurt so much worse.

"You've got to be fucking *kidding* me!" Dominic snapped. "Give me the vial of my blood."

"Of your what?"

"My blood on the necklace around your neck—give it to me."

I struggled to sit up. "What? Why?" My head and stomach were already reeling from the pain and adrenaline, and now, as I stared at the mess of my injured leg, which was only more a mess with my blood coating Dominic's mouth and cheeks, I couldn't hold the contents of my stomach back any longer. I turned my head and vomited on the sidewalk.

I took a moment to wipe my mouth with the back of my hand before facing Dominic and his knowing, penetrating stare. "Why am I not healing?"

He swiped his hands through his hair, his eyes shifting frantically over my wound. I got the distinct impression that the ever cool and in control Master vampire of New York City was panicking. "Another ability lost to the coming Leveling."

"Forget it for now. Whatever knocked us from the air is probably still nearby. We need to get Meredith, Greta, and Harroway and get out."

Dominic stared at me with his luminescent, nocturnal gaze, his expression pain-filled and creepy, but otherwise unfathomable. "I can't."

His eyes pinned on the center of my chest where the vial of his blood usually hung from my neck.

I swallowed. "What are you saying?"

"Nothing knocked us from the air; I fell all on my own."

I blinked, trying to focus on his words through the pain and dizziness and black starbursts beginning to dot my vision. "What?"

"I wasn't strong enough to carry you. I'm not sure I have the strength to fly at all anymore," Dominic's jaw ticked as he spoke through clenched teeth. "And now, just when we need it most, I've lost the ability to heal human flesh."

"You don't know that for sure. It might not be you; it might be my lack of night blood," I said, trying to be encouraging. It wasn't in me to admit defeat, but even I could hear the false cheer in my voice.

"Night blood has nothing to do with my saliva's ability to clot and heal human wounds," Dominic spat, and I could hear more than frustration in his tone. His anger bordered on disgust.

I bit my lip against the hopelessness in his voice. "We knew this was coming."

"It's still two nights before the Leveling, and already I've lost the majority of my abilities," Dominic said, shaking his head. "Without a Second, surviving the day in my coven is unlikely."

"Hey!" I snapped, nudging him with my uninjured leg. "Get a grip. We'll worry about you later. Right now, we need help. You might not have an official second in command, but you have peeps on your side."

Dominic raised his eyebrows. "Peeps?"

"Neil, Rafe, and Sevris. They have my back, if you remember, to protect yours."

"I don't think—"

"You called?" Rafe and Sevris materialized from the shadows and darkness.

I blinked. "That was fast."

Rafe grinned. "I'm not Beetlejuice. Say my name once, and I'll appear."

Dominic pinched the bridge of his nose. "Where is Neil?"

"Feeding," Sevris answered. "Once he's healed, he'll rejoin us."

Dominic nodded.

"Healed?" I asked, looking between Dominic and Sevris and wondering if telepathy was helping him connect the dots. "He's hurt?"

"Before this week is done, many will be injured, if not lost. Even the oldest, strongest vampires are no match for the Damned." Dominic met my gaze, and memories of my brother ripping Bex's heart from her chest slammed home.

"Right," I murmured.

"We came immediately because we thought you needed aid, but if you have Lysander to help you, we should return," Sevris said, jabbing a thumb toward Wingate Park.

I hesitated. Dominic was losing his strength and abilities—*he* needed help—but could we trust Sevris and Rafe enough to reveal Dominic's weakness? Could we really trust them with our lives and the lives of the coven, the lives of everyone in this city?

Could we afford not to?

"I need your help," Dominic said.

I sagged with relief. The starbursts had blanketed most of my vision, so Sevris and Rafe stood before me as if at the end of a long tunnel. I lay back on the sidewalk and groaned weakly. My head twisted and spun in somersaults.

"Cassidy?" Rafe's voice sounded suddenly closer than it had a moment before.

"She's losing a lot of blood," Sevris commented.

"Hand me the vial of blood on a pendant around her neck, will you? Touch only the glass vial. The necklace is silver."

I tried to open my mouth to speak, but before I could manage, I felt Sevris' cool hand reach down the front of my shirt. "There's no pendant."

I froze, waiting on Dominic's reaction.

"Of course not," Dominic said coolly. His voice shook with frustration and fury and something deeper, something akin to fear. I understood the former—he was almost always frustrated and infuriated with me about something—but I couldn't comprehend what Dominic could possibly fear. "Why would she be wearing my necklace, the very necklace she wears every night, on the one night I can't heal her?"

The silence after Dominic's words was a palpable weight in the air.

"How advanced are your abilities to fly?" Dominic asked.

"Me?" Sevris sounded shocked.

"Yes, you. Both of you," Dominic said.

"Master?" Rafe asked, his voice slow and deliberate.

Dominic sighed. "With the Leveling approaching, I no longer have the ability to fly or heal. I need to know here and now, do either of you have the strength to carry Cassidy to the hospital and guard her until I return?"

My heart jolted at the thought of being alone with not just one vampire, but potentially three, if Neil joined us. I swallowed and worked up the strength to speak. "No, I don't think—"

"Where's the necklace, Cassidy? Where's the vial of my blood?" Dominic asked.

I sealed my lips shut.

"That's what I thought," he said, "so I'll be thinking for the both of us going forward."

Sevris stepped forward. "I can carry her, and together, Rafe and I will guard her. But is the hospital necessary? I can heal her."

Rafe laughed. "You've never healed a night blood before. One lick, and you might lose complete control."

"I will *not* lose control," Sevris said, and the determination and confidence in his voice was unwavering. "She is your night blood, Master, and a future member of this coven. It would be a privilege to heal her on your behalf."

Sevris' sentiment would be heartwarming except for one pesky little detail: if Sevris were to heal me, he would taste my blood and know that I no longer had night blood. And with that unveiling, he would surely unravel Dominic's secret—that despite my lack of night blood, Dominic had allowed me, a human, to retain my memories and knowledge of their existence, breaking the very principle that had initiated his battle with Jillian, the battle against revealing the existence of vampires to humankind. He would lose what little support, loyalty, and respect his coven still had for him. He'd be dead before the Leveling even began, and I wouldn't be far behind.

All because I'd broken my promise.

I thought of the sample of Dominic's blood at the lab, being DNA tested and subsequently compared to the samples of the Damned's scales and their DNA, proving an impossible theory to Greta about the existence of vampires and the difference between them and the Damned, and I couldn't regret my decision, not even as my blood was pouring out on the pavement. If given the choice, I'd break my promise all over again if it meant protecting Dominic and his coven. Eventually, I'd write my article and expose the existence of vampires, and when that day came and people realized that creatures roamed the shadows of this city, they'd also know who was to blame for these massacres, and it sure as shit wasn't Dominic.

"May I have the honor, Master?" Sevris asked.

Dominic was silent. He met my gaze, and my breath caught. I bit my lip, feeling doom, like an impending thunderhead, shadow us.

"In another circumstance, yes, Sevris, you may have the honor, but not tonight. She knows better than to leave the safety of her home without the vial of my blood, and she must learn from those actions. She did not heed the advice of a vampire, so she will heal as a human. That is her punishment."

I blew out a breath, relief sweeping through me in a dizzying rush.

"Harsh," Rafe said, his grin saying otherwise.

Sevris nodded solemnly.

"I'll meet you before sunrise," Dominic said.

I blinked, caught off guard by the suddenness of his impending departure, and reached out to him before he could leave. "Where are you—"

"Greta, Meredith, and Harroway, remember? Or do you no longer care about their well-being?"

I opened my mouth and closed it, caught sideways by his abruptness. "Of course I do, but—"

Dominic placed a finger over my lips, interrupting me a third time, and I saw red. Sevris and Rafe were watching us; otherwise, I might have bitten his finger. Then again, knowing his propensity for mixing blood and foreplay, he might have liked that.

"I'm doing the thinking, remember? Greta and Meredith will meet you at the hospital shortly."

"But you can't heal anymore. What if they—"

"I'll take care of it."

"But—"

"Cassidy—"

"Stop interrupting me!"

Dominic sighed and stared at me in silence, waiting.

I breathed a deep, cleansing breath as my head spun. I wouldn't last much longer. "I'll see you before sunrise?" I asked.

I felt his lips brush my forehead and realized my eyes had closed of their own accord. "Before sunrise," he promised.

With every last ounce of will left in my body, I forced my eyelids open, but despite my effort, I was too late. He was gone.

Chapter 15

"They appeared out of nowhere, Cassidy. They literally material-ized from the darkness and shadows. Did you see?" Meredith asked.

"Yeah, I saw," I said.

She scanned through the dozens of photos she'd snagged while being attacked, the same batch of photos she'd been flipping through for the last hour—while getting X-rays, being stitched, and now, as we lay side by side on gurneys, waiting to be discharged. The beep of her sorting warred with the beeps of our heart monitors, and neither seemed inclined to stop anytime soon. The cast on my leg itched, and I couldn't decide which would drive me over the cliff first: the throb-bing swell of the stitches on my shoulder and forearm, the zing of my aggravated hip, the infernal itching of the cast on my leg, or Mered-ith's enthusiasm.

I'd share her enthusiasm—God knew I would—if only I didn't know how this would inevitably end.

"They were huge, at least twelve feet tall and nearly just as wide," she continued, "with pointed ears and reflecting black eyes. And their teeth! Did you see their rows of jagged teeth?"

I glanced at the doorway, where Rafe, Sevris, and Neil were standing guard at my curtain. The ER was flooded with victims from Wingate Park, but most of them couldn't recall any details. Dominic, or likely another vampire from his coven, considering his waning powers, had obviously already entranced them. I wondered how long they would wait before entrancing Meredith.

"Well, did you?" Meredith asked, her voice sharper than a mo-ment before.

I focused on her. "Did I what?"

She gave me a look. "Why are you not freaking out right now? This is your story, isn't it? This is why you gave Dr. Chunn the vial of blood to test. This will prove that these, these—" Meredith shook her camera at me, at a loss for words.

"Creatures?" I provided blandly, keeping a wary eye on my muscle at the curtain. They didn't react to anything Meredith was saying, but they'd heard me mutter their names to Dominic from blocks away in the thick of battle. They could obviously hear Meredith's ranting from five feet.

"Yes, creatures! You're trying to prove that these creatures exist, aren't you?"

"It's more complicated than that. We have to be careful about who knows and how we report their existence. There's so much that you don't know, that you couldn't possibly understand."

"That I don't know or understand—*yet*." Meredith squinted at her camera's screen, her thumb going crazy on the zoom.

"Knowing the truth is dangerous. People have been killed for knowing less."

"I have it here somewhere," she murmured. "I know I do."

I frowned. "Have what?"

"When we were in the park, one of the creatures lunged right at me. Faster than I could even think to scream, its talons swiped down at my chest, but someone caught me around the waist and threw me—literally threw me through the air, Cassidy—at the ambulance and medics at the end of the block. I landed hard on the pavement and broke my arm." She raised her casted arm as if in confirmation. "That person who threw me, he saved me from having my heart carved out by one of the creatures."

"Okay," I said slowly, feeling like I was playing catch-up over something I already knew. "And?"

"But before being thrown, I snapped a photo. I know I did."

"Even if you did, don't get too excited. We can't just plaster monsters across the front page of the newspaper. Carter will have a coronary."

"Good! Let Carter finally stroke out. Maybe you'll get a promotion," Meredith said, still clicking and zooming and searching through her memory chip. "People are being slaughtered. The world needs to know."

I bit my lip, thinking of Dominic. They weren't all monsters. People needed to know that, too.

"This will be better than what I found for Detective Wahl," she murmured.

I raised my eyebrows. "You found something for Greta?"

She nodded. "I finished the first file of photography they sent me from the original crime scene and gave my findings to Dr. Chunn this evening. Guess what I found scattered in the gravel when I heightened the resolution?"

"You didn't," I said, smiling.

"Oh, I sure did. It's raining scales all over this parade. It's just one crime scene, but where there's one, I'll find more."

"You know what this means, don't you?"

"That I'm the best investigative photographer ever. Yeah, I know."

"Well, sure, but this also means that we can finally tie the cases together with hard evidence."

Meredith went completely still, staring at her camera.

I waited a moment, but she didn't move. "Meredith?" I asked cautiously. "What is it? Are you okay?"

"Yes!" she erupted, shoving her camera at me and pointing at the screen. "I knew I had the shot! I knew it!"

I stared at her camera and blinked at the photo she'd captured, stunned. Seeing the creatures in person, being attacked and witnessing their kills, was horrific and stunning all on its own, but all I had of the creatures were memories and my belief that they existed. In Meredith's hands was undeniable proof. The pointed ears, the rows of sharp teeth, the reflective eyes, the flat nose and flared nostrils—all there in high resolution, digital clarity on Meredith's camera.

And next to the creature was Dominic, rushing to her rescue.

A floorboard creaked. I looked up, and Sevris was standing over me between our gurneys. He plucked Meredith's camera from my hands.

"Hey! Who the fuck are you?" Meredith snapped.

"Meredith Drake," Neil intoned from the other side of her gurney. "Look into my eyes."

I sighed, knowing what was coming next.

"I know who I am," Meredith snapped, meeting Neil's eyes. "I'm asking who the hell you are!"

"You don't care who I am. In another minute, you won't even remember we were here," he said.

Meredith's face suddenly went slack, and her eyes glazed over. "I won't even remember you."

"You won't remember that you took a clear photo of the creatures. In fact, you won't remember that you saw the creatures at all—not their pointed ears, not their jagged fangs, not anything. You're not sure what you saw because it was so dark and everything happened so fast."

"It was so dark. Everything happened so fast," Meredith repeated dumbly.

Rafe leaned in. "That's good. Being specific about the details helps the memories unstick. Keep eye contact and tell her that she's okay with not having the shot. She's lucky just to be alive."

"Is that really necessary?" I asked, the beeps of Sevris' thumb deleting Meredith's photos like stabs through my heart. "It's bad enough, controlling her memories, but you're controlling her feelings, too?"

Sevris looked up from the camera. "Do you want her searching endlessly for answers that she'll never find? Possibly asking the wrong people the right questions and putting herself in danger when she doesn't have any clue about the creatures she'd be up against?"

"No, but—"

"It's better this way. If she doesn't want answers, she won't search for them. We're protecting her."

I watched as Rafe helped Neil choose his words and erase not only Meredith's memories but her drive to find the truth. I watched him erase everything about her that made her a damn good journalist. Most of me was horrified, but the rest of me, the part I tried not to look too hard at, was relieved. Sevris was right about one thing: Meredith didn't understand what we were up against, and her enthusiasm and ambition would get her killed.

"I understand. I know the risks, and if the other witnesses are being entranced, it makes sense that you're entrancing her, too," I admitted. "But she's my best friend. On that level, I'm not protecting her. I'm betraying her."

Sevris dropped her camera back in my lap. "Lysander was right."

I raised my eyebrows. "About what?"

"Everything concerning you," he said.

Before I could reply, he turned to stand guard once more at my curtain.

I scanned through what was left of Meredith's shots, feeling the clench and drop of bitter disappointment. Her proof was gone, and all that remained were shadows and blurs of blood in the darkness.

"When I break eye contact," Neil said, "you won't care that you don't know us. We are Cassidy's friends, and that is a good enough explanation of our presence."

Rafe squeezed his shoulder. "That was great. You don't need to specify about breaking eye contact, though. It's kind of automatic; when you break eye contact, they'll snap out of it, and your commands become their new memories."

Neil nodded, watching Meredith expectantly, like a pet he'd just taught a new trick.

Meredith blinked her eyes into focus. She glanced at Neil, Rafe, and Sevris in passing, unperturbed, and then dropped her gaze to the camera on my lap.

She shook her head with a sigh. "There's no point. I didn't get anything worthwhile. It was too dark and everything happened so fast. We were just lucky to get out alive." She gazed out over the ER. "Not everyone here can say that."

"No, not everyone can." I handed her back the camera, feeling disheartened and resigned. Telling myself that erasing Meredith's memories was for her own protection might have been more convincing if I hadn't fought so hard to keep my own.

When the doctor returned with Meredith's discharge papers, I encouraged her to go home. I wasn't as alone as she thought; hell, I was safer here with Sevris, Rafe, and Neil than I'd ever been—being safer *with* the vampires, how the tides had changed—and honestly, I couldn't meet her eyes, knowing what had been taken from her.

Twenty minutes later, I was still waiting on my own discharge papers when Dominic strode through the emergency room's sliding doors. My breath caught. No matter how many times I saw him, even knowing his appearance was nothing but a mask, his presence spiked an indescribable need in me. Part fear, part anticipation, part reservation, and all-consuming, my feelings for Dominic, whatever they were, were undeniable.

He was so gorgeous during the night that sometimes it seemed impossible that he was anything but a beautiful, surly, magnanimous man. Then he growled or grinned with those very real, very lethal fangs or looked at me in that disturbing way he had, like he was mesmerized by the movement and flow of my blood pulsing through my beating heart, and I was reminded in no uncertain terms of his true nature.

He didn't have X-ray vision, but with his strangely heightened senses, I wouldn't doubt that he was listening to the smell or tasting the texture of my blood. His senses were skewed in that way—I remember how confusing and debilitating the sensory collision had felt when I was high on Dominic's blood—but for Dominic, the kaleidoscope of sights, sounds, textures, scents, and tastes was the version of the world that he lived and understood.

As much as he was mesmerized by my blood and potential, I was mesmerized by the man beneath the monster.

He grinned slyly, just enough that the tip of his fangs gleamed from between his lips. If I was truly honest with myself, I'd admit that I was mesmerized by the monster, too.

"We have a problem," Greta said, and my heart hit the ceiling.

"Jesus," I rasped, hand to my chest. She was perched on the chair next to my gurney, leaning forward on her elbows, clasping and wringing her hands, worrying her knuckles. "Where did you come from?" I tried to adjust myself on the bed to face her and winced. My newly stitched leg and my hip did not approve of the movement.

"You sit tight. I'll move." She stood and leaned against the side of the bed, her back to Dominic as he approached.

I glanced at the curtains separating me from the other patients on gurneys, but my guards were gone. The emergency room was still hopping, and my doctor was still bustling patient to patient, sans my release papers. Somehow, from one moment to the next while I'd been drooling over Dominic, Sevris, Rafe, and Neil had disappeared and been replaced by Greta.

I blew out a breath. Greta's memories weren't as easily wiped as Meredith's, so maybe the boys knew to stay off her radar. I scanned the ER, hoping against hope that they'd made themselves scarce, but sure enough, far enough away that Greta wouldn't notice them but close enough that they would still hear our conversation, Sevris,

Rafe, and Neil congregated around a vending machine in the back corner of the ER. Rafe unwrapped a Twinkie, glanced over his shoulder at me, and bit it in half.

I must have looked as stunned as I felt, watching him eat whole, human, processed food, because he winked.

Greta snapped her fingers in my face. "Earth to DiRocco! We have a problem." She eyed me warily. "Don't tell me you're one of them."

I focused on Greta, despite the spectacle behind her. "One of who? What are you talking about?"

"What do you remember about tonight's attack?" she asked.

I narrowed my eyes. "What do *you* remember?" I countered.

She crossed her arms. "Not what everyone else remembers. It's happening—the witnesses are forgetting everything they witnessed, damn it—and I don't know how. I was right there with them in the fucking trenches, surrounded by their blood and death, and I couldn't forget the image of those creatures severing limbs and eating hearts even if I tried."

I nodded, reminding myself to play it cool. "It seems impossible, but this is exactly what happened upstate in Erin, New York," I whispered. "People didn't remember the investigation like it truly happened. You read the reports."

"Yeah, I did," she said, not looking happy about it.

"And you remember another case, about five weeks ago, that I wrote as an animal attack, but the department reported as gang violence, the wounds clean and caused by knives. You made Meredith write a retraction."

Greta shook her head. "That *was* gang violence. The perps used sharpened brass knuckles on their victims to make their wounds appear like animal claw rakings."

I raised my eyebrows.

She stared at me, and seeing my expression, cursed under her breath. "You've got to be kidding me."

Dominic sidled up next to Greta. "Nothing tonight seems like a joke to me."

Greta snapped her head back, and if I wasn't mistaken, she looked relieved. "Dr. Nicholas Leander, it's good to see you alive and on your feet. When I didn't see you at triage, I had my doubts."

Dominic unloosed his satchel from around his neck, wincing as he lifted his arms. "I had my doubts, too," he said, placing his satchel down at the foot of my bed.

Greta lifted her eyebrows. "Are you injured? Were you treated on scene or here in the ER?"

"On scene," he said.

Greta nodded. "How were you injured?" she asked, but I knew the real question behind her words. She wanted to know how much he remembered.

Dominic snorted. "The better question is how were you not? At least now we have some answers, witnesses, and solid proof, even if those answers only open a hot mess of more questions."

"All we've got is a hot mess, *Nicholas*," I said. "Witnesses are forgetting what happened, Meredith snapped photos of nothing but shadows and blood, and the only proof we have, as usual, is the body count."

Dominic frowned. "Witnesses are forgetting what happened? How can they forget twelve-foot-tall minotaurs devouring human hearts?"

"How indeed," Greta murmured. She looked out over the ER at the sea of gurneys and at the moaning victims in pain writhing on them, not one cognizant enough to further her investigation, and her expression hardened. "And however they're forgetting, what's different about the three of us that we haven't?"

Dominic sighed. "Like I said. A hot mess of questions."

I watched Dominic's on-point performance as Dr. Nicholas Leander and fumed. The Leveling obviously hadn't affected his ability to bullshit.

Dominic's laser-focused eyes pinned me down, as if he could hear my thoughts. Maybe he could. The intensity in the simple shift of his gaze made me feel as if he could peel away the layers of my flesh and bone to see the thoughts beneath. While he was at full strength, I had no doubt that he could.

"We have a seven o'clock meeting with Dr. Chunn in her office," Greta said, and I broke eye contact with Dominic gratefully. There was no telling, with or without his full powers, what that man was capable of. "She'll have the lab results by then, so maybe we'll actually get some answers." She pinned her eyes on me, which in some ways, wasn't much better than facing Dominic's stare. "How's your leg?"

"I'm fine."

"What about your shoulder and your arm and your—"

I sighed and held up a hand. "Don't worry about me. I'll be there," I said.

"Good. I'll be expecting you." Greta shifted her gaze to Dominic. "Both of you."

Dominic inclined his head.

Greta left us to talk to more witnesses in a fruitless attempt to find someone who remembered the truth. I knew better than to hold out any hope; Sevris, Rafe, and even Neil were very good at keeping their existence a secret.

Greta didn't have extraordinary hearing compared to Dominic or his entourage, now back on duty at my curtain; nevertheless, I waited until she'd crossed the ER and was engaged in her own conversation before speaking. I had so many questions and grievances and so much gratitude to express that I felt raw from the rub of emotions.

The moment Greta was preoccupied, I blurted, "Lift your shirt."

I wanted to take it back and start again on a more pressing topic, but if I was honest with myself, nothing was more pressing than the panic I felt at the thought of him seriously injured. I snapped my mouth shut and let my words scorch the air between us.

Rafe turned his head, glancing back at us with a curious lift to his brow.

Dominic grinned darkly. "If I'd known you weren't opposed to public fornication, I'd have capitalized earlier."

I leveled my glare on him. "How bad is it?"

"Not bad in the least. I actually prefer an audience. The more watching, the better the performance."

"Dominic—"

"Cassidy," he purred.

"—you're avoiding the point."

"No, I do believe you're avoiding *my* point."

Taking matters into my own hands, literally, I ignored the uncomfortable pull and twinge of pain from the stitches in my forearm and lifted his shirt myself.

And stared.

Whether on scene or here at the hospital, a human doctor had treated him. Four long gouges raked across his chest and abdomen, angry red, swollen, and perfectly mended with tiny rows of very human stitches. A cluster of additional stitches circled around his collarbone where the creature had impaled him with its claws to hold him still for the strike. And if I recalled correctly, his front hadn't even been the worst of his injuries.

Him going back for Meredith and Greta might have been as dangerous as going back for them myself. *I could have lost him,* I thought, and something cold and trembling and desperate rocked me. Caring about a creature as enigmatic as Dominic was dangerous enough, but the thought of losing him was unacceptable.

One of the perks of being a Master vampire was his inability to die and stay dead. If he got caught in the sun and burst into flames, human blood could restore him to health. If the Damned tore out his heart, I could just shove it back in his chest. Very few injuries would result in permanent death, and up until now, I'd resented his near immortality, had in fact used it as a barricade between us.

I reached out and grazed my fingertips gently over his abdomen, hovering over the stitches, and very slowly, very carefully, I touched his skin.

"Better me than Greta. I can survive this. She can't," he growled darkly.

"Turn around," I commanded, but of course, my commands didn't hold any weight.

Dominic shook his head and pulled down his shirt. "What's done is done, and we've all survived. Let it go."

I pulled my gaze away from his wounds to meet his eyes, and the tenderness in his gaze pierced my heart. He cared. Greta and Meredith weren't important to his plan to survive the Leveling—they were, in fact, hindrances to his plan and a risk to the secrecy of his existence— but he'd made them a priority because they were important to me.

"Thank you for going back to save them. It means more than—" I cleared my throat and shook my head, at a loss. Not five weeks ago, it wouldn't have mattered if Greta and Meredith had been my identical twins; he wouldn't have saved them. Six weeks ago, he might have killed them to ensure their silence.

"I know what it means to you," Dominic murmured. "That's the only reason I went back."

"I know," I said, my voice suspiciously thick. "Thank you."

Dominic inclined his head, and his selflessness on my behalf struck an uncomfortable chord in my heart.

Lusting over Dominic and appreciating the strength and protection he offered was one thing; anything more was something else entirely—and unthinkable. My experience with Adam had taught me that dreams of a happily ever after stayed in dreams. An ordinary man—beautiful, talented, and driven, but in comparison to the vastness of Dominic's existence, completely, humblingly ordinary—had stolen my heart and torn it to pieces. A creature as dangerous and duplicitous as Dominic would not only tear it apart, he would lick my blood from each finger and savor the taste of my demise.

My heart accelerated at the thought of Dominic's tongue and other places he might lick.

A clicking growl hummed from Dominic's chest, and I realized my fingers were still grazing his stomach under his shirt.

I hastily snatched my hand back and changed the topic before logic and love cleaved me in half.

"Agreeing to meet with Dr. Chunn this morning was bold," I stated. "How will you pull that one off?"

Dominic let my swerve in conversation go unnoted, but I could hear the barely withheld restraint in the clipped chords of his voice as he spoke. "I agreed to a meeting? Did you hear me utter such an agreement?" he asked.

I shook my head. "That's a fine line, *Nicholas*, one I don't think Greta will acknowledge."

He shrugged. "One challenge at a time. Let's get you home first. We'll discuss business later."

"That would be wonderful, except that I'm still waiting on my discharge papers. Meredith was released an hour ago." I craned my neck to see around Sevris and Neil. Although the ER was still flooded, my doctor was nowhere in sight. "I've been waiting, but—"

"Ms. DiRocco?"

I blinked. The middle-aged, blond doctor who had provided Meredith with her discharge papers, who had been alternately checking our vitals and triaging all night, was suddenly, unaccountably, standing at my bedside, papers in hand.

"Yes, that's me," I said dumbly.

"You're all set. Thank you for your patience."

I glared at Dominic. "No one has that impeccable of timing."

He shrugged, but someone snickered behind him. When I shifted my gaze to the goons still guarding my curtain, Rafe had joined them. Sevris was glaring at him with heavy disapproval. Rafe pointed at Neil, and Neil was gazing out over the ER, unaware of the blame being tossed at him.

I rolled my eyes. "You can't just entrance people at random. He'll discharge me when I'm ready to be discharged."

Rafe clapped Neil on the shoulder. "He needs the practice."

"Ms. DiRocco?"

I transferred my glare to the doctor.

"You're ready to be discharged. I'm sorry for the wait. As you know, we've had a busy ER tonight."

I sighed heavily against battles better left unfought and signed the paperwork. The doctor traded my consent forms for crutches.

The disgust on my face as I stared at the crutches must have been obvious, because the doctor chuckled. "I'm guessing this isn't your first rodeo."

I shook my head. "Been there, done that, and had planned on never doing it again."

"Well, these bad boys will be your best friends for at least four weeks."

He couldn't be serious. "Four weeks?" I squeaked. "Put me in a CAM Walker, and let me loose."

The doctor nodded. "You'll get a CAM Walker afterward, but right now, your leg needs rest. Stay off of it, and keep it elevated. It'll help with the swelling."

If I'd thought discovering the existence of vampires was a living nightmare, four weeks of immobility and crutches was going to be hell. I ground the heels of my palms into my eyeballs and groaned.

I felt a hand on my shoulder, and when I looked up, I was surprised to see it was the doctor. "Take care, Cassidy."

I opened my mouth, but before I could respond, he'd already turned his attention to Dominic. "Ibuprofen will help relieve the swelling and pain, but nothing beats good, old fashioned rest."

The doctor gave my shoulder a final squeeze before leaving me alone with Dominic, his gang, and the crutches. I wasn't sure which I resented more.

"Will you hold these for me?" I asked. I handed the crutches to Dominic and tried to scoot myself to the edge of the bed. My hip fired a shock of pain up my spine.

Dominic tossed the crutches behind him. "I will carry you."

"I can do this myself," I said, breathless from the pain.

"You heard the doctor. Rest is the best medicine." He leaned over the sidebars to scoop me up. "Let me help."

"Hands off," I snapped. I lowered my voice and said, "You're losing your powers. Soon you'll be at human strength, and then where will I be? I need to be able to care for myself."

Dominic snorted. "Even at human strength, I can still carry you."

I held out my hand. "Crutches."

He shook his head but complied, handing me the crutches.

I scooted slowly, painfully to the edge of the bed. By the time my legs finally swung over the side, I was sweating and trembling, but I didn't know pain until my legs dropped. Blood poured in a pounding rush to my tender shin; my entire leg throbbed.

I gripped the crutches like the lifeline they weren't, tucked them beneath my armpits, and stood. My hip screeched from the lopsided pressure of standing one-footed, and my swollen shoulder and forearm balked from the strain. I didn't even bother attempting the precarious hop-swing motion that was crutching. From experience, I knew my limits. If I didn't sit in the next two seconds I would collapse, so I sat down before I fell down.

"Shit," I gasped. "Give me a minute."

Dominic lifted his hands innocently. "Please, take all the time you need. The sun isn't rising. I don't have anywhere else to be. It isn't imperative to return to the crime scene for damage control, and that task will be brief."

I glared at him. "Sorry my body's healing never fits into your schedule."

"If you let me carry you, we could stay on schedule."

"Let it go, Dominic."

"How will you ambulate without my help?" he pressed. "How will you leave the hospital, hail a cab, and walk to your apartment?"

"I'll manage," I gritted. I didn't know how at the moment, but I'd find a way.

"Let me help you. The Leveling may be siphoning my powers and strength, but I'll always be strong enough to carry you. You need me."

"I said give me a damn minute," I snapped savagely, but a second failed attempt to simply stand, let alone swing on the crutches, only underlined my complete helplessness. After years of limping and gritting my teeth through the pain, my hip had finally won. I was completely immobile. If I'd been an otherwise healthy person, I'd have been able to crutch from the hospital of my own accord. But I wasn't otherwise healthy. I wasn't going anywhere without someone's help, whether or not I accepted Dominic's.

This is how it begins, I thought. I'd always known my hip would eventually limit my independence and lifestyle, but I'd never thought the end would be so soon. Today, it was my ability to walk. Tomorrow—

"Don't even think it," Dominic murmured.

"You can't read my thoughts anymore. You don't know what I'm thinking."

"I don't need to read your thoughts to know your mind. This pain is temporary. When you are a vampire—"

"I'll never be a vampire," I snapped.

"—your pain will be nothing but memories. You will be stronger, healthier, and more powerful than you can imagine. Until then, come back with me to my coven, Cassidy. I will be your legs. Let my strength be your strength."

His words hit a little too close to home, and I lost what little control I'd maintained on my temper. "For someone with such heightened hearing, you don't listen to anything I say. I will *never* be a vampire."

"Then you will never find relief from the pain," Dominic said harshly.

My breath hitched. I'd known the truth for a long time now, but hearing him say it confirmed it on a level that hadn't solidified completely in my mind. I would be in pain, possibly immobile, for the rest of my life. "I know," I whispered, and the weight of acknowledging that truth was crushing.

Dominic reached toward me and brushed his knuckles over my cheek, his gaze suddenly shamed and imploring. "You're injured and in pain, but you're wallowing. You're nowhere near the end."

I shook my head.

"Please, Cassidy, don't—"

"Don't make me gag," someone behind Dominic said, and the interruption was capitalized by the rapid beep of a horn.

I leaned away from Dominic's touch to see around his body. My brother was driving a motorized scooter toward us, and despite the light tone in his teasing, Nathan's expression looked anything but amused.

"Cassidy doesn't need your legs or strength or anything else you have to offer. She has a home to come back to, not your damn coven, and this scooter to get there. So use that extraordinary hearing of yours; I believe the lady said hands off."

Dominic turned his head to face Nathan, his jaw flexing. His hand didn't so much as twitch from where it rested on my cheek.

I beamed. Nathan had impeccable timing all on his own. "A scooter?"

"I'm a genius, I know. And the best brother ever." Nathan narrowed his eyes on Dominic's hand. He stopped the scooter next to the bed and stood. "Your legs," he said, gesturing grandly to the scooter.

I didn't want a scooter. I hated that my body was betraying me, slowly at first and now completely, but being mobile on a scooter beat not being mobile at all. "How did you know?" I asked quietly.

Nathan's expression turned suddenly bland. "That's not important."

Dominic raised his eyebrows, but remained silent.

For the amount of anger rolling off him, Dominic was being uncommonly reserved.

I bounced my gaze between the two of them, but when it became apparent that neither of them intended to speak, I pushed. "Nathan, what's going on?"

Nathan's face shut down. "Some people, when presented with a scooter, would just say thank you."

"I am thankful, but I'm not most people. How did you know that I'd need a scooter?"

"Does it matter?" he snapped.

"It does now. Why won't you tell me?"

"Because it doesn't matter," he said stubbornly.

"If it didn't matter, you would simply tell me." I leaned forward and tipped my voice low, so anyone eavesdropping who wasn't a vampire or didn't know about vampires wouldn't overhear. "Did you retain some of your vampire abilities from being Damned?" I asked.

Nathan blinked. "What are you talking about?"

"I understand why you've been distant. If I'd experienced every-thing you've experienced, I'd crawl inside myself, too, but even though I've never been Damned, I know what it's like to resist addiction. You can talk to me," I said. "If you're struggling with cravings or height-ened senses, you can tell me. You were there for me when I needed you most. Let me be there for you now."

"There's nothing to tell," Nathan said, but his expression said otherwise. "Just drop it."

I shook my head. "I can't."

"Why the fuck not?"

"Because I'm losing you. Whether or not it's cravings or height-ened senses or something unforeseen that I haven't put my finger on yet, something is wrong. You can't eat. You barely sleep. You hardly talk. You're living a shadow of the life you once lived. I didn't find you and bring you back from the Damned only to lose you all over again."

Nathan crossed his arms. "It's not what you think."

"Then enlighten me."

He made a strangled noise in the back of his throat. "I knew you were injured because Dominic called me," Nathan said, jerking his thumb to the right.

Following the direction of his thumb, I met Dominic's laser-focused gaze.

I frowned, jerking my head alternately between Dominic and Nathan, but Dominic's expression remained impassive, carved from decades of experience.

"He called you?" I asked. "He still has mental ties to you? Is that why—"

"No, Cassidy, he doesn't have mental ties to me. He has a phone."

I stared at him, not comprehending the words coming out of his mouth.

Nathan sighed. "He picked up a phone, dialed my number, and told me about the attack. He told me you were hurt and would need crutches, and we both knew what that meant."

"I—You—" I stammered, trying to catch up. The fact that Dominic had had a full-blown conversation about me with my brother over the phone was throwing me off my game. "He called you?"

"I would have text-messaged him," Dominic interjected. "But you once said that it's more considerate to call someone with bad news."

"I, well, yes, that's true," I said, flabbergasted. "But normally you wouldn't bother with a phone at all. You would just—" I waved my hands in the air, words failing me. "—appear from the darkness and talk to him in person."

"Normally, yes," Dominic said. "But with the Leveling drawing nigh, I need to conserve my resources. I already can't heal and fly. Who knows what ability I'll lose next?"

The man could text, but he still said phrases like "drawing nigh." I shook my head. "I don't understand. Why would you call my brother to pick me up from the hospital if you wanted me to return with you to the coven? Without Nathan, I'd certainly need your help." I indicated the scooter with a swipe of my hand. "Now, I just need to sign my release paperwork, and I'm ready to rock."

"Ah, Cassidy, when will you understand?" Dominic touched my cheek again, his face so weary that I wondered if his hard-won, everlasting patience wasn't as everlasting as he'd like to believe. He leaned in close, so close that I could almost feel the whisper of his breath on my lips as he spoke. "I don't want you to choose me because you have no other choice. Despite the many choices at your disposal, I want you to choose me because I'm what you want."

I opened my mouth to reply, but I didn't have the words. Five weeks ago, I would have said, "I'll never want you," but that was before he'd saved my life and preserved my humanity, before he'd helped me find Nathan and risked his own life to bring him back from the Damned, and long before I'd realized that, besides our dietary preferences and his physical and mental abilities, we actually had more in common than I'd ever thought imaginable. After five weeks, fighting one another had somehow transformed into fighting beside each other. Never was a long time, and as Dominic had reminded me multiple times, he was very patient.

I couldn't examine my feelings for Dominic too closely because, after five weeks, I feared I knew exactly what I wanted. But knowing something, especially something about myself, and admitting it were two very different things.

Dominic swiped my cheek with the pad of his thumb one last time before letting his arm drop back down to his side. He turned away and walked out of the hospital at a human, very un-Dominic-like pace. I watched him leave, feeling oddly bereft considering I'd gotten exactly what I'd wanted. He'd left me with my brother, a scooter, and nowhere to go but back home to my vampire-proofed apartment. Except after all this time, the one thing I wanted might just be the very thing I'd proofed my apartment against.

One Day before the Leveling

Memory is necessary to our survival, as much as air is necessary to you and the consumption of blood is necessary to me. It composes our personality and mood, determines our capacity to learn from experience, and dictates our ability to function, to recognize objects and people. For something so essential to a person's existence, it can be easily molded, tweaked, and for some, completely eradicated. Off the record, I respect the power of memory and the debilitation of losing it, but if the choice lies between an individual's existence and my own, I choose mine every time. Besides, most people, when faced with the unexplainable, would prefer to forget.

—DOMINIC LYSANDER, on wielding the power of mind control

Chapter 16

The sun rose over the horizon and flooded my southeast-facing, window-lined bedroom with light. I enjoyed its warmth and comforting safety from inside a blanket-wrapped burrito on my bed for a blissful moment before reality slammed home with the sudden, debilitating pain of my injuries. If the sun was up and I was still in bed, that meant only one thing.

I was missing my meeting with Greta and Dr. Chunn.

Despite the scooter, getting washed, dressed, and applying makeup—simple, daily tasks that would normally take half an hour if I couldn't decide on an outfit—were made excruciating by the power-punch combination of my throbbing broken leg, the sting and pull of the stitches on my shoulder and forearm, and the ever-present and even more persistent ache in my hip.

An hour later, I gave up on makeup and any hope of being on time. The only item of clothing that I could physically pull over my cast was a pair of loose yoga pants. I topped the pants with a baby-T and twisted my hair into a bun. The air was still cool this morning, but by ten, the unforgiving summer sun would beat down on the city, ratcheting up the heat and my temper. Leather and jeans were better protection against fangs and claws than yoga pants, but the weather was too sweltering for the first, and my cast wouldn't fit into the latter. I stuffed the leather pants in my side satchel for later, along with several pens and silver sprays inside my cast. The damn thing was clunky and itchy as hell but ideal for hiding weapons.

I left a voice mail for Greta, apologizing for being late and letting her know that I was on my way, just not moving as fast as usual. She'd been there last night. She'd understand.

Supervisory Special Agent Harold Rowens, however, hadn't been there, and honestly, after everything that had happened, I'd forgotten he was sleeping on my couch. I left my bedroom and tried to roll past him unnoticed on my scooter, but I couldn't avoid the squeaky planks of my warped, hardwood living room floors. They groaned and shifted under my weight.

Rowens' face had sunk deep into one of my plush couch pillows, but half his face and one eye were visible. That one eye opened, and he pinned it on me. "What's the rush? No time for hello before saying good-bye?"

"You might be on medical leave, but some of us still have to bring home the bacon, despite our injuries," I quipped.

He sat up, and the blanket fell from his bare chest and pooled in his lap, exposing the stitches and scarred, swollen tissue where his arm used to be. Nathan had ripped Rowens' right arm clean from the shoulder socket—one of the lesser nightmares that haunted Nathan from his time being Damned. Rowens didn't have much of a residual limb, but I'm sure if he really wanted a prosthetic arm, the bureau would pick up the tab, considering he'd been injured in the line of duty. Judging by the hard lines and angles of Rowens' expression, however, when his shoulder healed, he wouldn't want one.

Shoulder disartics needed a prosthesis with straps across their back; without a residual limb, he'd use the movement of his shoulder blades to control the movement of his prosthetic arm. The technology wasn't bad, but the straps might interfere with his shoulder holster, the weight of an arm he couldn't fully control might be a burden while running, and more important than learning to use a prosthesis, he needed to relearn to shoot with his non-dominant hand. The loss of his right arm, although devastating, wasn't the nightmare that kept him awake at night.

He'd lost weight since I'd seen him last week, but he still had that beefy, block-jawed, lumberjack look that made him so handsome—devastatingly handsome, with his clean-shaven cheeks, bright aquamarine eyes, and sharp features. He narrowed those aquamarine eyes on me now.

"Give me five minutes. I'm coming with you," he said succinctly.

I raised my eyebrows. "You don't even know where I'm going."

"You're working with Detective Wahl on the same case you were working on when we were upstate. The same case they covered up as a rabid-bear attack."

I sighed. Rowens knew just enough to be dangerous and more than enough to be in danger. "You don't know who 'they' are, and believe me, I've warned you once and I'll warn you again, you don't want to know."

"I didn't come all the way here for a warning. I came for answers, and I'm not leaving without them. Hell, if what I think is happening is really happening, wild horses couldn't drag me away."

"Wild horses." I shook my head. "I wish."

"Wherever you are today is exactly where I want to be," Rowens pushed. "I'm glue, DiRocco; whether you want me or not, you're stuck with me."

"It's your funeral," I muttered.

"Looks like it was almost yours last night," Rowens said softly, taking in my cast and the scooter.

I squirmed uncomfortably and winced. "Just a flesh wound."

"Right. Me too." He wiggled what little muscles he had left in his shoulder, and I wrinkled my nose.

"Shouldn't you be keeping that shoulder wrapped? Your flesh wound still has stitches."

"Yeah, I need to redress it. Thanks for the reminder, Mom. You gonna lend me a hand?" he quipped.

I rolled my eyes. "Next question."

"Rabid-bear attacks are less common in the city. How are *they,* whoever they are, covering up serial murders here?" he asked.

"Where did you pack the gauze and disinfectant?"

"Nice try. I came here for answers, and I'm not leaving, even after I run out of questions. Somehow, though, I have a feeling I won't run out of questions."

I sighed, knowing he wouldn't. It had been five weeks since I'd discovered the existence of vampires, and I still had questions. "Before our case upstate, they used gang wars to cover their kills. Now, everything's different. We're actually solving this one. They're still entrancing our witnesses, but they're not tampering with evidence."

"What changed?"

"It's more like *who* changed," I admitted. "I'll explain on the way to the hospital. We're meeting Greta and the medical examiner, so you might want to prepare yourself."

"For the dead bodies?" Rowens frowned. "I've seen worse in the field."

I shook my head. "For Greta. I doubt anyone at this meeting will thank me for bringing a federal agent into this investigation, especially the very agent who accused Greta and her team of withholding information and threatened her with obstruction of justice charges."

"I call it as I see it, and at the time, that's how it appeared. Now, I don't know what I see, but I know it's nothing like anything I've ever seen before."

I snorted under my breath. "It's nothing like anyone has ever seen before. What is the bureau making of all this?"

Rowens raised his eyebrows. "How should I know what the bureau does these days? I've been stuffed behind a desk, remember?"

"Which gives you more time to talk now that you're not wasting time dodging bullets and being mauled by bears," I said snarkily. "How much time do we have?"

"Time before what?" he evaded.

"Before your replacement pokes his nose into this case." I sighed. "Don't play dumb. You know how this works. You were the one who did the poking last time. This case has national and international coverage spotlighting it now. It's only a matter of time before the FBI joins the party again."

His mouth turned down in a grim line. "Yes and no. Everyone believed the report on rabid bear attacks. The bureau took a hit on that one, so they won't get involved in this case unless they uncover that the attacks are human-caused."

I smirked warily. "The attacks aren't human-caused."

Rowens shrugged. "If they discover the true cause of these attacks, I don't know what they'll do, but it won't be anything good, I can tell you that. Nothing good ever came from shit hitting a fan."

"Then we'd better solve this case and reveal the truth on our own terms before that happens." I revved my scooter and, with an anticlimactic twist of my wrist, rolled slowly across the living room floor toward my front door. "You've got five minutes to redress that shoulder, but try making it three. Greta is not a patient woman, and we're already late."

Rowens nodded. "My kind of morning."

Twenty minutes later, Rowens and I were sitting in Dr. Chunn's cozy office, him on the couch and me on my scooter, waiting for Dominic, who wasn't coming, Meredith, who wasn't answering her phone, and Dr. Chunn, who should have been the first person there. Needless to say, Greta was not pleased, but at least she had other people higher on her shit list than me.

Rowens shook her hand when I made the introductions, exuding the calm, stoic, professionalism I'd come to expect from him, despite the fact that he'd had his mind blown on the way here. I'd explained the difference between night blood, vampire, and the Damned, how the Master vampire of New York City was losing strength and power with the coming Leveling and a new leader was emerging and transforming night bloods into the Damned. I'd explained the benefits of night blood—resistance to mind control being the only reason he still remembered the true investigation in Erin, New York, unlike everyone else who'd been involved with the case—and the potential to become a vampire. I explained everything I could never outright admit to Meredith or Greta, or any other human for that matter, because Rowens was a night blood. Everyone deserved to know the truth, but he was the only one whom the vampires couldn't entrance the truth from his mind.

Five weeks ago, Walker had been the expert night blood explaining everything to me. Now, I was the one explaining everything to Rowens, but my five-week crash coarse didn't make me an expert in anything except barely surviving. Rowens deserved a better mentor—Yoda, I was not—but my measly five-weeks worth of firsthand vampire survival skills was all I had to offer.

Despite my newly reversed role as night blood mentor to Rowens, I hadn't explained my specific and deepening involvement with said Master vampire of New York City; nor had I revealed that Dominic was more involved in this investigation than anyone realized. Rowens was still in shock and taking stock; coming to terms with the existence of vampires and his own existence as a night blood was enough to swallow for one day, and honestly, my relationship status with Dominic wasn't something I could easily explain in a fifteen-minute taxi ride. Even if I flashed a spotlight on it, shoved it under a microscope, and dissected it, I'd never quite understand how Dominic, the most dangerous evil I'd ever encountered, had somehow become a trusted ally. I cared for Dominic, more deeply than I'd thought my scarred heart capable of. In some ways, this made Dominic more dangerous than I'd ever imagined.

In protection of Dominic and his secrets, in protection of my heart and the fragile, uncertain bond growing between Dominic and me, I omitted Dominic's specific involvement as our Master vampire completely from my explanations to Rowens. He was an agent of the Federal Bureau of Investigation, and I had no illusions that he wouldn't eventually piece the puzzle together, but eventually wasn't this morning.

Rowens had processed everything I divulged in silent, tight-lipped stoicism, met my eyes, and asked, "How do we stop the Damned from killing anyone else?"

I couldn't help but appreciate a man who could drill through the mess I'd given him to see the core of our problem. Unfortunately, I didn't have an answer to that particular question, but that's what we were here in Dr. Chunn's office to figure out.

Harroway shook Rowens's hand, too, but he was less distracted than Greta by the absence of Dr. Chunn, Meredith, and Dominic, and more focused on in-person targets: us.

"First Meredith, now Rowens. Anyone else you want to squeeze into this office? Carter? Nathan? A cousin, maybe?" Harroway glanced around the room, sizing up the interior of Dr. Chunn's office. "The doc will need a second couch."

"Space isn't a problem. I brought my own seating," I reasoned, patting my scooter. "We could easily add a few more experts to the team."

"We can't get the team we have to show for a meeting," Greta groused. "I doubt adding more people to this circus is the solution. Maybe adding different people."

I sighed. "It was a long night for everyone."

"Meredith and Nicholas walked out of the hospital on their own two feet, but you're the one who shows up." Greta shook her head. "If you were able to attend this meeting, they have no excuse. How are you feeling?"

"Fine, thank you. How are you?" I asked, being deliberately obtuse.

Greta shot me a stern look. "You know what I mean."

"And I told you. I'm fine. Me being here is a testament to my severe lack of self-preservation and my obsession to out-scoop the competition. Points for me, not demerits for others."

Harroway snorted. "You're the one who should be home, resting. Jesus Christ, you're just the reporter and you're here, but the environmental science expert flakes out. Twice."

I crossed my arms. "You couldn't have just ended that statement with 'should be home resting,' could you?"

"You're more than 'just a reporter' to this investigation," Greta said to me, her voice clipped. "And you have a point," she conceded to Harroway.

"I hate to be the one to ask the hard questions, but—" I interjected, and Harroway snorted. Greta raised her eyebrows, and even Rowens shot me a side-long glance of disbelief. "Okay, maybe 'hate' is a strong word, but just because I'm good at something doesn't mean I like doing it." I took a deep breath and asked my hard question, determinedly unflinching in the face of truth. "Does anyone know the whereabouts of Dr. Chunn last night?"

We all looked at each other in silence.

Greta sighed. "Harroway, have you checked medical records from last night's crime scene?"

"Just our department's. Not our partnering offices'."

She gave him a look. "Not the medical examiner? We could be waiting here, and she might not be coming?"

Harroway stood. "I'm on it," he said and left the room.

When the door closed behind him, Greta honed her focus on me. "Harroway doesn't remember the attack—not in detail, like I do. His memories are vague and fuzzy. Whatever force is influencing our witnesses is influencing our department, too."

"Remember when I wrote my original animal-attack article four weeks ago?" I asked. "I had recorded testimony from you concerning the bites, but the next day, you didn't remember giving that testimony, even when confronted with the recording."

Greta crossed her arms. "How could I forget? You caught evidence everyone missed, even the previous medical examiner. Even me."

I shook my head. "You didn't miss anything. I just remembered what everyone forgot."

Rowens opened his mouth, and I braced myself—God only knew what he would say, with his new knowledge of vampires, night bloods, and the Damned—when the door whipped open, and Dr. Chunn, whole and healthy, if winded, barged into her own office.

"I'm sorry," she gasped, trying to catch her breath as if she'd sprinted here from across the hospital. "I apologize for my tardiness, but I couldn't present you with the data I found until I'd retested some of my findings."

Greta raised her eyebrows. "Was something wrong with the first round of data?"

Dr. Chunn shook her head. "I would have sworn something was wrong, but no, my second tests came back consistent with my original findings." She blinked. "Which only creates more problems instead of solving the ones we already have."

"Sounds par for the course on this investigation," Greta grumbled.

"Harroway wanted me to tell you that we should proceed without him, that he's confirming the whereabouts of your partnering offices' staff?" Dr. Chunn said, obviously relaying the message, but not quite understanding its implication.

Greta nodded. "By all means, please proceed. Where should we start?"

"Well, I—" Dr. Chunn looked up from behind her stack of files and paperwork at the three of us and hesitated when her eyes met Rowens.

"Sorry, Doc, we have an additional expert on this case, if that's all right," I said by way of introduction. "Dr. Chunn, this is Supervisory Special Agent Rowens. He's taking a medical leave of absence from the FBI and graciously decided to offer his expertise on our investigation. He spearheaded the similar case in Erin, New York, last week."

"I remember," Dr. Chunn said neutrally. She shook his hand. "Pleased to see you again, Harold, although I'm sorry for the circumstances. And your injury."

"A pleasure to see you again as well, Susanna," Rowens said, and his craggy, typically stony expression lightened. I blinked, wondering when Rowens had learned to smile.

Dr. Chunn blushed prettily from his regard, and I eyed the two of them curiously.

Dr. Chunn cleared her throat and looked around at our small group. "Should we wait for Dr. Leander and Miss Drake?"

Greta sighed. "No. Please proceed without them as well. The creatures out there killing people certainly won't wait, so neither can we."

Dr. Chunn nodded. "Then let's start with something that, if it doesn't make complete sense, at least isn't as crazy as some of my other findings."

Greta gestured to files that Dr. Chunn had dropped in three towering stacks on her desk. "By all means."

"I've reviewed Miss Drake's findings, and they coincide with my own. Although I can't corroborate the evidence found in her photos with hard samples from last week's crime scenes, last night's soil samples have the same scale-like fragments as Monday's crime scene. And traces of those scale-like fragments were found beneath a majority of the victims' fingernails."

Greta raised her eyebrows. "Beneath their fingernails? So the victims are scraping their fingernails through the ground at each crime scene?"

"Fragments beneath fingernails typically indicate defensive wounds. We usually find skin and blood. Dirt and grime are common, too," Dr. Chunn explained, "but considering the manner in which these victims were attacked, I'm leaning toward defensive wounds."

"What exactly are the scales? Where are they coming from?" Greta asked.

I exchanged a quick glance with Rowens. Maybe the gleam of the creatures' obsidian scales hadn't been as obvious last night as I'd thought, even under the glow of moonlight and crime-scene spotlights.

Or maybe Greta hadn't remembered as much as she thought she did.

"That's where the facts start to sound like fiction," Dr. Chunn said with a hefty sigh. "The scales aren't reptilian or fish, like you would expect. They're mammal."

"What mammal has scales?" Greta asked.

"Cursory research indicates that the pangolin is the only mammal on earth with scales."

Greta raised her eyebrows. "Pangolin?"

"Indigenous to Asia and Africa, it's nocturnal and resembles an anteater with scales." Dr. Chunn handed Greta a printed photo from a web search. The animals on the page were adorable, with long snouts and small, tucked ears. Granted, they had long claws, but they were roughly the size of a large pillow and just as cuddly. In some of the photos, by the set of their little lips, they appeared to be smiling.

Greta looked up from the photos. "This doesn't resemble the creatures from last night."

"I wouldn't think so," Dr. Chunn said, looking bewildered. "Like I said, they're indigenous to Asia and Africa."

Greta placed the photo back on Dr. Chunn's desk. "Then why do I need to know about pangolins?"

"I'm not particularly familiar on pangolins, so I need to perform more research and contact some zoology experts to confirm my findings, but pangolins may be one of the only mammals on record with scales," she said, giving Greta a sharp look.

"What are you saying? That we were attacked by an *unknown* mammal last night?"

Dr. Chunn shrugged. "This is just the tip of the iceberg. The part that makes sense."

"Right. Too bad we don't have an environmental science expert consulting on this case," Greta snapped.

"I've e-mailed my findings to Dr. Leander. I'll let you know when I hear from him."

I blinked, nonplussed at the thought of Dominic checking e-mail in the underground lair of his coven. I didn't think he had a computer, let alone Wi-Fi.

"Furthermore," Dr. Chunn continued, but her expression had changed slightly. She looked nearly embarrassed at the thought of more. "The scales are not a direct DNA match for the blood sample that Ms. DiRocco provided, but they do share some commonalities."

Greta's and Rowens' heads swiveled to stare at me.

"Please, just DiRocco," I insisted.

"How common?" Greta asked, but she didn't take her eyes off me.

Dr. Chunn shook her head. "Likely at the level of Genus. I've sent the samples to our lab to confirm, but the turn around on that will take some time."

"What exactly does that mean?" I asked.

"Horses and zebra are both equine, but they're not the same species. Although they share many similar traits, they are different animals. The same applies to the scales we found at the crime scene and the blood sample you provided me," Dr. Chunn explained. "The scales and the blood came from two separate species but may be of the same genome."

I nodded. "Interesting."

"It gets more interesting, I assure you," Dr. Chunn said, looking grim about that fact.

Greta still hadn't taken her eyes off me. "You're not surprised that the blood sample you provided is related but not identical to the scales found at the crime scene," Greta said. Considering the accusing look she was drilling at me, she didn't look much surprised herself.

I shrugged. "I had my suspicions."

"If you know who is responsible for these murders, you need to come clean. Right now."

"We both saw what attacked us last night," I reminded her. "After seeing them, do you know what those creatures are and who's responsible?" I gestured to the piles of files stacked on Dr. Chunn's desk. "Now we have scientific proof that they're not anything we've ever seen before."

Greta narrowed her eyes. "You know exactly what these creatures are, don't you?"

"All I know is that, even after seeing them and having the scientific proof to back it up, you're still second-guessing your gut." I shook my head. "Seeing really isn't believing."

"DiRocco." Greta said my name like a warning.

I held up my hands. "Let's just hear out Dr. Chunn's findings and go from there. She said it only got more interesting, isn't that right?"

Dr. Chunn nodded grimly. "Unfortunately, yes, there's more."

"Jesus, how much more could there possibly be?" Greta asked.

"Never ask that question," Rowens muttered.

"I sent our samples to a wildlife service forensic laboratory, and the findings indicate that both the scales and the blood, likely from mammals, share genetic traits similar to those of humans and bats."

"Whatever attacked us last night was not human, and it certainly wasn't bat," Greta said, not looking pleased in the least.

"I didn't say the creature was a human or a bat. I said the scales and blood samples indicate that the creatures were similar to humans *and* bats." Dr. Chunn licked her finger and tabbed through several pages of her report. "According to your statement, the creatures who attacked last night had long talons, sharp fangs, pointed ears, and a flat, point-tipped nose; stood upright on legs with posterior hinges; and drank large amounts of blood during their hunt."

"And ate human hearts," Greta added.

Dr. Chunn nodded. "Maybe Dr. Leander can better account for the human hearts—I certainly can't—but as extraordinary as it seems, bats do share all of those characteristics. Granted, bats have wings, not arms, they don't stand upright, and they don't have the mass or musculature of the creatures that attacked last night, but humans do. And some species of bat survive on a blood diet."

"What exactly are you implying?" Greta asked. "That a man-sized bat with pangolin scales attacked us?"

"My findings are based on your own descriptions and science. This is our evidence. These are the facts," Dr. Chunn defended.

"You saw it with your own eyes," I reminded Greta. "What did it look like to you?"

Greta cursed. "This is crazy."

I nodded. "It is. And it's supported by physical, forensic evidence."

Greta looked up at Dr. Chunn, and she nodded reluctantly. "I can run the data a third time, but working with what you've given me"—Dr. Chunn shook her head as she gazed down at her pile of findings, at a loss—"as unbelievable as it is, these are the hard, empirical facts of this case."

"What about sewer residue?" I asked. "Was there any evidence in your samples or on the victims that the creatures may be living in or in contact with the sewer or drainage pipes beneath the city?"

Dr. Chunn shook her head. "No, the lab results didn't indicate anything that might suggest that."

Greta stared at me. "What's rattling in that mind of yours, DiRocco?"

"I don't know for sure, but when I do, I'll let you know," I said. "For now, let's just stick with the facts we already have. They're unbelievable enough as it is without adding conjecture to the table."

Greta and Dr. Chunn nodded, but Rowens knew too much to be fooled. He stared at me, knowing I knew more than I was saying, more even than I'd confided in him, but he knew better than to speak his mind in front of everyone. He'd grill me in private, night blood to night blood, and he'd use that bond against me to leverage the truth because that's what I'd do if I were him. Unfortunately, I'd been grilled by him before and knew how good he was at his job.

Almost as good as me.

Chapter 17

I should have just sucked up my pride and taken a taxi to Meredith's apartment. At full speed, my scooter was faster than walking, or at least faster than I was able to walk, but her apartment was ten blocks west of the hospital. The sun was high and bright, and the lure of remaining in sunlight coupled with my aversion to asking a cabbie for help with my scooter had solidified my decision; I left Rowens with Greta to help her investigation and scooted all ten blocks to Meredith's apartment by myself. The five-minute drive turned into a thirty-minute scooter ride, and by the time I reached her apartment, ambulances were already on scene.

The ambulances aren't for Meredith, I told myself. I'd just seen her last night. She'd just survived the impossible—not just a vampire attack, a Damned vampire attack. How could she be hurt in her own apartment in broad daylight?

By accident. Home invasion. Armed robbery. Rape. Kidnapping. Assault.

The possibilities were endless, and I'd drive myself crazy thinking of the many traditional ways a person could die that had nothing to do with me or the danger that followed me every night. Add to those the many ways her association with me as her best friend and co-worker could put her at risk, and there was no telling the many ways Meredith could potentially be hurt in her own apartment.

I called Meredith's phone again, holding my breath and hoping against hope those ambulances were for someone else in her apartment complex.

I'd just passed the first ambulance and was driving up to the second when a paramedic jumped out the back, blocking my way. I considered running him over, but then I looked up, met his gaze, and stopped the scooter millimeters from his shin. The paramedic was Nathan. The implications of him being present at a crime scene were many and unpredictable, but one fact was undeniable.

He'd been crying.

His eyes were red-rimmed, his nose was running, and he had that stubborn, pinch-lipped expression that he wore when he was struggling not to flat-out weep. I didn't want to think about why he was on driving duty instead of on scene, helping to stabilize the patient.

Because he knew the patient. Or worse, the patient was already dead.

Nathan nodded at me, and we just stared at each other in silence for a long moment, me shaking my head and him nodding, and I wanted to rip his damn head off.

"No," I said aloud.

"It doesn't look good, Cass," Nathan whispered.

My breath caught. "So there's a chance."

Nathan shook his head.

My anger, hot enough to cauterize my wounds, exploded in Nathan's stupid, nodding face. "Bullshit. What are you even doing here? You haven't worked in weeks. No one at the hospital remembers you, and technically, thanks to Jillian, you're not an employee. She wiped you from their system as effectively as she wiped you from their memories."

"I showed them my badge and told them I'm a new hire. I blamed them for losing the paperwork." Nathan's expression hardened. "I have to do something with my life. I can't live off milk and cereal and your generosity forever."

I shook my head. "That's the dumbest plan I've ever heard," I said flatly.

"It worked, didn't it?"

"For now, but when they check the system, you won't be there. That's what happened to me with that first article on the animal bites. Meredith even had a photo, and—" I had to clear my throat at the mention of Meredith. "—and still, no one believed me."

"I'm not you, and this isn't about some stupid article. This is my life," Nathan snapped.

"Fine. Whatever," I snapped back. "Let me through."

"It's too late, Cassidy."

"It's never too late," I snarled, and ran over Nathan's feet as I scooted past him.

I made it into the apartment building, up the elevator three floors, and halfway down the hallway before a paramedic saw me. I blinked back tears, cleared my throat, and threw on the mask I'd perfected from years of reporting difficult and gruesome cases. I wouldn't get in as Meredith's friend or a reporter, but I might get in if I was on assignment from Greta. And officers on assignment didn't cry.

The paramedic strode over to me, a soft, sympathetic expression on his face. I resisted running over his feet like I had Nathan's. Officers on assignment played nice in the sandbox, at least for as long as it took to get what they wanted.

No crying. No hit-and-runs. No being my usual prickly self. I took a deep breath. I could do this. For Meredith, I could do anything.

When I stopped in front of him, the paramedic knelt down, so we were at eye level.

"I'm sorry, miss, but unless you live on this floor, you'll need to step, um, go back downstairs for another ten minutes until we clear the area."

I nodded, taking advantage of his hesitation. He'd misspoken, and his stutter, coupled with his fresh face and darting, uncertain eyes, were just what I needed to talk my way through. "I heard. There's been an accident in 304?"

His expression further softened. "I'm really not at liberty to discuss it, but if you'll just go back downstairs, we'll only be ten minutes."

"Actually, Detective Wahl called me in to check it out."

He blinked. "Who?"

"Detective Greta Wahl, NYPD."

The man's gaze darted down to my scooter before meeting my eyes again. "Can I see your badge?"

"Greta will vouch for me."

He shook his head. "Unless you have a badge, I can't let you—"

"Give her a call. Let her know I'm at Meredith Drake's apartment on official business, and like I said, she'll vouch for me." I cocked my head. "Unless you want her to charge you with obstruction of justice. If you don't let me through, you're impeding our investigation."

"I—Well—" the paramedic stuttered. He glanced at Meredith's apartment and rubbed the back of his neck, looking torn.

I bit my tongue, waiting out his response.

The man turned to face me again, looking resolute. "Wait here. I'll call it in," he said. He walked into the elevator I'd just rode up in and disappeared behind its closing door.

The moment he was out of sight, I scooted down the rest of the hallway and eased open Meredith's apartment door without knocking. Despite Nathan's warning, I wasn't prepared for the total destruction of her place. Part of me was still in denial. The stupid, optimistic part that should have died along with my parents still hoped against all odds that maybe someone else needed medical attention. Maybe, just maybe, it wasn't Meredith who was dead.

If I hadn't already been sitting on my scooter, I might have fallen to my ass on the floor.

Blood was everywhere. Soaked into the carpet. Sprayed across the walls. Smeared over the couch and chairs and tables. Puddles where she'd stumbled and streaks where she fell marked the hardwood. Handprints where she'd tried to crawl and pull herself up stained the cabinets. Proof that she'd fought her attacker and struggled to stay alive painted the entire apartment red. Proof that she'd failed.

I bit my lip.

"Clear."

A long, high buzz filled the room, and I swallowed down bile. I didn't know which was worse: the sight of so much of Meredith's blood or the sound of her still, lifeless heart.

Did she still even have a heart?

It couldn't have been the Damned, I thought, trying and failing to assure myself. She'd left the hospital early this morning and would have arrived home just before sunrise. The Damned would have had to wait at the hospital, follow her home, attack, and return to wherever they hide during the day in the mere minutes between early morning and dawn. That was a tight window, assuming the Damned had the cognizance to stalk their prey—which, according to my experience with Nathan, they didn't.

I covered my mouth with my hand to hold back a sob. Assuring myself that a human had killed her didn't change the fact that she was dead.

"One more time."

"But it's been—"

"Again."

A low, double pound shook the room. I bit my lip, wanting to die myself, but then the long, high buzz suddenly stopped and was replaced with a steady beat.

"We got her back. Let's move."

The paramedic moved out of my line of sight, revealing Meredith. She was lying on her back in the middle of a puddle of her own blood on her living room floor, her shirt split from hem to neck and the pads of the portable, external defibrillator stuck to the middle of her chest and left ribs. Her body had been slashed by deep cuts in rows of four across her wrists, neck, stomach, and thighs, and if I hadn't known better, I'd have said that the slashes resembled the same raking of claw marks on all our other victims. But her chest was smooth and unmarked. Whoever had attacked her hadn't taken or eaten her heart.

Her hair was plastered to her head with blood. Her face was tipped limply to the side, her eyes half open and unseeing.

Looking at her like this made me want to curl into myself, shrivel, and die.

"There's not enough time, damn it." One of the paramedics cursed. He was young and lanky and had been performing chest compressions before they'd found a rhythm. "With so many nicked arteries, there's no way she makes it to the hospital without going back into v-fib. She doesn't have enough blood to keep her heart pumping."

"We have fluids in the ambulance," his partner answered. She was calm and experienced, but I recognized the hard look in her eyes. The younger paramedic was right. Meredith wasn't going to make it.

"You think that'll be enough?"

"We'll make it work. Let's go," the female paramedic looked up and met my gaze. She scowled. "Who the hell are you?"

"I, um." I had to clear my throat before I could speak. I wiped my cheeks, realizing that tears had tracked down my face while I'd been watching them work on Meredith. So much for being here on assignment. When my throat was clear, or at least as clear as it was going to get, I spoke through the rasp in my throat. "I'm her best friend. We had a date. When she didn't show, I came to get her."

"I'm so sorry, miss, but you need to move outside. We're leaving now, and we need to move fast to save your friend's life. Do you know if she has any allergies? Any adverse side effects to medications?"

"No, she doesn't have allergies." I backed up my scooter as they picked up her stretcher between them.

"What's her name?"

"Meredith. Meredith Drake."

"Okay, we need to take Meredith down to the ambulance, so we can take care of her. Meet us at the hospital, and you can see her there."

"Can you—"

The steady beat of the portable defibrillator cut into a high buzz.

"We're losing her!"

The paramedics turned away from me to work on Meredith. They were taking too long. By the time they eventually carried her out of her apartment, drove to the hospital, and got her on the operating table, she'd be dead.

I gunned my scooter into full throttle down the hallway to the elevator and hit the down button.

"Come on," I urged. "Open."

Miracle of all miracles, the elevator doors opened before the paramedics could notice my retreat, but when I reached the ground floor and drove outside, the paramedic I'd lied to was waiting for me. I bit my lip. Greta had obviously not vouched for me and my investigative privileges.

I turned away from him and drove in the opposite direction.

The paramedic was faster than my scooter. He cut in front of me, and when I tried to run over his feet, he grabbed my handles and squeezed my scooter to a stop.

"Excuse me," I snapped.

"I don't think so. Detective Wahl's on her way, and she told me to keep you on scene. It's a federal offense to impersonate a police officer."

I rolled my eyes. "I did no such thing."

"Sure you did. You said—"

"I said that Greta would vouch for me. I never said that I was a police officer."

The paramedic narrowed his eyes. "You never denied it."

"Rule número uno, kid. Never assume someone belongs on scene just because they act like they belong. People can act really well."

His face turned hot red. "Listen, you—"

"Hey, what's going on over here?" Nathan asked. His eyes narrowed on the paramedic and his hands over mine on my handlebars.

"This man is harassing me," I accused.

"I certainly am not! She broke into a crime scene! She impersonated a police officer! She—"

"She's obviously handicapped, and you're scaring her," Nathan reasoned. All eyes turned toward me.

It wasn't hard to feign terror when the scene in Meredith's room had certainly terrified me.

Nathan turned back to the paramedic. "I'll take it from here."

The young paramedic looked unsure and confused again, obviously not accustomed to being accused of anything, let alone terrorizing handicapped young women. He looked between Nathan and me and eventually nodded. He released my handlebars.

"If you've got this, I'll just head back upstairs to see if they need more hands."

"You do that," Nathan said, but the paramedic had already disappeared into the apartment complex.

With the paramedic out of earshot, Nathan and I turned to each other and spoke at the same time.

"What the hell are you thinking?" he asked.

"When the paramedics come down with Meredith, I need you to drive the ambulance to the coven," I said.

Nathan blinked for a second, dumbstruck, but when he finally recovered, he exploded. "Dominic's coven? The *vampire* coven?"

I nodded. "One and the same."

"Are you insane?" Nathan shouted.

"Shut up before they hear you," I snapped. "Meredith isn't going to make it."

"I told you that," Nathan muttered.

"Her only chance is with Dominic," I reasoned. "Vampire saliva heals wounds. If the paramedics give her fluids on the way, and one of Dominic's vampires heals her when we get there, she might survive."

Nathan wiped his hand over his jaw as he thought about it. "It's a long shot."

"A long shot is better than no shot."

Nathan shook his head. "What about the paramedics? They're going to open the ambulance doors and realize we're not at the hospital. And then they'll freak when they see Dominic and the others in their true vampire form. Then what?"

"Altering memories is the vampires' specialty. The paramedics can freak all they want. They won't remember what happened or who they saw. They won't remember any of us."

Nathan shook his head, unconvinced. "You're putting all of us at risk, especially the paramedics."

"This is Meredith we're talking about, Nathan. She's dying. You don't think it's worth the risk?"

Nathan's expression fell. "Fuck," he spat, rubbing his hand over his jaw. "Take a cab. I'll meet you there."

"Thank you!" I squealed, tears flooding like twin waterfalls down my face in relief.

Nathan rubbed his own eyes. "Yeah, well, like you said, it's not like I have much of a choice. It's Meredith, after all, and she's worth the risk. Any risk."

He bent down, and I wrapped my arms around Nathan in a brief, fierce hug. Now she'd have a chance, however minuscule. The odds weren't in her favor, but hell, I'd managed to save Nathan against worse odds. I'd saved Dominic after he'd been staked through the heart and spontaneously combusted head to toe in flames. I'd saved Bex after she'd had her heart ripped from her chest. I'd survived after being bled nearly dry. Twice. If there was one thing I could fall back on it was my stubborn refusal to give up in the face of overwhelmingly bad odds. And if it was the last thing I ever did, I'd make sure Meredith survived, too.

Chapter 18

"Dominic!" I shrieked at the top of my lungs, hoarse now from screaming his name in a litany, like a prayer.

A prayer that had gone unanswered.

The cab had weaved and cut through the traffic in New York City style, beating the ambulance downtown. I'd waited until the cabbie had driven off—smiling, with an exorbitant tip in hand for helping me and my scooter in and out of his cab—before beginning my search. Typically, I'd go out of my way to avoid this seedy, secluded section of the city, but this was a likely neighborhood to find a manhole with a missing cover. With metal prices on the rise, people would steal the covers and resell them for scrap, but their greed was my godsend. A few minutes into my search, I found exactly what I needed: access to the sewer and Dominic's coven.

After messaging Nathan a pin to my location, I dropped painfully to my knees beside the open manhole. I'd been screaming Dominic's name through said sewer system for a full minute, but my efforts, though herculean, had been ignored.

Something was wrong.

Dominic could sense when my hip ached over the phone from three hundred miles away. Certainly he could hear me screaming for him when we were in the same city, less than three miles apart.

I gripped the edge of the manhole, inhaling and about to let loose another bellow, when a sharp, stabbing pain encircled my wrists and ankles. The pain was electric. I gasped and looked down at my hands, but in the time it took for me to react, the pain was already gone.

The injury wasn't my own. Considering my metaphysical bonds with Dominic and what that implied, something was definitely very wrong.

"Cassidy?"

That timid, nervous voice was not Dominic. I squinted into the darkness, but I couldn't see anything but shadows within shadows.

"Cassidy DiRocco?"

Something shifted, I heard the suction of a boot lifting from slimy sewer muck, and the glint of deep, plum-colored eyes blinked in the darkness.

Of all the vampires to respond to my call, I thought, *anyone but Neil.*

"Yes, it's me. Where's Dominic?"

"This had better be important, Cassidy," a deep, confident voice replied. Neil wasn't alone, but neither was Dominic with him.

"It's more than important, Sevris. It's urgent," I said. "It's a matter of life and death."

"Good. Those are the only matters I care about," Sevris said. "Come down."

I blinked, staring down into the sewer pipe. "I can't. You come up."

"*I* can't. It's still daylight. I'd burst into flames. In this, even if I wanted to, I can't compromise. You must come to me."

I blew out a long breath. There was a time when willingly crossing the threshold into darkness was unthinkable. They'd dragged me—sometimes kicking and screaming and oftentimes bleeding, broken, and unconscious—but I'd never gone willingly. I squinted into the sewer, their silence as damning as the approaching siren. Now, remaining in sunlight was the unthinkable option.

I crawled around the manhole on my hands and knees, and using the utility ladder, I tried to lower myself into the sewer.

The shards of my left hip ground into frayed nerves, my right leg burned in agony, and between the two, my legs gave out. I gripped the ladder rung with both hands and struggled to pull myself back up, but the rungs were slick from condensation and mildew. I'd never been particularly athletic. Even now, when I needed it most, my body failed me. My hands slipped, and I fell.

For a split second, I thought, *He'll catch me. Dominic would never let me fall.*

But Dominic wasn't here.

I hit cement. Hard.

The fall knocked the air from my lungs. I struggled to breathe, to move, to live with the pain splitting my body.

"You know I can't heal you, Cassidy. Lysander's orders," Sevris said, his voice strained. "This is your punishment for disobeying him. My punishment for disobedience would be much worse."

I coughed and gasped, my own inhalation strained as I dragged air into my reluctant lungs. Taking slow, even breaths to manage the pain throbbing through my body, I looked up. Sevris and Neil were still shrouded in darkness. The only indication of their presence was their voices and the glow of three pairs of reflective, nocturnal eyes. Three pairs, not two.

"Who else is with you?" I rasped.

"Who else?" Rafe's mocking voice echoed from the shadows, nearly giddy. "You think I'd miss all the fun?"

The siren cut short. I glanced up and watched as Nathan parked the ambulance next to the manhole. "Yeah, fun," I whispered.

Sevris inhaled deeply. A menacing growl echoed from the darkness. "A human? You want me to heal a human?"

"She's my best friend."

"Do you realize what you've done by bringing her here? Do you realize the danger to which you've exposed our entire coven for one human woman?" he spat.

"You said if I needed help," I reminded him, "that you were just a call away."

"Yes, if *you* needed help," he said roughly. "This is asking too much."

"You entrance dozens of people to cover up mass murder in the name of protecting the secrecy of your existence," I snapped. "Healing one woman to save her life is nothing in comparison."

"A life that doesn't matter," Sevris growled harshly. "She is nothing but a fleck of dust on the wind compared to the longevity and permanence of our existence."

"She matters to me," I said softly.

"What's it worth to you?" Rafe interjected.

"Excuse me?"

"What's Meredith's life worth?" he asked again.

I narrowed my eyes in Rafe's general direction in the darkness. I'd do just about anything to save Meredith's life, but that wasn't something I'd admit to these creatures. Then again, I'd just thrown myself ass-first down a sewer drain into the darkness with vampires. They probably already knew. Hell, they could probably smell the desperation wafting from my pores.

"This sounds vaguely like extortion, and I don't like it," I said.

"What are you doing?" Sevris hissed. I had to strain to hear his question, and I realized he was no longer talking to me.

"I'm helping," Rafe answered. "You're not happy about the rock and the hard place she's crammed us into. I don't like it either, but I'd not like it a little less if I got something out of it."

"Just shut up."

"What's your problem?"

"When you speak, the words that come out of your mouth make me want to kill you."

I took a deep breath and tried to think while they argued. This was how my partnership with Dominic had begun. Bartering. I'd allowed Dominic to use me as bait to find Kaden in exchange for his promise to keep our city safe. I'd traveled to Erin, New York, to speak to Bex on Dominic's behalf in exchange for his help to find and save my brother.

Now I wanted them to save Meredith. What was I willing to give them—and capable of giving them—in exchange now?

"What do you want?" I asked, interrupting their bickering.

"You're the only female night blood we've met in decades," Rafe said, obviously bitter over that fact. "Do you know how rough life is when no one you meet is allowed to remember you? If I heal Meredith, you introduce me to one of your friends."

"Seriously?" Sevris asked. "Of all the things—"

"Let me get this straight. You'll save my best friend's life in exchange for a date?" I asked dryly.

"I just want an introduction, that's all," Rafe said, confidently. "I'll take it from there."

"Cassidy?" Nathan called, his voice sharp.

"Where the fuck are we?"

The paramedics. Fuck indeed.

"It's now or never, Cassidy," Rafe said, and I could hear the grin in his tone. "Will you hook me up?"

"I'll see what I can do."

Rafe clicked his tongue, a precursor to the rattle of his growl. "You've got to do a little better than that."

"Cassidy?!" Nathan called.

"Fine," I snapped. "I agree. I'll introduce you to one of my friends. Happy?"

"Ecstatic. Get everyone down here, and we'll take care of the rest."

"Nathan!" I called. "Down here!"

Nathan looked around, up, and behind him, and finally, after looking in every other direction, he looked down.

"How did you get down there?" he asked, looking first at me and then at my abandoned scooter on the street.

"The same way everyone else is getting down here," I said. "Through the manhole."

Nathan shook his head. His lips moved, and I could just barely hear the curses he grumbled under his breath. The three paramedics surrounded Nathan, their expressions varying degrees of confused and angry.

Oh God, he doesn't stand a chance, I thought, dread like an anchor, weighing down my stomach. Three against one weren't good odds, but for my slender, emo little brother, one against one wasn't good. Three against one was impossible.

The older, more experienced paramedic didn't waste any words on Nathan. She pushed past him, ordering the others back into the ambulance as she climbed into the cab.

Nathan rushed her from behind, not in the way that Dominic could move—so fast that he was nothing but a blur of movement—but still, Nathan moved with more strength and ruthlessness than I'd ever thought him physically capable of. He picked up the paramedic by her waist and dropped her into the manhole. Her scream echoed through the pipe as she fell, but the crack of her head hitting concrete when she landed cut her scream short.

The other two paramedics gaped at Nathan and then down into the hole at their boss's unconscious form lying next to me. They glanced at each other warily, but something passed between them, so when they looked back at Nathan, their expressions were resolved. The young man who had worked on Meredith rushed for the ambulance cab, while the other paramedic dove for Nathan.

Nathan tripped the first paramedic and used the momentum of the second to knock him into the manhole next. The first paramedic was still finding his feet when Nathan kicked him in the ribs. He lost his balance, fell into the manhole, and landed on top of the others.

Nathan disappeared from view, but I was still gaping. I'd never seen Nathan like this before. Sure, I'd witnessed him as a nine-foot, heart-eating creature, but he'd transformed back from that hell. He was just Nathan again. My Nathan.

Except, he obviously wasn't.

Nathan reappeared above with Meredith strapped to a backboard. He lowered her carefully into the sewer and climbed down the rest of the way himself to drop her top half gently to the ground.

"Nathan, how did you—"

"I did what you needed, didn't I?" he snapped, and the ferocity in that one sentence was breathtaking.

I jerked, taken aback. "Yes, you did, and thank God you could, but how—"

"I hate to interrupt this lovely revelation, but the paramedics are reviving. Drag everyone to us before they gain full consciousness," Sevris said from the shadows, his voice grim and urgent.

"Where's Dominic?" Nathan asked me, ignoring Sevris.

"I don't know, but he sent backup," I said, pointing my thumb in Sevris', Rafe's, and Neil's general direction.

Nathan pursed his lips, but otherwise, he didn't move.

"Nathan?"

"I have enough innocent blood staining my soul. When we agreed to do this, I didn't realize there would be three more."

I frowned. "Three more what?"

"Murders, Cassidy. Even for Meredith, I can't do this."

"What are you talking about? Just drag them over there and—" I glanced toward the darkness, and the words died on my lips. I could see Nathan's perspective. We couldn't even discern Sevris, Rafe, and Neil from the shadows. They were still hiding, the glow of their eyes hunting us from the abyss. "Sevris will heal Meredith, and Rafe will entrance the paramedics," I assured Nathan. "No one is being murdered, I promise."

Nathan shook his head warily, but despite his reservations, he took hold of the backboard and dragged Meredith into the darkness. He reappeared and, one by one, dragged the paramedics toward Rafe and Sevris as well, until I was left alone in the gloom.

I still couldn't see anyone, but I could hear the paramedics' moans as they slowly regained consciousness. I listened as Rafe said, "Look into my eyes," and I knew what would come next.

Guilt gnawed at my gut. I remembered how it felt to be attacked and entranced. Only a few short weeks ago, I'd been frightened and confused by Dominic's attack, unaware of the nocturnal war raging beneath the city. Yet somehow, in that short time, I'd become the one who attacked and entranced. I'd become one of the vampires without ever undergoing the physical transformation.

"You brought Meredith to the hospital, and the doctors saved her life," Rafe told the paramedics. "You never saw Nathan, Cassidy, or this sewer, and after dropping Meredith off at the hospital, you came to this neighborhood to check on a prank call. Nothing came of it, and you will return to the hospital."

They repeated what Rafe said, word for word.

Nathan reappeared in the light. "You too?" he asked.

I bit my lip. I didn't really want to. I was still safe under my sliver of sunlight, but how could I not go where I'd willingly sent Meredith?

I nodded.

Nathan bent down, scooped me up under my back and knees, and stood with me in his arms. The contact with my leg and hip was agony; I clenched my teeth and bore the pain in silence, but I couldn't stop my body from trembling.

Being held by Nathan was strange. He'd always been slender. Not necessarily weak—he'd been unaccountably more athletic than me growing up—but he was more lean than muscular. Now, he held me with ease, and I realized with some shock that, despite the fact that he was twenty-seven years old, I was just now realizing that he was a man.

He carried me to Sevris and Rafe, plunging us into full darkness.

My heart knocked against my chest so fast and hard that breathing was physically uncomfortable. Nathan didn't seem nervous. He wasn't winded or sweating or hesitant, just unwilling, and it made me wonder what else I'd missed about him. I'd thought he was depressed from the lingering memories of his time being Damned—from the horrors he'd seen and done and the resulting loss of his identity—but maybe his illness was more than depression.

My eyes adjusted to the darkness, and when they absorbed the scene before me, I completely forgot my concern over Nathan. I flinched violently and choked on my tongue in an attempt not to scream.

I shouldn't have been surprised. How many times had Dominic warned me about the danger and depravity of vampires during the day? I'd seen him and Kaden in their fully transformed, gargoyle day forms. I'd lain beside Dominic as he newly woke from his day rest, frigid and skeletal and blindingly craving my blood. I'd even witnessed Jillian after she had been released from her confinement; having been burned by silver and starved for three weeks, she'd been nothing but bones and the tatters of tendons. I'd thought I'd seen just about every horror imaginable.

But I'd never seen this.

Sevris, Rafe and Neil reminded me of a deep-sea lamp fish—all needle teeth and glazed eyes—minus the hanging headlight. Their skin was stretched thin, nearly translucent over their knobby bones. Their muscles physically worked, proof of their movement and strength, but from appearances alone, they were nothing but skin-wrapped bones. I could overlap my thumb and pointer finger around Rafe's bicep. Hell, I could wrap my hand around the circumference of Neil's thigh. Not that I would want to approach close enough to touch either of them.

Sevris' legs were especially hideous; as he squatted on the ground, his legs hinged back and behind him like those of a praying mantis. Meredith was cradled in his elongated, gently curved claws, his glazed, reflective eyes devouring her, his forked tongue inside one of the many wounds across her stomach, his fang-stuffed mouth scant millimeters from her right bared breast. Given the length of his ten claws around her body and the uncountable fangs of various lengths protruding from both his upper and lower jaws, his ability to hold and heal her without hurting her was incredible. One misplaced movement of his head or hand, and he'd slice her open.

I'd come here for help from friends—if not technically friends, allies—but the creature savoring the taste of Meredith's blood wasn't anyone or anything I recognized. And it was holding my unconscious, half-naked best friend like a lover—a nocturnal, praying-mantis, cannibalistic lover.

Sevris met my gaze, snorted lightly under his breath at my expression, and refocused on Meredith and her wounds.

I took a deep breath. *This is Sevris*, I reminded myself. *No matter how hideous, monstrous, or murderous he looks, he's my ally, and he's healing her.*

And he was. Half her wounds were already closed. She was still unconscious and impossibly pale and vulnerable and maybe already gone, but where Sevris licked, her wounds healed.

Rafe broke eye contact with one of the male paramedics, the alien sheen of his shark-like stare seeming to look through me rather than at me. His eyes were buggy, too large for his emaciated skull. "What? Do I have something in my teeth?" he asked, smiling.

He rubbed his long, thin tongue along the razor edge of a fang.

I shook my head, beyond words.

Maybe it was something in my expression. Maybe it was my speech-lessness or the scent of my kaleidoscope feelings, but Sevris retreated from a particularly deep wound under Meredith's collarbone, swallowed, and said, "She's still alive. Weak and not out of the woods, but alive."

I blinked, surprised by the soft, caring quality of the voice emitting from that needle-toothed mouth.

The paramedics chanted, "She's alive. Weak and not out of the woods, but—"

"Oh, shut up," Rafe snapped.

"How could you know that for certain?" I whispered.

Neil cocked his head. "Even I can hear the slow, steady beat of her heart."

Of course he could.

Sevris continued licking—inside cuts, tears, punctures, and breaks—and she mended from the inside out. Bones, muscle, and skin became whole again until, miracle of miracles, when Sevris probed into a particularly sensitive wound across her face, beneath her eye, Meredith flinched slightly, minutely, and moaned.

I covered my mouth with my hands, hope shattering my composure.

"You'll have to babysit these bozos until dark," Rafe said, indicating the paramedics. "Until I can carry them out to their ambulance."

"Okay," I said numbly.

"Dispatch and the hospital will worry if they don't check in soon. I can carry them back up now," Nathan offered. "When you're finished with them."

I nodded.

"You'd better get on it, then. I'm done with them, and when Sevris finishes with Meredith, we need to return to the coven. Lysander needs us."

That more than anything else stole my attention from Meredith. I met Rafe's glowing eyes head on and forced myself not to flinch in the face of his grotesque appearance. "Why does Dominic need you? What's going on?"

"He's fighting—" Rafe began.

"He's indisposed at the moment," Sevris interrupted.

I blinked. "Who's he fighting?"

"Who isn't he fighting?" Rafe murmured.

Sevris growled.

"It's nothing she doesn't already know," Rafe said unapologetically. "His Leveling is in two nights, and the city's in chaos. It's a miracle they didn't visit sooner."

"They?"

Sevris cut his head to the left, looking murderous. "Don't—"

"The Day Reapers."

Sevris closed his eyes.

I breathed. I didn't know what else to do or how to react to that statement, so I just breathed. Eventually I whispered, "The Day Reapers. They're here? In the coven? Right now?"

Rafe nodded. "And fighting Dominic."

My brain shorted out at those three words, and the next thing I new the words, "I'm coming with you," spilled from my lips. "Nathan can care for Meredith and the paramedics. I'll return with you to help Dominic."

"Absolutely not," Sevris said. "We are under express orders to see you safely away from the coven."

Rafe snorted. "Lysander won't survive tonight, let alone the Leveling, without help. She saved him during Jillian's uprising. Maybe she can do the same against the Day Reapers."

"No one faces the Day Reapers and lives," Neil said morosely. "None of us will survive tonight."

"With Cassidy here we might," Rafe said.

Sevris didn't respond, but neither did he look completely convinced.

"I'm Dominic's night blood," I lied, using my only leverage against them. "I'm coming whether you want me to or not."

"What are you doing?" Nathan hissed. "Meredith's healed. We're done here. Dominic can clean up his own damn mess."

I touched my wrists, massaging the unharmed skin that had burned with electric fire when I'd called for Dominic. I'd known something was wrong, very wrong, for him to send Sevris instead of saving me himself. I couldn't help him anymore, not like I once could, not without night blood, but neither could I turn my back on him and retreat into the safety of sunlight knowing he was in such grave danger.

"You go," I told Nathan. "Take care of Meredith for me, and make sure the paramedics recover." I leaned back and met Nathan's conflicted, wary expression. "I can't let him face the Day Reapers alone. Dominic would risk the same for me."

Nathan tightened his arms around me—his hold, like his expression, fierce. "I don't like it."

"Neither do I," I agreed. "But I'm going anyway."

"Be careful. I'll take care of Meredith, but she'll want you by her side, not me. You better be there for her when she wakes up."

I nodded, knowing a warning when I heard one. "I'll be there."

Sevris' lips thinned around his protruding fangs. I couldn't read his expression, couldn't tell whether he was grimacing, growling, or smiling, but something in my own expression must have reassured him. He nodded. "If you're coming with us, follow me."

My compulsion to protect this city and its inhabitants was stronger than my instinct for self-preservation. That compulsion was what originally drove me to partner with Dominic, to help him find and stop Kaden and the other rebel vampires. It's what drove me now to venture underground during the day, even knowing the creatures I'd encounter would be more volatile and dangerous than their nighttime counterparts, which were volatile and dangerous all on their own. But if I was honest with myself—a habit that I'd always practiced but that had become increasingly difficult to continue lately—I'd admit that endangering myself wasn't just for New York City and its inhabitants anymore.

It was for Dominic.

Chapter 19

Much to my chagrin, I couldn't immediately follow Sevris whether or not I wanted to join him in the deep, dark bowls of his coven. I couldn't walk. After a little finagling and a lot of foul language, Nathan managed to manipulate my scooter through the manhole, so I could drive behind Sevris; he led me away from everything sane and safe, through abandoned sewer drains, and into the coven's elaborate tunnel system. I looked back, just once after giving Meredith a final hand squeeze and hugging Nathan good-bye, but I'd turned around too late. My eyes couldn't penetrate through the darkness to see anything but a pinprick of light at the end of what seemed like an unending tunnel.

An hour later when we finally reached the main hall of their coven, our entrance didn't catch anyone off guard. A few weeks ago, when I'd been mobile and capable of silently sleuthing through his coven, Dominic had sensed my presence despite my discretion; with his strangely enhanced sight, smell, and hearing, not much could surprise Dominic. Now, the whining hum of my scooter echoing through the sewer drains announced my approach like trumpets before a procession.

And what a macabre procession we made.

Sevris entered first, and I followed on my scooter, with Rafe and Neil covering my six. The three of them were looking increasingly like skeletal zombies and less cognizant by the moment. Healing Meredith and entrancing the paramedics without actually drinking their blood had taken its toll. And between my starving, skeletal zombie escorts was me, bruised and scraped from my fall into the manhole, my hair a tangled, matted mess from landing in sewer muck and mildew, my complete absence of makeup debatably more frightening than my companions' appearance, and rolling in at a sedate two miles per hour. Despite my painfully slow progress, they kept pace.

They knew as well as I did the power of solidarity against an opponent, and we needed every scrap of power we could get.

When we entered the hall, I recognized two of the vampires, one of which was Dominic. Even though he was half-transformed, with pointed ears, razor teeth, a flattened nose, and claws for hands, I recognized him; those piercing, otherworldly blue-and-ice eyes were unmistakable, not that I had a particularly excellent view of his eyes from that distance. He was on the far side of the room, behind a long, wooden banquet table that hadn't been present during my previous visit. A dozen vampires sat around the banquet table, drinking from wine glasses in silence.

The low rattle of Dominic's growl permeated throughout the hall, blending with the hum of my scooter. Everyone—from the dozen vampires seated around the banquet table to the hundreds of vampires watching from the honeycomb-like rooms that lined the walls nearly floor to ceiling—turned to stare at me.

I rubbed the front of my teeth with my tongue and twisted to ask Rafe, "Do *I* have something in my teeth?"

Rafe snickered.

The vampire on the near side of the banquet table, opposite Dominic, was the first to recover. He cocked his head at Dominic and said, "Please, extend me the pleasure of introducing me to the lovely woman who just interrupted our meeting."

The words were exceedingly formal, but despite the 'please,' the tone of his sentence was not a request. His voice was measured and mild—kind, even—and oozed sincerity, so it must have been something other than the sound of the words coming from his mouth that made my skin tighten across my body like shrink wrap.

The man steepled his fingers over his lips as he awaited Dominic's response. I frowned, staring at his hands. He wore silver-colored nail polish.

Dominic wasn't looking at the man. His gaze had unwaveringly set and fixed on me. Without my night blood, I couldn't call upon the mental and physical connections between us to discern his thoughts, but I didn't need to read his mind to know what he was thinking. He was angry. Arguably more angry than I'd ever seen him, and I'd seen him murderous.

He'd expressly ordered two of his last, most loyal vampires to keep me away. Yet here I was, and they'd escorted me personally.

Dominic had a choice to make: he could either order me to leave or introduce me to the scary, silver-nailed vampire, but we both knew that those options weren't really choices at all. He couldn't order me to leave, because as his night blood, I had the right to be here. The vampires would question his anger, and eventually they would question my night blood. We would both be exposed for the frauds we were and punished, tortured, and killed accordingly.

I smiled—because what else was there to do in the face of certain death—and waited on Dominic's next words.

Dominic cleared his throat, but when he spoke, his voice still scraped like gravel.

"I am honored to present Cassidy DiRocco, the newest night blood to the New York City coven. Cassidy DiRocco, I present you to Lord High Chancellor Henry Lynell Horrace DeWhitt, Master vampire of London and Lord of all vampires."

"Wow, Lord of *all* vampires. Not just North America or the Western Hemisphere. To what do we owe this honor?" I asked, and God help me, I tried to sound sincere, I really did.

Dominic froze. If it hadn't been for the glow of his reflective, nocturnal eyeballs, he would have disappeared like a chameleon into the wall behind him from the suddenness and completeness of his stillness.

Lord High Chancellor Henry's gaze turned on me so fast, the length of his thick, dark, chestnut-colored ponytail whipped over one shoulder. A shock of white streaked from hairline to tip, no split ends in sight, and I wondered idly, despite the danger and tension of the moment—or perhaps because of it—if his hair was natural or if he used a straightening iron. He stared at me in silence with his very human, strangely normal, unreflective eyes, and then turned back to Dominic. "Is she serious?"

Dominic opened his mouth.

The vampire sitting at the Lord High Chancellor's right hand interrupted before Dominic could defend me. "I assure you that nothing Cassidy says is serious. Her sarcasm is an armor even I have found impenetrable." She smiled sadly. "Rene adored her for it."

I gaped at the second person I recognized in the room.

Bex.

Being a Day Reaper looked good on her. Her eye no longer bled to white toward the pupil nor reflected with that otherworldly glow. Her yellow-green iris was as beautiful as I remembered, but like Lord High Chancellor Henry's, her gaze was strangely human. She wore a bedazzled, dark purple eye patch, which matched the purple and black dress that clung to her every curve, over her missing eye. And her curves were considerable. Bex normally wore jeans, cowboy boots, and flirty, barely there tops in an attempt to humanize herself and entice Walker. From the looks of her and her company, she had different priorities now that she was a Day Reaper that had nothing to do with acting human.

She eyed me just as thoroughly, taking in my bedraggled appearance, cast, and scooter before her expression darkened at the sight of my wristwatch.

I struggled against the natural reaction to squirm under her predator's regard.

She met my eyes and smiled coyly. "A pleasure, as always, Cassidy."

I could think of dozens of responses, each more inappropriate than the last. *Thank you for saving my life. Why haven't you returned to your coven? Why are the Day Reapers here? Do you need help escaping them?*

But even I, who'd made a name for myself in the journalism world for asking the hard questions when no one else would, couldn't voice any of those questions now. Too many ears and eyes and twitching talons were honed in on us, waiting on my response.

Bex and Lord High Chancellor Henry were staring at me, along with the rest of their entourage around the long banquet table, their human eyes gazing from inhumanly perfect faces, deceptively creepy for their masked civility.

Dominic was staring at me, disapproval and fear sharpening his already pointed gaze, and stacked above him in the honeycomb-like rooms that lined the walls were his coven. Hundreds of vampires, several in each room, were gazing down on us, waiting with bated breath for the tone, delivery, and nuance of my response. What I said and how I said it would solidify the current of this meeting and determine whether my presence only rippled the water or drowned them in undertow.

Moments like this were delicate, like a carefully choreographed high-beam routine; one misstep would tip our delicate balance.

I met Bex's eye and said the only thing I could say to her, the one thing I'd never had the chance to say because at the time I'd been dying and scared and grieving, too. "I'm so sorry about Rene. I wish I could have done more, but I never even saw it coming. If I had just—" I lifted my hands and let them fall back to my sides in a help-less gesture. "I could say 'if' about a lot of things, but the one thing that still kills me when I think about my visit to Erin, New York, is Rene's unnecessary death. I'm so very sorry for your loss."

Bex blinked; the long lashes of her carefully shadowed and lined eye swept over her cheek like the flutter of a butterfly's wing. Just as I used anger to hide my pain, Bex used beauty and sexuality to hide hers, and she looked stunning.

"I have many regrets about my time in Erin, New York, as well," she said. "Your visit and losing Rene being two of many, but I ap-preciate your condolences." She turned to the Lord High Chancellor and grinned again—a salacious, sexual grin that made the gloss of her shimmering lipstick sparkle temptingly. "That, my Lord, is about as much sincerity as we'll get out of our little Cassidy DiRocco."

"I'm always sincere. You just don't always like what I have to say," I said.

Lord High Chancellor Henry stood and was suddenly in front of me in one smooth motion. He was taller than I'd expected. Most of his height was in his legs, and considering I was still sitting and short to begin with, I had to crane my neck at an impossible angle to meet his gaze.

"And what is it you have to say to me?" he asked.

I swallowed the instinctive scream that leapt through my throat at the suddenness of his appearance. "May I call you Henry?"

He narrowed his eyes. "Pardon?"

I held out my hand, hoping I wouldn't lose it. "Most people call me DiRocco. Lord High Chancellor Henry Horrace DeWhitt—"

"Lord High Chancellor Henry *Lynell* Horrace DeWhitt," he cor-rected.

"Right. I'm sure that's not what your friends call you."

"We are not friends." The Lord High Chancellor looked at my hand, eyeing it as I might a critter that unexpectedly crawled out from beneath the bed.

I wiggled my fingers and forced a smile. "Does that mean we can't be friendly?"

The Lord High Chancellor glanced back at Bex. "Surely, she's joking."

Bex waffled her hand in my direction. "Her humor and wit can be an acquired taste; if you allow her to live long enough, you may learn to like it. Or not. Even the most exquisite wine can't agree with everyone's palate."

"You like the taste of her," he said, and it wasn't a question.

Bex licked her lips. "I do."

"Lysander?" the Chancellor asked.

Dominic let the silence stretch into a cavern between us. He locked eyes with me, but I couldn't decipher the fathomless depths of his expression. At one time, I could lock eyes with him and pluck the threads of his mind with my will, but even then, I'd only been able to glimpse a blush of his thought. He'd always kept his deepest, most cutting emotions buried where no one, not even himself, could feel them.

I held my breath as the silence lengthened, wondering what words Dominic could possibly utter to bridge its breadth.

Finally, mercifully, Dominic broke the silence. "The future of this coven is tenuous, as the future of any coven is tenuous during any Leveling, but unlike my past Levelings, a contender has risen against me to usurp my rule. Her intentions align with those of a great many vampires, more than just the intentions of a minority here in my coven, but she is the first to have the means, support, and power to make those intentions a reality. If she comes into power, more of those in power will follow suit, and you will have a much larger problem to wrestle with than the acquired taste of my night blood."

My jaw dropped.

The Lord High Chancellor disappeared from my side and reappeared with his clawed hand around Dominic's throat. The skin around Dominic's esophagus, under his chin, and behind his neck—anywhere the Chancellor touched—bubbled and steamed. The noxious smell of burnt flesh filled the room as the Chancellor's claw embedded itself inside Dominic's neck. Dominic was making strange, wet, struggling noises I'd never heard him make before, and although Dominic didn't necessarily need to breathe to live, losing the use of his throat was still debilitating.

The Lord High Chancellor waited until his claw was solidly embedded in the meat of Dominic's melted flesh, and then he ripped it out.

Dominic bowed over the table, a gaping hole where his throat used to be. Had Dominic suffered such an injury last week, he would have promptly healed and counterattacked like I'd witnessed him miraculously heal countless times. But Dominic no longer had the strength to defend himself. He remained firmly seated. He didn't counterattack. He didn't even move except to make horrible, gagging and coughing noises.

And he didn't heal.

Ropes of dark, viscous blood poured from the wound, across the table, and onto the floor in a widening pool at our feet.

The Chancellor's hands transformed from claws back to fingers, but the silver on his fingernails had taken on new meaning. His nails weren't polished silver. They were *actually* silver.

I should have kept my distance—what defense could I provide against the Lord of all vampires—but being a bystander had never been my strong suit. As usual, I did what I shouldn't do and scooted to Dominic's side. I placed my hand on Dominic's shoulder and gently squeezed the base of his neck, but if he noticed my presence behind him, he didn't acknowledge it.

Without the table obstructing my view, I could see that it wasn't choice that had kept Dominic immobile in his chair. His wrists and ankles were locked to the chair by silver cuffs, and all that remained of his arms, from the elbows down, was bone.

His skin had been boiled clean from muscle, and his muscles had been roasted clean from the bone. I shifted my eyes to the floor, not wanting to know but helpless not to look, and sure enough, twin puddles of blood and chunks of nearly liquefied, unidentifiable parts had piled beneath each chair arm—the remnants of flesh and muscle that had been burned from the bone.

I swallowed bile and tried not to breathe too deeply. I could only imagine the state of his ankles.

The Chancellor bent over Dominic and spoke directly in his ear. "If I were you, I wouldn't concern myself with the destructive properties of anyone's power but my own. Check your tongue before you speak, or next time, you'll lose more than just your throat."

The Chancellor straightened, adjusted his now blood-spattered dress shirt, and held out his hand.

"It's a pleasure making your acquaintance, Cassidy DiRocco," he said, as if he hadn't just mangled Dominic's throat between one sentence and the next.

"Lord High Chancellor Henry Lynell Horrace DeWhitt," I said with a nod of acquiescence. I didn't take his hand. We would not be friends. "I wish I could say the same."

The Chancellor wiggled his fingers at me, as I'd done to him only moments before.

I pointed at Dominic's wrists. "This is not friendly," I said. I glanced at Dominic. "Looks to me like our guests have worn out their welcome."

"They only just arrived," Rafe murmured.

I started, having forgotten that we weren't alone in the room.

"And what do you think, Rafe Devereaux?" the Chancellor asked, wielding Rafe's name like an incantation. "Have we worn out our welcome?"

Rafe bowed low and deep in supplication. "I have no thoughts on the wear or freshness of your welcome. I only know that you have just arrived. Literally—" Rafe glanced at his wrist, "—twenty minutes ago." Despite his formal, unflappable tone, Rafe wasn't wearing a watch.

The Chancellor narrowed his eyes first at Rafe, then inexplicably at me—as if I could in some way be blamed for Rafe's behavior—and then his eyes settled with disturbing finality on Dominic.

I squeezed Dominic's shoulder in warning. His throat was still bleeding out, although, remarkably less than a minute before. I could lend him my support and loyalty, but without night blood or physical strength, I had nothing else to offer.

I clenched my teeth against my own uselessness.

The Chancellor tapped a silver-coated fingernail against his lips. "Why is it, Dominic Lysander, that you always seem to surround yourself with vampires whose throats I'd like nothing more than to tear out?"

Dominic's mouth moved, but as he tried to speak, blood spurted from his torn throat.

The Chancellor lifted his palm for silence. "Please, you're spraying everywhere."

"If I may, my Lord?" Bex asked, raising a delicate finger in the air. "Lysander and I are allies once more, and I'd like to speak on his behalf."

The Chancellor turned to her and nodded once.

"I, too, was one of those vampires whose throat you would have loved to tear out. I hid in my cave for decades, rejecting my birthright, rejecting all Day Reapers."

"Are you defending Dominic or condemning yourself?" the Chancellor asked, raising an arched brow.

Bex blinked that one, perfectly lined, long-lashed, beautifully shadowed eye at the Chancellor. "I'm merely pointing out that I, too, was one of the strong-willed and stubborn, and here I am now, your strongest asset. Your deadliest weapon."

The Chancellor stroked his chin. "Continue."

She smiled coyly. "The best of our kind are not meek. We do not follow or surrender. And we do not fail. You may want to tear their throats out, but Dominic has undeniably allied himself with strong, brave, obstinate vampires. Not necessarily loyal," she added, "but the best of our kind, nonetheless."

"Your point is valid," the Chancellor said.

Bex nodded.

Rafe nudged Sevris in the ribs. "Hear that? I'm the best of our kind."

Sevris rolled his eyes heavenward.

The Chancellor honed his eyes on Rafe like two lasers. Best of their kind or not, Rafe was about to lose his throat.

Before the Chancellor could act on his impulses, I took his still-outstretched hand and shook it. "Friendly or not, you are our guest, and as the Lord Chancellor of all vampires—"

"Lord *High* Chancellor," he corrected.

I had to physically force my eyes not to roll. "—it's an honor to meet you," I lied, thinking, *Please, no more bloodshed.*

His strike was lightning fast and just as debilitating. I'd prevented him from shedding Rafe's blood, but instead, he'd chosen to shed mine.

His fangs pierced my wrist and drove deep through muscle and bone, so deep they punctured through to the other side. My mind remained clear—there was no orgasm like Dominic's bite could induce; no peaceful, pulsing cloud like Rene's bite had prompted; no grisly savageness like with Kaden and Ronnie—just an impersonal, nearly mechanical, stab, the quickest, easiest means to get to my blood. He sucked a long pull of it into his mouth. I tried to yank my hand free from his grip, but his jaw locked around my wrist, tighter than I could imagine a jaw could tighten without further breaking the skin.

He swallowed another mouthful, and I swayed on my seat. Dominic jerked at the cuffs that held him immobile, but his arms remained bound fast. He couldn't help me any more than I could help him. I laughed to myself. Despite the enormity of his usual power, he was useless, too.

Oddly enough, it was my sense of humor that saved me. The Chancellor pulled back from my wrist, gave my wound an impersonal lick—healing me was obviously an afterthought—and cocked his head. "Something funny?"

I shook my head. "Not really. Just ironic."

"Care to share?"

"Not particularly, but I will if it means you'll stop sucking my blood."

The Chancellor smiled. The cracks between each tooth were stained with my blood. "Do I frighten you?"

"Yes, but more importantly, I prefer to keep my blood in my body, where it belongs."

"Hmm," the Chancellor said noncommittally. "You were right, Bex."

"Of course I'm right," she said, examining the perfect points of her polished claws. They were dark red, nearly black, and more claw than nail even in nail form.

"Right about what?" I asked, knowing I probably didn't want to know the answer, but asking anyway.

"You're not a night blood."

My heart dropped, and I glanced at Bex. God only knew how she'd known. Maybe she'd suspected all along after saving me, knowing how thoroughly I'd been drained of blood. Maybe with her enhanced senses—more enhanced than those of Rafe and Sevris and the others—she could smell my humanity, just like Dominic could smell the truth of my existence.

How she'd known really didn't matter so much as the fact that she'd told the Lord High Chancellor and blown any hope we'd had of surviving this visit.

"So much for being allies," I muttered.

She waved away my words. "Much has changed since we first met. I've changed." She grinned. "You're about to."

I narrowed my eyes at her, confused and not wanting to show weakness, but like all predators, the vampires could sense my fear, no matter my bravado. They could taste the salt of sweat on my skin and feel the accelerated beat of my heart in that disjointed, over-sensitized way that they sensed everything. I was terrified, for myself and Dominic, and that was as much an admission of guilt as anything.

Dominic must have thought so too, because he gargled a few mangled words through what remained of his vocal cords. "I can explain—"

With one swipe of his hand, the Chancellor clawed open Dominic's throat again, reopening the wound and silencing his feeble attempt to speak.

"Explanation isn't necessary," the Chancellor said.

"Henry Lynell Horrace DeWhitt," I intoned, commanding the full strength of his name and hoping my mind would lock on his now that he'd ingested my blood. Last week, that might have been enough for me to jerk him like a puppet on the strings of my will, but last week, I'd had night blood.

Now, nothing happened.

"*Lord High Chancellor* Henry Lynell Horrace DeWhitt," the Chancellor corrected. He sliced a look at Bex.

"The more you insist, the more creatively she'll find ways to annoy you," she said, unconcerned. "Her sarcasm and grit are her strength and best defense."

He laughed. "I would never harm one of my own."

Bex's eye looked away. She didn't believe him. Or maybe she

knew otherwise. There must have been a reason she'd hidden from him for decades.

I glanced pointedly at Dominic and then back to the Lord High Chancellor, expressing my own disbelief.

"He is not one of us."

"I'm not even a night blood. If Dominic, a Master vampire, isn't one of you, then who the hell am I?"

"You, Cassidy DiRocco, are a Day Reaper."

Chapter 20

I looked back and forth between Lord High Chancellor Henry and Bex, but besides a sly little twist to Bex's lips, they both remained deadly serious. The Chancellor didn't have a sense of humor, but this was too much. I thought he'd kill me for not tasting my night blood, but no, he didn't think I was human or night blood; he thought I was a Day Reaper. I couldn't help it. I clutched my stomach, doubled over in my seat, and laughed.

Despite having had his vocal cords ripped from his throat twice in the last fifteen minutes, Dominic emitted a painfully wet growl.

"She's insane," the Chancellor said. "She can't handle the facts. We broke her."

"Ha!" Bex barked. "You have a sense of humor after all, my Lord." He cut a glance at her.

Bex smiled, the curve of her lips a slash of red against her porcelain features. "Cassidy DiRocco lives and breathes by the facts. She can handle them, and if she can't, she'll adapt. No matter what must be done, Cassidy will do it to survive. Rene recognized that instantly in her," she said, snapping her crimson-tipped claws. "She's an unapologetic survivor."

That I was. I shook my head, wiped my eyes, and pulled myself together. "I'm sorry for the outburst, but you must be mistaken. I'm not a Day Reaper. I can live in the sun, sure, but that's because I'm human . . . er, I mean, a night blood."

Dominic's glare was like a laser target aimed at my back, but I ignored his heat.

"You'd better hope I'm right about you. That is the only thing at this very moment preventing me from dismembering and disemboweling you in front of this captive audience." The Chancellor gestured to the hundreds of vampires watching us from the catacombs, their eyes a thousand glowing pinpoints in the shrouded darkness as they cowered in their rooms, watching, waiting, analyzing. Making judgments. Choosing sides.

And as far as I could see, with Dominic chained and bleeding and me in a veritable motorized wheelchair, our side wasn't looking too hot.

Their growls blended with Dominic's, a low tide that, with the least provocation, could rise to drown us all.

I raised my eyebrows. "I'd prefer you not do that. I like keeping my limbs attached and my innards inside my body, along with my blood, where they function best."

The Chancellor grinned. "And I'd prefer you didn't expose our kind by giving samples of Dominic's blood to the city's medical examiner, but we can't all have what we prefer, now can we?"

I froze. Dominic's growl cut off into sharp silence, and his stare, if I'd thought it laser-pointed before, sliced me in two.

I swallowed, trying and failing not to let my heart race or my forehead break out in a cold sweat, when Bex's words of praise echoed in my mind: *Accept. Adapt. Survive.*

"I didn't expose our kind," I said, deliberately including myself in that category, so he'd think that I saw myself as one of them. I was part of the coven, not humanity, so exposing them would be exposing myself, too. And who in their right mind would expose themselves as a party to this insanity?

"But you did give samples of Dominic's blood to the city's medical examiner?" Sevris asked, his voice a low growl.

"We are in the middle of a serial-murder investigation, and our vampires aren't responsible. But something is responsible, something not human," I reasoned. "If the humans discover the Damned, they'll discover us next, but in their fear of beings they don't know or understand, they might not distinguish vampires from the Damned. They'll think we are mindless, murdering animals, just like the Damned, and it'll be war against us all."

"And yet, you're helping them discover us," the Chancellor accused.

"No. I'm helping to exonerate you," I explained. "The police took DNA evidence of the Damned from the scene, but without something to compare it against, we had no way to identify it. With Dominic's blood as a baseline, now we can empirically separate vampires from the Damned. They know two separate creatures exist, one whose DNA matches evidence at the crime scene and one whose DNA doesn't."

"That's not how we do things here," the Chancellor said, as if speaking to a child. "The humans don't get to empirically categorize anything because they don't get to remember anything. We are but shadows in the night they swore they saw but can't place. We are but legends and nightmares. They get to forget, and we get to clean up the mess. That's how it's been done for centuries before your time, and that's how it will continue to be done if you expect to live centuries from now."

Good thing I don't expect to live that long, I thought, but there was no need to speak my mind on that subject. I did expect to live a few decades from now. Instead, I said, "I understand, and I see your point, but—"

"If you truly understood, there would be no 'but.'"

Rafe shook his head. "Buts don't bode well."

I sighed. "*But* vampires are rebelling, powerful vampires that may take control of this coven and tip the scales on what is and isn't possible to hide. Are you willing to kill hundreds of vampires in this coven with the same unflinching stoicism with which you kill humans and alter their memories? Is keeping your existence a secret worth such destruction?"

"Keeping our existence a secret is worth everything. It's bigger than you or me or the hundreds of vampires in this coven. It's worth millions of vampires."

The hundreds of vampires watching our conversation from their honeycomb-like rooms flinched back at his words. Their collective inhale was nearly an audible gasp followed by the low hum of their growling disapproval.

I smiled to myself and continued. "But if you were to take the reins of exposure and lead it instead of fighting against it, you could control it. You could reveal yourselves on your own terms, as a separate entity from the Damned, not on the whim of a heartbroken vampire who—"

"We won't be revealing ourselves at all," the Chancellor said calmly, so calmly it was creepy. But then, everything about the Chancellor was a little creepy.

"I'm not saying you should reveal yourselves, but of the two, who would you rather have reveal your existence: Jillian or yourself?"

"You took it upon yourself to give Dominic's blood to be examined, and between you and Jillian, I want neither of you revealing our existence. Once I find her, she and the Damned she created will be eradicated. Unfortunately, you are a different matter entirely."

"Unfortunately?" I said warily.

The Chancellor grinned. "I'd prefer to eradicate you as well, tying everything up nicely and tidily before I return home, but as rare as night bloods are to find, future Day Reapers are even more rare, nearly impossible to find. Despite your blood, however, your crimes against this coven and vampirity cannot go unpunished." His eyes settled on Dominic. "I'll have to make an example of someone else in your stead."

I opened my mouth to counter argue his logic, but the Chancellor was done talking. His arm was a blur of silver, his claws fully extended, his eyes sparkling with relish. Even if I could walk, which I couldn't, I wasn't fast enough to block the talons that bore down with invisible speed on Dominic's prone body, that threatened to rip through his flesh and muscle and organs, that would spill his intestines across the stone floor. Dominic would be the example I was supposed to have been. He would pay the ultimate price for my misdeeds, for my betrayal. I'd never be able to live with myself.

I may not have been fast enough, but Bex was not only faster than me, she was stronger. Without even a blur to reveal her movement, she was instantly, near magically, in front of Dominic, her hand catching the Chancellor's wrist in midair.

"If I may—" Bex said politely, almost cordially, as if they were having a conversation over tea.

"You may not," the Chancellor growled. His incisors had lengthened, along with his talons, so his mouth was crowded with too many too-sharp teeth. His lips curled back in anticipation.

"Dominic is my ally, and Cassidy has proven beyond a doubt that—"

"You waited over twenty years for Ian Walker only to lose Rene, your eye, and your heart—literally and figuratively. I don't trust your judgment of others."

"Cassidy returned my physical heart to my body. She could have let me rot, but instead she—"

"Release my wrist and step back," the Chancellor growled, his voice grating.

"—saved my life. She saved her brother at great personal risk, and though she is a handful, she is fiercely loyal once you've earned her trust. Dominic has earned—"

"Move aside, or I will move you," the Chancellor warned.

"—that trust. Maiming him will make Cassidy DiRocco your permanent enemy. If you intend to earn her loyalty and have her stand beside you, as you now finally have me, you must show mercy. In this moment and toward Dominic Lysander, you must be merciful."

The Chancellor stilled.

Bex didn't release his wrist, and she didn't step back.

I didn't dare even breathe. My heart was a desperate, caged creature inside my chest, pounding for escape.

The Chancellor's incisors shortened. His talons receded to fingernails, and he stepped back from Bex.

"I will show mercy this once, in this moment, to Dominic Lysander." The Chancellor enunciated very specifically, his words clipped. He met my gaze. "For you."

I wanted to argue that it didn't matter if he showed Dominic mercy or not, I would never be loyal to him, but I swallowed my words. Bex had won. Dominic wasn't going to be fileted in his own dining hall—at least not in this moment—and I wanted to keep it that way, even if it meant giving our dear High Lord Henry false hope.

The Chancellor honed his gaze on Dominic. "I want the physical and forensic evidence of vampires and Damned eradicated. Memories must be erased or altered, witnesses who refuse to comply killed. Numerical data, photos, videos, social media—by this time tomorrow, it will no longer exist. Am I understood?"

"Yes, my Lord," Dominic said. His voice was a wheezing rasp, but this time, blood didn't spray from the effort.

"We play this like we always have: the right way, the way I thought you supported."

Dominic nodded deeply. "I will right the wrongs of this coven and restore order, I assure you."

The Chancellor leaned down until he was nose to nose with Dominic and patted his cheek. "Excellent. Because if you don't, make no mistake, I will assume responsibility for this coven and everyone in it—" His eyes flicked to me. "—and restore order myself. Am I clear?"

"Translucent," Dominic said, his tone stoic and deadpan, but despite the delivery, even I could detect the fire of defiance in his word.

I bit my lip to keep from smiling.

The Chancellor narrowed his eyes, unsure if he was being mocked. Bex squeezed the Chancellor's shoulder—similarly to the way I'd squeezed Dominic's—and the Chancellor schooled his expression.

"Until then." The Chancellor straightened.

Bex turned to us, her lips a dark slash of a grin. "Knowing you two, sooner rather than later." She winked. At least, I think she winked with her remaining eye. "Have a good day rest."

The Chancellor, Bex, and their entourage disappeared in a veritable gust of wind, punctuated by the spring of Dominic's wrist and ankle cuffs opening.

Chapter 21

"I don't know what to say to you," Dominic said, not once breaking stride as I followed him through the coven. "I can't even look at you!"

He was walking humanly slow, but my scooter barely kept pace with his long stride. A soft, high-pitched whine came from its little motor; it needed a recharge, but as usual with everything in my life—my hip, my friends, and now even my appliances—I was pushing it to the breaking point.

"I send my most trusted vampires to help you while I'm imprisoned by Day Reapers in my own coven, and this is the thanks I receive for my sacrifice," he continued.

There were so many wrongs I'd committed that Dominic could potentially be upset about—interrupting his proceedings with the Day Reapers, giving his blood to Dr. Chunn for DNA testing, being bitten and discovered as a fraud, although not the fraud we'd both thought I was—that I didn't know how to respond. An "I told you so," concerning Bex's Day Reaper status didn't seem appropriate at the moment no matter how badly I wanted to broach that particular subject, so for the second time in as many minutes, I swallowed my pride and kept my silence.

Now that Dominic's vocal cords had regenerated, he was saying enough for the both of us anyway.

"Of all the ways to betray me, you use the gift I bestowed upon you, which was meant to protect you, *to expose me*." Dominic stalked forward even faster, his voice a low, grinding snarl. "Unthinkable!"

Ah ha, I thought. *He's most upset about my giving his blood to Dr. Chunn for DNA testing.*

"Expose you?" I asked, nearly shouting to project my voice down the hall. I tried to throttle faster to keep pace with his stride, but my efforts were wasted. If anything, the scooter was moving even slower. "I didn't—"

"You deliberately broke your promise to—" He whirled around to face me but sputtered to a halt when he realized how far back down the hall I was from him. "What the fuck are you doing?"

I threw my hands in the air. "My scooter needs a recharge. I can't move any faster, and I can't walk, so unless you—"

Dominic was suddenly beside me, scooping me from the scooter and into his arms.

"Put me down!"

"We don't have time for this," he said quietly, the underlying thunder in his growl more dangerous for its restraint. "My rooms are the only place safe enough from prying ears to continue this conversation, and I'd like to reach my rooms before nightfall."

"You can't just—" I gasped, trembling from the pain shooting up my leg. "My leg—"

He adjusted his hold, relieving some of the pressure. His wrists had healed enough that muscle and skin had formed over the bone, but the wounds were still freshly scabbed. I imagined his ankles were in much the same state. He was healing—slowly, but healing all the same.

That was more than I could say about my leg.

I sighed. "What's happening at nightfall?"

Dominic shot me a look. "If the pattern continues, another slaughter. We need to prepare ourselves, so when the Damned attack again, we can follow them back whence they came."

I bit my lip at his use of the word "whence." Such formal vernacular didn't bode well for his mood once we reached his rooms. "A stakeout?"

"Precisely. It's a better and more precise plan than revealing my DNA to the FBI," Dominic hissed.

"I didn't—"

Dominic covered my lips with his finger. "Whatever you are about to say, swallow it and regurgitate it when we reach my rooms." He looked around. "Here is not the place."

I rolled my eyes but swallowed my words all the same. The coven was filled with beings whose extraordinary hearing could detect even the barest of whispers. Not to mention that we had absolutely no idea where Bex, the Chancellor, and their Day Reaper entourage were taking their day rest. They could still be somewhere in the coven, waiting. Watching.

Listening.

No matter how much I wanted to defend myself, I'd have to wait.

We reached his rooms a few minutes later. Dominic knocked the door open with his elbow, strode in at a sharp clip, and promptly deposited me on the bed. Despite his fury, he took care to deposit me gently and prop my back and leg with various pillows. I tried to school my expression to hide the pain, but the set, pinched expression on his own face told me he knew exactly how much my leg and hip were killing me.

Despite the pain, I was keenly aware of being back in his bed.

I ignored the blush flaming my cheeks and asked cockily, "May I regurgitate now?"

"No." Dominic dropped to all fours and let loose a deep, pain-filled howl that shook the bed. His ears pointed, his teeth sharpened, his fangs lengthened, and his nails grew to talons. Both knees snapped back into hind legs with a wet double pop.

I eased forward fractionally. "Dominic?"

He held up a hand. "Don't." His voice was gravel through a grinder.

I stilled, waiting on his next move.

Several minutes passed before he pulled himself together, before his ears, talons, and fangs receded and his legs clicked back into place. I waited silently, warily, as he stood to face me. When he eventually met my gaze, his expression was guarded and stoic.

I had a flashback to a similar moment between Walker and me, when he'd perceived my alliance with Dominic as a personal betrayal. We'd looked at each other like strangers, like Dominic was looking at me now. I never thought Walker would be my enemy, but currently, we weren't even on speaking terms. If he ever saw me again, I had no doubt that he'd consider the merits of killing me to kill Dominic through our metaphysical bonds.

I'd labeled Dominic my enemy from the moment we'd met—the enemy I aligned myself with for mutual benefits, but an enemy nonetheless. Now that I was at risk of losing that alliance, I realized how close we'd really grown, how far we'd come since that first night, and how much of myself I'd lose if I lost him.

More than I'd lost when I lost Walker.

A chill ran through me, and I shuddered with self-doubt.

"I've controlled my rage enough that I won't rip you to shreds," Dominic said dismissively. "I won't harm you, I promise. Unlike some, I honor my promises." He sneered.

His casually spoken "rip you to shreds" was a little disturbing. "I'm not afraid that you'll hurt me."

He snorted. "There's no use lying. I can smell your fear. One of the few senses I've still maintained," he said bitterly.

"I'm afraid, but not that you'll hurt me," I began, but when I tried to find the words to continue—to explain that I'd lost enough people in my life, I couldn't lose him, too—my throat ached. I cleared my throat, but it only squeezed tighter. I couldn't speak.

"You should be," Dominic hissed. He turned to look at the far wall. "If we'd met a few decades ago, you'd already be dead. Only my self-control and curiosity have saved you. Not much else."

He was lying. I could tell by the way he'd looked at the wall instead of me, by the stubborn set to his jaw and the pain in his eyes. I'd hurt him, and he was lashing out, trying to hurt me back.

"I didn't betray you," I whispered.

"You promised to keep my existence a secret, and then you exposed my existence using my own blood, the blood I gave you to protect you." He locked eyes with me. "Betrayal."

I shook my head. "You're generalizing. I promised not to expose your existence to humanity, and I haven't. The public doesn't know that vampires exist. We need Greta and her team working on this case to help us find where the Damned are hiding. You're a part of that team now, if you remember, *Dr. Leander*, and as such, you need to be a team player. For the rest of the team to be effective at their jobs, they need all the facts."

"You're nitpicking details," he said dismissively. "You broke your promise, and now the Day Reapers are here to clean up the mess."

"They're here because the Damned are murdering people by the dozens."

"They could care less about murder. They're here because people remember the murders, and now, thanks to you, they suspect vampires."

"They don't suspect vampires. That was the whole point of—"

He held up a hand. "They suspect an undiscovered being is responsible for the murders, and they have forensic evidence to prove it, which is much worse. And the Day Reapers know it's your fault. They're here for you, Cassidy, which is exactly what I was trying to avoid!" He smashed his hand into a dresser, and the wood split.

I winced. "I didn't mean for the Day Reapers to come. I didn't think that using your blood to help this case was a betrayal. I wasn't trying to expose your existence. I was trying to help."

"You were trying to find a loophole," Dominic snapped. "How could you not? You're a reporter through and through, and it's killing you not to report the facts. How could you know the truth and not share it with the world?"

"I gave you my word, and as a reporter, I stand by that. I protect my sources."

Dominic crossed his arms. "Then what was Dr. Susanna Chunn doing with my blood?" he asked. He narrowed his eyes at me. "The truth between us, Cassidy. Only truth."

I sighed, hoping he'd understand and knowing from the hard ball of dread in my stomach that he wouldn't. "That is the truth. Without a basis for comparison, Dr. Chunn would have discovered the DNA composition of the Damned and assumed that an unclassified creature roaming New York City is responsible for the massacres, but there are actually two unclassified creatures roaming New York City: the Damned and the vampires. Thanks to your blood, Greta knows the difference, and the Damned will take the blame for their crimes, as they should."

Dominic narrowed his eyes. "You mean four."

I raised my eyebrows. "Four what?"

"There are four unclassified creatures roaming New York City: the Damned, the vampires, the Day Reapers, and the night bloods. When you expose the existence of vampires, will you expose your own existence?"

I stared at him, at a loss.

"I've warned you several times about Greta's perceptive nature and how imperative it is to keep her in the dark," Dominic growled. "You essentially signed her death warrant as far as I'm concerned."

"You wouldn't," I whispered, but I knew better. I recognized that gleam in his eyes. He was angry and thirsty, and at heart, no matter his more tender feelings toward me, he was still a predator. And a predator threatened is dangerous.

"If you push me further than I'm willing to bend, I will break. But it's not me who will feel the pain."

My closest friends and family were always the ones who suffered the most for my mistakes. I could see the pain in Dominic's eyes beneath the anger. Under the unbearable weight of everyone I'd nearly lost and could still lose—Meredith, Nathan, and now Dominic—I lost my composure.

"You're right," I whispered. My throat clamped shut against the sudden threat of tears.

Dominic froze, nearly blending into invisibility from sheer immobility. "Come again?"

"I'm sorry you feel betrayed, I really do, but you're right. I can't keep my promise. I can't protect both you and my loved ones." I shook my head, feeling torn and heartsick. "Meredith nearly died because I kept her in the dark. I'm her best friend, and I didn't tell her the truth about the creatures stalking this city. I let her be ignorant and vulnerable, and because of me, she couldn't defend herself. She had no way of knowing she even needed to defend herself!"

The dam burst, and words spilled out of me faster than the tears drenching my cheeks.

"I wrote an article," I admitted. "I've been writing it for weeks now, draft after draft—editing and shaping and perfecting—and it's almost done. I just need quotes. I just need witnesses. I need your permission, too," I added when Dominic's eyes widened. "But maybe I can't wait on that. Maybe the world needs to know the truth, so people can protect themselves and not die like Meredith nearly died!"

He was silent for a long, tense moment. Maybe he would tear me limb from limb after all.

He wiped his hand down his face. "Is Meredith all right?" he asked.

Of all the things he could have expressed, I hadn't expected genuine concern. I burst out crying in gut-wrenching sobs, beyond words.

He walked to the bed, bridging the distance between us, and held me. He just leaned down, wrapped his arms around my back, pressed me gently against his chest, and held me against him, offering me the comfort and haven of his body.

I cried harder. His arms tightened fractionally. His hand moved over my back, in gentle circular motions, but still only offering, not demanding, and I was undone. He'd never offered anything, gently or otherwise—only demands from Dominic Lysander—but for the first time, he gave without expecting anything in return. No deals. No quid pro quo. Just his arms around me and my tears between us.

Finally, reluctantly, I pulled away and answered his question. "Sevris saved her. I think. The last I saw, she was alive, and Nathan was taking her to the hospital."

"What happened?" Dominic asked. An intensity sharpened his gaze, and I couldn't tell if he was angry because of my distress or his own helplessness. Another attack had occurred in his city, under his watch, and he didn't have the power or means to control it anymore.

"I don't know exactly what happened," I admitted. "She skipped our meeting with Greta, so I visited her apartment afterwards to see why she'd missed it."

Dominic nodded, encouraging me to continue.

I took a deep breath, trying to smooth the quaver in my voice. "When I arrived, the paramedics were already there, and she wasn't responsive. They were shocking her with the defibrillator when I walked in. Her heart was so weak from all the blood loss, but—" My voice broke.

"Take your time," Dominic murmured, his hand still circling my back gently.

I cleared my throat. "—but she still had it. Her heart was still in her chest. She'd been stabbed or sliced by something, but her body hadn't been dismembered or torn apart."

"It couldn't have been a vampire or the Damned if she was attacked during the day," Dominic reasoned. "And it doubly couldn't be the Damned if she still had her heart."

"Day Reapers don't need the cover of darkness," I pointed out.

Dominic covered my mouth. "Lower your voice."

"You said your rooms were safe." My voice was muffled against his palm.

"They are, but discretion never killed anyone. Don't accuse them unless you know for certain," Dominic grunted. "Even then, don't accuse them. Not that you could ever know for certain."

"Now that Dr. Chunn has both vampire and Damned blood for comparison, I'll certainly know for certain," I said, watching him carefully. "I'll know exactly what happened. Uncovering the truth is kind of my specialty, Dominic."

His hold on me loosened. He let his hands drop to his sides and took a step back. "I believe this is precisely the reason why we are required to entrance all humans, no matter the circumstances. Your memories and conflict of interest make you a liability," he said dryly.

I stilled. "You said that entrancing me was unthinkable."

"So I did. It seems we both gave promises we now regret."

"Didn't you hear what High Lord Henry said? I'm not human. I'm a Day Reaper."

"High Lord Henry?" Dominic coughed. "Dear God, don't call him that. Ever." Dominic shielded his eyes with his hand as if pained. "And yes, I heard exactly what he said."

I frowned. "Why do you look sick at the thought of me being a Day Reaper?"

He glared at me from under his hand as he continued to massage his temples.

"Do you have a headache?" I asked, curiosity getting the best of me. Dominic could usually heal catastrophic wounds instantly, but with his Leveling approaching, maybe he was susceptible to daily aches and pains, like headaches.

"What?" He looked at his hand, surprised, and then let his hand drop to his side. "No."

"You were massaging your temple with your fingertips," I pointed out. "Do you typically suffer from headaches?"

"I don't typically suffer from anything," he growled.

I tapped my chin, thinking. Walker suffered from headaches and seizures regularly. One too many concussions, and his brain hadn't recovered. It made me wonder how many head wounds Dominic had sustained through the years and if his weakened state would surface past injuries. If he was susceptible to headaches, could he be susceptible to seizures, too?

"The thought of you as a Day Reaper disturbs me profoundly, as it should you."

I snorted. The thought of Dominic having a seizure was infinitely more disturbing. "At least they didn't accuse me of being human. We came this close"—I pinched my fingers until they nearly touched—"to being discovered, and we sneaked past on a technicality. That's a win as far as I'm concerned."

"Only the Chancellor is permitted to transform a Day Reaper. When you transform, you won't be a member of this coven. You won't be mine." He locked eyes with me, his expression more intense than I'd ever seen it. "You'll be his."

I shrugged. "I don't plan on transforming, so no worries there."

Dominic sighed, but the expulsion of his breath was more growl than air. He was frustrated and, for once, not appreciative of my obstinacy.

"I tolerate your insolence because I'm confident of my ability to eventually persuade you to see reason and agree to the transformation. You tolerate our relationship because you know I won't transform you without your complete, exuberant consent."

I nodded, not particularly agreeing with the word "relationship," but without another word coming to mind, I let it go. Dominic's tone was deceptively peaceful, like the silent drop of an impending bomb.

"The Chancellor won't wait for your consent nor attempt to convince you. When he feels the time is nigh, he will transform you. No questions asked."

And there it was: detonation.

"Oh," I breathed, and the cold bite of fear perforated my heart. "How could he know for certain what I am?" I asked. "You've fed from me. You've forged lifelong bonds with me, and you thought I was nothing more than a normal night blood." Had my heart not physically ached at the thought of my consent being ripped away, I would have chuckled at the oxymoron: normal night blood. As it was, I crossed my arms over my stomach and shivered.

"You are a night blood, but as usual, there's nothing normal about you. When you transform, you will become a Day Reaper. You will be able to tolerate sunlight. You will have superior senses, and despite your current physical ailments, you will be the strongest of our kind."

"I don't trust High Lord Henry. You've tasted me, and you never said—"

"I never knew. Only other Day Reapers can taste a potential Day

Reaper. You taste like a night blood to me, or at least, you used to before your blood transfusion. I'm told that a Day Reaper's blood crackles on the tongue, and that if other Day Reapers listen closely enough, they can hear the pops and snaps of the power in your veins, begging for release. But that's just what I'm told." Dominic lifted his hands in a helpless gesture.

"Oh," I said again, searching for another excuse, any excuse, for why the Chancellor was wrong, because if he wasn't, or at least if he believed he wasn't, he thought I was his. And that was unacceptable. "What would happen if you transformed me? Would I turn into one of the Damned?"

"No, nothing like that," Dominic waved away my concern. "You would be fine. The catalyst to becoming a Day Reaper is within the night blood, not in the vampire blood used during the transformation. I, on the other hand, would be death walking with the first swallow of your blood."

I raised my eyebrows. "The transformation would kill you?"

Dominic shook his head. "The Chancellor would kill me for such insolence, and take my coven with him," he said dryly.

I crossed my arms. "You'd think that since I no longer taste like a night blood to you, I'd no longer taste like a Day Reaper to him."

"The Day Reapers have enhanced senses, and the Chancellor himself has the most enhanced senses of all our kind, while my senses are weakening by the day. It's no surprise that I can't detect the slow regeneration of your night blood."

"But I still can't control your mind! I can't block your commands! I can't—"

Dominic held up a hand for silence. "Obviously you are not regenerated enough to utilize your natural abilities, but just enough for the Chancellor to detect the nuances of the Day Reaper in your night blood."

"He's mistaken," I insisted. "He must be."

Dominic's face turned sympathetic, and a wash of panic doused me. Worse than his anger was his pity. He truly believed I was a Day Reaper.

"He would have no reason to lie, and he's too powerful not to detect the truth," Dominic said gently. "You annoyed him enough that had you been anything but a Day Reaper, you would be dead."

I shook my head, feeling numb. "What should I do?"

"What can any of us do? We survive."

"That's precisely my problem, Dominic! I don't want to survive my brother, my co-workers, Meredith, Greta, and Harroway. I've already survived my parents. I don't want to survive anyone else, let alone *everyone* else."

"You wouldn't survive me," Dominic murmured.

I met his eyes, and something passed between us, a commonality that seemed obvious, but one I'd never previously considered. Dominic was lonely. He'd outlived the family and friends he'd known and loved during his human lifetime and wanted someone with whom he could share his current existence. The thought that I could fill that void was irrational—he'd built an entire city of vampires, transformed hundreds of other night bloods, made new friends and formed fresh alliances. If none of those connections could fill that void, how could I?

Irrational or not, however, I knew the pit of loss and the need to fill it with something, anything to bury the pain deep enough that not even an excavator could unearth it. I'd filled mine with work, and my single-minded focus to drive away that pain had made my career blossom. Except that, beneath my success and drive, the pain still festered, deep beneath the surface, unseen but still present.

Adam had been too full of light to follow me down into the darkness. Walker had been too stubborn and would battle against it with his dying breath.

But Dominic lived in darkness. He breathed it, thrived on it, and would follow me anywhere in it.

"Unless you reveal my existence to the humans and the humans eradicate us," Dominic teased, his voice husky but not rattling. His voice wasn't being affected by animal instinct but the instincts of a man. "But then, you wouldn't survive either."

I bit my lip. His eyes honed on the minute movement of my teeth on my lips, and my breath caught. The air was suddenly charged between us, his loneliness and my fear transforming into a different, all-consuming flavor of adrenaline.

"People deserve the truth. The people I love have the right to know they're in danger, so they can protect themselves."

Dominic made a scoffing noise in the back of his throat.

I could feel the heat of my blush light my entire face. "They deserve the chance to *try* to protect themselves," I amended on a whisper.

Dominic shook his head. "And what is it that I deserve? What about my rights?" he asked. "Eradication," he accused softly.

"When I reveal your existence, it won't be to eradicate you," I reasoned. "I wouldn't reveal you otherwise."

"How would revealing me not eventually eradicate me?" he asked snidely. I could feel the ties between us stretching beyond their ability to bend.

"You're helping to solve the case, providing essential forensic evidence. You can be the face to the name, so when people think 'vampire,' they think of someone who saved them from the Damned. You'll be the hero of the night, not the creature who stalks it."

"I didn't choose this life, but I damn well won't lose it. I've lost enough through the years, and if there's anything I've learned, it's to keep to the shadows—unseen, unheard, and forgotten if noticed. I'd rather live as a creature who stalks in darkness than die a hero."

"Then you made a huge mistake," I whispered.

He raised an eyebrow in challenge.

"I noticed you," I said. The spice of his pine scent wafted toward me as he leaned closer, and I shivered. "Some things simply can't be forgotten."

"You'd risk my life for a scoop," he said accusingly.

"Nothing I wouldn't risk myself," I reasoned. "For the bigger picture."

The tension between his brows and his pursed lips released, and my breath caught. He understood my reasoning for everything I'd done, everything I'd planned to do. Yet he didn't come any closer. He was waiting on me. He might understand the logic behind my actions, but he still felt betrayed by them.

I'd have to show him through action that even if I betrayed my promise, I wouldn't betray him. And I knew exactly how he wanted me to show him; it was exactly what I wanted, too.

I leaned forward and pressed my lips to his.

He didn't respond at first. Although it wasn't quite the cataclysmic experience I'd had while high on his blood, kissing him moved me nonetheless. In fact, being grounded in reality, with my very human senses and desires and knowing they were all mine, his lips against mine affected me more than I'd ever imagined a kiss could. I felt the softness of his lips and the brush of his stubble against my chin and upper lip. I smelled the heady pine scent of his skin. I heard the sharp intake of his breath and the deep, instinctual growl in his chest. And everything I smelled, felt, and heard rooted and grew inside me until, just as a flower blooms in the warmth of the sun, despite our shared darkness, my body basked in light.

Then he responded.

And my body incinerated.

He was on me, in bed on top of me, and although he took care with my leg and hip, he devoured every inch of me. His lips rocked over my lips, raw from his teeth and tongue. His arms surrounded me, his hands on either side of my face, urging me closer, tipping my head and angling our mouths to kiss deeper, anchoring me to him in the gale force of his desire. His lips and hands and hips demanded, and I conceded.

The fierceness of his response ignited a matching response inside me—a visceral, instinctual, predatory response that I didn't recognize—but I reveled in the power I had over him even as I was swept away by the equal power he had over me.

I made an indecipherable noise in the back of my throat. "I should have told you the truth about my article sooner."

"They say honesty is the best policy," he murmured.

The heat of his breath against my neck raised goose bumps down my side. I shivered. "You've never lived by that motto before."

"I'm starting to see its merit." He nibbled my neck.

"Thank God," I gasped.

"You're welcome," he said, and I could feel his smile against my skin.

I would have smacked his shoulder except he was doing something distracting with his tongue to the curve of my neck where he'd just nibbled. "No. I just, um—"

"Pardon?" he asked when it was evident I couldn't finish my sentence. His voice trembled with restrained laughter.

"I can't think," I snapped.

"Then stop trying. Use your mouth for something more useful than talking."

"I just wasn't sure you'd still want me. When you didn't respond right away, I thought—"

"Less thinking."

He sealed my lips with his, effectively cutting off my words and short-circuiting my thoughts.

A few minutes later, I tore my lips away to breathe, to catch my-self before I hit bottom, but Dominic nibbled my ear, and my brain shorted out again. "Why did you"—I gasped, chills zinging from my ear and down my side—"hesitate?"

Dominic groaned. "You're not going to let this go, are you?"

"Nope," I whispered against his neck.

He shuddered, and it was my turn to laugh to myself. "This is the first time you've ever kissed me."

I snorted. "Your memory is failing you, old man. We've most definitely kissed before."

"I've always forced you. Or coerced you. Or seduced you," he said. "This is the first time you've initiated and kissed me willingly."

I pulled back and met his gaze, the playfulness in both our eyes gone.

"Like you said," I murmured. "You and me, whatever this is be-tween us, it's come pretty far."

"It's far in coming, that's for sure," Dominic grumbled.

"The expression is 'long in coming,'" I said "And I don't think—"

"*Less thinking*," Dominic insisted and captured my lips with his again to shut me up.

I stopped thinking.

Minutes later, his hand shifted from my back, traveled over my shoulder to my stomach, and slowly worked its way over each rib. His hand didn't stop when he reached the underwire of my bra. I tore my mouth away and shook my head, having lost my words along with my mind several minutes ago.

Dominic frowned.

"My leg is throbbing," I said, which, according to our new hon-esty policy, was true if not accurate. My leg was throbbing, but that wasn't why I wanted to stop.

Dominic was quiet for a long moment, and I wondered if he would push me this time, demand an explanation or express his frus-tration. I braced myself for his reaction.

He lowered himself beside me in bed and held me.

I blinked, surprised. "What are you—"

He covered my lips with his finger. "It was a long night and an even longer day. There's not much time to regain our strength before sunset, so if we aren't going to continue what we started, we need to rest while we still can."

"I hadn't planned to stay here all day," I said, but his arm around my shoulders, pulling me to his chest, and his chest, so firm and warm against my cheek, were difficult to resist. Maybe I shouldn't have stopped him. Maybe I should have let myself finally feel again.

"I hadn't planned on you losing your night blood, being a Day Reaper, *or* staying here, but my very long existence has taught me that if we want to survive, we must adapt," Dominic simultaneously tightened his hold on me and relaxed into the mattress. "This once, adaptation feels just fine to me."

I yawned, exhausted despite myself. "Nathan probably needs me. Meredith might—"

"Meredith has survived thanks to you, and Nathan will ensure her safety. He will be fine on his own for the rest of the day. You'll see them both tonight."

"Greta might—"

"Be waiting for you with more questions than you can possibly answer. You infiltrated a crime scene, hijacked an ambulance, kidnapped a patient, and disappeared for several hours afterward." He ticked my actions off on his fingers. "You should rest and think about your situation before facing her," Dominic reasoned. "But that's just my opinion, whatever it's worth to you. Feel free to leave if you must, but take this with you."

He stretched back and opened the bedside table drawer. I blinked, stunned at its contents. Inside were dozens of little glass vials filled with blood and strung on silver necklaces.

He pulled one out, closed the drawer, and turned back to me, the necklace dangling in his hand. The vial of his blood swung in a gentle arc between us. I stared alternately at the vial and at the closed bureau drawer, dumbfounded by the sight of so many necklaces.

"Seriously?" I asked.

Dominic glanced down at the necklace and then back up at my expression. A frown slowly puckered his brow. "You've worn this necklace for weeks. Why are you balking now?"

"I'm not. I just wasn't expecting you to be stockpiling an entire drawer full of them."

Dominic gave me a withering look. "How many times now have you wasted my blood on someone other than yourself?"

I blinked. "It's not as if I'm keeping count."

"Three times," he promptly answered. "You healed me, for which I'm thankful. You healed Bex, for which I know she is also thankful. And then you allowed Dr. Chunn to run tests on my blood, for which you are forgiven. After you healed Bex and me, I had to open a vein to refill your necklace. Without my forethought, I wouldn't have anything of worth to give you this time."

It was my turn to frown. "What do you mean?"

"In my current strength, thanks to the approaching Leveling, I can no longer heal," he reminded me. As if I needed the reminder. My leg was throbbing because of it. "My blood would still make a beautiful piece of jewelry, but it would no longer be helpful for its intended purpose: to heal you. *You* being the operative word and the only one you can't seem to understand." Dominic unhooked the clasps and draped the chain out before me.

I leaned forward and allowed him to clasp the necklace around my throat, his fingers already steaming from the silver exposure. At one time, it would have taken several minutes for his skin to react from contact with silver. Now, after only a few seconds holding the necklace, his fingers were burning.

"After you used my blood to heal Bex," he continued, "I realized that wasting my blood on others instead of healing your own injuries would be a recurring pattern with you. So I filled a dozen vials with my blood before I lost the majority of my abilities, to prepare for the day when you would need a replacement vial and I would no longer have the strength to provide it." He gave me a knowing look. "You're welcome."

I touched the vial of his blood where it rested in the center of my chest between my breasts. His blood was thick and dark, nearly black, like lava, and when the light passed through the etched glass vial, it fractured into dozens of sparking crimson hues.

"I would argue that using your blood to heal you and Bex was not a waste."

He nodded.

"But I appreciate your forethought. Thank you," I murmured.

"You're very welcome." He hunkered down in the sheets and gathered me close.

I raised my eyebrows. "What are you—"

"Like I said, do as you please," Dominic said, closing his eyes on a deep sigh, "but I, for one, need rest."

I stared at the ceiling and sighed. Dominic knew damn well that I couldn't leave the bed, let alone the coven, without help. Unless I convinced him otherwise, I was stuck in bed with him until sunset. I glanced down at his thick, black hair, the slope of his straight nose, the plump curves of his lips, punctuated by the jagged scar across his chin. He was dangerous and beautiful and even more dangerous for that beauty.

And he was snuggling with me.

I could think of worse ways to spend the rest of my day.

I closed my eyes, let my head relax against the curve of his shoulder, and tried not to let the taint of longing and regret ruin the serenity of this moment. I could hear my heart beating in the silence. His arms, with hands that could transform into talons sharp and powerful enough to disembowel me, gently curved around my waist. The scent of Christmas spice surrounded me, reminding me, as always, of my parents and the sharpness of their loss, but the comfort of his arms made the pain bearable. The pain was still there after all these years, and always would be, but his body against mine made it easier to breathe without them.

And that unthinkable thought kept me awake long after Dominic stopped breathing and went limp beside me.

Chapter 22

The rhythmic vibrations of both our cell phones woke me. I reached my arm out from beneath the covers to silence them and shivered. Dominic was a shield of ice at my back. He hadn't moved yet, but I knew better than to think he was asleep. He claimed to rest, but he was always aware of his surroundings. Always alert and ready to strike. If I hadn't known before, I knew for certain as my backside slid away from him and his front followed me, not allowing even an inch of air between us.

The last time I woke in this precarious position, I hadn't had much choice, or so I'd told myself. The last time, Nathan had been Damned and waiting for us outside the coven, just daring us to face him to our certain deaths. The last time, our lives had been at stake, and the illusion of me as Dominic's loyal night blood demanded that I stay the night, no matter my discomfort at such close and intimate proximity to Dominic.

This time, nothing was at stake, certainly not our lives, and I was anything but uncomfortable.

I ignored those feelings even as my stomach warmed and my toes curled, and I distracted myself by checking our phones. The five missed calls from Greta effectively doused any residual, comfortable heat.

"We need to move," I snapped. "Can you get my scooter?"

Dominic growled.

The hairs on the back of my neck instinctively stood on end, but I ignored them. No matter what my instincts thought, the truth was that Dominic wouldn't hurt me. No matter his own instincts to hunt and feed, he wouldn't feed from me because I was injured, still blood-deprived, and I needed as much strength as possible to face the challenges waiting for us aboveground.

"Stop it," I admonished. "The sun will set in a few minutes, and we need to meet with Greta and Dr. Chunn, determine where the creatures are likely to strike next, and plan a stakeout before they attack."

"Need blood," Dominic said, his words halting between his growls.

I eased back and winced when my leg flared in pain. "Not from me. Feed on someone else. Anyone else."

His chest continued to rattle. "Your blood smells—"

I rolled my eyes. "I smell delicious, I know. One can smell a hamburger, and despite his hunger, have the willpower not to eat it."

Dominic smiled, but his pointed, elongated teeth were less than comforting. His growl stalled and became stilted, and I realized he was laughing.

"Would you get my scooter?" I asked, and softened the demand by adding, "Please."

Dominic's snake-like laughter stopped abruptly, and the ensuing silence was deafening. "Your scent hasn't altered from last night."

I frowned and unobtrusively smelled under my arm. "Should it have? After falling into the sewer, I doubt I could smell much worse."

"I'm not denying you need a shower before we meet with Greta. So do I. But you don't smell like fear. I can still smell the wet musk of your desire."

I blushed at his frank perception. "No hiding anything from you," I groused.

Dominic raised an eyebrow. "I'm not at my most desirable after waking."

I ran my gaze over the skeleton skinniness of his limbs; the boney protrusions of his temples, cheekbones, and ribs; the pale, nearly translucent ice of his skin; and the frightening chill of his dilated eyes. Had I not known him, I'd have been terrified. He was a creature born of nightmares and horror movies. He was living death.

He was also the man who had saved my life without transforming me into a vampire. He was the man who had risked losing everything—his coven, his position as Master, and his life—to help me save my brother. He was the man who had allowed me to keep my memory when he'd thought I was no longer a night blood, no matter that he was breaking the very laws he was charged with enforcing.

He was Dominic Lysander, and no matter the skin he wore, I trusted and desired him.

"Yeah, well—" I picked up a strand of knotted hair and flicked it behind my shoulder. "I'm not my most desirable after waking either."

Dominic reached up and touched my cheek briefly before getting out of bed to retrieve my scooter, but that brief press of his cold palm to my face spread inexplicable warmth through my chest. I closed my eyes and took a deep breath. More than Damned vampires, Day Reapers, and Greta's unanswerable questions, the most deadly danger I'd face today was unequivocally the realization that I was helplessly and unforgivably falling in love with Dominic Lysander.

Chapter 23

The steady beeps of Meredith's heartbeat monitor put me on edge. When our roles were reversed and I'd been the injured friend lying nearly unconscious in the hospital bed, I'd found the beep of my own heart a comforting confirmation that I was still alive. The sound of Meredith's heart monitor, however, made me uncomfortably aware that her heart could potentially stop beating. I ground my teeth together and tried to push aside the anxiety that she wasn't out of the woods yet, even as she pulled out her IV.

"Would you stop being a crazy person and just relax?" I snapped. "Lie down. You're not going anywhere."

"I'm fine," Meredith snapped right back. "You can't keep me cooped up, not after everything that's happened."

"You need rest, precisely because of everything that's happened." I tipped my voice low, hoping she'd do the same. "You were attacked, Meredith. You nearly died."

"I know. That's why I need to come with you to meet Greta. I saw my attacker."

I blinked. "You did? And you remember it?"

She nodded. "He's a man, about five-eleven, one hundred and ninety pounds. Curly blond hair and brown eyes. Features as handsome and fierce as an angel, even as he stabbed at my chest."

I closed my eyes against the person her description brought to mind. I knew a man with curly blond hair and velvet brown eyes. He'd stood over me as I nearly died, the outline of the sun a halo around his blond head, except Ian Walker was no angel.

Walker was many things—brave, loyal, prepared, unforgiving, driven—but for all the good and the ugly inside Walker, he did not hunt humans for their hearts. Granted, Meredith still had hers, so that begged the question: what creature would attack Meredith in broad daylight, claw at her chest, not take her heart, and leave her for dead?

For the first time in my very short experience dealing with vampires, I hoped that Meredith had been entranced, because the alternative was unthinkable.

I opened my eyes to meet Meredith's fierce expression.

"I know what I saw," she insisted. "Greta can give me a sketch artist and we—What? Why are you shaking your head?"

"Do you remember how fuzzy your memory was after being mugged? You said that it felt as if the memories were slick, and just as you'd recall the sound of his voice or the shape of his mouth, the features of your attacker would slip away before they could take root in your mind."

She nodded. "This is the opposite. I know exactly what happened this time. My memory is crystal clear."

"You were brutally attacked and unconscious. Between blood loss and concussion, your memory shouldn't be crystal clear, even if you did see your attacker."

Meredith leaned back against the bed, frowning. "What are you saying, Cassidy?"

"I'm saying that these creatures have the ability to twist the evidence and change memories. It's why I can't find a credible witness for my article and why you can't remember who mugged you five weeks ago. It's why I'm questioning whether your memory of yesterday is really your memory or the memory that they wanted you to remember."

Meredith's eyes widened. "Are you saying that whoever attacked me changed my memory of what happened? Is that even possible?"

"Yes, it is," I whispered.

Meredith glanced around the room, her eyes wide. "Like men in black?" Meredith asked.

I laughed. I couldn't help it. My nerves were strung on a fraying string, and her innocent question—the image of Dominic in shades and using MIB technology—was the final stretch that made it snap.

"I was being serious," Meredith said, exasperated.

I wiped my eyes. "I'm sorry. I know you were, and so am I. The truth is just so unbelievable that saying the words out loud is crazy.

But after all this time, and everything we've been through, I think not telling anyone is the thing that will actually drive me crazy."

"Just tell me," Meredith said. "I'm your best friend. Let me be crazy with you."

In the end, I didn't tell Meredith the truth because of her pleading or the fact that she was my best friend. I didn't tell her because I needed desperately to tell someone on the outside, although that was true, too.

I told Meredith the truth because she should have known weeks ago. She should have never been ignorant of the risk in this city, and as her best friend, I should have entrusted her with that knowledge to protect herself.

Keeping the truth from her had nearly killed her, and I wouldn't make that same mistake again.

When I was done, Meredith met my gaze for a long moment and said, "I think it's time you got over Adam."

I blinked, both relieved and exasperated by her response. "After everything I just said, your priority is me getting over Adam?"

Meredith grinned. "When has your love life not been my priority?"

"I think you missed the part when I told you that Dr. Nicholas Leander is actually Dominic Lysander, Master vampire of New York City."

"I missed no such thing, and if that's reason enough not to love the man, then great, but that's not what's holding you back, is it?"

I opened my mouth to deny my true feelings for Dominic and hesitated. I'd just spilled my guts to Meredith. No more lies. But that didn't necessarily mean I was ready to admit the truth. I closed my mouth and ground my teeth together.

Meredith leveled me with a look. "Adam tore your beating heart from your chest and ate it for breakfast; I get it. You survived a death-blow and understandably protected your heart from future heartbreak. But that was five years ago, Cassidy. You're not the same person you were back then."

I snorted. "I'm not the same person I was last week."

"Exactly. So as this new person, where's your heart now?"

The truth, I reminded myself. This was the time for only the truth. I took a deep breath and said, "I'm not sure. My heart is somewhere

I'd never in a million years would have anticipated it being, and I don't know how I feel about that."

"Maybe it's time you figured it out," Meredith said.

"Maybe." I shook my head. "After we figure out everything else."

"No time like the present," Meredith said, resuming her effort to get out of bed.

I groaned. "What are you doing?" I asked, exasperated. "Lie down. You need rest."

"I told you. I'm fine. I feel better than ever, and after everything you just told me, I know why. It's as if I was never even injured!"

I rolled my eyes. "That's a lie, and you know it. Your wounds might be healed, but you lost a lot of blood. You're weak and in no condition to participate in a murder investigation."

"I'm in better condition than you," Meredith pointed out. "Your leg is broken. At least I can still walk."

I threw up my hands. "Fine. If you can walk down to the meeting of your own volition, who am I to stop you?"

I turned the handle of my scooter, about to leave her in the dust.

"Cassidy?"

I paused mid-turn and met her eyes. My breath caught at her expression. Her face was solid, like granite, but I could tell how upset she was by the quiver of her chin.

"Oh, Meredith—"

"Thank you," she said. She had to clear her throat to continue. "Thank you for finally telling me. You were right. The truth is crazy. If Dr. Chunn's test results hadn't confirmed the DNA of another species, I never would have believed it. I still don't quite believe it," she said, shaking her head. "But I believe you."

"No, I'm sorry," I said, and this time, I had to clear my own throat. "I should have told you earlier. You should have known and been able to protect yourself. I should have—"

"You didn't do anything wrong, Cassidy," Meredith interrupted. She stepped away from the bed and knelt in front of me. I leaned into her, and we wrapped our arms around each other. I clung to her, hanging on tight to her and what was left of my sanity.

"I'm so, so sorry," I whispered against her neck.

Meredith pulled back to meet my eyes. "I don't know what I would have done in your shoes, but I know one thing for sure. You're not the one who attacked me and tried to kill me."

"I know, but—"

"And you fought for me and found a way to save me." She squeezed my shoulders tight. "You saved me, Cassidy."

I nodded numbly; the relief that Meredith didn't blame me for her attack was almost as overwhelming as the relief that she'd survived.

She smiled. "Good. Now, let's go help Greta find the bastards who attacked me and make sure they never attack anyone else again."

Ten Hours before the Leveling

Only one thing hurts worse than having your heart ripped from your chest, and that's having your maker do the ripping.

—NEIL CAROLE, on the pains of servitude

I didn't sign up for this power struggle bullshit. I don't care who leads the coven as long as I don't have to.

—RAFE DEVEREAUX, on the pains of servitude

My every thought, every choice, every action and breath—if I so choose to breathe—occurs only after I've considered the potential benefits and threats that may impact the coven as a result of my decisions. Recently, what benefits the coven is not what the coven desires, and they resent me for it. But their desires are not my priority. My priority is our survival, and the majority of my vampires will see the wisdom of my intentions. If they don't, then they can go to hell.

Ruling on a pedestal is lonely, but I've endured enough servitude to know that I wouldn't have it any other way but my own.

—DOMINIC LYSANDER, on the pains of masterdom

Chapter 24

Dominic, Rowens, Meredith, and I stood in front of Greta, Harroway, and Dr. Chunn, and the tension between us made me feel like we were facing a firing squad. Well, technically, I wasn't standing, but Greta didn't seem to care if I was unofficially handicapped or not. She could kill with the fury in her eyes.

"Detective Wahl," Dominic began, "if I may—"

"You may not," Greta cut in. "You've missed two of our meetings, one of which I expressly told you to attend. You don't get to talk."

"I can explain—" I began.

"And you," Greta said, shifting her target to me, "sweet-talked your way into a crime scene using my name as leverage. That is inexcusable."

"But she—" Meredith began.

"And don't even get me started on you." Greta's face softened as she shifted her gaze to Meredith. "You should be home, resting."

"I can't. My home is a crime scene," she said.

"Perhaps we should just focus on the case," Rowens said, the voice of calm reason. "You can crucify your team later."

Greta turned her fury on him. "Meredith's attack *is* the case."

"We don't know that for certain," I reminded her, hoping to temper her anger with the facts. "The attacks at Harry Maze Playground and Wingate Park weren't personal. They occurred in public places with multiple victims of convenience. Meredith's attack was at her home, not in public, and she was a specific target, not convenient in the least."

Harroway nodded. "That's true."

Dr. Chunn shook her head. "I found evidence that says otherwise."

"Oh?" I said noncommittally, wondering whether Dr. Chunn's evidence would be real or fabricated by whoever had attacked Meredith.

"Hit us with the facts, Susanna," Rowens encouraged her.

Dr. Chunn blushed prettily behind her thick, gray and yellow hipster glasses. "As with all the forensic evidence in this case, the facts only open a host of questions instead of answering the ones we already have."

Greta frowned. "I'm not going to like this, am I?"

Dr. Chunn grimaced. "Scales were found at the scene and beneath Meredith's fingernails—the same scales that were found at our other scenes. But they weren't an identical DNA match."

"Translation?"

"Whatever species of animal attacked Wingate Park last night also attacked Meredith at her home this afternoon, but not necessarily the same exact animal. Granted, we don't have DNA samples from every animal from last night, not for lack of trying."

"So the only thing we know for certain is that one of our mysterious, human-sized, bat, heart-eating creatures, potentially from Wingate Park but not necessarily, attacked Meredith without eating her heart, their signature mark."

"That's correct."

Greta closed her eyes and squeezed the bridge of her nose.

"Maybe it was interrupted before it could finish its feeding," Harroway offered.

"Was there evidence of anyone else in the apartment?" Rowens asked.

Dr. Chunn shook her head. "If someone interrupted, you would think the animal would have attacked whoever had interrupted as well, but only Meredith's blood was found at the scene."

Harroway crossed his arms. "Unless whoever interrupted knew the assailant."

Dr. Chunn frowned. "The scales found on scene were from one creature. There's no evidence of a second assailant."

"Maybe the second assailant didn't attack, only interrupted the attack, like a lookout or a partner or—"

"Or their leader?" Dominic asked.

Harroway nodded. "Exactly."

I shook my head. Dominic was trying to pin this on Jillian and the Damned, but the timeline didn't fit. "Can you estimate the time of Meredith's attack?" I asked Dr. Chunn.

"To the hour?" Dr. Chunn laughed. "I'm good, DiRocco, but unfortunately even the most advanced forensic technology isn't that good. Based on the amount of blood loss from Meredith's injuries, I'd estimate the attack took place anywhere between late morning yesterday to early afternoon."

I nodded. "During the day."

Dr. Chunn nodded. "Based on Meredith's wounds, she would have bled out relatively slowly. She was incapacitated, but no major arteries had been severed. Meredith was very lucky."

Rowens frowned. "Or someone wanted her to suffer."

I glanced at Meredith. She was biting her lip, probably trying to revive a memory she didn't have anymore.

"The incidents at Harry Maze Playground and Wingate Park were random hunts, not strategic attacks," I said, thinking out loud. "Why would they suddenly have an agenda? Why would they target Meredith specifically?"

"Whether or not the attack was premeditated and personal, Meredith's survival is nothing short of a miracle." Dr. Chunn met Meredith's gaze. "Given the extent of your injuries and the time you spent bleeding out—" She shook her head, baffled. "According to science, you should be dead."

Meredith shrugged. "I must have someone watching over me."

I coughed to cover up my bark of laughter and shook my head. "I'm sorry, but I'm not convinced that the same creature who attacked Meredith is responsible for the previous attacks at Harry Maze Playground and Wingate Park. Despite the scales, this attacker has a completely different MO."

Greta opened her mouth.

"If I may," Dominic interjected, "I have a suggestion."

Greta spread her arms out. "By all means, don't show up for my other meetings, but please, contribute to the ones you deem worthy to attend."

Dominic ignored her sarcasm and took her at her word. "We have only ever been reactionary to the attacks on this city. I think it's time we anticipate their next move and plan a course of action to either stop them or catch them in their own game."

Harroway raised his eyebrows. "Like a booby trap?"

"No, like a stakeout," I said. "We don't have the manpower, weapons, or means to stop them, but I have silver-plated tracking devices. If we stake out their next hit and shoot trackers into a few of the creatures, we can follow them back to the location where they hide during the day." I turned to Greta. "Instead of just waiting around for them to attack, we'd be able to take the fight to them."

Greta was nodding, the cogs in her head turning in sync with mine. "If we discover their daytime hideout, we could plan a raid and take them all out at once. We could finally play our game, not theirs."

"Planning a stakeout is great if they give us fair warning," Harroway interjected, "but how will we anticipate the location of their next attack? Does anyone have a creature in their back pocket with a tip?" he asked, pinning his eyes on me.

I crossed my arms. "Funny."

"I'm not laughing," Harroway said.

I opened my mouth, not sure if Harroway was playing nice or just twisting the knife, but Dominic clamped his hand on my shoulder and squeezed.

"We need bait," Dominic said.

I glared at him and struggled not to roll my eyes. Every plan he'd ever suggested used me as bait. Why should this one be any different? "We need inside information," I said.

"They're creatures who hunt. Their attacks aren't premeditated, so there isn't inside information to be had," Rowens chimed in. "We need to determine how they choose their hunting grounds and either anticipate their next attack or stage a scenario that will draw them to us."

"Like I said," Dominic murmured. "Bait."

I tapped my lips, thinking. "For argument's sake, let's say that Meredith's attack was separate." I held up a hand when everyone in the room opened their mouths to argue. "I'll concede that her attack is related in some fashion, but everything about it breaks their typical pattern. We need to analyze their patterns to predict their next move."

Greta made a circling gesture with her hand. "Fine, assuming that, for argument's sake, what's your point?"

"What do Harry Maze Playground and Wingate Park have in common?" I asked, working through my process out loud. "They're both wide open, yet enclosed areas. They're both tucked away in the borough, yet have high foot traffic. They—"

"They both had events," Meredith said.

I frowned, thinking. "Harry Maze Playground had the Night Owl literacy fund-raiser, but Wingate Park didn't have an event."

Meredith nodded. "The crime scene was the event. It drew more people than would normally be in one location. It could have been a trap, set by the creatures to ensure a crowd, but if these creatures are led purely by instinct and the thirst to hunt, they don't have the mental awareness to plan a trap. Maybe a few creatures attacked initially, and then when we came on scene for the investigation, it drew the rest of them. Maybe we unwittingly created a bloodbath."

I nodded along with her. "Maybe. All those heartbeats migrating to one centralized location. . . . It would have been like a homing beacon."

Everyone was staring at me, silent.

Dominic cleared his throat. "They can hear hearts beating?"

"Well, of course, I mean you—" And then I realized what I was saying with everyone in the room. "Don't you think they could? They're more animal than human, more instinctual than intellectual. Their senses, including hearing, are probably more acute."

Dominic nodded sagely, but I could see the slight smile tugging the corner of his mouth.

Greta snorted. "From what I saw at Wingate Park, that's damn true."

"Well, there's another public, outdoor event at Prospect Park tonight," Harroway said. "A festival. Something about the sun god and body paint?"

"Tomorrow is the summer solstice," Dominic said. "The longest day of the year."

Dr. Chunn nodded after a few keystrokes at her computer. "Yes, it's a celebration of the summer solstice."

"They're celebrating the sun at night?" I asked.

"They're celebrating the sunrise. It's the longest day of the year, and apparently they're celebrating it all day," Dr. Chunn said, scanning an online article.

Harroway snorted. "Sounds like an excuse to get drunk to me."

"Sounds like our next hit to me," Rowens said.

"The festivities began at sunset tonight and continue until sunset tomorrow," Dr. Chunn continued, sticking to the facts.

Greta nodded curtly. "Harroway, research parks and outdoor venues for other possible events tonight. If there are multiple events, find out which has the highest head count."

"You got it," Harroway said.

"So we're officially planning a stakeout?" Meredith asked, her tone suggesting a possible barbeque instead of a mass murder.

"*We're* planning a stakeout," Greta corrected, circling Harroway, Dominic, Rowens, and myself with her finger. "You've had enough excitement for the week."

Meredith frowned. "Cassidy's had more excitement than me. She's in a wheelchair, for heaven's sake."

"Scooter," I corrected with a glare. "And I was injured in the line of duty. You can't exclude me for that."

"And I wasn't?" Meredith asked, obviously affronted.

Greta looked between the two of us, just as obviously not liking what she was seeing. "You're both out."

"I'm the one with the tracking devices," I said. "I'm in."

"Tell me again, because I must have missed it: Where did you get those tracking devices? And why is it important that they're silver-plated?" Greta nailed me in place with the suspicion in her eyes.

I snapped my mouth shut.

"That's what I thought. The trackers are mine, and you're out."

"Rowens only has one arm," I said, dragging him under the bus along with the rest of us. "He should be out, too."

"I was an ambidextrous switch shooter with FBI training." Rowens pointed at Dominic. "And I've shown up to more meetings than him."

Dominic didn't point the finger at anyone. He just stared Greta down with those creepy eyes in silence.

Greta and Harroway looked at each other, knowing they were toast. They couldn't stake out an attack of the magnitude we were anticipating by themselves. The rest of her department would be on patrol, protecting the festival participants and bystanders. We were a ragtag team, but we were all she had.

"Fine, you're all in," Greta conceded grudgingly. "But I want on the record that I'm not happy about it," she grumbled. "Pair up. We need—"

"I call DiRocco," Dominic said.

"Not a chance." Greta eyed the two of us warily. "Neither of you can shoot. As I was trying to say, we need at least one person in each pair who can aim the trackers." She eyed the lot of us with her hard, decisive gaze and said, "Cassidy, you're with Harroway."

"Wonderful," I grumbled. "Just like old times."

Harroway scowled.

"And Nicholas," Greta said, ignoring us, "you're with Rowens."

I glanced askance at Rowens and tried to remember if I'd told Dominic that I'd told Rowens the truth about vampires.

"What about me?" Meredith asked. "Who's my partner?"

"Dr. Chunn," Greta said. "I need you here to continue the good work you're doing with our crime-scene photos."

"But you said everyone was in. I can take photos. I can—"

"We have police on staff who know how to point and shoot a camera if needed. What we don't have is your eye and software. I need some people on scene, and I need some people in the lab. We need both to compile a successful case, and right now, you're one of the people I need in the lab."

"We'll have more fun in the lab anyway." Dr. Chunn glanced up from her computer and smiled at Meredith. "Do you like sushi?"

"Do I like sushi?" Meredith asked and laughed. "Never mind, I like the lab."

I shook my head. "I'm going out to face heart-eating monsters with Harroway, and you get to play with your photos and eat sushi."

"Doesn't seem fair," Rowens muttered, but from the way his eyes lingered on Dr. Chunn as she bent over her computer, I'd say it wasn't the sushi he wanted.

I glanced at Dominic and recognized the same longing on his face that I'd just glimpsed in Rowens' expression. His gaze ignited something hot and feral inside me. I looked away before my expression could give away my own longing. None of us would be getting what we really wanted tonight.

Chapter 25

An hour into my stakeout with Harroway, I realized that if the Damned didn't attack him soon, I would. In the five years since our last fateful stakeout together, I'd forgotten how much he liked to bite and spit out his cuticles. We were across the street from Prospect Park on the top floor of a fifty-story high-rise. Rowens and Dominic were in a similar location across the park on the north side, and Greta was covering the west end. Harroway had already locked and loaded the tracking gun. He'd checked his rounds three times, set up the tripod, and tested the angle of our location. He had a clear view of the southern half of the park through the window at this location, just like he'd thought he would. He couldn't do anything about the areas obstructed by trees, and Rowens should have a clear view of the north half of the park. There was nothing left for Harroway to do but sit and wait.

And spit his cuticles out the open window.

I pointed at the mostly naked festival revelers as I watched them through my binoculars. "Does this bother you?" I asked. Honestly, I couldn't be less interested in his opinion, but I needed him using his mouth for anything besides a nail trimmer, even if that meant small talk.

"I've never been inclined toward public nudity myself, but it doesn't necessarily bother me." He raised his eyebrows as a group of women rode into the park on bicycles, the only thing between their nipples and the air a thin coating of orange paint in the shape of sunbursts. "In fact, I think we should have solstice festivals more often."

I rolled my eyes. "Not the festival. The people and their ignorance. We know the creatures will attack, and here we wait and watch, not giving them warning."

"We need the creatures to attack so we can track them back to wherever they're hiding. If we warned people and prevented the attack, the creatures would just attack somewhere else where we're not waiting and watching. What good would that do?"

"I know," I said, but gazing out at the mass of painted fanatics enjoying their night, anticipating the sunrise, unaware that they were vampire bait, made my heart sore. They would die tonight if we were right about the Damned. Not telling them felt wrong, even if Harroway was right.

"You can't save everyone, DiRocco," Harroway said. I met his gaze, and the bitter gratefulness in his eyes was still there even after all these years. I'd saved his life. He'd lived when he should have died, but I'd been the one to sacrifice my health.

Being a cop, he thought it should have been his sacrifice and my life saved.

Being his partner, I didn't care what he thought. Partners had each other's backs—literally, if necessary—whether they were cops or not. Whether they were friends or not.

"Besides," he continued, "we have a perimeter of police on the ground to protect the civilians. You and I might be waiting and watching from a distance, but the rest of the force will jump to the rescue if the creatures attack."

I looked out over the night warily. "They'll attack. Whether we chose the correct location is questionable, but they'll attack somewhere tonight."

"I did my research," Harroway defended, not for the first time. "There are no other outdoor events occurring in Brooklyn tonight. This is our best bet, just like Meredith said."

Something moved in the night sky, a slight shadow behind the clouds. The movement was too fast and too faint to see, but if I didn't blink, I could almost see it again. Something.

"Harroway," I whispered.

"I even reached out to my contacts at the Chamber of Commerce and had them check their calendars. Unless an unsanctioned public event occurs tonight, this festival is our crime scene."

The shadow movement multiplied, still too fast to really see and into too many forms to differentiate one from another. Something had to cast those shadows, and I realized with a grim sort of resignation that that something was the Damned; they were soaring high above the clouds, the moon casting their shadows under them. They were coming. Dozens of them. And they were closing in fast.

"And a personal party, even outside, wouldn't be bigger than this, anyway. We—"

"I believe you." I pointed to the sky. "Look."

"Up? What could possibly be—" His mouth fell open in silence.

The Damned broke through the clouds. More than the dozens of them we'd anticipated—nearly a hundred of them. Moonlight beamed over their swarm through the holes they'd punctured through the clouds, spotlighting their descent. They converged on the park like locusts—like ten-foot-tall, taloned, fanged locusts—and the moment their back-hinged hind legs pounded down into the earth, they didn't waste any time on foreplay. I could hear the screams from the festival-goers even from fifty floors up.

"Are you ready?" I asked, but I should have known better. Harroway had already abandoned his binoculars in favor of his sniper scope.

But he didn't shoot.

"Do you have a good shot?" I asked.

"I have thirty good shots," he snapped. "I picked this location for the very purpose of having a good shot, remember?"

"Then what are you—"

"What are they, DiRocco?" he asked, still gazing down on the bloodbath through his sniper scope. I didn't need my binoculars to know the nightmare that he was seeing. The carnage. The sudden, certain, widespread death. The solstice revelers had been enjoying the night moments before, and now they were dead, just like I'd known they would be, despite the police perimeter. The police were probably dead too.

"Just take the shot," I said, my voice as cold as I felt.

"With the tracker gun or my real gun?" he asked, and he was looking at me this time. It was a legitimate question.

"Regular bullets won't penetrate their scales," I reminded him.

"Bullets can't penetrate, but the tracker will?" he asked.

"According to my source—" I began.

"If you found trackers that penetrate their scales, you should have found bullets that could, too. This is bullshit," he grumbled, but his eyes were back on his scope.

"You agreed to this plan just like I did. We knew the risks." I pointed at the festival. "You knew we were using them as bait. So don't let their deaths be for nothing. Take the damn shot."

Harroway's lips thinned to a straight, hard line. He stared down on the scene through the scope, his breathing slowed as his body stilled, and he squeezed the trigger.

I stilled, too, waiting on Harroway's reaction, but he didn't move.

"Well?" I asked.

"It penetrated the scales," he said, his voice flat. He shifted his stance and squeezed off another few shots.

"Good," I said.

"Nothing about this is good," he murmured.

"Had the trackers not penetrated, that would *really* not be good," I reasoned. "Sometimes you take the good wherever you can get it."

"Yeah, well, I—" Harroway's voice cut short. He whipped around, his face feral. "Get away from the window!"

He scooped me off the scooter and knocked me to the floor a second before the window shattered.

Glass rained over us. I tucked my face into Harroway's shoulder, and he protected my body from the blast with his own.

"Are you okay?"

"What the hell was that?" I snapped.

"Let's go. We need to move. Now." Harroway was already on his feet and dragging me across the floor by my bicep.

"Your leg is bleeding." I pointed to his thigh and the glass shard protruding from it. "How—" I looked back, over Harroway's shoulder at what was left of the window, and my heart dropped.

One of the Damned was standing behind him. As it stared at us, panting, the tracker Harroway had just shot into its flesh expelled itself from the creature's shoulder with a wet, suctioned pop. It fell with a hard clank onto the hardwood floor at its feet.

The creature's body had ejected the tracker and healed itself, like Dominic's body could expel and heal from silver bullets. I stared at the now-useless tracking device with numb incredulity. This was not happening. Nathan had been shot with silver-plated bullets, and they'd stayed in his body where they'd belonged. The tracker was silver-plated and should have worked under the same principle, damn it!

The creature reached out with its massive claw and struck Harroway. I heard the rip of Kevlar, felt a warm, liquid gush of blood, and then Harroway was ripped off me. He was airborne for a heart-beat before slamming into the far wall and landing hard on the floor.

I reached for Harroway's dropped tracker gun, but instead of aiming between the eyes, I aimed directly for the creature's eyeball. It had worked for Walker against Bex. It could work for me, too. I remembered what had happened to Rowens when his kill shot hadn't killed Nathan, and it wasn't just my own mistakes that I could learn from. I planned on keeping my arm.

I squeezed the trigger.

The creature's eye exploded. It reared back with a shrieking howl that made the glass shards dance across the floor. As it backpedaled away from me, I shot it again and again without mercy, forcing it back step-by-step until it ran out of floor, slipped on the shattered glass, and disappeared out the broken window.

I didn't waste time watching it fall. I knew better. I'd watched Nathan fall while he was Damned, but he'd never hit bottom. Those were precious seconds we didn't have, because if one enraged creature could jump fifty stories to kill us, so could a second. And a third. And however many more Harroway had shot, giving away our location.

I crawled to him, debilitating pain radiating from my hip and down my leg. Hand over hand, I dragged myself across the floor until I reached Harroway. He hadn't moved since being slammed against the wall and falling to the floor, and when I was finally at his side, I could see why. My breath hitched, and I covered my mouth as my brain refused to accept what my eyes were seeing.

The creature's claws had gouged his back in four slices, but the Kevlar had provided some protection; the wounds weren't deep. They could have been stitched, and he would have been fine, except that the shard of glass in his thigh had slammed home when Harroway had been knocked into the wall.

My hand trembled as I touched the wound, but I didn't dare pull the glass out. Judging by the amount of blood pulsing from his thigh, it had severed the femoral artery. If I removed it, he'd bleed out in moments. As it was, he probably only had minutes.

I laid my head down on the floor next to his. "Harroway?"

He was still breathing, but just barely. His inhales were slow and labored, and his exhales were hard, fast drops. He was struggling and suffering. His eyes were wide and glazed.

I yanked the phone from my pocket and called Greta. Her phone rang, but five rings later, she still hadn't answered. My hands shook as her phone transferred to voice mail. Greta always answered her phone. Especially on a stakeout when everything was going to shit, she would answer or die trying.

Unless she was already dead.

I called the precinct and ordered backup and paramedics before ducking back down to eye level with Harroway.

"Harroway!" I tapped his cheek. "Please. Come on, don't do this to me."

His eyes focused on my face and something between a sob and a whimper escaped from my lips. "You saved my life," I said. "You covered my body with yours and shielded me from the glass."

His eyes glazed and fluttered. I touched his cheek to make him listen. "You saved me, Harroway."

"'Bout time," he whispered.

I let out a harsh little laugh. "I've already called for backup. More police and medics are on the way."

"No more people," he whispered.

I frowned. "Yes, more people are on the way. Just hold on."

Harroway didn't speak for a long moment. It took everything in him just to keep breathing. "No," he finally said, "more people—" He gasped between words. "—means more victims."

I cupped his face in my hands. "You listen to me. Don't worry about other people. You just hang on and keep breathing. You got that?"

The wet, tearing noises of his gasping breaths slayed me.

"Run," he whispered.

Tears scalded my cheeks. I swiped them away with the back of my hand before he could see. "I'm not leaving you," I choked out.

His eyes were unfocused, staring through me rather than at me, and he repeated, "Run."

"Even if I wanted to, you know I can't. I'm not going anywhere," I snapped, but even as I said it, I smelled what he'd probably already seen. He wasn't looking through me. He was looking behind me.

The putrid stench of feces.

The Damned was behind me. Breathing on me. I hadn't heard its reptilian, clicking growl over the noise of Harroway's labored breaths, but now that I was listening, I could hear it like a death toll.

"Run," Harroway whispered one last time, and then he exhaled and didn't inhale again.

I didn't have time to run. I didn't even have time to scream or cry or rage at his loss. My back was a sudden, sharp, blaze of pain as the creature's claw slammed into my side, and I was airborne.

I soared across the room, over thirty feet of hardwood floor, shattered glass, Harroway's spattered blood and our tracking equipment. The creature had broken all the windows on the far wall, so there was nothing between my body and the street below except fifty floors and air. There was nothing to grab, nothing to slow my momentum. I only had time to think, *No!* And then my body hurtled through the shattered window and out into the open air.

I did the only thing I could do.

I screamed.

Air whirled around my body, tumbling me head over foot as I fell. Sky swapped with building and building swapped with the insanely shortening space between me and the ground. I stretched my arms wide, as if that would help, as if anything could help, and just seemed to fall faster.

Of all the ways to die by vampire—bite to the carotid, bite to the brachial, throat slashing, exsanguination, heart consumption—and all the lengths I'd gone through to protect myself from those outcomes, I'd never imagined that falling fifty stories from a city building would be my demise.

But something smashed into me before I smashed into asphalt. It bruised the side of my body, and I thought for a moment that I'd hit the side of the building.

Maybe I'll die before even hitting the ground, I thought, but then arms wrapped around my waist and stopped my body from somersaulting.

Dominic.

He slowed our fall and controlled our trajectory, but he'd lost the ability to carry me while flying two days ago. Hell, he probably couldn't even fly solo anymore.

"What are you doing?" I shouted at him.

"What does it feel like?" he shouted back. "I'm saving you."

I looked down at the fast-approaching street and concrete sidewalk below. "I don't feel saved."

The ground met us in a sudden rush, Dominic twisted, and I

screwed my eyes shut. We hit the sidewalk, not nearly as hard as I would have hit without him, but just as hard as the last time we'd crash-landed from midair. This time, however, Dominic hooked my legs with his, preventing every part of me, even my extremities, from scraping the ground. Despite his effort, the impact jarred every bone in my body, punched the air from my lungs, snapped my head back against Dominic's chest, and clanked tooth against tooth, but as I lay immobile, cradled on Dominic's stomach, my back on fire, and struggling to breathe, I realized that I was alive.

I'd plummeted fifty floors and lived.

I was starved for air. Something was pooling in my mouth, something sticky and metallic, and I realized belatedly that I must have bitten my tongue. It ached dully, but as the adrenaline slowly faded and as my lungs inflated and I finally gasped sweet, essential air into my body, the pain became sharp and penetrating. Worse than my tongue, however, was my back.

"Dom-nic," I whispered, but with what was left of my tongue, my words were garbled.

Dominic didn't move behind me. He wasn't breathing either, but that didn't mean anything from a man without a circulatory system. I craned my neck to see his face.

He was staring straight up at the night sky, unmoving, unseeing, and unaware.

On the concrete sidewalk beneath us, a widening pool of blood was spreading beneath him. Some of it was mine—I could feel its sticky wetness gluing my back to his front—but not nearly all of it. He was injured, egregiously injured, but thanks to the extent of my own injuries, I couldn't discern which pain stemmed from his wounds and which were mine.

I heard its rattling growl before I saw its movement. Turning away from Dominic and his bleak stillness, I looked up. The creature was just a speck of a shadow from the distance of fifty stories, but as I stared, the speck became larger.

I could discern its massively muscled arms and its hinged hind legs, and, as it drew rapidly closer, its snarling, rage-filled features. But it didn't fall with the somersaults and crazy airborne acrobatics of my free fall. It fell with controlled focus, its eyes honed with laser-targeted precision.

And that target was me.

Chapter 26

The creature was closing in, close enough that I could see the anticipation and hunger in its rage-filled expression. I could barely find the strength to breathe, let alone move. Dominic wasn't in any condition to duck and run either, but if we didn't do something in the next three seconds, the creature would skewer first me and then Dominic through the chest with the foot-long talons on its horror-movie, back-hinged, bat legs.

I closed my eyes and braced for its impact.

Someone wrapped a punishing grip around my wrist and yanked me sideways. Dominic moved with me, and the agony of his wounds scraping over the sidewalk scored my back.

The creature landed. Its talons missed my body by inches and embedded into the concrete from the force of its impact. Blood oozed from its toes where its talons jammed into its own skin. It howled.

I gritted my teeth against the pain of moving and glanced up at the hand still gripping my wrist, the hand that had just saved me. Petite, with red, chapped skin, its dainty fingers tapered to pale pink nails bitten down to the quick. I blinked, shocked. I wouldn't have thought that such tiny hands could pull my weight, let alone the combined weight of me and Dominic, but I recognized those hands. She wasn't as strong as other vampires, but she was stronger now than most humans. She was certainly stronger than me.

I looked past her hands to the arm and then higher to her face.

"Ronnie?" I slurred. I tried to say more but my tongue stung, and I couldn't form the words fast enough.

"Get up," Ronnie said. Her words were for me, but she wasn't looking at me. She was looking at the creature next to me.

I knew the creature was still there—I could hear the blare of its howls and smell the foul stench of its breath—so I didn't need to look. I probably shouldn't have looked, because anytime I glanced at the horrors of the Damned, I gained a new nightmare to keep me awake at night. Nathan eating hearts. Rowens losing an arm. Scattered body parts and spurting blood. But my natural reaction after seeing Ronnie's expression was to look.

I turned from Ronnie and looked at the creature. I wouldn't be sleeping tonight.

The creature had hit full speed into ground, anticipating the double cushion of Dominic's and my bodies to break its fall rather than sidewalk. Its back-hinged legs, horrific and grotesque all on their own, had suffered multiple compound fractures. The femurs, fibulas, and talons in both legs had pierced through the skin. The exposed bone was a shock of white through the dark, nearly black blood oozing like honey from the wounds. Its blood was thicker than even Dominic's blood and moved like creeping lava as it spread over the cement.

Even as I watched the creature bleed and scream in rage and pain—between the three of us, we were creating a veritable sea of blood—I saw the impossible. Its skin was regenerating and healing over the wounds before my very eyes. One of the breaks that hadn't broken the skin straightened back into place with a sickening crack. The creature howled, but although the injuries were debilitating, they weren't from its maker. They would heal.

Wound by excruciating wound, in another minute or two, the creature would be hale and hearty, while Dominic would still be unconscious and I would still be immobile.

Ronnie pulled hard on my arm, yanking back my attention and pulling my arm nearly out of its socket. "Get *up!*"

I looked down at Dominic. He was still staring blankly at the night sky, unmoving.

"I can't just—" I gagged as the puddle of blood in my mouth clogged my throat. I turned my head, spat, and tried again. "I'm not leaving him."

"He's dead. You don't have to be." Ronnie grabbed both my wrists and let loose a long cry as she pulled me from Dominic's embrace. She wasn't strong enough to carry me, but that didn't matter as much as the fact that she was stronger than me.

"He only looks dead," I ground out on a gasp. My words slurred, and I spat more blood before speaking. "You can't drag me out of here faster than the creature will heal. We need a plan."

"Running is the best plan I've got," Ronnie said, and despite my misgivings about her strength and fortitude, she bent down, picked me up over her shoulders in a fireman's carry, and true to her word, ran.

I cringed. As much as my leg and hip pained me, my entire body was one sensitive bruise. "Wait. You can't just—"

"I promised Nathan that if I came here instead of him, I wouldn't let you die," she said fiercely, but despite her determination, she really didn't have the strength she needed. She'd only run a few yards, and she was already gasping for air she technically shouldn't even need. "I keep my promises."

I blinked. So many things were wrong with that explanation that I didn't know where to start. "When did you talk to Nathan? Why would he come here? How did either of you know where I—"

"He was at your apartment when I arrived for my lesson," she said, as if she had been learning to play the flute or piano. "But you weren't there. He told me where to find you."

"Why would he—" I began and took a deep breath. Snapping at Ronnie wouldn't help. Even though she was a vampire, yelling at her was like kicking a puppy. She peed on the carpet because no one had trained her otherwise. "You shouldn't have come. It's dangerous. I—"

"That's exactly why I'm here, because it's dangerous. *You* shouldn't have come."

I bit back a curse and changed the subject. "Where are Keagan and Jeremy? You didn't bring everyone, did you?"

"Keagan wanted to come, but Logan wouldn't risking losing another son. And when you didn't show, Jeremy half-convinced everyone that you don't care about us anymore now that we're vampires. They think you feel the same way that Ian feels about us," she said, and when she mentioned Walker, her voice broke, "but I know better. I was there when Ian came to the house. You hid me from him. You protected and fed me, and helped me in every way you could. We were friends as night bloods, and being vampires hasn't changed that now, right?"

I'd only known Ronnie for less than forty-eight hours before she'd been attacked and transformed into a vampire, but the guilt over her attack still weighed heavily on my conscious. I hadn't protected her the way I should have, the way Walker had asked of me, so whether or not we were friends before, she was undeniably my responsibility now.

And if that meant giving her blood, teaching her to entrance, and being her friend, that's exactly what I planned to do.

"Right?" she asked, sounding frantic.

"Yes, we're friends. Nothing, certainly not you being a vampire, will change that," I said. I craned my neck to see how much time we still had to escape before the creature fully healed . . . and cursed.

Time was up.

The creature didn't seem remotely interested in Dominic—maybe his unconsciousness coupled with his unbeating heart was unappetizing. It wasn't howling in pain or disoriented by the fall anymore. The large compound fracture in its right femur healed over as I watched, the last break to snap into place. I winced as the jagged, unnatural bend in the middle of its thigh straightened, but the creature didn't so much as flinch. It didn't have eyes for anything or anyone else except for me.

It charged.

I didn't even have time to give Ronnie warning. One moment our eyes were locked from twenty yards out, and the next moment, the creature and I were eye-to-eye, scant inches from each other. I opened my mouth, but before I could scream, its claw swatted Ronnie aside, and we were airborne.

Ronnie fell flat on her back, losing her grip and spilling me in a log roll into the middle of the street. On a regular day, we'd have been road kill, but the police must have been successful in some semblance of damage control and diverted traffic.

I struggled to sit up—the double weight of pain and dread nearly paralyzing—to see how badly Ronnie was injured. She wasn't as strong as other vampires. Strength or not, it might already be too late if the creature had gone for her heart.

Before I could move or find Ronnie—I'd barely even caught my breath—the creature was on me. Its claw wrapped around my throat and held me immobile against the asphalt. I tried to think past the rushing panic of choking, but I didn't have anything with which to defend myself against this creature: my vision was becoming too spotted and double to accurately aim the silver spear inside my wrist-watch, the wooden pen stake was useless against the Damned, and I couldn't reach my cast for the silver nitrate spray. I couldn't compete with it physically, and I didn't have night blood to try to control it mentally.

The creature tightened its grip. Blood from my bitten tongue pooled and spilled from my mouth as I choked.

Harroway was dead. Dominic was dying. I'd lost Ronnie. Greta and Rowens were MIA. And I couldn't scream for help. Even if I physically could, calling Sevris and Rafe into this bloodbath was a suicide mission, and I'd lost enough friends to these monsters. I'd lost nearly everything but my life, and now, I was about to lose that, too.

No more weapons. No more allies. Under the pressure of the Damned's crushing grip around my esophagus, this was the end. The creature raised its other claw and struck down in a hard, swift jab at my chest, aimed directly over my heart.

I'd have screamed if I could, but I couldn't even breathe.

A second Damned appeared from thin air, which was obviously impossible, but in the way that Bex seemed to materialize from the shadows, the Damned was suddenly, incomprehensibly beside me, its own massive claw around the first creature's wrist, blocking its strike.

The first creature stared at the second, and although seeing past its fangs and scales to decipher facial expressions was difficult, I would swear that it stared at the second creature with shock. And that the second creature, with its saber-toothed fangs, grinned back.

Taking advantage of its hesitation, the second creature used its other claw to rip four long gouges into its opponent's chest.

The injured creature howled. It released my neck to counterattack, and the moment the Damned released me, my protector drove it back with a frantic, selfless rage I'd only seen from mothers protecting their children. Disregarding its own safety, the second creature lunged between me and my attacker. It pinned the Damned on the asphalt with its powerful jaws and, with one mighty shake of its head, tore out its throat.

Blood poured from the wound like a geyser, drenching the creature and showering me with its spray. I winced back, trying to protect my face from the spatter, but I could barely move. My throat was still convulsing as I relearned to breathe and swallow through the bruises.

Ronnie's face swam into view over me, and with the knowledge that she was on her feet and mobile, a tiny, clenched part of my heart relaxed. She looked panicked and rumpled, but otherwise untouched.

She scanned my body, first with her eyes and then patting me down with her hands, and I realized she was looking for injuries on me, too.

I waved her hands away. "Help me up," I whispered. It sounded more like a croak than actual words, but Ronnie must have understood because she placed one hand under my back, the other holding my hands, and helped me sit up.

The city somersaulted around me. Roads pirouetting with buildings. The sky twirled and twisted, and the ground rocked sideways. Ronnie's hands tightened on my shoulders, keeping me upright. I closed my eyes for a moment, took a few deep breaths, and tried again. The world still hadn't steadied, but it settled enough that I could focus on the scene in front of me without vomiting.

The second creature, my protector, shook my attacker by its throat, nearly decapitating it. Small bits of flesh were flung out from the violence, and I swallowed, my stomach roiling again. Maybe vomiting wasn't out of the question.

"What the hell?" I whispered. Maybe the Damned weren't as mindless as we all thought. First, Meredith was singled out in a targeted attack, and now this? A Damned vampire had attacked one of its own to protect me? None of this made any sense. The Damned were vicious, blood-thirsty, insatiable creatures incapable of thought or reason. Their attacks weren't premeditated, and they weren't capable of the depth of emotion necessary to risk their own safety in protection of another.

Ronnie shook her head. "I promised to protect you. He obviously didn't believe me." She bit her lip. "Not that I was doing a great job."

The second creature turned its head toward us, and I froze. It had finished its assault on the Damned vampire and was coming for us next.

Before I could give warning to Ronnie, before I could even brace myself, it snorted and turned back to its meal.

I gaped.

The second creature wasn't interested in us at all. In fact, if I hadn't known any better, I'd have said it had snorted at Ronnie. But worse than the creature being uninterested and having the capacity to understand language and the personality to snort derisively, almost worse than being choked to death and nearly having my heart ripped from my chest was what I saw pierced through the creature's flat, pointy-tipped nose: a diamond-stud nose ring.

Despite the creature's protection, seeing that nose ring punched a hole through my chest and ripped out my bleeding heart.

The creature was Nathan.

"How—I don't—" I stuttered, shaking my head as a wide canyon of hopelessness yawned inside me. "No," I said, refusing to accept the horror in front of my eyes. "No!"

"Cassidy?" Ronnie asked tentatively.

I pointed accusingly at Nathan. "I transformed him back into a night blood."

Ronnie nodded. "Yes, you did. For the most part."

"For the most part?" I asked, but my voice was more shriek than words. "What the hell does that mean? *For the most part?*"

"No one could completely recover from the creature he became. There's no going back. That's what you told me, remember?" She tugged on my arm. "That and his maker is still alive. Dominic was supposed to kill Jillian, but she escaped before you could actually seal the transformation."

I turned my head and gaped at Ronnie. My jaw might never close again. "How do you—"

She pulled harder on my arms when I didn't budge. "He transformed. It happens. We need to move before more creatures come."

"It happens?" I asked, and even I could hear the hysteria in my voice. "It does not just *happen*. Did he transform at will? Did Jillian get to him again?" Ronnie yanked on my arm, violently this time, but I fisted my hand in her shirt and screamed, "What the fuck is going on with my brother?"

"I don't have any answers, Cassidy. You're the one who lives with him." She cocked her head as she watched him. He was looking back at us again and jerking his head to the side. If I didn't know any better—which at this point it looked like I didn't—he was telling us to run. "He seems cognizant now. When he's finished with the creature, maybe you can ask him."

I let loose a noise, something between a laugh and a sob. "Sure, when he's finished tearing out that creature's throat, I'll just ask him why he's Damned again. Problem solved."

Ronnie shrugged. "Creature or not, he saved us. As long as he's attacking them and not us, who cares?"

"Me," I whispered, but the outrage seeped out of me as I watched Nathan feed. "I care."

I hated to admit it, but if I put aside love and tender, maternal instinct, Ronnie was right: Nathan had saved us, and if he was on our side, we had other, more pressing problems to worry about than him being Damned again. But I couldn't put those feelings aside. My little brother was once again in full, Damned vampire form, from the top of his shaggy black head to the tip of his taloned toes. Unlike last time, however, the recognition and love in his beautiful, Siberian Husky-blue eyes, were irrefutable.

Nathan wasn't completely Damned, but even that was a bitter pill to swallow. I thought I'd saved him, but here he was, saving me. I'd failed.

I must have murmured as much under my breath, because Ronnie squeezed my shoulder. "That doesn't look like failure to me."

I looked up again and blinked. Nathan was nearly back to normal, except for his claws. And the blood smeared across his mouth. And the creature dead on the road behind him, a neat, nearly surgical hole in its chest.

I glanced between that hole and the blood smeared across Nathan's mouth and gagged. He'd saved my life, protected me, and killed the creature trying to kill me. And then he'd eaten its heart.

Nathan licked his lips, clearly savoring the taste like he'd been starved. Considering he hadn't been able to keep anything, not even cereal, down for an entire week, he probably had been starving. Just not for cereal.

I sighed hopelessly, and Nathan looked up sharply as if just realizing I was still there. He looked down at his claws, suddenly self-conscious, and wiped his mouth with his elbow, even though a moment before he'd wanted to lick his mouth clean.

I didn't know how to handle a half-Damned brother, but as with everything else, I'd fake it until I figured out how to fix it. "Good timing," I said.

He just stared at me.

"Thank you," I said, still trying for normal.

His claws receded back into his very human hands. If it hadn't been for the blood gloving his palms and smeared across his mouth, and the fact that he was completely naked in public, we might have passed as normal siblings.

"I'm so sorry," Ronnie gushed. "I tried to get here before they attacked, but by the time I reached her, they were already here and she—"

Ronnie bit her lip, and I wondered if she was about to say, "—and she was falling from the top floor of a fifty-story building," but couldn't work up the nerve. It was a lot to admit to a man who had just killed a creature three times our size and devoured its heart.

Nathan knelt next to me, eyeing me critically. "Are you okay?"

Nothing about this was okay. "How did you know I needed you?" I asked.

"I could hear them long before they actually attacked. I knew they were coming," he said, his voice hesitant and uncertain.

"Can you hear where they're coming from and determine where they might be hiding during the day?"

He shook his head and looked away.

"Why didn't you tell me that you were still Damned?"

"How could I tell you something I didn't even know myself? I knew something was different. I was weak and starving, but food simply wasn't appetizing. It made me sick. Then you came home with those vials of human blood, and suddenly I knew exactly what I was craving. And I hated myself. I don't want to hurt more people. I don't want to kill anyone else." He looked down at his blood-gloved hands and shook his head. "But I don't want to die either."

"You saved me, Nathan." I reached out a hand to comfort him, but my hand shook. There was nowhere for me to touch—not his cheek, shoulder, arm, hand—that wasn't drenched in blood. I let my hand fall to my side, the gesture forgotten.

He jerked his thumb at the dead, unmoving creature behind him. "That creature was a night blood, just like you and me. He was a victim of Jillian's lust for power, just like me, but unlike me, that creature didn't have a sister to fight for him. He could have come back from that hell, just like you brought me back, but I didn't give him that chance. I killed him, I ate his heart, and I loved every moment of it."

I shook my head. "There are too many of them now. Saving you was almost impossible, and you were just one Damned vampire. Now, there are at least a hundred Damned. We can't possibly save them all, not when they're all trying to kill us."

"Shouldn't we try? You weren't sure that you could save me, either, but I was worth the effort, wasn't I?" Nathan looked out over the scene behind me. "Are they not all worth the effort?"

I didn't want to look, but God help me, I couldn't help it. I craned my neck back, and sure enough, I regretted it the moment I did. The Damned were swarming the park and bathing in their victims' blood. People were screaming and running and being dismembered. Their hearts were beating in their exposed chests, and I couldn't bear to watch as one of the creatures nearest us severed its victim's aorta with one clean slice of its claw, upended the artery into its mouth, and squeezed the heart until it burst in a gush of blood down its throat.

Yet, I couldn't bear to look away. Nathan was right on a philosophical level—all of the night bloods that Jillian had turned into the Damned were just victims who needed saving—but I couldn't be everyone's savior. I'd only been able to save Nathan because I'd known the man beneath the monster. Even then, I obviously hadn't done a great job of it.

It had taken Dominic, Bex, Rene, Jillian, and me to subdue and transform him, and every last one of us, including Nathan himself, nearly died that night. If saving Nathan had been nearly impossible, saving them all was unthinkable.

"Before we plan how to save everybody, maybe we should just figure out how to save ourselves?" Ronnie asked. "I hate to point out the obvious, but the Damned are running out of living victims. At the rate they're hunting, it won't take them long to finish festival-goers and move on to fresh prey." Ronnie gave me a look. "Us."

I cursed under my breath. Ronnie was right; we were sitting ducks, literally, since I couldn't stand.

Nathan and Ronnie started talking at the same time.

"If you found a way to save me, we can—"

"If we move now, we can make it back to—"

I ignored both of them as they fought for my attention. Dominic still hadn't moved. His eyes were fixed on the night sky, his limbs limp, and his wounds still seeping blood in a slowly expanding puddle around him. At least the rate at which his wounds were bleeding had slowed. That wasn't much comfort, but since I couldn't determine his health by his breathing or heartbeat, I'd have to settle for his rate of blood loss.

"Would both of you just shut up?" I snapped. I glanced at Nathan. "The night bloods who were transformed against their will into the Damned deserve to be saved. But that's a fight for another night." I turned my gaze on Ronnie. "Tonight, we survive." I glanced at Dominic. "All of us."

"That's a wonderful sentiment," Nathan said drolly. "But how do you suppose we accomplish that?"

"With a little help." I took a deep breath. "Rafe! Sevris!"

Nathan raised an eyebrow. "Seriously? You think if you just scream out their names, they'll—"

"You rang?" Rafe asked, appearing from the darkness directly behind Ronnie.

Ronnie shrieked and ducked behind me.

I grinned, but my smile was short lived. "Where's Sevris? We need him, too. All hands on deck."

"Somewhere in the thick of things. It's a losing battle," he said, jabbing a thumb toward Prospect Park, "but we'd lose it faster with both of us gone." Rafe's eyes fell on Dominic as he spoke, and he froze. "No. It can't be."

"It's not," I said dryly. Why was I the only one who believed in him? Granted, he looked like death—the hollows beneath his eyes and cheeks were sunken, his skin was stretched tight against the skeletal knobs of his temples and jawline, and the scar across his lips and chin was stark against the sickly, pale gray hue of his complexion—but that's how he always looked until he fed. If he'd been truly dead, I'd be dead, too, thanks to the metaphysical bonds connecting us. Unless Dominic had found a way to sever those bonds without telling me—which, considering he'd created them without telling me, was a distinct possibility.

I brushed aside that thought and its accompanying spike of panic and said, "Being injured this badly the night before the Leveling, he needs help healing."

Rafe rushed to him, scowling. Maybe I was wrong. Maybe—

"He needs blood. Human blood," Rafe said, locking eyes with me.

Of course he does, I thought, cursing under my breath. My head was already swimming from my own injuries. "Can't you just heal him? A few licks usually do the trick."

"A few licks usually do the trick for you. Vampire saliva heals human injuries," Rafe corrected. "Lysander needs your blood to heal."

"Fine," I said, reluctantly holding out my wrist. "If you puncture my skin, I'll—"

"No," Dominic growled. His voice was nothing but a rattling rumble, but the command in his voice was undeniable. "Not Cassidy."

Rafe frowned and looked down on his Master. "You're dying. You need blood to heal, and as your night blood it's her duty to—"

"She's lost—" Dominic began, and then there was nothing but the swell of his growl. "—too much blood," he finished.

Rafe shook his head. "Cassidy is the only human here to heal you. Beggars can't be choosers."

"Cassidy!"

I turned, dread punching through my stomach as Rowens ran toward us, Greta hot on his heels. I shook my head, but they were sprinting. There was no stopping them, and there was no stopping what I knew would happen.

Rafe looked up, too, and smiled. "Never mind."

"Don't even think about it," I warned, but I was too late.

In the seconds between one precious heartbeat and the next, Rafe had disappeared from Dominic's side and reappeared with Greta bound in his arms, her neck bared and inches from Dominic's lips.

"Dominic, don't!" I screamed. He was injured and barely conscious, and considering his injuries and his weakened condition from the Leveling, he might not even know who he was about to bite. "It's Greta! Please don't, it's Detective Greta Wahl."

Rowens had his gun up and aimed. "Freeze! Nobody move."

Greta's eyes widened, but otherwise, she managed to keep her composure. "Dr. Nicholas Leander?"

Dominic let loose a growl so loud it vibrated the insides of my own chest, but to his credit, he listened to Rowens. He didn't move.

"Dominic, take me instead," I reasoned.

"A little bite never killed anyone," Rafe admonished. "Chill out."

"No one is biting anyone," Rowens said, unflappable in the face of chaos. "Release Detective Wahl. Now."

"Don't need the entire cow," Dominic said breathlessly, "to make a hamburger."

"The cow dies nonetheless," I reminded him.

"Not this one," he said.

"Shoot him," Greta said. Her eyes were locked on Rowens, her gaze just as cold and ready as his. "Don't hesitate, Rowens. If you have it, take the damn shot."

"As if even silver bullets could stop us." Rafe laughed under his breath.

Dominic bared his fangs, about to strike.

"The greater good," I reminded him. "Greta has a sticky memory. She'll never forget this, no matter how you twist it."

He hesitated.

"She's on our team, and we thought you were on ours," I pleaded. "Don't prove me wrong now."

Dominic released a thready growl. "Release her."

Rafe's eyes widened. "You don't want Cassidy. You don't want this human." He shook his head, shocked. "You were never this picky before."

Dominic met Rafe's eyes. He didn't have to ask twice. Rafe released her.

I exhaled in shaky relief.

Greta backed away from Rafe warily. She knew how quickly he could move. Keeping her distance wouldn't save her, which was probably why Rowens hadn't lowered his gun.

Greta glanced at me. "What the fuck?"

"I didn't think you would believe me," I said.

Greta's eyes darted toward the dead creature lying on the ground behind Rafe, then to Dominic lying on the ground at Rafe's feet—the rumbling growl from his chest now a constant rattle—then to Ronnie next to me, propping me upright, looking more and more like a rotting corpse than a vampire, and shook her head. "After tonight, I'll believe anything."

I swallowed. When baby birds get pushed from the nest, they either fall or fly. I'd been nursing this scoop for weeks—growing it slowly, laboring overtime in the long hours before sunrise, and nesting the facts and forensics in place as cushion for the hard truth. I'd done everything I could in preparation for this moment.

Time to take the plunge.

"There are some humans, myself included, with a rare blood condition capable of transforming rather than clotting when mixed with the blood of another species. This species appears human, but they have enhanced, animal-like senses, incredible strength and healing abilities, and they feed on blood," I said, evading the truth in the smoothest, surest way I knew how: sticking to the facts. "But if our blood mixes with a creature too weak to complete a proper transformation, we become one of the Damned," I said, gesturing to the ten-foot-tall, scaled, fanged creature for courage.

Greta snorted. "Next, you'll tell me they're allergic to the sun."

My heart dropped. Even with everything in place—my facts and forensics, my ten-foot-tall proof lying at her feet—the truth was too large to swallow. She didn't believe me.

"Is this really happening right now?" Rafe asked. "Are we being exposed to humans by our own night blood?"

Dominic growled.

I bit my lip, knowing I'd gone too far. And yet, somehow, I'd not gone nearly far enough.

I opened my mouth, the mix of anxiety and anticipation like a wasp buzzing inside my heart, but Nathan placed his hand on my shoulder and squeezed, silencing me.

"Maybe we should finish this conversation in private," he murmured.

I followed his gaze, and the buzzing in my heart turned to stings. I didn't know which was worse: nearly a hundred Damned vampires flooding from Prospect Park—finished with the festival-goers, like Ronnie had predicted, they'd left the park grounds to hunt new prey—or Lord High Chancellor Henry descending from the night sky, Bex and their flock of Day Reapers in V formation behind them.

The unyielding expression on Lord High Chancellor Henry's face made my insides shrivel. I didn't know how he knew, but with that one look, I had the sudden, horrific realization that he knew I'd planned to expose the vampires to the public, that I'd in fact planted my seeds, watered them fondly, and, with my admission to Greta, encouraged my first flower to bloom.

Based on the chiseled tick of his clamped jaw and the growing length of his fisted talons, I gathered that he didn't just intend to destroy the garden. He intended to destroy the gardener along with it, so the seeds I'd tended and sprouted would never grow again.

Bex followed in his wake, her expression serene, nearly bored, until her gaze swept over our motley party of injured, half-starved, vampire and human rebels. If I wasn't mistaken, she rolled her eye. The sequin-covered patch covering her other eye sparkled under the festival lights.

Beneath the shadow of Day Reapers descending on us from above, the charging riot of Damned vampires drove toward us by land. We were the only beings stupid enough, or alive enough, to be left standing on the street, our hearts beating like a siren song within our chests, beckoning them.

After everything I'd experienced with Nathan when he was Damned—after surviving the battle that had nearly killed all of us and saved him, or so I'd thought—and everything I'd witnessed from Jillian and her unyielding drive for power, I would have said that her army of Damned were nearly invincible. Five against one, we'd liked our odds against Nathan, yet Nathan had almost won, and Jillian had escaped in better health than she'd arrived in.

The odds were not in our favor this time.

Dominic was injured, Ronnie was still a liability despite being a vampire, Rafe was unpredictable, Sevris was still MIA, Harroway was gone, and Greta and Rowens were as fragile as I was, if more mobile. The only one of us physically capable of going head to head with the Damned was my little brother, but just because he could kill one Damned didn't mean he could single-handedly protect us from the stampede of them raging toward us.

The Day Reapers landed in front of the Damned, facing the swarm and blocking their charge. Like an unstoppable current meeting an unmovable dam, the Damned and the Day Reapers collided.

We weren't alone. And the Damned weren't invincible.

Lord High Chancellor Henry was a force of nature. His lethal claws ripped through the Damned's front line, and his silver claws didn't just scratch their scales. They gouged through them. The Damned shrieked and broke formation. The creatures behind them tripped and stumbled over their fellow Damned in the confusion as their front line fell.

Bex took advantage of the break and clawed through their ranks. I'd witnessed Bex's unimaginable speed and awe-inspiring power before, but I'd also witnessed her nearly die, her speed and strength no match for Nathan's when he'd been Damned.

Bex displayed no such weaknesses now. Her talons gouged their scales as easily as a hot knife slicing through butter. Her fangs drove deep into skin and muscle and tore through throats in a spatter of blood and gore and thicker things. Her speed and strength were unmatched. This time, with a hoard of strangers vying for our beating hearts instead of my brother, I couldn't help but feel relief in the face of their suffering and deaths because it wasn't our suffering. It wasn't our deaths.

"Tell me they're on our team," Greta muttered.

If the Day Reapers had been led by Bex, perhaps. But they weren't. My relief quickly soured. "No," I said warily, "they're not."

With the Day Reapers fighting our battle at the moment, we had a short reprieve, but eventually, the Day Reapers would force the Damned to retreat back to wherever they'd come from. And when they did, we needed to be somewhere else, anywhere else but here, still sitting ducks.

"We need to get out of here," I said.

Greta shook her head. "We can't. We need to finish what we started here. The trackers didn't work. Their skin simply repelled the devices."

"Not one tracker remained inside their host?" Rowens asked.

"Not a one. A hell of a lot of good they'll do us now, scattered across the field instead of tracking their monsters."

"What the hell happened?" Rowens snapped, turning on me. "I thought they were silver-plated. I thought you knew what you were doing!"

"They *are* silver-plated," I said calmly, trying to keep my cool as all eyes turned on me. "They should have worked. Silver-plated bullets worked on the Damned before, so I don't know why silver-plated trackers didn't work now."

Dominic opened his mouth to speak, but all that emerged at first was a low growl. Slowly, painfully, the gravel of his growl turned into words. "Jillian. Has my powers and strength now. Didn't think. Damned have power and strength Nathan didn't have."

"Whether they're tracked or not, we need to move," Nathan said. "Now."

"We risked our lives to track these things. I'll be damned if all of this was done in vain." Greta snapped. "Figure it out. We're not leaving until we do."

"Then you'll be the only one here to face the Day Reapers," Nathan snapped right back. "'Cause I plan to live through tonight. We can figure out a new plan and fight them tomorrow. Tonight, we escape with our lives, and gratefully. Others weren't so lucky."

"Day Reapers?" Greta asked warily.

I didn't like the feeling of pointless defeat any more than Greta did, especially considering that Harroway had given his life for this stakeout, but I agreed with Nathan wholeheartedly. If we didn't survive today, who would fight them tomorrow?

As I watched Lord High Chancellor Henry and Bex fight and win against the Damned, something snapped into place. The Day Reapers could penetrate the Damned's scales. Their talons and teeth left permanent wounds, or at least wounds that didn't heal instantaneously.

And I was a potential Day Reaper.

The idea probably wouldn't work. We would likely be wasting our time, precious time better spent creating distance between us and the Day Reapers, but we wouldn't have another opportunity like this. The Day Reapers were distracted, fighting the Damned, and the Damned were distracted, defending against the Day Reapers.

I glanced at Rowens. "Do you have any trackers left?"

He nodded. "When we realized how high they could jump, I stopped shooting. We were only giving away our position."

"Unload a round, please," I said.

Rowens glanced at Dominic, considering his options. To do as I asked, he'd have to put up his gun.

"Dominic is too weak to attack, and Rafe won't ignore a direct order," I reasoned. I pointed at the Damned and the Day Reapers battling behind him. "It's them we need to worry about."

I could see the indecision in Rowens' gaze turn to reluctance. He put up his handgun and stepped forward as he unsnapped a round from the tracking device.

"Coat the tracker in my blood and then shoot it."

Rowens lifted his eyebrows. "How will that help?"

"It might not, but it's worth a shot." I smiled to myself. "One last shot, literally. My blood might keep the wound from healing and therefore from expelling the round, but whether it sticks or expels, we move out. Once you shoot, there's no telling what the Damned will do. Last time, one of them jumped fifty floors to kill the shooter," I said quietly.

"Move out where?" Rafe asked. "Even if the Day Reapers beat back the Damned, they can follow us anywhere. There's nowhere safe on this earth to hide from them if they want us found."

"There may be one place," Nathan said, meeting my gaze.

My apartment, I thought, my hopes rising momentarily.

I squashed that hope before it could take root, because no matter how much it chafed to admit it, Rafe was right. Even Walker's house, impenetrable by Dominic and supposedly the safest place against vampires, had fallen to Bex. I'd fortified my apartment against vampires, hoping to create a measure of safety and privacy, but even Walker's house, which had been fortified over two generations of night bloods to become a veritable fortress, couldn't withstand the onslaught of a Day Reaper.

"My coven," Dominic rasped.

I snorted. "The Day Reapers can enter your coven. They've proven that."

"They enter everywhere," he said, breathily. "Safest in numbers. With coven. Show of strength."

I pursed my lips, unconvinced, but we didn't have time to argue. The Day Reapers were herding the Damned back steadily, which was good, but when they won, there would be nothing to distract the Day Reapers from turning on us.

I thought of Lord High Chancellor Henry's thunderous expression as he'd descended on us and shuddered.

"Let's get this over with," I said. I lifted my shirt to expose the wounds on my side for Rowens.

"There's not much blood there to work with," Rowens commented blandly.

"What are you talking about? I—" I glanced down at my side and stared, shocked into silence. My wounds were healed.

I narrowed my eyes at the growing puddle of blood around Dominic. He wasn't bleeding from his injuries alone. He'd used our metaphysical connection to take mine into himself, too.

I cursed. "I need a knife." I looked around in the telling silence. "Anyone?"

Rafe smiled. "You can have my fangs, but you must heal Dominic if I help you coat the tracker."

Dominic growled, and the noise sounded painful, like his insides were tearing apart. "Don't—"

"Agreed," I said, holding my wrist out for his bite. I'd planned to help heal Dominic anyway, so agreeing for Rafe's cooperation wasn't much of a concession.

Rafe smiled, not unlike the Cheshire Cat—all fangs and anticipatory pleasure—and before I could even blink, his fangs were buried gum deep in my wrist.

I swallowed back a scream, more startled at the suddenness of his strike than in pain, until he didn't let go.

"Rafe?" Blood was running down my wrist—precious blood that I could use to heal Dominic, coat the bullet, or keep inside my body. "You have to let go," I reminded him.

His tongue flicked out to catch the stream of blood before it could drip on the asphalt.

Dominic growled.

"Back off," Nathan said. As he stepped forward to confront Rafe, I noticed his ears had pointed and his nose had flattened at the front and flared at the tip.

Rafe ignored both Dominic and Nathan, his eyes lost in my wound. "You smell like cinnamon and sweet spice. Like home," he growled.

Shit, I thought, but before I could warn Rowens to re-aim his handgun, Rafe sealed his lips over the wound and sucked a long pull of my blood into his mouth.

The world tilted and my vision blurred into a million starbursts.

Nathan tackled Rafe away from me, forcing his fangs, still embedded in my skin, to tear my wrist.

Dominic bellowed, "Ssssevrisss!" in a hissing rattle.

Sevris was beside Nathan in an instant, helping to dislodge Rafe from my wrist before he could take a second swallow.

Rafe thrashed, trying to fight past him to reclaim my wrist even as Sevris' claws gouged deep into his arms, holding him back.

"Control yourself, Rafe Devereaux," Sevris commanded in a cold voice.

Rafe blinked several times and, after a moment, regained his head. He looked away nearly apologetically. "I've never tasted anything like her. None of the other night bloods smell that tempting, that irresistible," he said, and by the end of his sentence, his tone had transformed from contrite to accusatory.

I ignored him, and before I lost any more blood than necessary, offered my wrist to Rowens.

"Coat the tracker," I said.

"Won't work," Dominic said, his voice a frail thread.

Rowens stepped forward, tracker in hand, and dipped the tracker's projectile in my wound, coating it from top to tail in my blood.

"Well, we're about to find out." When Rowens was done, I squeezed my wrist to help staunch the flow of my bleeding.

As Rowens reloaded his weapon, I looked out over Prospect Park. The Day Reapers had won against the Damned, and those who still remained were tucking tail and fleeing, disappearing into the night even as we spoke. They leapt into the air, soaring through the night sky—more flying than jumping, even if their size and stature belied that ability. Rowens would only have moments to aim and fire.

"They'll be gone in another minute," I warned.

"I've got it," Rowens said, but he hadn't pulled the trigger yet. He was breathing, deep and even, and then he exhaled slowly. Just as I was about to tell him to pull the damn trigger, he fired.

The projectile was too fast for me to track its flight, but I saw one of the last Damned still standing wince as the round hit behind its shoulder blade. Rowens had aimed at one of the Damned's already existing claw rakings from the Day Reapers, which was good fore-thought on his part, but before we could determine whether the tracker would stick or expel itself from the wound, the Damned leapt from the ground and soared through the midnight sky, following its brethren high over the cityscape and disappearing to wherever it is they hid the day away.

As the last of the Damned fled, Lord High Chancellor Henry turned toward us. His expression hadn't changed. He'd arrived, fought for his life, and killed several dozen Damned vampires, but his chiseled jaw was still clamped and the growing length of his fisted talons still showed his displeasure. But now, enhancing the appearance of unyielding anger, was the spatter of blood and gore from his kills. His left cheek was dotted with blood spray, and his right was painted with it. His clothes were ruined and soaked with thicker things. I didn't want to look at those things too closely, but neither could I look away from his expression. In his eyes, we were already dead as punishment for our transgressions; it was simply his duty to carry out the sentence.

Bex was suddenly at Lord High Chancellor Henry's side, her lips moving against his ear.

Something in his expression changed. It stiffened slightly. I froze, too scared and too resigned to dare hope that whatever Bex was whispering to him would make him reconsider the horrors he'd had in store for us. What could possibly make a man as infallible and un-yielding as Lord High Chancellor Henry Lynell Horrace DeWhitt change his mind?

He nodded in response to whatever Bex had whispered—a curt, barely discernable incline of his head. He never untrained his eyes from the target slightly behind me and to my left. His eyes blazed with that same unyielding promise of retribution, and I knew that whatever Lord High Chancellor Henry had just agreed to, it hadn't pertained to whomever his eyes were fixed on with the heat of a thousand suns.

I turned my head to see the target of his wrath and caught my breath.

Dominic.

When I turned back to face the Chancellor and Bex, they were gone.

Chapter 27

Nathan was watching the empty night sky, the same as me, waiting for the thunder and lightning from Lord High Chancellor Henry's unfathomable power to strike us all dead. But the longer we waited, the longer the silence stretched, and the more I felt like we were standing in the eye of the storm.

"I said it before, and I'll say it again," Nathan whispered to me under his breath, "we need to get out of here."

I nodded. "You read my mind."

"No one is going anywhere," Greta said. "Ambulances are on their way, and I have questions. So many damn questions my head is spinning." She crossed her arms in front of her chest, but I had the distinct impression it was to cover the fact that she was trembling. "Everyone better get damn comfortable."

"Cassidy and I," Dominic said, his voice brittle and biting, "must return to the coven."

"And where might that be?" Greta asked, her voice saccharine sweet.

Dominic growled.

"That's what I thought," she said. "You can't just disappear into the night like everyone else. I have questions, and you'd better have answers. Lots of answers."

Sevris stepped up next to Dominic. "Your will is my command, Master," he said, and he wasn't talking to Greta.

Rafe joined Sevris at Dominic's side, eyeing Rowens and Greta thoughtfully. "There's been so much slaughter tonight, we might not even need to entrance the medics when they arrive if we match the injuries the Damned inflicted on their victims."

It took me a moment to understand the line of Rafe's reasoning, but when it hit me, I froze. Greta and Rowens wouldn't forget what they'd witnessed tonight. The only way to silence them would be to kill them, and everyone would think their loss was just part of tonight's slaughter if their hearts were ripped from their chests, too.

Nathan stepped in front of Rowens and Greta without me having to ask. He met Rafe's eyes squarely, his features already shifting in preparation. "You can try."

I turned to Dominic, knowing that Rafe and Sevris would act on his command, and found Dominic staring at me, his expression inscrutable. He'd warned me over and over again that Greta's stubbornness and sticky memory would get her killed, but he also knew that if he killed her, no matter the provocation, our relationship—partnership, whatever crazy bond that had inexplicably grown between us—would be permanently severed.

"Convince her," Dominic said.

My breath caught. He was giving me a chance. He was giving *us* a chance.

I didn't know how to convince Greta, but meeting Dominic's gaze in that moment, looking into the piercing depths of his icy eyes, over his proud, protruding brow and across the sneer of his scarred lips, I felt like I could do anything.

I turned to Greta and took a deep breath. "Dominic's right."

Greta raised an eyebrow. "And I'm sure you're about to tell me why."

I nodded. "Until you and I have time to talk, to plan how best to release this—" I waved my hand at the ten-foot-tall, fanged, scaled monster lying dead on the ground behind me, "—to the public, I think it's best we let Dominic and his coven do what they do best."

Greta raised her eyebrows. "And what do they do, exactly?"

"They alter the evidence to make it look like something plausible, something the public can digest and understand." I gave her a look. "Something besides Damned monsters, Day Reapers, and vamp—" I swallowed my tongue, but when Greta narrowed her eyes on me, I finished, "—and nocturnal creatures that drink human blood."

Greta digested my reasoning for a moment. "Like animal bites that suddenly look like clean slices from knives?" she asked.

I bit my lip. "Yes, exactly like that."

"You knew about all this five weeks ago," she said, shaking her head in disbelief. "It's crazy. How is any of this even possible?"

"Show her," Dominic said.

I blinked. "What?"

"Sevris, will you please demonstrate your healing abilities for Detective Wahl? Cassidy has suffered her injuries as punishment long enough."

"Really?" I asked. The jubilant possibility of being healed made my voice squeak.

The lines bracketing Dominic's mouth tightened, and I remembered what Dominic had once said about never willingly or unnecessarily allowing me to suffer. He was accustomed to healing me. Leaving me immobile for so long may have actually hurt him more than it did me.

"Yes, really."

Sevris stared at Dominic blankly. "Master?"

"I'll do it," Rafe interrupted enthusiastically.

Dominic ignored Rafe and continued to stare at Sevris. "Heal her."

"In front of humans," Sevris said, the flat tone of his voice speaking volumes.

Dominic grimaced. "That's the point."

"You have changed," Sevris said. "Not necessarily for the worse. You might actually survive the Leveling."

Dominic growled.

Sevris knelt beside me. With the elongated talon of his pointer finger, he carefully sliced my cast in half and peeled it from my leg. Three pen stakes and two silver nitrate sprays fell out with a clatter onto the street.

Rafe let loose a long, high whistle. Dominic raised his eyebrows.

I shrugged, fighting back a grin. "A girl can never be over-armed these days."

Sevris ignored our banter. He unwrapped the ace bandage and gauze around my calf and exposed the red, angry lines of stitches that held my skin together. The wounds were clean but swollen and obviously irritated from not receiving the rest the doctor had prescribed. A few of the stitches had torn through the skin and were trickling blood.

"Is this really the time or the place?" Rowens asked, eyeing my leg speculatively. "Wound care should wait until we're in a sterile environment."

"He's worried about you catching an infection," Rafe said. He laughed. "How cute."

"What are you doing?" Greta snapped, obviously in agreement with Rowens. "What will exposing Cassidy's injuries prove?"

Dominic didn't respond. He knew that Sevris would convince her more thoroughly with actions than he could with words.

Sevris' expression never wavered despite their conversation. His face was composed and focused, but I wasn't fooled. Beneath the calm exterior, he was triumphant inside. I could see the anticipation in his eyes. Master vampires rarely allowed others to drink from their night bloods—with good reason—and Sevris planned to savor the experience.

I held my breath and hoped that Sevris would be able to control his urges better than Rafe had. The irresistible, savory spice in my blood made it impossible for most vampires to stop drinking once they started. As much as Dominic wanted to see me healed, I didn't completely trust Sevris not to lose control. Hell, sometimes I second-guessed Dominic's ability to maintain control, and he was Master vampire of New York City.

Sevris cupped my bare calf in his hands and pricked each stitch with the razor edge of his fang. As the stitches severed, the tension holding my skin together relaxed, and the wound gaped open.

I gritted my teeth against the sight and the pain.

"Stop," Greta snapped. "I don't know what the hell you think this proves, but I've seen enough."

Sevris licked deep inside my wound, allowing excess saliva to pool from his mouth into my leg.

"I suppose my suggestion for a sterile environment was 'cute' after all," Rowens said faintly.

Sevris' tongue probed my wound, his movements swift and bone deep. His saliva burned as it healed. Coupled with the sharp slice of his tongue as he licked, the typical discomfort and near sexual heat of being healed by Dominic instead bordered on pain with Sevris.

Dominic must have seen some indication of that pain in my expression. "Cassidy?" he asked.

I opened my mouth to reassure him, but Sevris licked even deeper. He tore through healthy muscle and tissue to reach the fractured bone beneath, and my eyes rolled back.

"Stop," Greta said again, and this time, her voice wavered. "She's had enough."

The blaze of Sevris' healing shot through my tibia. I heard my nails crack and break as I gripped the sidewalk, searching for an anchor to keep me from drifting off.

The click of a bullet prepped in its chamber. "You heard the lady," Rowens said, his voice low, cold, and resolute. "She's had enough."

I wrenched my eyes open, not sure when I'd screwed them closed. Sevris was eyeballs deep in the meat of my calf, literally, healing me from the inside out. I understood the necessity—he couldn't heal my skin before healing muscle, and he couldn't heal the muscle before healing the bone—but knowing the reason behind his actions didn't stop the agony they caused.

"Cassidy, you must speak before Rowens shoots Sevris in your defense and Sevris kills Rowens in self-defense." Dominic's hand was suddenly in mine, his fingers uncurling my grip from the sidewalk and lacing through my fingers. I squeezed his hand to find the strength neither of us had and focused my pain-blurred gaze on the scene before me.

Rowens had his gun aimed on Sevris. Greta looked about to draw her own weapon. Rafe was growling, his features half-transformed. Nathan eyed us all warily, obviously unwilling to test his strength against bullets or vampires.

And Sevris, bless him, was ignoring them all.

"Stand down, Rowens. I'm fine," I ground out between clenched teeth. "Better than fine. You'll see."

Rowens didn't move. He didn't shoot, but he didn't put up his gun either. "I'm not seeing much of anything but your blood spilling across the pavement and Sevris thoroughly enjoying your pain. Show me otherwise."

"You'll see," I said on a gasp. "Patience."

"I'm at the end of mine," Greta snapped.

Sevris moved on from my bone to the muscle. The pain was still there and still debilitating, but the burning sensation and needle-like sharpness of his probing tongue was different somehow, like the subtle nuance of a scalpel's surgical incision rather than the frenzied stab and twist of a kitchen knife. "Just a minute longer," I lied. "You'll see."

Dominic tightened his grip on my hand. I took a deep breath and squeezed back.

Several minutes passed in tense silence, and I forced myself not to react to the movement of Sevris' tongue. Finally, eventually—taking longer than I imagined Dominic would need to heal me but working just as thoroughly—Sevris pinched the edges of my skin closed and licked over the seam to seal the wound.

He glanced up, meeting my gaze over the nearly healed sliver of scar on my calf. The lingering, throbbing memory of pain was exhausting, but presently gone. Even so, my smile, though genuine, felt strained.

"Thank you," I said, grateful that he'd healed me, and even more grateful that he'd done so without allowing instinct to override reason. Mentioning that I was relieved he had the strength to resist eating me seemed insulting, so I let the gratitude stand without explanation.

Keeping eye contact, he flicked his tongue over the remaining wound, and in two quick swipes, the scar dissolved too.

He straightened. "You're welcome."

I turned to face Greta, but she wasn't looking at me anymore. Neither was Rowens, and although he still hadn't technically put up his gun, he wasn't aiming it anymore, either. His arms had dropped, along with his jaw. Both he and Greta were staring at Sevris with a strange mix of fear, disbelief, and wonder.

Sevris extended a hand to me, the barely-there smirk of anticipation back on his face.

I took his hand for the help, despite the grin, and stood.

Everyone's eyes and expressions of fear, disbelief, and wonder shifted to me.

Greta was shaking her head. Even as she opened her mouth and inhaled to speak, she continued shaking her head back and forth in denial. "How?" she finally asked.

"An enzyme in their saliva enhances blood clotting and healing in humans. Handy when human blood is their main source of food; they can feed from an artery and heal it before the person loses too much blood."

"They feed on humans," Greta said dryly.

"They feed on human *blood*," I corrected. "Humans don't necessarily need to die for them to eat," I said, but my defense sounded weak, even to my own ears.

Rowens recovered and re-aimed his gun, training his sights steadily on Sevris. Greta didn't look convinced either.

I glanced at Dominic. "Maybe we should demonstrate feeding as well."

"How are you feeling?" he asked, and the fact that he was still more concerned for my well-being than his own moved me like nothing else could.

"Better than ever," I lied. My head still spun from blood loss, my hip still ached as usual, and my back still stung from the residual pain of his injuries, but compared to the agony and immobility I'd experienced in the last five minutes, I felt brand-new.

He narrowed his eyes at me. "Try the truth this time."

I sighed. "I'm feeling better than before. Better than you," I pointed out. I eased myself back down to sit on the ground next to him and offered my still bleeding wrist at his mouth. "Heal yourself," I encouraged him. "We'll convince her together."

Dominic's growl was low and rattling. He didn't want to bleed me—he certainly didn't want to hurt me—but he was weak and injured, and that meant he was also ravenous. He opened his mouth, baring the long, protruding length of his fangs.

"You attack, and I shoot," Rowens said calmly. "Simple action/reaction."

Dominic pulled back from my wrist and glanced at Rowens. "Attacking requires resistance. Do you see any resistance from Cassidy?"

Rowens shook his head. "She's suffering from Stockholm syndrome."

Dominic laughed, further baring his fangs, his expression anything but amused. "She is not being held captive, against her will or otherwise."

Greta placed her hand on Rowens' arm and squeezed his bicep. "I trust Cassidy. Let this play out," she said.

Rowens didn't drop his aim, but his finger relaxed minutely on the trigger.

That must have been permission enough for Dominic. He sealed his lips around my wrist and sucked at the tender wound there from

Rafe's bite. Typically, his bite was electrifying, consuming, and orgasmic. Literally, he could bring me to orgasm by piercing my skin with his fangs and sucking my blood through the wound. Every swallow brought waves of dizzying, soul-baring pleasure.

With the approaching Leveling, he'd lost many abilities, and the power to produce an orgasm with his bite was obviously one of the abilities he no longer possessed.

I gritted my teeth against the uncomfortable suction of his mouth on my wound as he drank. He glanced up at my sharp intake of breath and, realizing I wasn't distracted by pleasure, made short work of his meal. He drank quickly, without savoring my taste, and was careful not to tear my skin with his fangs.

The sting of Dominic's shredded back faded with his every swallow of my blood. I tried to focus on the recession of his pain, but as his pain became more faint, the discomfort of his fangs embedded in my wrist became more prominent. Just when I might have asked him to stop, the sting of Dominic's wounds faded entirely, and he pulled away.

We stared at my oozing, bloody wrist between us. The edges of Dominic's mouth pinched grimly.

"Sevris," he said, offering up my wrist to him, "would you, please?"

"With pleasure," Sevris said. He bent over my wrist and, with two quick swipes of his tongue, healed the jagged wound.

I stood to face Greta, albeit a little more shakily than a moment before, and extended my hand to Dominic the way Sevris had extended his hand to me. Unlike Sevris', however, the hand I extended to Dominic visibly trembled.

Dominic took my hand for appearances' sake, but he stood without my help. We turned to face Greta and Rowens together, our hands still locked, our fingers laced, more than just allies. I felt the pain of his injuries. He bled from the depth of my wounds. We had each other's backs as partners, but more than that, we bled and recovered as one person. We'd rise and fall and struggle our way back to the top, and we'd do it together.

At one time not that long ago, such a realization would have terrified me. Being intertwined that deeply and certainly with anyone, let alone a vampire, would have been incomprehensible. Now, the very fact that it was Dominic with whom I was intertwined made it acceptable. A warmth and strength I'd never before possessed swelled through my chest.

Greta was still shaking her head at us. She moved to step forward, and Rowens blocked her.

"I don't think you should—"

Greta knocked his arm out of her way and stepped toe to toe with Dominic. "Turn around."

He raised an eyebrow, ever cool and collected.

"I need to see your injured back," she explained. "You're alive and standing, which should be proof enough, but everything you're telling me and showing me is unbelievable. I need to see it for myself."

Dominic hesitated, obviously uncomfortable giving anyone his back, especially now that he wasn't at full strength. He glanced down at me.

The weight of implicit trust in that one action was humbling. Something warm and lingering and nearly suffocating swept through me, and I hoped against everything sane and precious in this world that I had the strength to bear that kind of trust.

I nodded.

Dominic let go of my hand and gave Greta his back.

Her jaw went slack as she stared at the blood-soaked tatters of his shirt and the untouched, baby-smooth perfection of his skin beneath. She was still shaking her head as she raised a hand to touch what her eyes couldn't accept. I wasn't the only one trembling.

Dominic's jaw clenched when Greta's hand grazed his scapula, but otherwise, he remained stock still.

Greta closed her mouth, stepped back, and tightened the pieces of herself that had fallen slack with disbelief. "What do we do now?" she asked.

I took a deep breath. "We let Dominic and his, vamp—um, *people*, alter the scene, so the public has a rational, sane explanation for what happened. No one is ready for this." I gestured to the dead Damned behind us. "Not yet, anyway."

"And then?" she asked.

"And then Cassidy and I take shelter in my coven in preparation for the coming dawn," Dominic said. "As you now know, I'm nocturnal, and where I go, Cassidy goes."

Greta didn't look convinced.

"We all need to rest and recuperate," I added. "The Damned included. They took a huge hit, thanks to the Day Reapers." I gestured to the mutilated body of the Damned behind us. "If we take the dead Damned back to the lab, maybe Dr. Chunn can learn more about their strengths and their weakness. They're difficult to kill, but obviously not immortal."

"How was that one killed?" Greta asked.

Silence.

Even Rafe and Ronnie held their peace. I struggled not to glance at Nathan and give him away.

Nathan let loose a snort of disgust. "With my bare hands."

My head jerked up sharply. "Don't," I muttered.

He shook his head. "Every other secret is out. Why not mine?"

I turned back to Greta, ignoring Nathan. "Once we've had the chance to rest and recuperate and Dr. Chunn examines the remains, then we can discuss our next move," I reasoned. "There's no point in planning a counterattack before we know all the facts."

Greta eyed us critically, her gaze flicking between Dominic and me. "I agree to your plan, Cassidy. We'll rest and reconvene in a few hours, giving Dr. Chunn the opportunity to examine the bodies. Dominic and his *people*," she said pointedly, obviously not missing my earlier hesitation, "can fix the scene in the way they see fit for now, but we need a press conference to release this information, sooner rather than later. After Dr. Chunn figures out what we're dealing with. And after I notify the feds. And after we—" She swiped her hands down her face. "This is a fucking nightmare."

I nodded. "Agreed."

"And I take Nathan back to the lab," Greta added.

I jerked, taken aback. "I don't think so."

"We need all the information we can get to use against these creatures: their strengths and their weaknesses, like you said. Considering that Nathan killed one of them, he's obviously one of their weaknesses."

"He's not a body for experimentation. He's my little brother!"

"Not so little anymore." Nathan placed a hand on my shoulder. "It's okay, Cassidy. I'll go."

I blinked. "But you can't just—"

"I need to help," Nathan said. "I need a purpose."

"You have a purpose," I scoffed. "Just because no one remembers—"

"I was erased!" Nathan exploded. His ears pointed, and his fangs elongated. He closed his eyes, and I could see his desperate struggle for control in the deep crevices at the corners of his lips, crevices that hadn't been there a few months ago. He covered his face with his hands to hide his transformation, but his fingernails had sharpened to talons.

Dominic placed his hand on my waist and urged me back, but I patted his hand in reassurance. Even as a rampaging, heart-eating, psycho killer, Nathan had been my little brother. I wasn't giving up on him now.

"You weren't erased. Only forgotten, and not by everyone. Not by me," I reminded him.

When Nathan dropped his hands and looked up, his face was once again composed and perfectly human, but he wasn't looking at me.

"I used to be one of the Damned," he told Greta. "I was transformed by Jillian into one of those soulless, heart-eating creatures, but Cassidy tracked me down and transformed me back the best she could."

Greta raised an eyebrow. "Back into what?"

Nathan shrugged. "Isn't that Dr. Chunn's job to find out?"

Greta inclined her head.

"I don't like it," I insisted, but from the satisfied look on Greta's face, the matter was settled.

Nathan grinned at the sourness in my tone and stepped forward. Dominic tensed, but I knew better. I met Nathan halfway and wrapped my arms around his waist. He hugged me back, his arms resting on my shoulders.

"I'll be fine in Dr. Chunn's care," he murmured in my ear. "If the Damned can't kill me, she certainly can't."

"Be careful. Take care of Meredith, and call if you need me," I said, my voice muffled in his shirt.

"I will."

"I'm serious. You didn't ask for help with Jillian last time, and look what happened." I pulled back to meet his eyes. "We're a team, and that means we play the game together, got it?"

He nodded. "I'm not the same person I was when I sought out Jillian. I won't make the same mistakes."

"Good. I love your dumb ass, but I'm sick of saving it," I said, letting my arms drop.

Nathan let his arms drop, too, but he didn't laugh like I thought he would. His expression was deadly serious. "I love you, too."

I watched Nathan walk away with Greta and Rowens, back to their cruisers and what remained of their task force, and my throat tightened uncomfortably.

"He'll be fine. Dr. Chunn wouldn't deliberately harm him, and if anyone tried," Dominic glanced at the dead Damned behind us, "he can defend himself."

"I know," I said, but my voice was nothing but gravel. I cleared my throat and tried again. "I know." But knowing a thing and feeling it in my bones were two entirely different things.

"Are you ready?" he asked, taking my hand.

"What about me?" Ronnie asked in a small voice.

Chapter 28

Ronnie's question cut through the illogical grief of losing Nathan. I'd forgotten she was even there, but refocusing on her was startling. I hadn't had time to really take note of her appearance in the panic and chaos when she'd first arrived to save me, but what I saw now didn't look capable of life.

She was very nearly completely bald now, the straggles of remaining hair on her scabby, emaciated skull pathetic and dull. Her cheeks were sunken. The hollows beneath her eyes made them bulge, and even her sad little fangs were too big for her mouth. Every bone, every rib, every knobby joint was shrink-wrapped with, pale, nearly translucent skin.

Ronnie had been beautiful when I'd met her. She was concerningly skinny even as a human, but she'd hidden her disorder behind a pretty smile and beneath baggy sweaters. She'd made the best banana nut pancakes I'd ever eaten in my life, and even though she'd never had a bite of them herself, she'd fed an entire household. She'd been suffering even then, but to the unobservant eye, she did a fabulous job of faking it.

She couldn't fake it anymore. She needed help, and she knew it.

And she'd come to me.

I'd failed her when she'd been attacked and turned into a vampire, and by the looks of her, I was continuing to fail her. Ronnie was another anomaly I didn't know how to fix, but unlike Nathan, Ronnie needed a solution now, before she crumbled into a pile of ash at our feet.

My mind came up blank.

"Well?" she asked.

Dominic squeezed my hand, reminding me that I needed to respond.

"Well, what?" I asked.

She stared at me like *I* was demented. "*Well*, Nathan is going to help Greta and Rowens find the Damned's weaknesses, if they have any. Rafe and Sevris are going to cover up the evidence of vampires at the crime scene. And you and Dominic are going back to the coven to pretend to rest while you devise a plan to save us, right?"

I gaped. I couldn't help it.

"Right," Dominic said, and by the faint lilt to his tone, I could tell he was amused.

"Well," she said, looking back and forth between the two of us, "what do you need me to do?"

My God, Ronnie didn't want help. She wanted *to* help.

Rafe snorted. "What *can* you do?"

Dominic sliced him in half with his gaze.

Rafe cleared his throat. "Sorry. But look at her." He waved his hand at Ronnie as if she were on display, and she shriveled in on herself. "She can barely stand."

Despite the horror of Ronnie's existence, or maybe because of it, I snapped. "Shut the fuck up, Rafe. She can more than stand. She saved my life."

Ronnie's expression brightened. She might have even smiled. Her lips thinned and pulled up at the corners, exposing her needle-sharp fangs.

Rafe snorted. "And tried to leave Lysander for dead."

Her expression froze. "I didn't leave him for dead. I thought he *was* dead." She met Dominic's eyes and then quickly looked away. "You looked dead," she whispered in her defense.

Dominic's voice was gentle when he spoke, the voice with which one speaks to a person flirting with the ledge. "It's okay, Ronnie. I'm not angry with you. I'm proud of you."

She looked up and held his gaze this time. "You are? But I'm"— she looked down at herself, and the movement caused the few remaining hairs on her head to fall and flutter to the ground—"pathetic."

"In the face of adversity, and despite your lack of strength, you tried to save Cassidy. I commend you for that."

"She left you for dead," Rafe muttered under his breath.

"I can live through trauma that Cassidy cannot. Ronnie chose to save Cassidy over me, and that was the right decision," Dominic said, his voice brooking no argument. When he spoke to Ronnie again, his voice turned soft and sweet, like he was speaking to a child. And I suppose in a way he was. "Now, Ronnie, why are you not eating? I know you must feel the burn to feed. The scent of Cassidy's blood must scorch your every breath."

Ronnie nodded. "It does," she admitted softly.

"Then why haven't you fed?"

"I never received my lesson," she said softly.

I closed my eyes. *Shit*, I thought, as Ronnie unwittingly threw me head first under the bus.

"Her lesson?"

I peeked up at Dominic at his question. He raised his eyebrows, waiting for me to enlighten him.

Ronnie wrung her hands nervously. "You didn't tell him. I thought you'd tell him. He knows everything."

Dominic made a noise in the back of his throat, almost a growl, but the sound wasn't menacing in the least. If I didn't know better, I'd think he was quelling a laugh.

I glared at Ronnie, but I couldn't remain stern for long in the face of her deterioration.

"Let me help you, Ronnie," Dominic said. "I'm your Master's ally, and my night blood is your good friend. There's no reason to be frightened. We are all in this together."

"You're not angry that I'm here, in your territory, without your knowledge or permission?" Ronnie asked.

Dominic sighed. "I'm more angry that Bex has allowed you to remain untrained, unfed, and uncared for."

"It's not just me," Ronnie said softly, and something in Dominic's expression must have encouraged her, because she took a deep breath and continued. "I'm not the only newly turned vampire who's starving. We all are. Jeremy and Logan didn't want to come here for help, but I knew Cassidy would know what to do. She always seems to know the next step."

Dominic blinked. "Jeremy and Logan are here, too?"

"And Keagan and all the night bloods that Bex transformed that night," I murmured. "She abandoned her coven for the Day Reapers, and the coven hasn't helped much with the transition."

"They're angry and grieving and lost," Ronnie said, her voice pleading now. "Bex attacked, transformed, and abandoned us. If I don't find someone to help us, they'll go off on their own to help themselves."

Dominic's face hardened. "Newly transformed vampires finding their way alone never ends well."

I sucked in my breath. "Your brother."

Dominic inclined his head deeply. "He set out on his own after being transformed, and without the guidance of other vampires, he lost his way."

Sevris, who had been silent until now, nodded his agreement. "To build a better future, we can't allow history to repeat itself."

"It's already repeating itself with Jillian," I reminded them.

"It's up to us to break the cycle," Dominic said.

I glanced at Sevris and Rafe to my right and Ronnie in front of us, and sudden inspiration hit.

"Your lessons are important, Ronnie, but I don't think I'm the best person to give them. I'm not even a vampire."

Ronnie's face fell. "But you promised."

"Yes, I did," I said quickly, before Ronnie could crumble, "but I'm not the best person for the job. Rafe and Sevris can take over your lessons."

"We can?" Rafe asked.

Dominic nodded. "You will."

"Ronnie, I'd like you to meet Rafe. He's a member of Dominic's coven, has a wicked sense of humor, and can tell time without a watch." I glanced back at Rafe and grinned. "You're welcome."

Rafe glanced at Ronnie and then back at me, and I knew the moment he put the puzzle together. He shook his head frantically. "Oh no. I don't think so. This does not count as an introduction. She's not a night blood anymore. And she looks like hell."

Dominic rolled his eyes. "She needs our help."

"Ronnie is female, my friend, and she will remember your existence. Those were your stipulations," I argued. "It counts."

Rafe crossed his arms, petulant.

"Introduction?" Ronnie asked warily.

"Never mind that." I waved her concern away. "Make allies. Make friends. Forge alliances and all that. It's a predator-eats-predator kind of world out here, and let's face it, Ronnie, you're prey."

"You're not much of a predator yourself," Ronnie grumbled.

"No, I'm not, but I've surrounded myself with friends and allies who are. Right now, all you have is me," I said, looking down at my own prey-like body. "Make friends with people your own species, okay?"

Ronnie crossed her arms and glared at Rafe, looking pretty petulant herself. "I don't think—"

"You wanted my help, right? You wanted to know your next step, didn't you?"

"Well, yes, but this isn't it. Not with him," Ronnie said, still giving Rafe the stink-eye. "He's an asshole."

"Yes, he is. But he knows how to entrance and feed without killing anyone. You can learn from him, Ronnie, and be stronger for it. Dominic wasn't a picnic when I first met him, either, but now, we are better for having taken the time to know one another."

"Thanks?" Dominic asked, his grin lopsided.

I shrugged. "I only speak the truth."

"I wanted *your* help, Cassidy. I trust *you*," Ronnie insisted.

"Then trust me when I tell you that I can't give you the help you need. But they can," I said, pointing to Rafe and Sevris.

Ronnie glanced at them. Rafe glared back, and Sevris, bless him, just stared, stoic and unreadable as usual.

"Okay." Her voice was a small, hesitant whisper, but her expression was resolute. "I'll try."

"Wonderful," I said, feeling a small measure of accomplishment that I'd solved one of my unsolvable problems. "Now, I can go back to my apartment to grab the rest of my weapons and—"

"Excuse me?" Dominic interrupted. "You're coming back to the coven with me."

"Yes, I am," I said calmly, despite the crazy suddenly lighting his eyes. "But I can't face the Leveling with only three pen stakes and two silver nitrate sprays. Give me twenty minutes to pack some real weapons."

Dominic shook his head. "I need to return to the coven without delay, for my own safety as well as the safety of the coven. When Lord High Chancellor Henry returns, I am the one he will be returning for."

I nodded. "I know," I said softly.

"Do you?" he asked, and his tone was more challenge than question. "If I'm not present in the coven before the Day Reapers arrive, they will torture whomever they deem necessary to find me. I can't come with you to the apartment and risk destroying the coven with my absence."

"I'm not asking you to come with me to my apartment. I can pack a bag of weapons on my own."

"If I'm wrong, and the Lord High Chancellor comes for you instead of me, you are the one who will be tortured in my absence. And I won't be there to stop him."

I shook my head. "Even if you were there, you're in no condition to stop him anyway." I shot him a look. "Just twenty minutes. I'll be fine."

He cupped my jaw gently. "You've got five."

I rolled my eyes. "The elevator ride to my third-floor apartment takes five minutes."

"Five minutes," he repeated in no uncertain terms. "You do what you need to do, and I will send Sevris to get you." He stepped closer. "If he doesn't return with you in five minutes, I will come for you myself."

I groaned. "You just said that you couldn't leave the coven to come with me. It's too much of a risk for you and the coven."

His thumb brushed over my cheekbone. "Then don't make me risk it."

Chapter 29

I looked over the clothes, bathroom accessories, and weapons piled on my bed, and then at the TSA-approved luggage next to said pile, and thought, *I need a bigger suitcase.*

My hip protested as I squatted to reach for the large duffle under my bed, but since being healed, I could actually squat. I could walk, climb stairs, and pack a bag without help, without a scooter, and I couldn't have been happier, protesting hip or not.

I took that back, sobering. I'd have been happier if the Damned and the Day Reapers weren't hunting us, but the relief of being mobile again was making me uncommonly optimistic.

Even mobile, however, I was still moving at my typical, snail-slow pace. Five minutes had already come and gone sometime between packing my toothbrush and my silver-threaded gloves, but I wasn't the only one who was late. Sevris hadn't arrived to pick me up, either.

I should have been worried, except that I wasn't ready for him. If he showed up late and I still wasn't ready . . . I shuddered and tried to speed up the packing process.

Ten minutes later, someone pounded on the door. I quickly dumped an armful of tuna cans and ammo boxes into the side pocket and zipped the luggage, fully intending to rip Sevris a new one for making me wait, until I peeked through my apartment door's peephole; the person pounding on my door was none other than Dominic himself.

"Sevris never came to pick me up," I shouted through the door, neatly throwing Sevris under the bus. "I've been ready for over ten minutes now."

"I don't care if you're ready. We need to move. Now," Dominic said. He was looking down the hall as he said it, and I sucked in my breath at the worried planes of his profile. He was scared, nearly panicked, even. "Open the door!" he shouted at me.

I unlocked and opened the door.

"What's going on? Why didn't Sevris show? Where—?"

Ignoring my barrage of questions, Dominic reached out to grab my arm. "Less talking. More moving."

A flare of heat burst between us. Dominic's arm dropped to his side, and my face felt fried from the sudden backdraft. A rotting sizzle lit the air; the putrid smell reminded me of Dominic's allergic reaction to silver.

I wrinkled my nose. "What is that?"

Dominic frowned, looking puzzled, but when he raised his hand toward me again and the same burst of heat and rotting sizzle flamed the air between us a second time, Dominic lost his composure. He pounded the air with both fists and cursed in frustration as punches of heat and putrid steam clouded the hallway.

I stared at him, confused at first by his antics and misplaced anger, and then in wonder at the doorway between us. Dominic couldn't cross the threshold.

I'd succeeded in vampire-proofing my apartment.

I would have danced in glee if I could dance without my hip giving out, but at that exact moment, when all my efforts and hopes and dreams had blossomed in sweet fruition, Lord High Chancellor Henry stepped out from the shadows behind Dominic.

I opened my mouth in warning, but my words weren't fast enough. The Chancellor knocked Dominic aside and lunged for me.

He must not have witnessed Dominic's inability to cross the threshold, because logically, if he had, he wouldn't have tried to cross it himself. Or maybe he thought, being the Lord of all vampires, he'd be exempt, but the moment he came into contact with the threshold, he blew back from my doorway in a sizzling blaze of flame and fireworks. He smashed into the opposite hallway wall, knocking Dominic back with him. I didn't have time to think or reason or weigh the pros against the cons. My mind filled with Lord High Chancellor Henry's unyielding expression as he glared at Dominic with death in his gaze, and I just reacted.

"Dominic Lysander, I give you permission to enter my apartment," I commanded.

I reached out to drag him across the threshold with me and safely away from Lord High Henry's wrath. Dominic tried to help, but he was still stunned from the blowback. I scooped him up beneath his arms and yanked him into my apartment with all my strength and body weight. He tumbled on top of me on my kitchen floor, our legs tangled, my knee catching beneath his ribs, his face smothered in my chest, and I lost my breath from the double hit of his weight and proximity.

Over Dominic's shoulder, I watched as the Chancellor rose from a heap of broken plaster on the hallway floor. He bared his fangs at me in a furious sneer and charged. I braced myself for his impact.

Dominic shifted his body over me, covering me from head to toe with his own.

The Chancellor attacked, battering my threshold. Dominic and I both tensed at the violence of it, but the harder the attack, and the more violent the Chancellor became, the more explosive the blowback.

I gaped at the damage to my doorframe and hallway, at the impressive display of power and rage from the Chancellor, and at the fireballs, sparkling firework explosions, and billowing clouds of rank steam from his assault. A slow, smug smile curved Dominic's scarred lips.

Henry could unleash the full pent-up fury of his unimaginable, unnatural long life on that threshold, but no matter his strength and power and rage, no matter his Lord High Chancellor status, or perhaps because of it, he wasn't getting through.

The silence that followed his attack was punctuated by the staccato barking from a few of my neighbors' dogs. The man across the hall, kitty-corner to my apartment, had the gumption to not only look through his peephole, but to actually open his door. Henry didn't even glance behind him. He didn't speak a command or break eye contact, and he didn't need to. One nonchalant wave of his hand, and the man's gaze dulled to a glassy stare. He stepped back into his apartment and shut the door.

But Henry's expression was anything but nonchalant as he stared at me through the threshold he couldn't cross. Dominic kicked the door with his foot, slamming it shut on the Chancellor's red, rage-filled face.

"No matter how hard he huffs and puffs, he'll never blow that door down," I said, succumbing to a little smugness myself.

Dominic turned away from the door and looked down at me.

I lost my breath at the look on his face.

"Sevris never came to pick me up," I reminded him.

In everything that had just occurred in the last half second—realizing that I'd created a sanctuary from Dominic's inescapable reach in my own apartment, granting him access to said sanctuary, and now having him bodily flattening me on the kitchen floor of my apartment, which against him was now no sanctuary at all—Sevris' tardiness was the only thing that made sense. Everything else had happened in fast-forward, and now the irresistible press of Dominic's body against mine and the heat in his icy eyes made time suddenly pause.

Dominic inclined his head. "Sevris was detained. They think you are the key to my power, so they don't want you anywhere near me for my destruction."

"They?" I asked, in favor of questioning his word choice: his "destruction," not "death."

"The Day Reapers. High Lord Henry in particular," he said with a smirk. Given the Chancellor's roar from the hallway, I got the distinct impression that Dominic was purposefully goading him.

But we're metaphysically bonded, I mouthed to him, hoping against hope that the Lord High Chancellor wasn't so powerful that he could read my lips by the feel of their movement on the air.

Little do they know, he mouthed back, *that your survival means my survival.*

Little do they know, I agreed, *that your destruction means my destruction.*

"You transformed your apartment into a fallout shelter," he stated aloud, his icy eyes scalding me with their heat. "You learned a great deal during your brief visit with Ian Walker."

It burned to hold his gaze, but for the life of me, even if I were to spontaneously combust under the heat of his regard, I couldn't look away.

I swallowed and nodded.

He broke our gaze, but as his eyes darted around my apartment, scrutinizing God knew what, I felt just as stripped and charred. "It's certainly not where I had anticipated settling for the Leveling, but it prevented the Chancellor from entering. It will do just as well as my own fallout shelter, I think."

"Glad to know it meets your approval," I said dryly. "I thought you were taking me back to your coven."

"I made preparations for the unthinkable, and as the Leveling comes to pass, the inevitable, it seems. But thanks to you, your apartment will suffice." His eyes met mine again, and I squirmed. "I'm sure you would have preferred to restrict my permission to enter as well," he murmured, "but you gave me access, sharing your sanctuary from vampires with me, a vampire."

"As if I had a choice, with the Lord High Chancellor beating down my doorstep," I snorted.

"You had a choice," Dominic whispered. "There's always a choice."

I pursed my lips, and his eyes darted down to stare at them. I was suddenly very self-conscious about my mouth.

"I, well . . ." I stuttered, struggling between the uncertainty of my emotions and the very certain pressure of his body flattening mine. I stared at his lips, just as fixated on their movement as Dominic was on mine. "I prefer you alive . . . er, well, as alive as you are. Not destroyed," I finished lamely. I couldn't possibly be less eloquent.

His lips were suddenly, unfathomably closer, scant breaths from my own lips. I hadn't thought he could draw any closer.

"I can smell your desire and the barest spice of your fear, as usual, but there's something more. Something I've never smelled on you before," he whispered. His lips skimmed mine, more movement than kiss, as he brushed past them to bury his face in my neck and inhaled.

The soft tickle of his breath on the sensitive curve of my neck curled my toes. "The remnants of sewer sludge, perhaps?" I asked, trying to create some distance, any distance that I was capable of creating, since I couldn't do anything about his physical proximity. And if I was honest with myself, I didn't want to do anything about it as much as I wanted to do everything about it. My body thrilled from his closeness.

"Hmm," he murmured and the vibration of his lips made me shiver. "I think not."

The scent of his skin breezed against my face as I struggled to catch my breath, unsure when exactly I'd lost it. Like Christmas pine, as always, his scent was poignant and nostalgic, but despite the confusing kaleidoscope of old grief and new desire that his scent inspired in me, the consistency was comforting if not telling. He could probably discern the confusing nuances of my contradictory feelings for him in the scent of my skin, but his scent wasn't contradictory nor confusing in the least; his scent surrounded me like warm arms welcoming me home.

Arms that could transform into talons and sever aortas, rip through throats to the bone and decapitate bodies. Arms that had killed in defense of me, held me gently as I shuddered in pain, and caught me as I fell. His arms had saved me in more ways, more times, and with more sacrifice than I'd ever thought a person could be capable of.

"I think your scent stems from the same emotion that would motivate you to give me access to your vampire-resistant apartment." Dominic breathed in deeply. "More than your desire, even perhaps more than your fear, it's the sweetest scent of all."

I wasn't ready to admit the true depth of my feelings for Dominic to myself, let alone to him, but I knew in that moment what he was trying to tell me because I felt the same way.

Dominic Lysander loved me, too.

I leaned up, closing the scant millimeter distance remaining between us, and pressed my lips firmly against his.

He reacted instantly and intensely, moving his mouth over mine, pressing his body firmly against my body, locking his hands behind my neck and waist. His mouth was heat and need, and the demanding forcefulness of his embrace heightened my own need and stoked my own heat. I circled my arms around his body, feeling the ridges of his back muscles shift and contract under my fingers. I scraped my nails over his skin through his shirt, and he groaned.

He tore his lips from my mouth and buried his face in my neck, his breath harsh. I breathed in his scent, too, desperate for him and everything I'd never dared to consider wanting from him. I wanted more. I wanted all of him.

I'd denied my feelings for Dominic for weeks that felt like years. The doubts had been too vast and the risks and the differences between us too great to even consider the possibility of something more. Now that we were here in this moment, reveling in how far we'd come, how much we'd grown, and how perfectly combustible we were together, I wanted so much more, more than I'd allowed myself to have in a very long time, from anyone.

And I wanted it here and now with this man, Master vampire of New York City, my worst nightmare turned grudging ally, now my greatest protector. Meredith was right; it was time to get over Adam.

I bit his neck.

Dominic reared back in a growl, the sharp intensity in his eyes cutting. He wanted me as much as I wanted him, with so much need and desire that it hurt to want it. It hurt so much that it was terrifying to consider having it.

But for the first time, not nearly as terrifying as considering not having it.

"Foul play," he growled. "I can't bite you without piercing your delicate skin." He licked said delicate skin, and goose bumps shivered over my neck and down my spine. I shuddered in his embrace.

"I've suffered your bite before, and it wasn't so bad," I murmured.

He snorted at my understatement. He knew the power of his own bite. He could make me come—hard, instantaneously, and continuously—reducing my body to a twitching, mindless, exposed nerve with one swallow of my blood.

"With the Leveling unfortunately upon us, my powers are severely diminished. As you experienced firsthand while healing me, I can no longer heal my own bite, and you wouldn't take any pleasure in it."

"Poor you," I teased. "For once, you'll actually have to work for it."

Dominic crushed his lips against mine, licking the seam of my lips with his tongue. I opened my mouth, and he nibbled my lip, careful of his fangs. I stretched down to grab his ass and winced. My damn hip was getting in the way of living my life as I wanted to live it, as always.

Granted, it didn't help that he was crushing me with the full weight of his body against the hardwood of my kitchen floor.

No sooner had the thought crossed my mind than Dominic stood. He picked me up with him, cradling me against his chest as he swung me off the kitchen floor and into his arms. He walked the few steps between the kitchen and the living room and promptly deposited me on the couch.

I squeaked, shocked at the sudden drop when I'd anticipated him carrying me to the bedroom—my thoughts had certainly gone there—and I had the immediate, horrified realization that his hadn't. Despite his kisses and touches and incorrigible innuendoes, he actually did not want everything I wanted in this moment.

The piece of me I'd thought had fully callused from the scars of past wounds ripped wide open.

Dominic dropped to his knees before me and eased his hands under my shirt.

I was so confused by the duality of my disappointment and desire that I didn't do or say anything while he tugged my yoga pants over the generous curve of my butt and peeled them from my legs. It wasn't until he slid my thong aside and spread my bare legs open to him that I balked.

"Wait, what are you doing?" I squeaked.

He glanced up at me from between my thighs.

"I'm working for it," he said, but despite his cocky tone, I could detect a wavering in his expression. It would break a little piece of him if I didn't want him, just like it had broken a little piece of me thinking he'd meant to stop.

"Oh. Good," I said, nodding like a bobblehead.

He raised an eyebrow at me. "Was I doing something to your dissatisfaction?"

I shook my head, embarrassed now that we were talking instead of doing.

"Then what's wrong?"

"It's nothing. Let's just—"

He grasped my chin, gently forcing me to meet his gaze. "Cassidy," he interrupted, his voice chiding. "No more secrets. What is it?"

"Really, it's nothing. It's just that, well, I thought you were stopping," I admitted.

Dominic raised both eyebrows at that, glancing at my pants on the floor. I stared at him kneeling between my bare legs and blushed.

"What could have possibly given you an indication that I intended to stop?" he asked.

I glanced at my bedroom door and shook my head. "My own insecurities."

He followed my gaze to the bedroom and laughed. "The bed would be my preference as well, but I couldn't make it that far." He looked back at me, and our gazes locked. "I want you now. Here. For hours."

My body ignited at the heat behind his words. He was everything

I'd never wanted, and everything I now couldn't bear to live without. How many times had I felt crushed by the thought of losing him? How many times had he risked losing everything for the chance to save me? How much more proof did I need to untangle the uncertainties of my own heart?

Dominic didn't wait for me to untangle anything; he slayed my thoughts with a kiss. His lips were fire, his hands were magic, and Jesus, his hands were everywhere—in my hair, stroking my jawline, squeezing my hip and wrapped around my back, urging me closer, making me hotter, driving me wild. When my breasts suddenly dropped from the cups of my undone bra, I pulled back, gasping. I hadn't even felt his hands unclasp my bra hooks.

His teeth nipped at the skin beneath my jawline, kissing, licking, and carefully biting across my neck and down my collarbone. He rucked my shirt up and continued his conquest over my stomach. I bucked at the shock of sensation, wanting more, never wanting him to stop, drowning in so much want that I couldn't think.

His lips kissed past my navel, drifting lower, so damn close to where I wanted him most—I could feel the exhalation of his breath over my clitoris and leaned into him desperately—but his mouth continued lower still, passing over my throbbing heat in favor of my inner thigh.

I groaned in frustration.

And then immediately gasped as his tongue found the underside of my right knee.

"Dominic, please," I begged.

"More?" he asked. He swirled his tongue in that same sensitive spot.

"Dominic!"

My heat throbbed even harder. The inner muscles of my vagina clenched and ached, and if he didn't touch me, really actually physically touch me, I might turn violent.

He turned his head, giving equal attention to the underside of my left knee, and I lost my grip on sanity. I fisted my hand in his hair and moaned. He chuckled, and the vibration of his lips against my bended knee made me squirm and gasp.

"I must confess, I rather like having to work for it," he murmured.

"Dominic, *please!*" I screamed, but the tail end of my cry turned into another shivering moan as he lapped at my knee.

"Tell me what you want from me," he demanded.

I shook my head from side to side in desperation. I'd been confused about Dominic and his intentions and my feelings for him for so long, but in this very moment, the clarity of my feelings and his intentions was like inhaling fresh, clean air after holding my breath for weeks. Exhilarating. Freeing. So damn alive we were electric.

"Cassidy, tell me what you want," he demanded. His voice this time wasn't a metaphysical pull on my mind, forcing his will, but I bent to his will nonetheless.

"I want you to kiss my clit!" I shrieked, every part of my body from cheek to cheek, flushed from frustration and desire and embarrassment at my outburst.

"My pleasure," Dominic growled, and I didn't have time to stay embarrassed. He took me at my word, draped both my knees over his shoulders, buried his face between my thighs, and kissed my clit with the same body-rocking, mind-blowing, heart-stopping, all-consuming expertise that he used to kiss my lips.

My back arched, my toes burned, and I nearly catapulted off the couch, a woman possessed.

I gasped, my shouts an unintelligible garble of his name, a curse, and a prayer.

"Pardon?" he asked, his tongue doing a flick, flick, swirl dance that reduced my body to nothing but nerve endings. "Is there something else you wanted?"

"Just." I gasped. "Stop." I moaned. "Talking. Oh, God!"

Flick. Swirl. Flick. Flick. Flick.

And no talking.

With or without the use of his full powers, Dominic's mouth was cataclysmic. He didn't need an orgasm-inducing bite or the ability to entrance to control me. He had me.

I came.

Hard.

My toes curled, my body throbbed, and I bucked off the couch, twitching and gasping and clutching his hair in my fists.

He straightened, still kneeling in front of me, and met my eyes as I caught my breath. A hush fell over us as we stared at each other, my labored breathing the only sound in the apartment. I lifted my hand and brushed my thumb over his mouth, tracing the deep, jagged scar that cut through his chin and pulled his lower lip down into a permanent pout.

His hand reached out to touch my stomach. The flat of his palm was gentle on my side, his calluses rough as he felt the curve of my hip and the indents of each rib, then traveled higher in a slow slide toward my breast.

My breath hitched. Despite everything we'd shared, although the desire was still there, my heart pounded in panic. Instinctively, I tensed.

He froze, undoubtedly sensing the shift in my heartbeat.

"I'm sorry," I murmured, not wanting to stop, but just as unable to stop my reaction.

"You're frightened," he said, sounding perplexed. "You weren't a moment ago."

"It's not you. I—"

"It's not you, it's me?" Dominic's grin was wary.

"Let me explain. You—"

He shook his head on a sigh. "I understand, Cassidy. There's no need to explain. Your virginity isn't something to justify."

I blinked. "My what? I'm not—" I groaned. "Believe me, I need to explain."

He pulled back and stared at me, the epitome of patience, but I knew that flat, noncommittal stare better than anyone. He was bracing himself in case my explanation crushed the fragile, precious bloom that had just flowered between us.

I worried my lip with my teeth, uncertain where to begin. I'd never told anyone about my last fight with Adam. Not even Meredith knew all the details. I'd locked it away in my tiny lockbox and hidden it among the other horrors I'd stashed out of sight—among murders and rapes and gang violence, the stress of climbing the rungs of my career—so it'd become lost and forgotten and minuscule compared to everything else I'd experienced.

But that's not how horrors work. No matter how long or steadfastly I'd tried to ignore them, they don't easily hide. They'd grown in the darkness, taking shape and strength from my wounds, and transforming me into a person with fears and triggers I didn't even recognize anymore.

Adam had been my first, my college sweetheart, the man I'd planned to marry. My entire future had revolved around our life together, but when my parents died, the future I'd wanted died along with them.

The dark, sarcastic person I'd become after my parents' death wasn't a person Adam wanted a future with anymore. I'd been the one to pull away. I was the one who'd supposedly broken *his* heart, but he'd walked out on me after our last time together, still naked and shivering in the sheets without him, because he didn't recognize me anymore. How could he, when I didn't even recognize myself? I'd felt used and hollow and abandoned, and I swore never to feel that way again. I had my career, and I threw myself into that fateful Mars Killington drug trafficking case to forget everything I'd lost.

If only I'd known at the time how much I still had to lose.

The hurt and loss I'd suffered from Adam was a part of me, interwoven into the person I'd become over time as surely as my parents' deaths had hardened me and overcoming Percocet addiction had strengthened me. The person Adam had devastated all those years ago wasn't the same person in this room with Dominic. Even if Dominic hurt me in the exact same way with the exact same weapon, my injury would be different. I wouldn't turn away, naked and shivering, to staunch the hemorrhage; this time, I'd fight back until we were both bleeding. And Dominic, being Dominic, could heal my body head to toe with a lick of his tongue afterward.

Adam's presence had been a bright, shiny beacon high up on a hill, but after the pain of my parents' deaths, the light I'd once basked in became a spotlight for my wounds. Instead of leaning on him for comfort, I'd turned away from him in grief, and Adam, the beacon that he was, couldn't dim his light, not even for me.

Dominic wasn't bright and shiny. His presence was like a shroud, and I could willingly lose myself hiding in the cover of his darkness. He understood my wounds because, like me, his own pain had needed time and space and solitude to subside. He'd helped me find an anchor in the storm and had the patience to wait until that storm passed because he knew the truth about wounds and living with them. He understood the burden of choosing to live despite them.

I took a deep breath and pressed his hand firmly against my breast. "I'm not a virgin. I've suffered heartache, just like you and everyone else who's ever loved, and I've been afraid to feel. I've been afraid to live. But I've never felt more alive in my entire life than I feel here with you."

The tense, pinched expression in his eyes wilted, and in its place, the bloom growing between us turned its face to the sun and basked in its rays.

Dominic's lips quirked. He was struggling to keep his expression neutral and failing. "Tell me what you want, Cassidy."

I inhaled sharply. He was going to make me say it.

He must have felt my hesitation, because he tsked his tongue and shook his head at me in gentle rebuke. "You must tell me exactly what you want of me. Not only do I want to hear the truth of us on your lips, but I refuse to endure false accusations later tonight or tomorrow or next week when you decide I somehow seduced you with my wicked ways." He gave me a look. "I want this as much as you do, but I refuse to take liberties if you're not willing to admit that you want liberties taken. You must say what you want, Cassidy. Exactly how you want it."

He really is wicked, I thought, but despite my reservations, I relented. "I want you, Dominic," I whispered.

The heat of my blush burned my face from hair root to chin as I finally admitted the truth to him.

He made a circular gesture with his hand for me to continue.

I sighed, digging deep in my reservoir for courage and strength. Why were words so much more difficult than actions? Ask me to jump in front of a bullet or open a vein for the man, no problem. But admit my true feelings? The risk of bodily injury, dismemberment, and death were obviously not as frightening as the risk of embarrassment and rejection.

"I want you to finish what you started and make love to me," I said, my voice soft but unwavering. "I want your bare skin against mine and your hands on my body. I want you inside me." I swallowed at the look on his face, like that of a child on Christmas morning. Granted, a child with fangs, but the glee and unadulterated joy of witnessing a miracle was there in his expression just the same. "I want all of you."

Dominic was on me in an instant, executing my every want. He stripped me of my shirt and bra, and I ripped the shirt from his body, buttons springing out in every direction and raining over my hardwood floor. He pressed his bare chest to my bare chest and the dual exhalation of our groans swelled the apartment with need.

"Another shirt bites the dust," he commented. "You're hell on my wardrobe."

"You're hell on my sanity, but do you hear me complaining?" I unzipped his pants, finished with being the least-dressed person in the room.

"Yes, I hear your complaints all the time," he said, breathing his dissatisfaction across the shell of my ear. "I don't respect your boundaries or your privacy. I bound you to me metaphysically without your knowledge. I won't let you write the article that would expose me, ruin you, and kill us all." He nibbled on my earlobe and simultaneously moved the hand I'd pressed to my breast, massaging my nipple between his thumb and forefinger. "All you do is complain."

I gasped and shuddered. "Are you trying to dampen the mood?" I asked, not feeling dampened in the least despite the recitation of his worst faults. I shoved his pants down to his knees and squeezed the long, firm length of his erection in my hand.

His body stilled. His lips on my neck paused their nibbling, and I could feel a tremor wrack his body with a sharp inhale.

"My point—" He tried to continue, but as my hand stroked over him, distracting him, his words were stilted and breathless. "You managed to transform your apartment into a fallout shelter to secure your privacy." He groaned as I squeezed tighter and stroked longer and faster. "Our bonds have saved us on multiple occasions; we've taken strength and life from each other that we otherwise would have lost, thanks to those bonds."

I shifted my hand so my strokes pulled him high and taut, his balls bouncing from the motion. He cursed softly.

"And no matter what I do," he continued steadfastly, a man determined, "you will be the end of me, the end of us all, and write your article anyway. You don't need space, apology, or permission from me to attain what you want."

"Is that right?" I asked, grinning. I could tell by the roll of his eyes into the back of his skull and the slack-jawed tilt to his head that he was lost in my touch. "What do I need from you?"

"Me."

Dominic forced my hand away and slid inside me, the thick length of his shaft stretching and filling the deepest parts of me, and we stopped arguing.

He remained stock still for a moment, his expression wide and full of wonder, and when he did finally move, just a slow retreat and even slower thrust, we both gasped and shuddered in pleasure and awe at the person we'd become.

He rested his forehead against mine and shook his head. "I can't believe we're finally here. I can't believe this is real."

"Don't let it end," I said, writhing my hips impatiently.

He chuckled softly and leaned back, gazing over the length of my body with hungry eyes. "I can't believe you're mine."

Mine, I thought, and everything about that thought and our bodies together as one felt right and whole and inexplicably freeing.

He moved again, slowly retreating and thrusting forward harder this time, again and again until I didn't know embarrassment or reason or reality from insanity. He filled me with such pleasure and promise that I didn't have room for anything else inside myself but him.

I came in a screaming, clenching explosion, and I thought I heard Dominic murmur, "Thank God," before his shuddering groans joined mine. I watched him over me, his furrowed expression focused and driven, nearly in pain, and I couldn't help but smile in wonder at the power I had over the formerly most powerful creature in the city.

I sighed. It was the same power he had over me.

Dominic withdrew from inside me and collapsed next to me, his upper half on the couch, his head resting on my chest, his arm slung over my stomach and his lower half kneeling on the floor, his legs intertwined with mine. He shook his head, and the soft wisps of his hair tickled my chin.

"That sigh better be one of lingering pleasure," he said, his voice still rasping, "and not your typical pessimism. Usually I appreciate your pragmatism, but in this moment, so close to divine perfection, I will not tolerate anything but satisfaction."

I smiled. "Okay."

Dominic lifted his head, his expression wary now instead of blissful. The huff of his breath blew across my chest as he grunted. My nipple puckered. "You never give in to me so easily."

"Enjoy it. It's not likely to happen again anytime soon."

He cocked an eyebrow.

"My easy acquiescence. Not this," I said, indicating us sprawled naked together on my couch. "We should most certainly do this again. And often."

Dominic chuckled. "How often?"

I shrugged. "Well, we never made it to the bed. And there's still the recliner, love seat, and ottoman left to test out in the living room."

His grin was swift and rakish. "Far be it from me to exclude a piece of furniture."

Dominic made good on his word. We kissed and licked and loved throughout my apartment, fighting over each other's body parts as intensely as we fought over everything else. When we eventually ran out of living room furniture, kitchen countertop, and area rug, we landed in an exhausted, blissful stupor on the bed, curled into one another. The strong, unyielding planes of Dominic's muscles pressed firmly against my curves. I luxuriated in the feeling, too sore to move, too thoroughly spent to care, and for the first time in a very long time, utterly content.

I'd been delightfully, delectably wrong. Despite all my efforts to distance myself from Dominic and his limitless reach by transforming my apartment into a fallout shelter, the sanctuary of Dominic's arms contained a warmth and sustenance I'd never thought could exist in a world without my parents.

And I'd found it in a world of monsters with one of the biggest, most badass monsters of all.

The Leveling

Our lives are nothing but a compilation of moments—snapshots of laughter, love, tears, blood, grief, pain, and joy—but the moments we choose to hold dear are the life we lead. I could choose a various number of snapshots in which I scoured civilizations and ruled kingdoms and bathed in my enemy's blood before drinking it, but that was the life I chose to lead before other moments in life became dearer.

Now, I choose you.

—DOMINIC LYSANDER, evading my questions on his morally corrupt past

Chapter 30

The smell of roasting meat woke me. My stomach growled, and I peeked one eye open under Dominic's arm against the single ray of sunlight beaming onto the bed through a crack in the blinds.

Both my eyes snapped wide open.

Sunlight.

I catapulted myself out of bed, ignoring Dominic's groan and the lightning bolt streaking through my hip to twist the blinds down, unsnag all the curtains from their sashes, and snap their seams closed against the light.

It wasn't enough. It wasn't nearly enough. I'd bought beautiful, gauzy curtains that didn't do much against sunshine, intending to protect apartment *from* vampires, not for them. Even with the curtains fully closed, light filtered through the fabric, glowing into my apartment instead of shining. Dominic would still cook in here; he'd bake instead of broil, but he'd burn just the same.

I ran to the linen closet—my version of running, which for anyone else might appear as hobbling, but for me was a dead sprint— and pulled my winter quilts and comforters from storage. Once they were draped over the curtain rods in addition to my ineffective curtains, the room was finally plunged into shadow.

Dominic had woken, either from the pain of being burned or from my own racket as I'd sun-proofed the room; his arm was flung over his face, covering his eyes as he groaned.

I stepped cautiously toward the bed. Dominic wasn't his best self during the day, often succumbing to his gargoyle-like form. He didn't look particularly transformed now—the hand attached to the arm covering his face appeared human—but if I'd learned anything from my time with Dominic, it was that appearances weren't reality.

"Are you all right?" I asked, careful to keep my voice neutral.

"No," he said, and his voice rumbled from his chest, not in a growl like it would normally rumble, but rather like he needed to clear his throat. "I have a headache. And my throat is parched. And I'm exhausted."

Dominic lowered his arm and looked at me. Gone were his reflective, nocturnal, icy eyes that bled from midnight blue to white in the center. His eyes had irises, which were midnight blue, but surrounding his irises was white sclera, and in the center, there was something I'd never seen in his gaze. His pupils contracted to absorb the light.

I gaped.

He broke eye contact with me and stared down at his own hands. He flexed his fingers into fists and then opened them wide, only to flex them again.

A minute passed in silence. He didn't move except to stare at his flexed hands.

"Dominic?" I asked softly.

"I once told you I'd feel bereft without my heightened senses, essentially blind and deaf compared to the visual and auditory acuity I'm accustomed to."

I nodded, hesitant to find out exactly where this train of conversation would lead us, but relieved he was at least speaking.

"It feels worse than I remember, worse than I could have imagined. I'm essentially crippled without my senses, and without you at your full strength either," he said, shaking his head. "I'm afraid we've lost the battle before it's even really begun."

I cupped his face in my hands, less afraid of him than I'd ever felt since meeting him all those weeks ago, and for that very reason, more afraid for him than I'd ever imagined feeling.

"We've had our backs up against the wall before, and when everything seemed lost, when you were shot through the heart and burst into flames and Jillian escaped and all that was left was me and insane hope, we still won," I reminded him. "No matter how lost things seem, you've got to hold on to hope. Sometimes that one, tenuous strand of hope is the harness that helps you climb the mountain safely instead of plunging down the ravine to certain death. And I should know," I said, forcing a smile, "I've gone rappelling, remember?"

He shook his head, trying to pull away, but he was so weak, at nearly human strength, that I could tighten my grip and keep my hold. "You didn't go rappelling. Ian Walker tried to convince you to rappel into Bex's coven, but you were physically incapable of bearing your weight in the harness because of your hip."

I blinked. "How do you"—I shook my head—"it doesn't matter. That doesn't change my point," I said sharply. "Someone once told me that you are not immortal. Nothing is. You're just long-lived and difficult to kill. One day, whether it's fifty years from now or another five hundred years from now, you will die just like everyone else, because nothing, not even the sun or this earth, will last forever. Eventually, you and I and the coven will no longer exist, but not today. Today, we live."

Dominic met my eyes, and the sadness in his very human gaze broke my heart. I wasn't accustomed to looking into his eyes and seeing his soul. Somehow, seeing Dominic stripped bare made me feel naked too.

"Today, Jillian officially has all of my strength and powers," Dominic said. "And in addition to her own army of Damned vampires, she now has control of my coven. Even the most loyal to me will struggle against the power of her direct command, and without the coven at my back, it will be very difficult to stay alive today. Or, how might you put it?" he asked, a light twinkling in his eyes. "To retain my existence."

I scrunched my nose at him.

"My death would seal the complete transfer of my Master's power to Jillian, but even if I do survive, there are many ways to lose my coven—if not by the transfer of power, than by crippling their will or poisoning their hearts."

I raised an eyebrow. "You think she could convince an entire coven of loyal vampires to just, what, have a change of heart?" I asked, letting my voice drip with doubt.

"She turned the tides of my loyal coven against me when she was my second and I in full command of my powers," he reminded me.

"And we stood against the tide and held strong. We—"

"We are in hiding," Dominic said. "Now that I am at my weakest, I have no doubt that she—leader of an army who feasts on beating hearts—will find a way."

"*We* will find a way," I insisted.

He rested his forehead against mine and sighed. "My reign as Master of New York City was by far the most agonizing and fulfilling endeavor of my very long existence." He expelled a breath, more sob than sigh this time, and shook his head. "The weight of responsibility and chains of leadership bound me as surely as my coven was bound to my rule, and those confines were both constricting and comforting. Each individual vampire was my family, and the coven was my legacy." He made a choking noise in the back of his throat. "How can I let go, Cassidy? If Jillian wins, whether by my death or by her own force of will, how can I leave them behind, bound to her rule?" He shook his head, the brief glimmer of light and humor in his eyes winking out. "I've failed them."

"Some things transcend time and death. Some things are eternal, lasting long after we're gone. Even if Jillian usurps your rule, even if you die trying to regain control of your coven, your reign as Master vampire of New York City transcends even you."

Dominic made a humming noise in the back of his throat. "Such sweet words said by an even sweeter mouth. If only they were true."

"I'm in the business of exposing the truth, remember?" I grinned. "Speaking of which, do you know what would help immortalize your memory?"

Dominic raised an eyebrow.

"Allowing me to quote you in my article."

His gaze was leveling. "Seriously? You want to do this now?"

"The article's main focus is the existence of a new, undiscovered species living in a city beneath New York City. It makes perfect sense for the leader of that species to be quoted. In fact, not obtaining your quote would be remiss of me. People will want to know your story, your history, how you survived and thrived undetected by humans. The people will want to know what you have to say."

Dominic scoffed. "I don't care what 'the people' want. They are human and insignificant."

"I'm an insignificant human," I reminded him.

"On the contrary, you're not human. You're a night blood, a future vampire, possibly a future Day Reaper, and I think worlds of you."

"Potential vampire," I grumbled. "What of when I had no memory of your name, when you thought I'd lost my night blood? Why did you remain loyal to me and protective of me when I was as insignificant as a human?"

Dominic shrugged. "You were injured during battle—in the line of duty, you might say. I couldn't fault you for that, no matter how insignificant you'd become."

I rolled my eyes. "You're impossible."

Dominic grinned. "You're no longer insignificant."

"Thanks?"

"Rafe was overwhelmed by the taste of your blood, and Sevris didn't notice anything amiss when he healed you. Unfortunately, in my current state, I lack the strength and skill to test the theory, but your blood may very well have finally regenerated enough to give back your night blood abilities."

I pondered the possibility. "I haven't sneezed in front of Meredith in at least a full day," I admitted. "Too little, too late, though," I said sadly.

Dominic touched my cheek. "What are you thinking? I can no longer sense the nuances of your thoughts in the pitch of your voice or the quickening of your heartbeat. You must confide in me with words."

I sighed. "I'm thinking it would have been nice to have my night blood abilities when the Damned attacked Harroway and me."

Dominic tightened his hold on my jaw and shook his head. "Even if you'd had your night blood abilities, they wouldn't have saved Harroway. You can't entrance the Damned. They are so consumed by their need to feed, they don't understand anything else. You tried with Nathan and failed because his thoughts didn't comprehend your commands, remember?"

"At least I could have tried," I said softly.

"Harroway finally returned the favor you did him all those years ago. He saved your life like he believed he should have the first time. He died a hero," Dominic said. "I dare say he's happy with himself."

"I didn't give him my life. He didn't owe me anything," I ground out. I had to clear my throat to continue talking. "You can't justify his death. Not to me."

Dominic raised his hands. "I apologize. I'm trying to comfort you, not upset you."

"I know. I just—" My phone vibrated on the nightstand, interrupting me. I glanced at the caller ID and then at the time. "Shit."

Dominic raised his eyebrows.

"It's Greta. And it's well past when I should have called her."

He gave me a little grin. "It's becoming a habit with you, ignoring her phone calls."

I grinned back, despite myself. "Only when I'm in your bed."

"We're in your bed this time," he pointed out.

I swiped the phone from the nightstand and got out of said bed.

"Where are you—"

"You know I have to take this. Stay put and out of sunlight," I said, shrugging on an oversized T-shirt and jeans. "I need fresh air to clear my head, and you in my bed isn't helping."

My words wiped the grin clean off his face. "You can't go outside. The Day Reapers—"

"Can't get into my apartment," I finished for him. "And the rooftop is part of my apartment. I'll get my fresh air and remain in the relative safety of my fallout shelter. I'll be fine." I cracked the door open, careful to allow only a sliver of light to breach the bedroom.

"No, Cassidy. It's an unnecessary risk," Dominic said, his voice sharp, near panic.

He jumped off the bed, fast for a human, but I was used to dodging vampires. I slipped out of the room and slammed the door behind me.

"Cassidy!" Dominic bellowed and nearly ripped the door off its hinges.

"Dominic, don't, you'll burst into flames!" I tugged the door shut again.

"I might not—not instantaneously, anyway," he argued. "I'm near human in every other way."

I made a rude noise in the back of my throat. "Now *that's* an unnecessary risk."

Dominic sighed deeply and stopped tugging on his side of the door. I leaned my forehead against the wood, and judging by the proximity of his sigh, he was likely doing the same.

"I'll be careful," I reassured him. "And I'll be right back after my conversation with Greta."

"An hour," Dominic said, his voice ringing with grave finality.

"Not a minute longer. You know what happens when you don't keep to schedule."

I pulled back from the door. "You can't come for me in daylight. You'll die."

"When have you known something so pesky as the threat of death to stop me from coming for you?" he asked, his voice low and more deadly than the rays of the sun.

Chapter 31

"It doesn't make any sense. The tracker must have been expelled like the others," Greta said, her voice grim.

I was on speakerphone with Greta, Rowens, Meredith, Nathan, and Dr. Chunn, but even with all our minds and combined expertise on this case, we were at a loss.

I blew out a long breath. "What doesn't make sense? Where's the tracker?"

"It's lighting up 432 Park Avenue."

I looked across the skyline, imagining 432 Park Avenue in the distance beyond my sight. "The tallest residential building in New York City," I murmured. The city was just rising with the sun, and somewhere, within or below or surrounding the building where people were just waking for the day, slept the greatest danger this city had ever faced.

"But recon reported that all is well at the tower," Greta continued, interrupting my rumination. "No disturbance, no deaths, and no Damned. Nothing."

I tapped my lips with my forefinger and squinted through the blinding morning rays and fog. "We've got to think about this from their perspective. They're nocturnal, and with the exception of Meredith's attack, they only hunt at night. They must hide somewhere during the day, not hunt, so wherever they are, there wouldn't be a disturbance." I double-tapped my lips, thinking. "What's beneath 432 Park Avenue?"

"Sewer, steam tunnels, and the 6 Train."

"There were no sewer particles found on our samples," Dr. Chunn reminded us.

"Right." I pinched the bridge of my nose, trying to expand my mind to consider the unthinkable and discover the truth. The fresh air was helping, but obviously not helping enough. Even without the distraction of Dominic gloriously naked in my bed, my mind was giving me nothing but facts, and the facts we had weren't offering me any answers.

"We're just so out of our element," Dr. Chunn said. "We've never seen anything like these creatures before. We have nothing as a basis for comparison."

I blinked in realization. We certainly did have a basis for comparison. My brother. "Feel free to pipe in anytime now, Nathan," I said, calling him out. "Where did you hide during the day when you were Damned?"

He didn't speak for a long moment, but when he did, his voice was deadpan. "High in the trees where no one could see me."

I frowned. "How did you avoid the sun?"

"The foliage blocked some of the sun's rays. My scales burn easily, but even in direct sunlight, I don't burst into flames."

"Burnt scales," I whispered, realizing something I hadn't considered before.

"We found burnt scales at several scenes," Dr. Chunn reminded us, having the same realization I was having. "And Meredith found evidence of scales at past scenes using her resolution-enhancing software on our crime-scene photos."

"They're not taking shelter out of the sun," I said, nodding in agreement even though she couldn't see me. "Wherever they're hiding, they're getting burned."

Greta's sigh across the phone was sharp and hard. "Where on earth could they be hiding that is open to the sun that my recon team can't find them?"

I shook my head. "I have no idea. Nathan, where did you hide in the city when you were Damned?"

He was quiet for such a long moment that I thought maybe I'd pushed him too far this time. His memories from his time as a Damned vampire were worse than nightmares. People often wonder how they would react in a crisis, if they would be the hero or the coward, but luckily, not everyone endures the experience to prove their worth.

Nathan's experience as a Damned vampire made him discover a side of himself that most people could go their entire lives not knowing. He discovered in no uncertain terms that he wasn't the hero or the coward. He was an exceptional murderer and the very monster that made others cower.

And the memories of his kills were killing him.

Finally, he answered. "I don't remember."

I frowned. "I thought you remembered everything."

"I do," he snapped. "I'm haunted by the memories every day, and I relive the nightmare of being Damned every time I close my eyes."

"You remember where you hid upstate," I pointed out. "But you don't remember where you hid in the city?"

"All my memories are of the time after I found you." Nathan made a pained noise in the back of his throat. "And they are quite enough memories for me."

I tried not to let the disappointment show in my voice. "Well, let me know if any come back to you."

"Will do."

We hung up a few minutes later, out of ideas. Dr. Chunn wanted to comb through the evidence again, but she didn't sound particularly confident. We'd gone over all the evidence multiple times, and she knew it. If we were all this city had against the Damned, New York City was out of luck.

I turned my face to the sun and closed my eyes, letting its rays heat my face. I sighed from the pleasure of it. Despite the over-whelming pressure of solving the puzzle of this case—and my inep-titude at solving it—the rooftop was still my oasis from the world. I could hide up here in seclusion and sunshine for as long as it took to fit the pieces together.

My eyes snapped open. I could see many of the other rooftops from my own rooftop terrace, but 432 Park Avenue was the highest rooftop terrace in the city: the perfect place to hide from the world but not the sun.

The Damned weren't in the building, and they weren't under-ground below it.

They were above it, on the rooftop.

Chapter 32

I listened to Greta talk about plans for evacuation, a SWAT raid, and tear gas—my allotted hour away from Dominic nearly up—and my numb, trembling fingers almost dropped my phone. My worst nightmare was spilling from her lips, and she didn't have a clue.

I'd wanted the public to know about vampires for weeks now. No matter the repercussions to Dominic and his coven and me as his night blood, I'd thought that revealing vampires to the public was necessary; I was in the business of exposing the truth, and the public deserved to know about the existence of creatures who hunted them night after night. Knowledge was power, and the public deserved the power to protect themselves.

Or at least, that's what I'd thought.

The public was woefully unprepared for the reality that vampires existed. I'd only survived this long thanks to Walker, who had introduced me to basic survival skills and given me access to weapons. Dominic did his part to help me survive, too, but in the beginning, before I'd fallen down the rabbit hole and in love, when Dominic was still a creature to guard against, I'd survived on Walker's weapons and knowledge and willingness to share both.

Greta had neither, and she was going to get herself, her police force, me, and possibly all of New York City killed with her plan to raid 432 Park Avenue. She didn't have weapons designed to specifically take down the Damned, and even if she reached out to Walker for his weapons, we were overwhelmingly outnumbered.

Fighting the Damned by force was suicide; we needed to focus our efforts on Jillian. If we could stop Jillian, their maker and hopefully their leader, maybe she would rein in the Damned, assuming they could be reined. Or transform them back, assuming they could be transformed.

If reining them in or transformation failed, despite Nathan's adamant reservations, we'd have to find a way to force Jillian to kill them. Nothing was immortal, only long lived and difficult to kill. The Damned just happened to be the most difficult creatures to kill of all.

"That won't work," I interrupted Greta, somewhere between her discussion of evacuation and a mention of tear gas. "Our weapons won't work against them. You could blow up all of Brooklyn and the Damned would smile at the destruction, the last living thing standing. But their leader has more weaknesses than the Damned. She's highly allergic to sunlight and silver, and we can use that against her. But we need weapons made specifically to target Jillian's weaknesses."

"We don't have time to build custom weapons," Greta said, her tone sharp.

I was loath to drag Walker into our investigation—he had a bead on me as surely as any vampire—but I couldn't deny the usefulness of his extensive arsenal. He had the best toys, and against the Damned, we couldn't afford anything less.

"Ian Walker can help," I said grudgingly.

Greta was silent for a long moment. "He knows about all this?" she asked, her voice carefully reserved.

"He doesn't know about this case, specifically, but he knows that these creatures exist. And he makes custom weapons to kill them." I sighed and finally admitted, "He made the tracking devices."

"And you're just telling me this now, DiRocco? Get in touch with Ian Walker and get him here pronto!"

"Walker made the trackers, but a mutual friend gave them to me. I haven't talked to him since returning from upstate. Walker and I, well, we had a falling out," I said.

"So I gathered," she said dryly. "Why do you think I hired Nicholas, or Dominic, or whatever the hell his name is?"

I blinked. "I don't know," I evaded. I'd thought Dominic had a hand in that as surely as Bex had had a hand in Greta originally hiring Walker.

"I reached out to Ian Walker after hiring Nicholas. I didn't want

Walker on this case, which was odd of me because I usually prefer working with people I know no matter my personal preference, but I called him anyway," Greta said.

I bit my lip. Another perfect example of Greta once again thwarting Dominic's mind-control abilities.

Her voice turned bitter as she continued. "Ian knew what we were facing, and because of a spat with you, he hung us out to dry."

"It was more than just a spat," I said. Although the bruise where he'd jabbed me in the rib with his sawed-off shotgun had only just healed, my broken trust in him hadn't even begun to mend; I had no doubt the feeling was mutual. He'd felt just as betrayed by me as I had by him.

"I don't care about his crimes against you," Greta said, on a roll now. "This investigation trumps personal conflict. Hundreds of people have died, and hundreds more are at risk. He should have come when I called. Or offered some advice, if he's as knowledgeable about these creatures and the weapons needed to kill them as you say he is. He could have done *something*. Anything's better than nothing, and with all that insight, he gave me a big ball of nada."

"He couldn't have known exactly what we were facing," I said, defending him despite my better judgment. He was, after all, a fellow night blood, and at one time not that long ago, a very good friend. "But in general, he knows more than I do about their weaknesses and how to build weapons against them," I admitted.

Greta was silent for a long moment. "We just don't have the time or resources to wait. We need this solved now, not a week from now."

"If we raid 432 Park Avenue today while we're unprepared, we'll lose, G. We can't—"

"It's Detective Wahl."

I blinked. "What?"

"We're close, DiRocco, but sometimes you forget that I'm lead on this case. If I say we go in today, we go in today."

"But you don't understand what we're up against. You don't have the means to—"

"I understand perfectly what we're up against," Greta interrupted, her voice sharp. "I watched as that creature jumped fifty stories and crashed through the window on your floor. I watched as you were thrown out the window and Dr. Nicholas Leander turned into Dominic Lysander before our very eyes and soared from his tower, caught you in midair, and saved you. And even though both of you fell fifty floors, you both survived."

"He slowed our fall. We didn't hit at full speed and—"

"Seven years of friendship, and suddenly, I don't even know who you are anymore. I'm not sure I know *what* you are."

My throat tightened. When I tried to speak, unshed tears and fear roughened my voice. "I know it seems crazy—I felt like I was going insane when I first met Dominic—but for the past month, ever since I discovered the truth about myself and the creatures that exist beneath this city, I've been trying to find a way to tell you without putting you or myself in jeopardy. That's why I brought Dominic's blood to the lab for testing. You never would have believed me if I'd only told you the truth; I had to prove it to you."

"You're right, DiRocco, I never would have believed you. No one would have. And you did a damn good job proving it to me. Unlike Ian, you stayed to help me solve this investigation. Knowing what I know about the danger we're up against, you did more than your part. Which is why you should evacuate with everyone else and leave the rest to me and my team."

I groaned. "G, please, hear me out. Your plan won't work. You can't—"

"Get Meredith, Rowens, and Dr. Susanna Chunn as far away from ground zero as you can. If we fail, there will be a bloodbath, and you're the only civilians who know the truth."

"Greta, please, I—"

"Get out of the city, and that's an order. I'll take it from here."

"You can't just—"

I heard the click on the line and realized I was talking to nothing but air.

"Fuck." I ran my hands through my hair and paced my rooftop, feeling desperate. I'd thought that giving people knowledge would help them protect themselves, but I was wrong. Greta knew enough to fight but not enough to win, and we would all pay the price. The ultimate price.

Unless I got to Jillian first.

Chapter 33

I sat in a cab at the base of 432 Park Avenue, looking up the enormous height of the tallest residential building in New York City, and trembled. Pedestrians hustled down the sidewalk, bustling around parked cars, cabs, and each other; cabbies honked, people whistled and waved for rides, and food vendors shouted "order up!" to hungry buyers. My cabbie smoked a cigarette, the stink of his smoke wafting to me in the backseat despite his open window. He tapped a finger against the steering wheel as I hesitated. People were living their lives as if today was any other day instead of their last, their hustle and bustle uninterrupted by the creatures hiding on the rooftop above where they stood. I watched dozens of people pass by, completely unaware of the destruction this city was about to face.

Completely unaware of the danger I was about to face for them.

I needed a damn good reason to approach Jillian, but I didn't have to look far to find dozens of good reasons.

The cabbie finished his smoke and flicked its butt out the window. "You're going on twenty dollars, ma'am. Should we continue to park?" he asked. "I am running the meter."

I glanced at the meter and then back at the cabbie through the rearview mirror and sighed. I was only delaying the inevitable. The Damned might be hiding on 432 Park Avenue's roof, but Jillian wasn't, and it was Jillian that I needed to confront. If I hesitated too long, Greta would be here with her SWAT team and tear gas before I could find Jillian, and I'd have missed my window of opportunity.

"Thanks," I said, handing the cabbie twenty-five. "I appreciate you waiting."

The cabbie nodded and took the cash.

I stepped out of the cab, waited with envy as the cabbie turned the corner, driving away from me and 432 Park Avenue, driving away from destruction and danger and the insanity of the world as I'd come to know it, and I walked under the building's overhang toward the front entrance.

No sooner had I crossed into the shade of the overhang than something with the speed and strength of a Mack truck slammed into my body, drove me back into the shadowed alley beside the building, and pinned me up against the wall.

The back of my head cracked on the brick, and a sense of déjà vu coupled with the blow to my head was disorienting. I blinked slowly, trying to find my bearings. I was dangling a foot off the ground, and the being who had slammed into me was holding me there by my upper arms.

I kicked out. My blows landed against something solid, unmovable, and unbreakable. I may as well have been kicking the brick wall behind me. Its claws dug deep into my arms as I struggled, and no matter how I kicked and writhed and fought, I remained pinned up against the brick, my arms aching.

My vision finally focused enough that the double blur in front of me solidified into one image, but I must have hit my head harder than I'd thought. I laughed at my own foolishness. I never should have wasted time worrying how I would find Jillian. I should have known that, the instant I stepped into the shadows, she would find me.

Jillian's blue-and-ice eyes were identical to Dominic's nocturnal gaze, and the memories of how I'd met Dominic all those weeks ago flooded through my mind: I'd been hit by the force of a Mack truck and pressed up against the wall of an alley just like this one, and he'd compelled me with his gaze and irresistible will to forget I'd ever met him.

But I hadn't forgotten, and now he was as vitally a part of me as my own beating heart.

"I'm sorry," Jillian whispered. "In another time, in another life, we would have been allies. Friends even."

Without further ado, small talk, or warning, Jillian dipped her face into the bend of my neck, pierced my skin with her fangs, and drank a long pull of my blood.

I gritted my teeth against the sudden, sharp pain.

"Don't," I said. "We can come to terms. That's why I'm here. Dominic agrees that the public should know that vampires exist. You don't have to kill more people to get what you want."

Jillian pulled back to meet my gaze. Her bite had been neat and precise, and only a small smear of blood stained the right corner of her mouth. She licked it clean with a quick flick of her tongue. Her hair hadn't grown much since we'd last met. It was still thick and healthy, but pixie short. Her bold, angular facial features and big, doe eyes suited the hairstyle. Just last week, she'd been a skeleton, literally, when we'd unearthed her from her imprisonment. Now she was back to full strength, more powerful and more beautiful than ever. We'd released her to save my brother, and here I was, confronting her in the attempt to save us all.

"You can get exactly what you want—freedom from the darkness—without killing more people. Call off your Damned, Jillian. You win," I said, and with the saying of her first name, I felt a tiny thread I hadn't felt all week pull taut inside my mind. If my night blood was finally, truly replenished, I might have enough power to entrance her.

Jillian shook her head. "Even if that were true, Dominic would only agree to expose vampires to the public because he lacks the power necessary to stop me. And if that's the case, why would I stop now when I've already won?"

"It *is* true. I'm writing an article. We can hold an international press conference. You can officially come out of the closet," I insisted. "Why continue fighting when you've already won?" I countered.

She was quiet for a long moment. When she spoke, I realized that I'd convinced her, but by the strained tone in her voice, I wasn't sure if that was necessarily a good thing. "He'd rather break the very vow of secrecy that turned me against him rather than risk losing you."

I blinked. "What does this have to do with me?"

"It has everything to do with you. He couldn't convince you to stop writing your article, could he?"

"No," I said, not liking where this conversation was heading.

"He could stop you, if he really wanted to. He couldn't kill you because of the bonds he's created with you, but if he really wanted to, he could imprison you."

I snorted. "Dominic wouldn't imprison me."

Jillian stared at me, the emotion in her gaze unfathomable. "He imprisoned me."

"You betrayed him. You led an uprising against his rule, attacked him, and left him to burn in the sun. You deserved imprisonment," I said.

"All I ever wanted was for him to release us from the prison of our secret existence. I wanted him to lead us to freedom, and if he had, I would have followed him to the ends of the earth. I loved him. But he turned his back on me when I tried to expose our existence. If he wouldn't lead the coven into the light, someone had to rise to the occasion, and who better than his second?" She tightened her grip on my upper arms, embedding her talons deeper into my flesh. I inhaled sharply. "But you," she continued, "you plan to write an article exposing our secret existence—the very secret that pounded a permanent wedge between him and me—and did he punish you? Did he lock you in a box for you to rot?"

"It isn't that simple. It took some convincing for him to—"

"Convincing?" Jillian laughed. The bitterness in her laugh was piercing. "I had decades to convince him. You bent him to your will in mere weeks."

"I didn't bend anything. If you've known him for decades, you know that Dominic's will is unbendable."

Jillian nodded. "I know, and as I suspected, the difference is you. He would lock me away to rot, risk losing his coven, endure the Leveling without the support of his second, and face his final death rather than break the secret of our existence, but he won't risk losing you." She shook her head, the sorrow in her gaze shattering.

"I'm sorry for everything you suffered," I whispered. "But we can do right by this city. There won't be anything left for you to rule if you don't stop."

"Dominic is allowing you to expose the existence of vampires as a last-ditch effort to save you, himself, and this city from me, unwillingly giving me exactly what I wanted in the first place: the secret of our existence exposed. But if I stop the Damned, alleviating the risk to you and this city, what guarantee do I have that Dominic will still allow our existence to be exposed?" Jillian smiled, and her teeth were stained with my blood. "Quite the conundrum."

"You have my guarantee," I said. "I promise, no matter what, that I will write my article and expose the existence of vampires."

Jillian's expression softened. "I believe you. No matter what, you would write your article. But I know Dominic, and without the physical risk of losing you, he would prevent you from publishing that article or, at the very least, prevent anyone from remembering that you published it. If I stop now, Dominic will go back on his word, and I'll be right back where I began, hiding and suffocating in secrets and darkness."

"That's not true. Dominic wouldn't—"

"It's a possibility, and that's enough for me. After everything I've done and how far I've come and everything I've endured and suffered and strived for to come this close to becoming Master vampire of New York City, I can't turn back now. No matter what you say or promise, I will stay the course."

My temper snapped. "If you're willing to destroy New York City just to rule it, you don't deserve that power."

"Fortunately for me, it doesn't matter what you think I deserve. It only matters what I can take."

"Fortunately for *me,* you can't take shit. You need to kill Dominic to permanently usurp his power, and Dominic is safely tucked away where no one can hurt him—not the Damned, not the Day Reapers, not even you."

"I'm so sorry, Cassidy, but I don't need to hurt Dominic to kill him," Jillian said, and the genuine sadness in her expression and tone made the hairs on the back of my neck stand on end. "Thanks to your metaphysical bond with him, I just need to kill you."

Jillian struck, embedding her fangs in my neck before I could even sense her movement. I screamed and fought back, but I was no match for her strength. She sucked on the wound, guzzling swallow after swallow of my blood. My head spun as I tried to sort my options: she wouldn't listen or see reason; the silver nitrate spray and pen stakes in my pocket were out of reach; and the watch on my wrist was trapped to my side by her unyielding grip on my arms. Without back-up to help me, I only had one last weapon with which to stop her.

"Jillian Allister," I intoned, using the full command of my voice and the power of my blood coursing through my veins, a part of me now inside her, to take back control. "Stop feeding from me, and—"

Jillian stopped feeding, compelled by my direct command, but I never finished my sentence. She bit into the front of my throat and sank her fangs deep into my esophagus. In one smooth, backward rip, Jillian tore out my throat.

I opened my mouth to scream, but a geyser of blood sprayed from my throat instead. I tried to cover the wound with my hands, instinctively wanting to staunch the bleeding, but Jillian was still holding me off the ground by my upper arms, preventing my movement, and her hold was unbreakable. She watched as I struggled, my screams nothing more than the opening and closing of my mouth and horrible, wrenching coughs that spewed blood across her porcelain features. My struggles quickly became twitches, and her grip on my arms finally loosened as my movements became sloppy and uncoordinated. My body wilted in her embrace.

She eased my body carefully from the wall and laid me gently on the ground, taking care with the back of my head. Between the metaphysical bonds tying my life to Dominic and my own ability as a night blood to survive catastrophic blood loss, there was no telling how long I could hang on to my last thread, assuming Jillian didn't go so far as to rip my heart out. I doubted even my bonds with Dominic could help me survive wounds that catastrophic.

Jillian leaned over me, the talons of her thumb and forefinger raised over my face mere millimeters from my open, exposed eyes.

If I could have moved, I would have flinched away. If I could have breathed, I would have held my breath, but I couldn't do anything as the razor-sharp, pointed blades of her talons passed over my face. Miracle of all miracles, she used the soft pads of her fingers to tenderly close my eyes.

"I'm so sorry, Cassidy," she whispered, and I could feel the soft breeze of her breath against my cheek. "In another life, we could have been sisters in this coven, but circumstances being what they are, my heart is too hardened for sisters. I must look beyond the now to the future, a future in which I am Master."

I couldn't breathe through what was left of my throat. My lungs were drowning in more blood than I could cough up, and my brain, which wanted to fight and scream and flee until my last breath, couldn't get my body to move, not one muscle. Maybe because this *was* my last breath.

"We are all just extensions of our Masters," she continued, "forced to bend to their will as surely as their own limbs. I learned early on that if I didn't agree with my Master, the only way to attain what I wanted was to become Master myself."

Jillian's voice was strangely soft, almost choked. Something warm and wet dripped onto my cheek, and I realized that Jillian was crying over me.

"I know my uprising seems like betrayal because I was Dominic's second. All those decades ago, he saved my life, but just as surely as he saved me, he stole everything from me: my love, my freedom, and my dreams of a better existence. I finally have a chance to claim my right to his power and regain the life I dreamed of having. That's what the Leveling is for, to equal the playing field between Master and coven, so a Master whose reign should end can end." Jillian took a deep, trembling breath, her voice wobbly and wet as she struggled to speak past her emotion. "I actually feel something I'd never thought to feel again, Cassidy. I feel hope. But I'm so sorry that reclaiming my life means taking yours."

Jillian swiped the soft pad of her thumb across my cheek. I couldn't see because she'd closed my eyes, but I knew how long and lethal her claws were, bare millimeters from my face. Maybe she knew I was still clinging to a thread of life. Maybe now that she'd spilled her soul and confessed her sobbed sorrys, she'd flay open my chest and rip out my heart to finish me, and Dominic by proxy, and seal her position as Master of New York City.

"Be at peace, little night blood. No more pain."

Her hand left my cheek, and she was suddenly gone.

A long time passed before I finally opened my eyes. I'd like to think I was being cautious, that I knew she might double back to check the permanence of my demise or that her Damned might report my movement from their watch atop 432 Park Avenue, but the truth was that the sun had shifted considerably higher in the sky in the moment I'd closed my eyes: I'd lost consciousness.

I drifted in and out; my phone vibrating in my pocket jogged me awake several times as I watched the sun move steadily across the sky and the buildings' shadows turn and lengthen. Someone must have discovered my absence, or maybe Greta was just pissed that I hadn't followed her orders; my phone seemed to vibrate every five minutes, and eventually, it became a constant vibration.

The sun was past noon when I could no longer feel my phone's vibrations. I could hear it shake against the sidewalk, but my body was numb. Without the feel of my phone, my drifts into unconscious-ness became longer, and my vision, though the sun was directly over-head, became darker. I imagined the Damned staring down the height of 432 Park Avenue into the crevice of the alley with their honed, sharp, focused vision, grimacing in glee at my death. I didn't know if it was my lack of strength to keep my eyes open or the lack of blood to remain conscious, but either way, darkness swallowed me in an unfeeling, unseeing, inescapable wave.

Chapter 34

"Cassidy!"

I heard the shout of his voice before I smelled the Christmas pine of his scent, but it was his scent that pulled me from the darkness. That and the smell of roasting meat.

I opened my eyes and stared at the bright blue sky in confusion. Maybe Jillian had won; maybe we were both dead, and in our heaven, Dominic could live in sunshine.

I tried to sit up, but my numb body didn't recognize how to move. I tried to speak, and although I swear I could feel the movement of my neck muscles, nothing came out but a squirt of blood. If Dominic's heaven included sunlight, mine surely included being whole and healthy.

I was still lying broken in the alley beside 432 Park Avenue. Either I was hallucinating or Dominic was searching for me in daylight.

"Cassidy!"

His shout was louder this time, closer than it had been a moment before.

I opened my mouth, instinctively wanting to respond to his call, but again, I couldn't produce anything but wet gurgles and vertical spurts of blood.

Someone coughed, someone besides me, but the noises were just as wet and gurgling as the coughs coming from my own throat.

"Oh, Cassidy," Dominic said, his voice no longer shouting and desperate. He sounded grave.

I opened my eyes, not sure when they'd closed, and stared up at Dominic. Although the alley was in shadow, the glow of the sun rippled the air around him, giving him a halo. That effect, coupled with the fierce, rage-filled expression darkening his features, made him look like an avenging angel hovering over me. Or maybe I was just that relieved to see him.

Dominic's expression was frantic as his eyes scanned over me, taking stock of my injury. I tried to speak, desperate to explain, but without a throat, without vocal cords, my muscles contracted, and my throat gurgled with blood instead of words.

Dominic coughed, and blood spewed in an arc over me. Some of the spray dotted my shirt. "Stop trying to speak. Preserve your strength. Our strength. Christ, if I had more time, more blood, maybe I could—" He shook his head, his eyes frantically searching our surroundings, but there was nothing at his disposal.

I waited until his gaze settled back on my face. Anger and frustration still twisted his expression, but the panic had dampened and been replaced with resignation.

How? I mouthed.

"Does the how of it really matter, Cassidy?" he snapped.

I didn't have the strength or means to hold an extended conversation, so I just stared up at him and waited.

He sighed deeply. "How am I here in daylight, how did I know you were hurt, or how did I know you'd be here, alone, after your prearranged hour of conversation with Greta had expired?"

I let loose a snort of derision, or rather I tried. Blood squirted from the ravages of my throat.

Dominic coughed up more blood. He was struggling to keep it together, to keep us alive, and if the deepening lines bracketing his mouth, the trembling of his hand, and his ghostly complexion were any indications, his struggle was a losing battle. The more I died, the more he took the injury into himself to keep me alive, and the more he died.

He'd obviously known I was hurt because he'd felt the injury himself, and how he'd found me wasn't nearly as impossible as the fact that he'd found me in the sun without bursting into flames.

I moved my lips: *daylight.*

"I have human vision and human strength. When I felt your throat being torn and I realized what you'd done, I just hoped that I had human skin as well." He turned his face to the light. The scent of roasting meat became more prominent in the air, but he didn't immediately burst into flames.

I raised my eyebrows. At least I thought I did. I couldn't feel my face. *Stupid risk.*

His expression darkened. "Look at the risk you took and where it got you. Look at us," Dominic said, and he began coughing from the overexertion. Blood sprayed in a thick arch over me. Smaller droplets dripped down his chin. He covered his mouth, but his hand trembled so badly, he only managed to smear the blood across his face. It embedded in the crevices of his scar, making him look savage. He met my gaze, and the intensity, even with human eyes, was searing. "No risk, no matter how great, could keep me from you at a time like this. We are one, you and I. Where you go, I follow."

I opened my mouth to explain myself, to justify what I'd done, but the explanation was too long and too much. Blood squirted from my throat, and Dominic coughed up more of it. A long moment passed before either of us was composed enough to communicate.

Maybe Dominic was right. I didn't have many words to spare, so the ones I took the effort to speak shouldn't be the how and the why. I should speak the truth.

I didn't have the strength to admit my feelings for Dominic before, but now that I was too weak to even speak, my heart had never felt more invincible.

I love you.

"Shut up," he snapped, suddenly seething. "Do *not* say that to me right now, not like that, not like you're saying good-bye." The panic returned to his eyes, and he looked around, searching the alley and his vast empire of nearly five hundred years' worth of experience and knowledge, but I knew what he hadn't yet accepted. The only other vampires able to withstand the sunlight were Day Reapers. No one willing to help from his coven could leave the coven, and no one who could withstand the light would be willing to help.

And I had to confess another truth—a horrible, inevitable, unthinkable truth, worse than admitting that I loved Dominic.

I didn't want to die.

I could try to fool myself into believing that what I was about to ask of Dominic was a selfless act for the bigger picture. Lives were at stake, an entire city needed protecting, and I couldn't leave now without putting up a fight, the biggest fight of my life. For my life.

But I'd be lying to myself, because the truth was that I simply wasn't ready to leave this life—or Dominic, not when I'd just found him. As always, unfortunately for my sanity and the bloating of his already bursting ego, Dominic was once again, unfathomably right. I'd never wanted to wear the vial of his blood on a necklace, but I couldn't deny that in this moment, the one moment when I actually needed it, I was glad I had it—not for Bex and not for Nathan, and not as proof of the existence of another species; I was glad I had it just for me.

I opened my mouth to speak, but I didn't have enough air in my lungs to coax my voice to form words.

Dominic noticed my struggle, and he placed his fingers over my lips. Their gentle touch trembled against my skin. "Shut up, and rest, damn it."

I tried to take a deep breath for courage and strength, but I didn't have a throat to breathe through.

Dominic coughed up more blood from my effort.

Vampire, I mouthed.

"Impossible. Where?" Dominic stiffened, his gaze snapping up to dart around and above the alley.

I waited until he looked down at me again before moving my lips. *No. Me.*

His eyes narrowed. "What?" he asked, and there was a mixed awe and horror in that one word that I wouldn't have guessed would be present in this moment.

Transform me into a vampire.

One Night after the Leveling

Never apologize for surviving.

 —RENE ROLAND, in remembrance

ABOUT THE AUTHOR

Melody Johnson is the author of the gritty urban fantasy Night Blood series set in New York City. The first installment, *The City Beneath*, was a finalist in several Romance Writers of America contests, including the "Cleveland Rocks" and "Fool for Love" contests.

Melody graduated magna cum laude from Lycoming College with her B.A. in creative writing and psychology. While still earning her degree, she worked as an editing intern for Wahida Clark Presents Publishing. She was a copyeditor for several urban fiction novels, including *Cheetah* by Missy Jackson, *Trust No Man II* by Cash, and *Karma with a Vengeance* by Tash Hawthorne.

Constantly striving to hone her craft, Melody is a member of Romance Writers of America and regularly attends conferences and book fairs. When she isn't working or writing, Melody can be found swimming at the beach, honing her blossoming volleyball skills, and exploring her new home in southeast Georgia.

You can learn more about Melody and her work at http://www.authormelodyjohnson.com and connect with her on Facebook and Twitter.

THE CITY BENEATH

THIS TURF WAR NEVER SLEEPS . . .

As a journalist, Cassidy DiRocco thought she had seen every depraved thing New York City's underbelly had to offer. But while covering what appears to be a vicious animal attack, she finds herself drawn into a world she never knew existed. Her exposé makes her the target of the handsome yet brutal Dominic Lysander, the Master vampire of New York City, who has no problem silencing her to keep his coven's secrets safe . . .

But Dominic offers Cassidy another option: ally. He reveals she is a night blood, a being with powers of her own, including the ability to become a vampire. As the body count escalates, Cassidy is caught in the middle of a vampire rebellion. Dominic insists she can help him stop the coming war, but wary of his intentions, Cassidy enlists the help of the charming Ian Walker, a fellow night blood. As the battle between vampires takes over the city, Cassidy will have to tap into her newfound powers and decide where to place her trust . . .

THE CITY
BENEATH

MELODY
JOHNSON

A Night Blood Novel

SWEET LAST DROP

TRUST NO ONE

Cassidy DiRocco knows the dark side intimately—as a crime reporter in New York City, she sees it every day. But since she discovered that she's a night blood, her power and potential have led the dark right to her doorway. With her brother missing and no one remembering he exists, she makes a deal with Dominic Lysander, the fascinating Master vampire of New York, to find him.

Dominic needs the help of Bex, another Master vampire, to keep peace in the city, so he sends Cassidy to a remote, woodsy town upstate to convince her—assuming she survives long enough. A series of vicious "animal attacks" after dark tells Cassidy there's more to Bex and her coven than anyone's saying. That goes double for fellow night blood Ian Walker, the tall, blond animal tracker who's supposed to be her ally. Walker may be hot-blooded and hard-bodied, but he's hiding something, too. If Cassidy wants the truth, she'll have to squeeze it out herself . . . every last drop.

SWEET LAST DROP

MELODY JOHNSON

A Night Blood Novel

Printed in the United States
by Baker & Taylor Publisher Services